The Wind Blows in Sleeping Grass

Books by Katie Powner

The Sowing Season

A Flicker of Light

Where the Blue Sky Begins

The Wind Blows in Sleeping Grass

The Wind Blows in Sleeping Grass

KATIE POWNER

BETHANYHOUSE
a division of Baker Publishing Group
Minneapolis, Minnesota

Published by Bethany House Publishers
Minneapolis, Minnesota
www.bethanyhouse.com

Bethany House Publishers is a division of
Baker Publishing Group, Grand Rapids, Michigan

Printed in the United States of America

Library of Congress Cataloging-in-Publication Data
Names: Powner, Katie, author.
Title: The wind blows in sleeping grass / Katie Powner.
Description: Minneapolis, Minnesota : Bethany House, a division of Baker Publishing Group, [2023]
Identifiers: LCCN 2023012861 | ISBN 9780764242007 (paperback) | ISBN 9780764242250 (casebound) | ISBN 9781493443772 (ebook)
Subjects: LCGFT: Christian fiction. | Novels.
Classification: LCC PS3616.O96 W56 2023 | DDC 813/.6—dc23/eng/20230410
LC record available at https://lccn.loc.gov/2023012861

This is a work of fiction. Names, characters, incidents, and dialogues are products of the author's imagination and are not to be construed as real. Any resemblance to actual events or persons, living or dead, is entirely coincidental.

Author is represented by WordServe Literary Group.

Baker Publishing Group publications use paper produced from sustainable forestry practices and post-consumer waste whenever possible.

23 24 25 26 27 28 29 7 6 5 4 3 2 1

To Andy
I love you forever and always

one

The garbage truck grumbled to life like a grizzly waking from hibernation. Pete Ryman stepped down, blew out a breath that hung suspended in the frigid air, and turned to the seventy-nine-pound pig at his side.

"I told you, Pearl." Pete tugged on the zipper of his insulated coveralls. "If the truck runs, the route runs."

Pearl grunted. Pete unplugged the block heater as they made their way back to the passenger side, which was on the left in this particular vehicle—a beat-up, hand-me-down Xpeditor that the town of Sleeping Grass had purchased from nearby Shelby when Shelby bought a new Kenworth T370. Pete opened the door and set Pearl's portable pet ramp in place. The floor of the cab was almost four feet off the ground, so once Pearl had grown too big for Pete to lift, the ramp had become a necessity.

He made an exaggerated sweeping gesture toward the ramp. "Your Majesty."

While Pearl pranced up into the truck like the Queen of England's prize swine, Pete puffed out another breath. At zero degrees, his coat stiffened when he walked outside. At ten below, his nostril hairs froze. At twenty below, the early morning seemed to be a still life painting with only the crunch of his boots and slow rise of steam off the creek to prove it wasn't.

It was twenty below.

Once his sidekick was safely in her seat, he folded the ramp and hurried over to the right side of the truck. Pearl sniffed at the makeshift outfit she was wearing and gave him a long-suffering look as he buckled.

"I'm sorry." Pete shivered as he laughed. "It was the best I could do."

Pete had always believed an animal should wear only the covering God gave it. He'd mercilessly teased Windy Ray about the sweaters the old man put on his scruffy little dog. But what kind of protection did a potbellied pig have against a morning like this? He'd shortened the sleeves of an old hoodie with scissors, then tied up the back with a rubber band to keep the sweatshirt from dragging underneath her. She looked . . . well, ridiculous.

A gust of wind rammed the truck, poking frozen fingers through the cracks in the old beast.

"Don't even think of leaving this house without a coat."

The words pelted him like sleet, and he shook his head. For most folks, February was the shortest month of the year. For Pete, it was the longest. In February, the wind carried his mother's voice.

He turned up the radio and glanced over at his partner in crime. "Ready to roll, oh Pearl of great price?"

She stomped the fleece blanket with her front hooves, spun a cumbersome circle like an overweight dog, and nodded before settling in. At least that was how he took it. After nearly three years together, they seemed to have an understanding.

"All right, then."

The Autocar Xpeditor shuddered into drive and rumbled onto Seventh Street. He should've gotten up earlier to let the truck warm up. Even with a knit beanie on, he could feel the cold seeping through the bald spot on the back of his head. It would be an hour before the cab was comfortable. In the meantime, he and Pearl would tough it out.

Lights were starting to come on in some of the houses, and Pete could see inside the windows that weren't covered by curtains. Mrs. Baker sat at her kitchen table, scooping the guts from half a grapefruit one spoonful at a time. Everett O'Malley sat in front of a giant flat-screen TV that flashed and flickered. Did that man ever sleep?

Pete knew their names because they left him Christmas cards. A handful of folks around here did that, even though he kept to himself and interacted with others as little as possible. One lady even left a neatly wrapped tray of homemade caramels every Christmas and a gift certificate to The Hog House in Shelby on the first day of every summer. She must not know about Pearl. She never signed the card.

Pete routinely caught glimpses of the private lives unfolding in Sleeping Grass, but folks rarely paid any attention to him. So long as he did his job, the garbage man remained largely unnoticed. He just drove and dumped, drove and dumped—week after week, month after month. Which was fine with Pete. He didn't want to be noticed.

"Hey, Pearl." He turned down his first alley and pulled up to the battered blue garbage bin waiting stoically for him like an old man at the bus stop. "What do you suppose we'd see if we ran the route backward one day? Just flipped it right around?"

She seemed to shrug. He'd be tempted to do it if it wouldn't send everyone into a state of panic and confusion. Folks would surely notice him then.

The hydraulic mast clutched the bin and dumped it effortlessly into the truck's hopper. At the next stop, a shabby-looking baby walker leaned against the bin, so Pete hopped out to grab it. Snake on a rake, it was cold.

This house had already used up their two "hand pickups" for the month, yet Pete never reported anyone if they went over the allotted amount. If the Sleeping Grass Public Works Department could look the other way when he had a potbellied tagalong in his cab, he could handpick a few extra items without complaining.

The walker was filthy—crayon marks covered the tray, and mashed Cheerios were crusted to the seat—but he saw no broken pieces. All four wheels were present and accounted for. No rips in the fabric.

It wasn't easy to wrangle the walker into the cab and over the center console. Thankfully it was collapsible. Pearl snorted irritably when Pete wedged it down in front of her seat, forcing her to reposition.

He quickly shut his door on the cold. "It's not my fault folks insist on throwing away perfectly good stuff."

Pearl snorted again, and Pete huffed. "And where would *you* be if I never rescued anything from the landfill?"

She nudged the chair with her snout.

"That's what I thought."

Pete was nearly two hours into his route when the sun peeked over the frozen prairie. It brought little warmth, but the temperature could rise to zero by noon. Maybe. On days like this, he kept the heat cranked up and recited Robert Frost's "An Old Man's Winter Night" to his unwitting cab companion.

Sleeping Grass was enduring one of the cold snaps common to February in the northern plains of Montana, an area along Highway 2 referred to as the Hi-Line. It had never bothered him when he lived here as a child, but now that he'd returned to the place where so many cold memories lived, the bitter chill weighed him down.

"Oh, February, you most unbearable and endless of
months,
cold and dark and empty with no sign of spring.
Why must you breathe your stinging breath
all over everything?"

He liked to recite his own poetry to Pearl, as well. Her expectations for his body of work were, thankfully, not very high.

Pete turned down another alley while repeating the words of his poem in his head. December was cold and dark, too, but there were glimpses through windows of Christmas parties and holiday lights and gingerbread houses. And January's cold and dark were tempered by the promise of new beginnings, the hope of starting over. But February?

February was the reason not everyone made it on the Hi-Line.

He stopped alongside the trash bin belonging to a tiny gray bungalow buttoned up tight against the cold. A wisp of smoke rose from the chimney. He maneuvered the joystick to lower the grabber while peering over the fence. Though run-down and nondescript, this was his favorite house.

The house where *she* lived.

There were never extra items to handpick here, only a bin full of beer cans and tequila bottles, week after week. He was sure those belonged to Jerry, the other resident of the house. He'd often seen Jerry out carousing, and Pete had faced him down twice now when he'd met Pete at the truck to chew him out over letting the lid of the trash bin hit the fence.

Pete had seen the hard set of his jaw and the mean glint in his eye. He'd never seen *her*, though, except for a few brief glances through the window. He'd never met her. Didn't know her name. But he knew it couldn't be Jerry who was responsible for the burgeoning flower beds in the backyard. The picnic table painted yellow with white daisies stenciled across its top. The bird feeders and wind chimes and well-kept crabapple tree with a barn-shaped birdhouse perched in its branches.

She had done all that. And she'd been the only reason Pete hadn't broken Jerry's nose that last time. That and the fact Pete was tired of never lasting more than a couple years at a job before being fired for losing his temper. Tired of having to find a new place to live. This time he was planning to stick it out, if only to watch her backyard stutter to life every spring like a foal finding its legs. He was getting too old for fighting.

There were no flowers now, not in godforsaken February. The picnic table lay under a tarp. But he could picture it all, and he believed the hands that nurtured this oasis must be beautiful hands indeed.

Surely they must be.

The hands that cultivate the seed
Must be beautiful indeed . . .

Pearl grumbled, and Pete blinked, his face warming as he realized how long he must've been staring at the house, hoping to catch a glimpse of her. Daydreaming in rhyme. Boy, was he ever stupid. Stupid!

He saw Pearl looking at him as he quickly drove forward to the next bin. He chuckled. "What are *you* staring at?"

Pearl tolerated him at least. Pearl and Windy Ray were his only friends in Sleeping Grass. He'd feared coming back here would mean running into all kinds of folks from his past, but he hardly remembered anyone. That was what almost forty years of being away did. It made it easier to pretend he had no past here at all. No history.

Except when February rolled around.

two

Pete helped Pearl down from the Xpeditor and into his twenty-year-old Dodge Dakota. She was a good truck, had taken him all over the country, but she wasn't pretty. Pete set the baby walker in the bed of the pickup and climbed into the cab. Pearl nestled into the blanket he kept on the passenger seat for her.

"Sit tight." Pete turned the heat to high. "We'll get your bacon sizzling in no time."

They drove to the outskirts of town to a small cabin that reminded Pete of a bunkhouse you might've found on a cattle ranch a hundred years ago. Pearl gave a squeal of protest when Pete opened her door and the cold air entered the truck.

"Don't give me that." Pete helped her down and hurried toward the front steps. "You know there's better food here than at our house."

Every Monday, rain or shine, Christmas or Fourth of July, Pete and Windy Ray played Chickenfoot at Windy Ray's house. It was the only game they'd both known when they first met, and they had honed their skills to the level of an art form.

Pete knocked twice and opened the door. "*Oki.*"

The Blackfeet greeting Windy Ray had taught him filled the small space, landing gently on the various piles of rocks placed throughout the two-room house. A pot that smelled of sage simmered on the stovetop.

"Pete the Poet." Windy Ray sat at a rickety card table, the dominoes already laid out. "I thought maybe your hands would be frozen to the steering wheel and I would have to come rescue you."

Pete smiled. "I might be able to stand on the back of your bike, but what about Pearl?"

Windy Ray didn't have a car. Wherever he went, his dog, Apisi, rode in the wire basket attached to the front of his red tricycle, and his oxygen tank rode in the rear basket.

Windy Ray eyed Pearl carefully. "Perhaps you would carry her on your back."

Pearl parked herself in front of the woodstove next to Apisi and gave Pete a look that seemed to say *You wouldn't dare*.

Pete settled into the chair across from his friend. "Let's hope it never comes to that."

Pearl had been a piglet when he found her at the dump, listless and covered in dog food. She'd weighed four pounds. The vet he'd taken her to said she was sickly and had probably been the runt of the litter and not expected to live. She'd likely been tossed to give the other piglets a better chance at survival.

That hadn't sat well with Pete. Against the vet's recommendation, he'd taken the pig home, and he and Pearl had been inseparable ever since. He was thankful she was a runt, however, or she might be twice her size.

Windy Ray had found the double-nine domino, so he made the first move. "I feel I must address Pearl's sweatshirt."

Pete's face scrunched. Windy Ray never let him get away with anything. "It was awful cold this morning."

Windy Ray turned his gray eyes on Pete. "And we wouldn't

want our beloved animal friends to be cold, would we? The friends we feel it is our duty to nurture and protect? Whom the Creator has given no one in the world but us as their humble caretakers?"

Pete grinned sheepishly and made a play on the table. "Okay, okay. I promise I'll never make fun of Apisi's sweaters ever again."

Windy Ray nodded solemnly as he took his turn, but there was a spark of humor in his expression. "Apisi would be grateful."

Pete played another domino. "What's in the pot? Smells good."

"Elk stew." Windy Ray stood and lumbered over to the stove, carefully arranging his oxygen tube as he went so he wouldn't trip over it. He was taller than Pete and, despite his advanced age, had long black hair that flew behind him like a raven when he faced the wind behind his house and shouted into it, letting it carry his heartache away. It all sounded like heartache to Pete. He'd never asked what the shouting meant, and Windy Ray never offered to tell. He merely accepted the nickname his behavior generated around town with a dignified air of inevitability.

Windy Ray stirred the contents of the pot. "I have it on good authority it's your birthday on Friday."

Pete's eyebrows shot up. He'd never mentioned that to anyone. "What good authority?"

"The wind never lies."

"Fine, don't tell me. When is *your* birthday?"

Windy Ray's eyes twinkled as he replaced the lid on the pot and returned to the table. "I was born before harvest."

Pete was used to such vague answers. His friend rarely spoke of his past. Pete knew he'd been born outside a town even smaller and more isolated than Sleeping Grass, to a Blackfeet father and white mother. He knew he'd been taught both Siksika and English, though the family hadn't had much contact with the tribe. Pete hadn't been able to pry out any other details, however.

"How old are you, then?"

"Old enough."

Pete shook his head and glanced in the direction of the woodstove to check on the animals. They were curled up together, napping. "How old is Apisi?"

Windy Ray's smile was like the break of dawn. "Nine years and four months as of two days ago."

Pete laughed.

With a clink, Windy Ray played his last domino and won the first round. "I need a ride to Great Falls next week."

"Oh?" Many folks in Sleeping Grass drove the two hours to Great Falls once a month to stock up at Costco and go out to eat—maybe spend the day at Electric City Water Park in the summer—but Pete rarely went there. He had no need for a forty-eight-pack of hamburger buns. Not to mention the years he'd been forced to spend in Great Falls as a kid were ones he'd just as soon forget.

"I have business to attend to in the big city." Windy Ray's large hands deftly mixed up the dominoes in preparation for the second round. "Will you take us?"

"What kind of business?" Pete's voice had a wary ring to it. The last time he'd driven Windy Ray and Apisi to the "big city," he'd ended up being thrown out of a KFC for defending Windy Ray against a punk kid who thought the old man was an easy target for whatever anger and fear were festering in his soul. Of course, Windy Ray had not been entirely innocent in the matter, having felt the need to comment on the young man's low-riding, baggy pants.

Windy Ray's face gave nothing away. "I need to see a man about a horse."

Pete harrumphed. "When do you want to go?"

"At your earliest convenience."

"Wednesday would be best. Would that work? I'm usually done by one-thirty."

Windy Ray bowed his head gallantly and made a big play on the table. "Thank you."

Pete scowled at his friend's dwindling pile of dominoes. "You're going to beat me again, aren't you?"

Pete lost these Monday matches more often than not.

"You don't focus. Your mind wanders."

Pete couldn't argue with that. "This time when we're in Great Falls, could you keep your comments to yourself?"

The corner of Windy Ray's mouth twitched. "Perhaps you should keep your fists to yourself."

Pete scowled again. He'd gotten better at that over the years, but it was still easier said than done. He turned to Pearl and jerked a thumb at Windy Ray. "We've got a wise guy over here."

Pearl did not so much as flick an ear in response.

"She agrees with me," Pete said.

"Yes." Windy Ray laid down his last domino. "I'm very wise."

Pete stared at his hands as he helped his friend mix up the dominoes for the third round. They were gnarled and scarred. They'd been in many fights. Some men aggravated and hurt others for the fun of it, but Pete didn't enjoy fighting. He never intended for it to happen. Yet sometimes it did, and his fists had cost him over a dozen jobs. It was becoming more and more difficult to find anyone to take a chance on him anymore, which was how he'd ended up back in a place he never thought he'd see again.

He tucked his hands away. Maybe all those folks who'd given up on him when he was a kid—families who had kicked him out of their homes, counselors who had added incriminating reports to his case file—had been right.

He would never amount to anything.

three

Wilma Jacobsen set her teacup on its saucer with a clink and let out a long sigh. Drinking tea was supposed to be relaxing. Herb always used to say so, but she didn't feel relaxed.

She carefully pushed away from the table and shuffled to the kitchen sink. She'd already done the dishes. She'd already wiped the counter . . . twice. Through the window, she eyed the blue trash bin in the alley, dumped earlier today. An eighty-two-year-old widow living alone didn't produce much in the way of garbage in the span of a week, but she was loath to give up her trash service. Knowing Pete would stop at her house every Monday, however briefly, made her feel like her connection to him hadn't been completely lost.

Even after all these years.

A knock sounded from the front of the house, followed by the low squeak of the door opening. "Miss Wilma? I'm here."

"Lily." Wilma stood a little straighter. "Is it four o'clock already?"

A boot stomp or two, then a young lady entered the kitchen. Well, Wilma considered her young. If she remembered correctly, Lily was in her early forties, which felt like a lifetime ago to her.

"Four o'clock on the dot." Lily smiled and set a pile of envelopes on the table. "I brought in your mail."

"Thank you, dear."

Wilma's family was always telling her she didn't make wise choices with her money, but hiring Lily last month to clean her house once a week had been one of the best decisions she'd made in recent memory. Her friend Gladys had recommended Lily when Wilma got her cane. Lily was Gladys's cousin's neighbor, and it had been working out splendidly. Not because Wilma couldn't keep a tidy house on her own—of course she could, she was an excellent housekeeper—but because she enjoyed the youthful company. Usually, Lily came first thing every Monday morning, though she'd asked to come at four today.

"You were busy this morning, hmm?" Wilma peered at Lily over her glasses.

Lily's expression remained steady and inscrutable while her hands tightened into fists that she quickly tucked behind her back. "I had some other things to take care of, is all."

"I see." Wilma's eyes narrowed. She often got the feeling Lily was hiding something from her, but having raised three children of her own, she knew better than to press. "Would you pull the trash bin in for me, please?"

Lily frowned. "Did you roll it out by yourself last night? You really shouldn't go out in this kind of weather, Miss Wilma. You can get frostbite in less than thirty minutes."

"Nonsense." Wilma waved away Lily's concern. "It was fine."

Lily still had her boots and jacket on, so she went out the back door and trudged across the yard to the gate. Wilma watched through the window. Really, it hadn't been fine. The cold had clawed through her heaviest coat and bit at her skin, which felt like nothing more than weathered wax paper these days. The ice on the back patio had been treacherous, even with that blasted cane. She had tried to take her time, but the freezing air compelled her to hurry and she'd almost had a fall.

No one needed to know about that.

Lily wrestled the bin through the gate and left it just inside the fence. It was easier for Wilma to carry her garbage across the yard to the bin than roll the bin across the yard, so she always left it near the gate. She'd never mentioned that to Lily, but Lily was very observant and thoughtful. There was a real gem hidden beneath that reserved manner and boxy, unfashionable wardrobe.

Lily's nose was red when she came back into the house. "The wind's picking up."

Wilma shuddered. "I hate to think of you walking home in the cold."

"It's only a few blocks."

"Still." The corners of her lips curled up. "You can get frostbite in less than thirty minutes."

Lily's laugh warmed her heart. "I promise I'll walk fast."

Twice now Wilma had asked Lily to pick things up for her from the grocery store, and she had walked the three-quarters of a mile to Murphy's Meat and Market in the cold. Wilma wasn't sure if Lily didn't have a car, didn't have a license, or just enjoyed exercise, but again . . . she never pressed. There were other ways to get information, however.

"You don't happen to have another trip planned to the Walmart, do you?" Wilma raised her eyebrows. "I'm all out of those frozen chicken-and-rice meals you got me last time. I'd love to have some more."

Lily shook her head. "Next time I catch a ride to Great Falls, I'll pick some up for you."

Aha. She didn't have a car, then.

"You can always borrow my Corolla." Wilma studied Lily's face. "It ought to be driven once in a while, and I avoid going out in the winter if I can."

"That's very kind of you, Miss Wilma."

Wilma waited for more, but Lily just gave her a small smile. "Shall I get to work?"

Wilma flicked her wrist twice. "Yes, yes, go ahead. Thank you, dear."

Lily knew where the cleaning supplies were located. While she busied herself, Wilma eased back into her chair at the table. Lily might be a tough nut to crack, but Wilma didn't mind having something to ponder besides her own problems. She poked at the stack of mail with a dull ache in her stomach. Bills, bills, and more bills. Why couldn't the credit card companies leave a poor old lady alone? She would pay them.

Eventually.

She *tsk*ed to herself. Her son Michael would have a fit if he saw these. Who knew when he'd come around to worry about it, though. Her kids had all left Sleeping Grass the moment their high school principal said, "I'm proud to present to you the graduating class of . . ."

She couldn't fault them for it. They had their own lives now, far away from here. They had high school diplomas, college diplomas, careers, hobbies, families. She thought of Pete and shook her head. He had none of those things. Why had he come back?

Lily peeked around the corner. "Did you clean the bathroom?"

Wilma shifted in her seat and pretended to study a piece of mail. "Of course not, dear, that's your job."

But she had.

four

By Friday, the temperature had risen to ten degrees. It felt downright balmy. Pete parked the Xpeditor at the end of the day and set the ramp in place for Pearl. She trotted out of the vehicle as fast as her stubby legs could carry her. It had been a long week.

"Good girl." He rubbed her bristly head. "I know the truck is boring."

She leaned into his hand and grunted happily. The vet had warned him that pigs were not easy pets. *"They're too intelligent and curious to be content staring out a window all day,"* the man had said. But Pete and Pearl had found a system that worked for them. Most of the time. Pete kept a small bag of toys and snacks in the Xpeditor and stopped every two hours for a fifteen-minute break instead of taking a lunch hour. Pearl would use the ramp to get out and go to the bathroom, and she and Pete would play for a few minutes.

This week had been scarce on the playtime, however. Even when Pearl was wearing her sweatshirt, the days had been too cold to spend fifteen minutes outside. Pete cringed to think what the vet would say if he knew how many snacks

Pete had given Pearl to compensate for the shorter breaks. Sometimes it couldn't be helped.

"Ready to go to Sunny's?"

Pearl's pointy ears perked up. He was sure that was a smile he saw. Every Friday, Sunny's Sweet Shop offered dollar-scoop ice cream from three to six. It was a more popular deal during the summer months, but neither Pete nor Pearl was inclined to miss it even in the dead of winter.

Pete helped the pig into the Dodge and chucked the ramp into the bed. "I won't tell the vet if you won't."

Windy Ray and Apisi were waiting at their usual spot when Pete and Pearl arrived at Sunny's. Windy Ray never had trouble bringing the cute and tiny three-legged Apisi into any businesses or eating establishments. The oxygen tank he lugged around took up more space than she did. The first time Pete tried to bring Pearl anywhere, however, he'd been met with resistance. The sweet-tempered swine had eventually won everyone over, except Julie at the post office. She made Pearl wait in the entryway—snow, rain, heat, or gloom of night.

As Pete pulled up a chair, Windy Ray nodded a greeting. "It's a happy day."

Pete groaned. He hoped the man might've forgotten. "Not really."

"For me it's very happy. I'm glad that you were born. It's something to celebrate."

Pete figured Windy Ray was the only person in the world who thought so, but he couldn't help a half smile. "I still don't know how you found out about my birthday."

"And you may never know."

A blast of wind threw itself against the window, and Pete looked out, staring at the wind turbines churning in the distance. On the northern plains, a person could see for miles.

"Today's a special day. A boy only turns eleven once."

He watched the turbine blades spin. That was the last time he'd had lemon pound cake. His mother had disappeared the next day.

"Here you go." The owner of the shop, Sunny herself, approached the table with two cones and two dishes. "I went with Rocky Road today."

"Thank you." Pete took the dishes and set them on the floor for the animals before accepting his cone.

"Rocky Road is my favorite," Windy Ray said.

Sunny grinned, her wide smile revealing a chipped tooth. "That's what you say every time."

Windy Ray nodded. "It's true every time."

Pete and Windy Ray had spent several weeks at the beginning of their friendship agonizing over the ice cream options and arguing over who'd made the better choice before Sunny had intervened. *"You're worse than a pair of old maids bickering over whose turn it is to do the laundry,"* she'd said. And she would know. A matronly woman in every sense of the word, she lived with her sister, and they fought over everything.

Sunny chose for them now, and Pete had never found reason to complain about the arrangement. Pearl and Apisi always got vanilla.

As he and Windy Ray ate their ice cream in silence, the wind continued to blow, and he found himself taking stock of his life. He had turned fifty today, after all. Half a century. If that didn't give a man something to chew on, what would?

The taking stock didn't take much time. He had a steady, if smelly, job, a pig, and one friend. It wasn't much to show for fifty years. Yet, despite his best efforts, he'd learned a few things. Such as how to look on the bright side.

Switching jobs every couple of years gave him the chance to see different places.

Pigs were more agreeable than most of the folks he knew.

He saved a lot of money on Christmas presents.

See?

In his contemplative state, he licked his ice cream scoop right off the cone. It hit the tiled floor with a splat.

"Snitch in a ditch." Pete hurried to wipe it up before Pearl could get at it. "Sorry, Sunny."

"I'll get the mop," she called.

"Snitch in a ditch," Windy Ray repeated. "That's a good one."

Pete chuckled. He'd been sixteen when Arnie had taught him an alternative to cussing that consisted of nonsense rhymes. Arnie was the only worker at the group home in Great Falls Pete had connected with. He'd heard Pete let loose some pretty appalling words and introduced him to the world of poetry. *"Language doesn't have to be ugly,"* Arnie had said and handed Pete a battered copy of Thoreau.

When your dreams spill out across the floor
When you just can't take it anymore
When the wolf is howling at the door
There's always Rocky Road ice cream.

Thoreau, he was not. But Arnie had taught him to love words. Poe, Silverstein, Kipling, Dickinson, Berry—Pete loved them all.

Sunny came over with a mop in one hand and another Rocky Road cone in the other.

Pete hopped up to grab the mop. "Here, let me. And you shouldn't have brought me a new cone. It was my own fault."

She let him clean the floor but waved away his protest. "It's no trouble. Besides, I heard it's your birthday."

Pete narrowed his eyes at Windy Ray. "You did, huh?"

"Sylvia always says you might as well celebrate birthdays while you have the chance because you only get so many."

Sylvia was Sunny's older sister. Pete sometimes heard them arguing in the back. They were around Pete's age but often acted like teenagers unhappy about having to share a bedroom.

Pete handed the mop back and reluctantly took the cone. "Thank you."

"Anything for my favorite customer." Sunny held his gaze for a second, then ducked her head under the table and patted Pearl's back. "Second favorite customer, that is."

Windy Ray cleared his throat.

Sunny straightened. "Okay, okay, you're all my favorite."

Windy Ray inclined his head toward her. "That's what you say every time."

Her eyes shimmered like sunlight on fresh snow. "It's true every time."

When Sunny had gone, Pete reclaimed his seat and determined to focus this time to avoid another mishap. Pearl nuzzled his shins from under the table, her ice cream long gone. He reached down and rested a hand on her head.

"Any big plans for the weekend?" he asked.

Windy Ray studied Apisi, who had settled on his lap, and gave this some thought. "Big? No."

"I hear it's supposed to storm next week."

Windy Ray frowned. "Will it keep us from going to Great Falls?"

"No, we should be okay. The storm's supposed to roll in Thursday night."

Windy Ray nodded. Pearl nuzzled Pete's shins again, this time with a little more urgency, and he scooted back to look at her.

"You getting antsy?"

She stomped her front hooves.

Pete pulled some money from his wallet and handed it to Windy Ray while popping the last bite of cone into his mouth. "I think we better go. See you Monday?"

Windy Ray nodded. Pearl scrambled to her feet to follow Pete.

"See you, Sunny," he called.

"Happy birthday" was the reply.

Outside, the wind stabbed at him like the sharp tines of a pitchfork. It didn't feel like ten degrees anymore. He and Pearl hurried around the corner to where the Dodge was parked. He didn't even bother with the ramp but bent and grabbed the pig around the waist to hoist her in. Oof. Either she was gaining weight, he was losing strength, or both.

She noisily protested his taking liberties.

"Sorry." He hugged her around the neck. "I should've at least warned you."

She forgave him with a magnanimous dip of her snout.

As he shut her door, he noticed a large cardboard box sitting beside the dumpster next to Sunny's back door. The air chilled him to the bone, but he felt himself drawn to the box. He'd been a garbageman—"waste management specialist," as his boss preferred to say—long enough to know folks don't typically leave boxes next to dumpsters unless they're too heavy to lift into the dumpster. What could be in there?

He approached with some trepidation, muttering to himself, "Please don't be kittens."

He'd faced that scenario once before and had no desire to do it again. His eyebrows rose as he peeked through the cardboard flaps. No animals.

"Books?"

There appeared to be all sorts. Cookbooks, spelling books, comic books. He growled his indignation. These didn't belong in the garbage. He tested the weight of the box to find it was at least forty pounds, but he couldn't leave it here.

The truck bed accepted the unexpected burden graciously, the Dodge's back-load extension springs hardly noticing the additional cargo. Pete hurried into the cab and started the engine. Pearl gave him a curious look.

"Shall we?"

When Pearl set her gaze straight ahead in anticipation of home, Pete laughed and swung the truck around. He hoped there would be something in the box he could spend the weekend reading.

Though his house was southeast of Sunny's, he drove southwest around the bank and down Clark Street so he could include a certain alley in his circuit. As he neared *her* house, he slowed. Would she be home on a Friday afternoon? It seemed like she was always home.

He spotted the tarp-covered picnic table before seeing the figure standing beside it, arms wrapped around herself in a futile attempt to ward off the dropping temperature. Pete's foot tapped the brake of its own accord. It was her. The hood of her ragged sweatshirt was pulled up, blocking his view of her face, but he had no doubt. What was she doing outside?

He inched the truck forward, transfixed. He shouldn't be here. He shouldn't be staring. A few loose strands of hair whipped across her downcast face while she paid them no heed.

She seemed far away, lost in whatever thoughts were holding her captive in the cold. The sleeves of her sweatshirt were pulled down over her bare hands, and she had nothing but socks on her feet. So strong was the urge to cover her frozen fingers with his—to lend her his warmth and his protection and his everything—that he couldn't swallow. Why didn't she move? Where was her boyfriend or husband or whatever Jerry was?

Just as the Dodge drew even with where she stood, she looked up. His breath caught as their eyes met. Hers appeared red-rimmed and watery and imbued with magic. His were surely dumbstruck and hopeless. She was thin and clearly distraught, but all he could think was that she was as beautiful as he'd always imagined.

He could feel her sorrow across the yard and over the fence and through the glass of the truck window. It blew over him like the wind, and something heavy and uncomfortable made itself felt in his heart as their eyes remained locked. Slowly, his right hand began to rise. What was it doing? Why would he wave at her? What was he thinking?

Put your hand down, Pete.

She blinked. She turned toward the door.

Then she was gone.

five

Wilma stirred a dab of honey into her tea Wednesday morning with more vigor than necessary. She really was *this close* to giving up the whole tea thing altogether. She'd tried every flavor available from the limited selection in Sleeping Grass and had yet to discover one she could say she enjoyed. But the hot drink did serve to chase away the chill.

Thankfully, the cold snap was about to end. If the discomfort in her joints wasn't enough evidence, the forecast was clear: a major winter storm was due to roll in by tomorrow night, and the incoming clouds were predicted to raise the temperature into the upper twenties. She'd already checked her fridge and cupboards to make sure she was well stocked in case the impending snow left her cut off from the outside world for an extended period of time.

She was.

The mail truck drove by, and she carefully rose from her chair. A trip to the mailbox would provide a fresh breath of air. The inside of her house had a distinct impression of staleness, she'd noticed recently.

It ought to have caused some level of chagrin, but instead

Wilma was inordinately pleased when she found a full thirty minutes had passed by the time she was back at the table, mail and letter opener in hand. It was those tall lace-up boots that gave her the most trouble. It took ten minutes just to get them on, but they were essential for February. Fleece-lined with nonslip treads. A gift from the kids a couple of Christmases ago.

It was almost ten o'clock. The morning was practically flying by.

Her stiff fingers sorted through the mail. A credit card bill. Another. A threatening-looking envelope that screamed FINAL NOTICE. No point in opening that one.

She tried to keep up on the minimum payments for all seven of her cards, but sometimes they got away from her and the fees began to pile up like heavy snow falling and choking out everything else. Maybe she should take Michael up on his offer to automate her monthly payments online. "*It's easy,*" he had said. But then he might see the shape her accounts were in. He only knew about three of her cards.

No, that wasn't going to work.

She raised her eyebrows at an envelope with a familiar return address. "Has it been six months already?"

She slid the letter opener under the flap and sliced it open. Inside, a single sheet of paper, a response card, and a smaller envelope awaited.

Dear Mrs. Jacobsen, the letter began. *Thank you for partnering with us to minister to women caught in the snares of addiction.*

The message went on in its usual way. A summary of the work Redemption House was doing to help drug addicts reclaim their lives. A personal story of how one such woman's life had been transformed through the recovery program. A plea for donations so the important work could continue.

Redemption House sent her these fundraising letters twice

a year. They were the same as all the others she received regularly from a variety of nonprofits specializing in serving vulnerable women.

"Now where did I leave my purse?"

She scanned the kitchen. It wasn't on the counter. It wasn't on the hook in the hall. Really, she must be more careful where she set her things.

Ah, there it was. Silly goose. It was hanging on the back of her chair.

She pulled out her checkbook. Her hand shook slightly as she filled out the check in careful, decorative cursive. *Redemption House*. When she reached the number box, she paused and squinted at her credit card bills. Her fixed income covered her living expenses, minimum payments, and Lily's wages. Thankfully, the final mortgage payment for the house had been made over a year ago. That was the money she now used to pay Lily.

She sighed. "Oh, Rosie. I wish there'd been a place like this for you. Maybe you could've gotten better. Maybe everything would've been different."

Her pen resumed its task. She hadn't been able to help Rosie, but if she could help even one woman escape destruction, she had to try. She was too old to volunteer with any of the Montana state programs for women like she used to, but she could write a check.

Three hundred dollars. It wasn't much in the grand scheme of things. It wouldn't make a dent in her debt, though that was what her son would say it should be used for. Yet it might make all the difference in the life of someone like Rosie.

"'Rosemary, Rosemary, cheeks like a cherry.'" She sang the old song softly. "'Eyes like the moon, what a treasure you are.'"

She tucked the check and response card into the return envelope and licked it closed. As she slid her checkbook back into her purse, the phone rang from the dresser by the fridge. The screen on the handset lit up as it jangled loudly, but she couldn't read the caller ID from the table.

Her sons, Michael and Steven, were both at work and couldn't possibly be calling. Her daughter . . . well, who knew what she was up to anymore. They hadn't spoken in ages. It could be Edna or Gladys, but Wilma decided to let the answering machine get it. She didn't want to be surprised again by a debt collector.

The machine message played, and the requisite *beep* sounded. A young lady's voice followed.

"Hello, this is Sadie from Financial Assistance Services. I'm calling to let you know about a new law that can reduce credit card debt by up to eighty percent. Here at Financial Assistance Services, we know that wading through the legalese can be daunting, but our goal is to assist you in navigating the ins and outs of this new legislation. Call us today to find out how we can help."

The woman left a phone number, and the call clicked off.

"A new law?" Wilma tapped her chin. She hadn't heard of such a thing, but she didn't exactly keep up on issues related to the government. She had better things to do. *Really.*

Michael would know what this woman Sadie was referring to, yet she couldn't ask him about it. He would scold her about her money problems and renew his request to become her financial power of attorney. Then she wouldn't be able to employ Lily anymore. Firing her would be the first thing Michael would do.

That was not an option.

She shuffled slowly to the phone and pressed the button to replay the message. She wrote down the number. It wouldn't hurt to call. If she could reduce her debt by eighty percent, she wouldn't need to keep thinking about selling her house. She could stay right where she was and continue watching over Pete. Continue praying that God would show her if there was something she could do for the young man. And maybe someday she'd even muster up the courage to face him again.

Pete could feel the promise of snow in the air as he parked in front of Windy Ray's cabin. Hopefully, it would hold off until tomorrow like it was supposed to. The thought of snow piling up conjured an image of *her*, standing alone out in the cold. Those eyes. He'd seen something in them that looked like need and had caused an unexpected stirring in his heart. What would it be like for someone to need him?

It was an absurd thought. He could barely meet Pearl's needs, let alone another human's. He had nothing to offer anyone.

Windy Ray came out of the house with Apisi tucked under one arm and his oxygen tank under the other.

"Come on, Pearl." Pete tugged on her blanket to coax her into the middle of the bench seat. "Make room."

She complied with a snort and a snuffle. The sparse wiry hairs on her back reminded him of an old man's comb-over. When Windy Ray opened the passenger door, Pearl stomped her hooves in delight.

"We must hurry." Windy Ray slid into the truck with no small amount of maneuvering, and the cab was suddenly crowded. "The store closes at five."

Pete put the truck into drive. "Why didn't you tell me that before? We could've picked you up sooner."

"It's soon enough."

Pete pointed the truck toward Great Falls. "What store is it?"

Windy Ray gave Apisi a long look before answering. "Glacier Nutrition and Feed. There's a special food there for Apisi's bowels."

"She's having stomach trouble?"

"Yes."

Pete studied Apisi from the corner of his eye. She did look a little out of sorts. "Do you know where the store is?"

Windy Ray pulled a piece of paper from the pocket of his coat. "I got directions from the internet."

Pete shot his friend a look. "You were on the internet?"

"I don't know how someone can be *on* the internet. The internet is not a sofa."

"You don't have a cellphone or computer."

Windy Ray smiled. "Sunny helped me."

Pete scoffed. "You told Sunny where we were going but not me? I could've looked it up."

"She gave me a raspberry Danish."

"Okay, well, that I could not do."

Pete neared the turn onto I-15, which would take them all the way to Great Falls. He checked the clock on the dash. Unless catastrophe struck, they would make it in time.

"How long has Apisi been suffering?"

"Long enough."

"The feed store in town couldn't order the food?"

In the ensuing silence, Pete heard the answer to his question and shook his head. This wasn't the first time the owner of the feed store in Sleeping Grass had made Windy Ray's life difficult. The man was a racist pig, no offense to Pearl. The next time Pete got the urge to punch something, he hoped that man's face was in the way.

"I would've ordered it for you. Or you could've had it shipped."

Windy Ray nodded. "I could have."

They fell into a comfortable quiet. Pearl occasionally sniffed at Apisi's ladybug sweater, and Apisi occasionally jumped to her feet to look out the window. Acres and acres of open prairie drifted by.

Pete turned up the radio and half listened to an NPR program about bison ranges in Montana. Would Windy Ray know the name of the woman who lived in the little gray house? Know her story?

He couldn't ask. Learning more about her would only torture him anyway.

And what if Windy Ray told Sunny he'd asked? Despite Pete's efforts to avoid as many human relationships as possible, he cared what Sunny thought of him. She was the only woman who didn't make him feel like a total loser, and the only person in Sleeping Grass who remembered him from before.

It was too risky.

Pete thought of Kipling's poem:

> If you can make one heap of all your winnings
> And risk it on one turn of pitch-and-toss,
> And lose, and start again at your beginnings
> And never breathe a word about your loss . . .

Yeah, that was a pretty big *if*. How many times had Pete already lost everything and started over? Now he had a rental he could afford and hadn't had to move in three years. He would be content with that. And he would keep Sunny far away from his personal life.

When Great Falls came into view, Pete switched the radio off so he could follow Windy Ray's directions to the store. Windy Ray recited them carefully, as if they were traversing the bustle of an overcrowded foreign metropolis rather than a city of barely sixty-thousand people. Neither of them felt comfortable in a place like this. They were more at home where the deer and the antelope play.

"There it is." Pete spotted it first. "Glacier Nutrition and Feed. With forty-two minutes to spare."

They piled out of the truck and onto the sidewalk, the fresh air welcome after two hours of breathing in close quarters.

Pete eyed the storefront. "It looks a little highfalutin."

The displays in the window and the crisp appearance of the décor gave the impression this was a store that catered more to the hoity-toity than the rough and tumble. He looked down at Pearl.

"Do you suppose they'll let her in?"

Windy Ray studied Pearl, as well. "Perhaps they won't notice."

Pete huffed. "Right."

Windy Ray's arms were full, so Pete turned the knob on the door and held it open for his friend. A pleasant chime announced their arrival as they entered the building. Pete sniffed the air appreciatively. He'd never been in a feed store that smelled like cinnamon apples.

"Good afternoon, gentlemen. I'm Evan." A man with a wide forehead and pointy chin appeared. His welcoming smile faltered as his gaze fell upon Pearl. "And who do we have here?"

six

Despite his initial uncertainty, which Pete conceded was only natural, the owner of Glacier Nutrition and Feed warmed quickly to Pearl's presence in the store. Once introductions had been made and Pete assured him she was potty-trained, of course.

"Can I take a picture of Pearl and Apisi for our Wall of Fame?" Evan asked. He pointed to a large bulletin board behind the cash register, where numerous photos of pets had been pinned.

Windy Ray tucked Apisi into the hood of Pearl's sweatshirt. "Apisi would be honored."

Pete nodded and stepped back to keep himself out of the frame.

Evan snapped a picture with a Polaroid camera he produced from behind the counter. "What brings you gentlemen in today?"

"It's a sensitive matter." Windy Ray lowered his voice to a whisper. "There's a special food for small dogs who can't move their bowels."

"Ah, yes." Evan immediately started toward the far corner of the store. "I know the one."

Windy Ray lifted Apisi from Pearl's hood and followed. Pete exchanged a glance with Pearl.

"After you." He held out his arm. "And behave yourself."

She was a good pig, but curiosity sometimes got the better of her. There were a lot of enticing sights and smells in a place like this. It would take no effort at all for her to knock over a display or small child, if one happened along. Potbellied pigs were not known for their finesse.

In all fairness, neither was he.

They met up with their friends at the far wall. Pete's eyes bugged out when he saw the price tag on the food Evan was showing Windy Ray, but he kept his opinions to himself. He had once spent $47.99 plus shipping on a bottle of hoof conditioner for Pearl. So there was that.

Evan rubbed his chin while looking Apisi over. "Have you tried wet food instead of kibble?"

"Yes." Windy Ray held Apisi up. She was small enough to sit in one of his large hands. "Apisi won't eat it."

"Huh," Evan said. "That's unusual."

"Apisi is unusual."

"That's a unique name."

"It means *coyote*."

Pete had laughed the first time he heard that, but after he'd gotten to know Apisi, he'd come to believe the moniker was fitting. If nothing else, the yips Apisi made sounded eerily similar to a coyote's.

"I can carry this to the counter for you if you'd like." Evan indicated the bag.

Windy Ray nodded, and Evan headed toward the front counter.

"Do you need anything else before we go?" Pete asked.

Windy Ray didn't answer at first. He was looking closely at a display of fancy winter dog booties. "It's a hardship for Apisi to do her business outside in the cold. Her paws don't like the ice."

Pete had promised to never joke about Apisi's sweaters again, but booties hadn't been part of the deal. "She can't wear those. They might clash with her outfit."

Windy Ray tapped his chin. "Style is not so important."

Pete's eyes narrowed. His friend was being serious. "There's no way you'll ever find booties small enough for those paws."

Windy Ray plucked the booties marked XS from the display and held them next to Apisi's feet. "I fear you are right."

His shoulders drooped as he put the booties away. Pete thought back to a garage sale last summer that had amassed a rather large free pile by the end of the day, including a doll with a backpack full of clothes and accessories. Surprised no one had wanted it, he'd taken it home because he didn't think it deserved to end up in the trash. He made a mental note to check through the backpack later to see if there was anything that could be improvised to work for Apisi's paws.

A real coyote would turn its nose up at booties, of course. But it was important to Windy Ray.

By the time the whole motley crew had reassembled in the Dodge, Pete's stomach was grumbling. He considered their options. He hadn't brought any food for himself, and home was two hours away. Not that there was anything worth getting excited about waiting for him at home. His cooking expertise did not extend past peanut butter and jelly and microwave dinners.

He started the truck to get the heat going and turned to Windy Ray. "Do you want to hit a drive-thru while we're here?"

The dine-in option wasn't tenable at the moment for obvious three- and four-legged reasons.

Windy Ray grinned. "I'd never turn down fried chicken."

Pete shook his head. "I'm not going within a hundred yards of that KFC, so you can forget about fried chicken."

"They won't remember us. It was months ago."

"The manager said if he ever saw me there again, he'd call the police."

"Fine." Windy Ray held up his hands. "We should go to a nice place, then. It's not every day we make it to the big city."

Pete gave him an incredulous look.

"We can place a pickup order." Windy Ray bobbed his head as if it had been decided. "There's this restaurant I went to once. They have pasta and chocolate cake. It will be my treat."

Pete's stomach grumbled louder. He *was* starving. . . .

"Okay, fine. What's the name of the place?"

"Giorgi's."

It took no time at all to bring up the menu for Giorgi's on his phone and place an order. Two plates of creamy chicken primavera, two orders of breadsticks, and two pieces of chocolate cake.

"It's going to take forty-five minutes," Pete said as he ended the call. "They said they're really busy, but they'll bring it out the back door."

"It's a popular place, I suppose. Everyone likes chocolate cake."

Pearl's ears perked up.

Windy Ray nodded gravely. "See what I mean?"

Pete began the journey to Giorgi's. The sun would be setting soon, which meant they'd be driving home in the dark. He pulled into the restaurant's parking lot packed with cars and drove around to the back door. Every few minutes, a teenager in a white apron came out carrying a large white bag and handed it to a waiting customer.

It seemed awfully busy for a wintery Wednesday night. Windy Ray must be right about the chocolate cake.

They waited in the truck until Pearl and Apisi began to fidget, then decided to take advantage of a small grassy area along the side of the building. It wasn't as cold here as it had been up in Sleeping Grass. Pete and Windy Ray watched couples come and go from the front door, holding hands and beaming into each other's faces, while the pets sniffed around and relieved themselves on the grass.

"I also need to relieve myself," Windy Ray said.

Pete squirmed. "Me too. Maybe they'll let us in the back door to use the bathroom."

The back door was located at the end of the patch of grass. The next time the kid in the apron came out with a bag, Pete was waiting for him.

"Hey, would it be all right if my friend and I ran in to use the bathroom?"

The kid handed off the bag to a man in a hurry and eyed Pete and his entourage skeptically. "I don't know. . . ."

"We've got a long drive home." Pete shifted on his feet, his bladder screaming now. "Please?"

The young man peered around him at Pearl. "Is that a pig?"

Pete held back a sigh. Why did people always ask him that when they could plainly see that it was? "Yes."

The kid made a face and took a step back as if she were an alligator instead. "The animals can't come in."

"Of course. No problem."

"Okay, I guess that would be fine. You'll have to go through the kitchen."

"Thank you." Pete turned back to Windy Ray and jerked his head. "You go first."

Windy Ray followed the kid inside, and Pete stomped his feet while he waited. His toes were almost numb. He was sure forty-five minutes had already passed.

Pearl rubbed her head against his knees, and he knelt to

look her in the face. "I know you're hungry. Just a little longer."

Evan had given her and Apisi a treat before they left the store, but Pearl wasn't fooled. She knew it was past her usual dinnertime. He would give her the apple and pig pellets he'd brought along while he ate his own meal. It wouldn't be easy to keep Pearl from his food, though, as she *loved* pasta and breadsticks.

Windy Ray slipped out of the building like a man who knew how to make himself invisible. "I don't remember it being so fancy in there." His eyes widened in wonder. "Red roses on every table."

"Wow." Pete didn't make a habit of frequenting establishments to which the word *fancy* could be applied. "No wonder they want guys like us using the back door."

A man in a wool-lined denim jacket joined them with a nod, evidently waiting for his pickup order, as well. He eyed Pearl curiously but said nothing.

"The bathroom is straight through the kitchen and to the left," Windy Ray said.

"Okay, thanks." Pete reached to open the door, but the kid beat him to it, appearing with a white bag in each hand.

"Peter?" he said.

"Yes, that's us." Pete gestured for Windy Ray to take the bags while he tried to maneuver around the kid to get inside.

The man in the denim jacket piped up. "I'm Peter."

Pete paused in the open doorway to look back. Uh-oh.

The kid frowned and looked back and forth between the two bags and the three men.

Windy Ray stepped up and waved Pete away. "I can sort it out."

Pete hesitated for a second before disappearing into the kitchen with a mumbled, "Be right back." He didn't care which bag they ended up with at this point, so long as they got some food and got out of here. It was going to be a long, dark drive home.

As he hurried through the kitchen to the men's room, he caught a glimpse of all the roses Windy Ray had mentioned—along with table after table of swoony-eyed couples—and something niggled at his brain. It was like he'd walked into a Hallmark movie. Hey, wasn't it February fourteenth? He mentally slapped a palm to his forehead. Today was Valentine's Day. He should've known.

A certain woman's stricken face appeared in his mind without warning, and he flinched. Why had she been crying? Would Jerry bring her roses today and make her smile?

He hoped so.

Pete would later swear up and down and halfway to Sunday that he was only in the bathroom for one minute. That it wasn't his fault, what happened next. But with *her* on his mind, he never could be a hundred percent sure.

When he came out of the bathroom, he saw and heard several things at once. A waiter in a white apron pushing a narrow three-tiered cart filled with slice upon slice of chocolate cake on shiny white plates. The sound of commotion from the kitchen. Windy Ray's voice calling his name. And a potbellied pig with her snout in the lone slice of cake on the bottom level of the cart.

Before Pete could process what was happening, a woman screamed. The waiter yelled. A man wearing a red tie dove at the pig.

"Pearl." Pete's senses returned to him, and he dove at the pig as well, prepared to fight the other man off her, but instead the man snatched the white plate and retreated with a look of panic.

"No!" He jabbed his fingers into what was left of the cake, his red tie flicking back and forth. "Where's the ring?"

The waiter's eyes bugged out. A dozen phone screens pointed in Pearl's direction.

Pete tugged Pearl away from the cart by her hood. "How did you get in here?"

Windy Ray appeared with Apisi. "I came to tell you I can't find Pearl."

"The ring." The man in the tie dropped the plate in despair. "I can't find the ring."

All eyes turned to Pearl's chocolate-covered snout, and Pete groaned.

This was way worse than the KFC.

seven

Pete stared Pearl down early Monday morning as they stood in the backyard. A single bare bulb above the sliding door cast a dim light on four inches of new snow.

"You've got to try." Pete crossed his arms over his chest. "It's been five days."

Yes, five days had passed without Pearl passing anything besides the usual manure. Philip, the man with the red tie from Giorgi's, texted Pete daily to check on the status of the engagement ring Pearl had gobbled up. *We're working on it*, Pete would text back.

Pearl snuffled and looked at the sliding door with obvious intent.

Pete heaved a giant sigh. "Fine. But we're going to try again during every single break today."

Windy Ray had found it boundlessly humorous when they discovered Philip had been planning a Valentine's Day proposal complete with a very expensive diamond ring hidden in a piece of cake. Pete had found it rather less humorous.

Philip had found no humor in it at all.

Pete slid open the door. "Come on, let's go."

They tromped through the house and to the Dodge. The

vet had said that as long as Pearl continued to eat, drink, and poop normally, there was no cause for concern. The ring would make an appearance eventually.

As Pete drove to work, Sleeping Grass was quiet and still, blanketed in the snow the predicted storm had left behind. Pete and Pearl had spent the weekend bumming around the house. Pete had sorted through the box of books he'd salvaged from Sunny's Sweet Shop and dug through that backpack of doll accessories. He'd been pleased to find a pair of fabric slip-on doll shoes made to look like red high heels that he was sure would fit Apisi. If he waterproofed the fabric and slid a rubber band around the tops, he was confident they would serve her well. They would even match her ladybug sweater.

The only problem was, she had three feet. One too few on the one hand—er, paw—and one too many on the other.

The Xpeditor had no trouble starting today, the temperature sitting at twenty-two degrees. Pete cracked his knuckles as he drove, then his neck. The inescapable Hi-Line wind blew a swirl of snow across the road.

"Good night, Pete. See you when the morning wind blows."

The same words his mother had spoken to him every night, but that time he hadn't seen her in the morning. Or any morning since.

Maybe if he knew where she was, where exactly she'd ended up, it would be easier to let her go. Decades had passed, after all. But she could be anywhere. Could've done anything. It was the not knowing that kept her stuck under the surface of his thoughts like a splinter.

He pulled up to a blue garbage bin and shook his head. He had arrived at *her* house already? He hardly dared look over the fence for fear she would see him and recognize him as the dolt who drove by and inadvertently spied on her a week ago. He hadn't taken the long way home since.

The hydraulic mast lifted the bin, then set it down. The lid stood up and swayed for a second before falling backward and slamming against the fence. Pete thought of Jerry and frowned.

"Hang tight, Pearl." He hopped out, shut the lid, and slid back into the truck without once letting his eyes stray toward the house. His face burned as he thought of her watching him, and for the first time he felt a twinge of embarrassment at being a garbage hauler. *Waste management specialist* or not, it was a dirty job. Smelly. He didn't mind the long tedious hours of driving, and he always put in an honest day's work, but what would she think of him if . . .

Well, it didn't matter. Their paths would never cross.

He dumped a few more bins before coming to a stop with another shake of his head. It was the Christmas caramel lady's house, but her blue garbage bin was nowhere to be seen.

There were people who regularly forgot to roll out their bins. People who would come running through their backyards in bathrobes and slippers, waving their arms as he drove by the empty space where their bins should've been. But in three years, this house had never missed a garbage day. Not once.

The Xpeditor's engine idled as he hesitated. Whoever lived here had probably decided to wait until next week because of the weather. The bin was never full anyway. Yet something kept his foot firmly planted on the brake.

"Ugh." He shifted the truck into park and pointed at Pearl. "I'll be right back. No monkey business."

He hopped out and looked around. There were no footprints in the snow by the fence. He cautiously tried the gate and found it unlocked. Through the slats, he could see the garbage bin up against the inside of the fence, giving nothing away. An uneasy feeling roiled in his stomach.

He looked over his shoulder at the truck. He had a route to run. This woman was none of his business.

It took three tries with his shoulder to get the gate open wide enough to slip through due to the snow.

"You're a fool," he muttered to himself as he crossed the yard. "You're going to scare this poor woman to death and get fired." But the feeling in his gut wouldn't go away.

He reached the back door and knocked, feeling like a complete idiot. He strained to listen but heard no reply. With his hands cupped against the glass, he peered through the window into the house. A light was on. He saw a tidy kitchen, a table with a teacup and saucer on it, and . . . a pair of legs sticking out from behind a chair on the floor.

His heart dropped a beat. "Hey." He pounded on the door. "Hey, are you okay?"

The legs moved. A heavy, winter boot–clad foot. The other boot was sitting on the chair. Why didn't she get up?

He tried the door. Locked. He ran back to the truck for his phone.

"Here." He quickly pulled snacks out for Pearl to keep her busy. "I'll be right back."

He dialed 911 as he raced back to the house. It only took a minute to give the address and explain the situation.

"Can you stay on the line until help arrives?" the dispatcher asked.

Pete sized up the door, wondering if he could force it open. "Yes."

"Can you still see movement?"

"Yes."

It was a heavy door with a dead bolt. It didn't budge when he rammed it with his shoulder. He growled and ran around to the front. That door was locked, as well.

He returned to the back so he could keep an eye on the woman through the window.

The dispatcher's voice was calm. "An ambulance will be there soon."

Pete hoped they would hurry, but he knew the emergency vehicles in Sleeping Grass were manned by volunteers who would need to be called away from whatever they were doing. He slammed a palm against the door in frustration, hating the feeling of helplessness.

A movement caught his eye. The shape of a person moving around the house. He cupped his hands to the glass again. Had the EMTs arrived already?

A woman stared back at him from mere inches away. Those eyes.

He froze, a sickening stillness like the eye of a storm overtaking the inside of his body.

It was *her*.

Wilma waved the EMT away. "Stop pestering me, please. I'm fine."

Her foot was cold—the one that hadn't yet had a boot on when she fell—but other than that, she really was fine. Physically, at least. Her pride was another matter.

Herb would have a fit if he were here.

"I strongly suggest you let us take you to the clinic." The EMT sounded exasperated. "I would feel better if we could get you checked out."

"Nonsense." Wilma shifted on her chair. "Nothing is broken, and I think I would know."

It took several more rebuffs before the EMTs finally packed up their paraphernalia and left the house, leaving firm instructions with Lily to keep an eye on her. Wilma breathed out relief when they were gone. So much hullabaloo over nothing. She had just wrestled one boot on when the phone rang, and she reached a little too far for it. She hadn't quite been able to get herself back up, that was all.

If she would've dealt with the trash bin last night instead of waiting until this morning, none of this would have happened.

She turned her eyes on Pete. After all the times she'd imagined him here, it was a shock to see him standing in her kitchen. To be this close. She wasn't ready. She didn't feel the courage she'd asked God repeatedly for.

"Can I make you some tea?" She hoped Lily and Pete would attribute the tremor in her voice to the morning's excitement.

Pete glanced at Lily before responding. "No, thank you. I need to get back to my truck."

He made a move toward the door.

"Wait." Wilma's mind churned through hundreds of thoughts, fears, and questions. She couldn't just let him go. Not again. "I want to thank you. You were very kind to check on me. Wasn't he, Lily?"

Lily nodded at Pete. "I'm glad you were here."

Lily had let Pete in the back door, and the two of them had carefully lifted Wilma off the floor. She still couldn't believe she had lost her balance like that. It was all that clunky old boot's fault.

"I'm glad I could help." Pete inched toward the door. "I'm sorry I tracked snow all over your kitchen."

"Nonsense." Wilma did her best to offer a reassuring smile. "Lily will set it to rights in no time. She's the best cleaning lady in town."

Pete's face contorted, and he hung his head. "I'm sorry, Lily."

"It's all right, Pete," Lily said softly. "I don't mind."

His ears turned red. Whatever was the matter with him?

"I'm glad you're okay, Mrs. Jacobsen. Now, I really need to—"

"No, um, you . . ." Wilma sputtered. If he walked away now, she might never get a chance like this again. "You must come for supper tonight. So I can thank you properly. Please. You too, Lily."

Pete gripped the back of his neck. "A friend of mine is expecting me tonight. We have dinner every Monday."

"Bring him with you." Wilma leaned into her offer. "The more the merrier. I insist."

"Ah, well, the thing is . . ." Pete's neck was red now, as well. "I've got a pet that can't be left alone in the house for long, and she—"

"I love animals." Wilma clapped her hands together. "She can come, too. It will be fun, right, Lily?"

Lily's face had that unreadable expression Wilma had grown accustomed to.

Wilma gave her an encouraging smile. "You'll come, won't you, Lily? Six o'clock?"

Lily looked at Pete, then the floor. "I'll try."

"Wonderful." Wilma waited for Pete to give an answer, her heart torn over what she hoped he would say. He was a grown man, but all she could see was the boy he'd once been.

"Okay," Pete finally said. "We'll be here."

When he had gone and Lily got to cleaning the house, conspicuously passing by the kitchen to check on her every five minutes even though she was fine, *really*, Wilma took a notepad from the drawer under the phone and tapped it with a pen. She must plan a first-rate meal for four. She must make a grocery list. She must figure out a way to tell Pete about . . . well, so many things. But she couldn't do *that* tonight. Not with other people around. She'd have to find a way to get him to come back.

Once they knew each other a little better—once she could assure herself she couldn't do any more damage than she'd already done—then she'd tell him.

eight

Pete turned down Mrs. Jacobsen's street with a sigh of resignation. It had taken no convincing at all to persuade Windy Ray to come with him to dinner. He'd been so curious and excited, he'd lost four Chickenfoot rounds in a row to Pete.

Pete was less excited. It had been a mistake, agreeing to this. He'd made a fool of himself in front of Lily, and somehow—*somehow*—now that he knew her name and had stood close enough to smell her hair, she seemed even more mysterious. What would he possibly say to her? What if Jerry was there?

Pearl snuffled as Pete parked in front of the well-kept yellow house, one of the nicest in the neighborhood. That was another reason he should've declined Mrs. Jacobsen's offer. What sort of person brought a pig with him to dinner?

"Maybe Pearl will finally give up her diamond ring tonight." Windy Ray scooped up his dog and his oxygen tank and opened the passenger door. "And maybe you'll keep her away from the dessert this time."

It was as if he could sense Pete's discomfort and was enjoying it. Pete helped Pearl down and hurried around the truck after Windy Ray. "Promise you won't say anything about that."

Windy Ray's long hair flew to one side in the wind. "I can't promise anything. I don't know the future."

As they reached the front door, Pete begged his friend, "Come on, please. Don't embarrass me."

Windy Ray fixed him with an exaggerated look of indignation. "I am not embarrassing."

"That's not what I meant. Wait, don't—"

Windy Ray knocked on the door with a smirk, and Pete groaned. He wasn't ready to face Lily. At the same time, she was the only reason he'd come back. A gust of panic blew over him. He bent close to Pearl's ear. "Be good."

Pearl's face seemed to say, *I'm always good*.

The door opened slowly, and Mrs. Jacobsen took in the sundry assortment on her doorstep with a steady smile. In a fancy, dark pink pantsuit that made him feel underdressed in jeans and flannel, she didn't seem nearly as old and frail as she had this morning. Her eyes glanced from person to person, creature to creature, without the surprise or consternation Pete had expected.

She pulled the door open wide. "I'm so glad you came, Pete. Please, come in and introduce me to your friends."

There was no turning back now. They lumbered inside, stomping their boots and crowding the entryway. Pearl sniffed the aroma of roast beef on the air with appreciation. Pete silently thanked the Creator Windy Ray always talked about that Mrs. Jacobsen had not chosen a pork roast.

"Thank you for having us." He jerked a thumb at Windy Ray. "This is my friend Windy Ray, and his dog, Apisi. This is Mrs. Jacobsen."

"Oh!" She flicked her wrist. "Please call me Wilma."

Windy Ray tucked his oxygen tank under his arm and

took hold of her hand, suddenly very serious. "It's an honor, Mrs. Wilma."

She chuckled. "Just Wilma will do. It's nice to meet you, Windy Ray."

He nodded gravely. "It's nice to be met, *wawetseka*. Perhaps you will call me Raymond."

Wilma smiled. "Certainly."

Pete's brow furrowed. *Raymond?* What on earth was up with his friend? He was acting as though he'd never spoken to a woman before. As if this dinner party wasn't weird enough already. Pete shook his head and gestured to the swine at his side. "This is Pearl. I'm sorry, I should've mentioned she was a . . ."

"Nonsense." Wilma's eyes lit up. "You said you were bringing a pet, and that's what you've done. Pleased to meet you, Pearl."

Pearl made a variety of noises as Wilma patted her head gently. Pete knew Pearl preferred a good hard scratch or rub that invigorated her rugged hide, but he wasn't about to tell Wilma that. He discreetly glanced around the house in search of Lily but didn't see her.

"Lily isn't able to join us, unfortunately." Wilma gave him a wink as if she knew his thoughts. "She called a few minutes ago to extend her regrets."

Pete swallowed hard and hoped the relief and disappointment he felt were not evident on his face. Had she decided not to come because of him? Because of how he'd acted this morning? It would make sense. No reasonable woman would want to sit by him at a table.

Wilma directed them to hang their jackets on the hooks in the hall and led them to the kitchen. "Where would your four-legged friends be most comfortable, gentlemen?"

Pete spotted a heating vent along the trim board behind

the table and pointed. "They'll be just fine over there. They like to snuggle up in the warmest place they can find."

"All right." Wilma nodded. "And have they eaten or . . . ?"

"Yes. They had dinner before we came."

"Wonderful. Please make yourselves at home."

Pearl and Apisi gravitated toward the vent with little coaxing, drawn by the warm air. Pete had taken Pearl on a long walk before they came, hoping to tire her out. He took a seat at the already-set table, feeling like he should be helping with something but afraid of ruining whatever plans Wilma had laid. This was nothing like dinner at Windy Ray's cabin, where they sometimes ate straight out of the pot while hunched over the stovetop.

Windy Ray took a deep breath through his nose. "It's better than the smell of seasoned venison cooking over a fire at twilight."

"My, what a compliment." Wilma blushed.

"Please allow me to assist you." Windy Ray bowed, and Pete puzzled. He'd never seen his friend act like this before.

"You may fetch the Jell-O salad from the fridge if you'd like."

Windy Ray eagerly retrieved a square glass container. Pete's heart lurched at the sight of the lime Jell-O and cottage-cheese concoction, but he didn't know why. Had he ever had it before? He remained helplessly and awkwardly at the table and wished he could disappear as Windy Ray and Wilma got everything ready.

When they finally sat down, Wilma held her hands out, one to Pete and one to Windy Ray. "Would one of you like to say grace?"

Windy Ray took her hand with a look Pete could only describe as reverent. "I would be honored."

Pete tried not to roll his eyes as he took Wilma's other hand. He'd heard Windy Ray pray before—every Monday for almost three years now—but it seemed different tonight. Fervent and deliberate.

"O Creator of heaven above and earth beneath, I thank you for this gift of sustenance and for the eyes to behold the beauty before me. May the Great Spirit guide us along the path of righteousness as surely as the *aapi'si* finds his way to his den. In the name of your beloved Son whom you sent to walk the dusty trail, amen."

Pete mumbled an amen as he stared at the feast before him. Windy Ray talked often of the Creator, the Great Spirit, and the Son. It never bothered him, but this time Pete thought of the fool he'd been in front of Lily and wondered, Why would the Creator make someone like him?

Wilma began passing food around. "Did Pete tell you how he came to my rescue, Raymond?"

Windy Ray dipped his head. "He's a great man, but he does not know it."

Pete inwardly scoffed. He gathered garbage for a living and had virtually nothing to show for his fifty years of life. *Great* wasn't the right word for him.

"Indeed." Wilma turned her gaze on Pete. "I hope you were able to finish the rest of your route all right after being so rudely interrupted by a clumsy old woman."

The town office had received four calls from folks wondering why Pete was late picking up their bins, but he wasn't about to tell her that. "It was no problem. Pearl was a little put out, though. She doesn't like to miss out on the action."

"Neither do I." Wilma grinned. "Now, tell me, how long have you lived in Sleeping Grass?"

He swallowed. "Three years."

She studied him and waited as if she knew there was more to it.

"But I lived here for a while when I was little. A long time ago."

"I see."

The expression she made reminded him of his mother. It was unnerving. If Wilma had been living in Sleeping Grass for a long time, she might remember his mom. Might've even known her. But he couldn't bring himself to ask.

She cut a minuscule piece of roast beef. "Where did you live before coming back?"

"Here and there." He slathered butter on a biscuit and avoided her eyes. "Anyplace that would have me."

"Pete is like the wind roaming the face of the earth," Windy Ray offered.

Wilma bobbed her head. "Sounds adventurous."

Pete hated talking about himself. He had no interest in sharing his life story, such as it was. He crammed his mouth full of biscuit and resigned himself to the inevitable. This would be one of the most uncomfortable dinners of his life.

Wilma held out two large Tupperware containers packed tight with leftovers. "Please, I insist. It's far too much for me to keep for myself."

It was true. The food would go bad long before she could finish it. She also hoped the containers would give Pete a reason to return to her house.

"We're grateful." Raymond took the containers from her and bowed. "You have blessed us this evening."

My, he was handsome, though she was too old to think such things. The lines of his face spoke of years of struggle that tugged at her heart. Herb had had lines like that.

"You're welcome anytime, gentlemen." She looked down at Pearl and Apisi. "You too."

Pete bobbed his head. "Thank you for letting them come."

"It was no trouble at all. They're so well-behaved."

Raymond's lips quirked. "It's not always so."

"Oh?"

A grin appeared. "A pig and her pastries are not easily parted."

Raymond gave Pete a sidelong glance. Pete's face turned red.

"Is there a story you're not telling me, Pete?" she teased.

He glared at Raymond. "No."

She raised one eyebrow but stuck to her policy not to press. As she hoped, Pete proceeded all on his own.

"It's just that, uh, she got into some cake last week that happened to have an engagement ring in it that happened to be for a proposal that happens to now be, uh"—he eyed the pig—"delayed."

Wilma's eyes widened as the implication of Pete's words sank in. A giggle worked its way up from her stomach. She couldn't remember the last time she'd *giggled*, of all things. "Oh my. So Pearl is something of a . . . a party pooper?"

Raymond's laugh boomed through the house. "Party pooper. Yes. Pete will have to drive all the way to Great Falls to return the ring."

Wilma stood a little straighter. *Great Falls?* Bless that cake-loving pig. This couldn't be more perfect.

"Lily was just talking about needing a ride to Great Falls, Pete. Something about stocking up at the Walmart. Do you have any idea when you might be going?"

Lily hadn't said she *needed* a ride, but this was too good of an opportunity to pass up. Wilma would love to see Lily get out more. Do more than clean her house. She'd been quite disappointed when Lily called to say she wasn't coming tonight.

Pete looked like he'd swallowed a fly, however.

"Hopefully soon." He glanced at Pearl. "I mean, any day now."

"Perhaps you wouldn't mind if I send my phone number with you, then." She retrieved a pen and paper from the drawer. "You can call me, and I can let Lily know when you're ready to drive down. I'm sure she would appreciate it."

Every time Wilma said Lily's name, Pete's eyes seemed to widen, and the wheels began to turn in Wilma's head. Despite being rather timid and wearing frumpy clothes, Lily was a lovely young woman. She deserved better than that man she was living with—Wilma was not impressed with *him*. It certainly wouldn't hurt Lily to spend time with Pete instead.

Herb's voice echoed through the years—*"Mind the meddling, Willy Mae"*—but she shooed it away and wrote her number down. Herb hadn't always been right about everything.

She held the paper out to Pete.

He stared at it. "I'm not sure she'd want to be seen with the likes of me."

"Nonsense. Any woman would be fortunate to ride with you."

He didn't seem convinced, but he took the paper. "Okay. Sure, if I can help. I guess I'll be in touch?"

"Wonderful."

She leaned on her cane as the men slipped on their jackets and boots. Raymond was ready first and turned to her with a spark in his eye.

"It was a beautiful evening, wawetseka." He bowed. She wished he would stop doing that. "I hope I will see you again."

She dipped her chin once. Raymond was pleasant company, but it was Pete she wanted to spend time with. Needed to spend time with. And what did wawetseka mean?

Goodbyes were said, and she waited until her new friends were all in the truck before closing the door with one final wave. She shuffled back to the kitchen and sank into her favorite chair. The dishes would have to wait until tomorrow. She was exhausted. From her early morning fall to entertaining a potbellied pig, it was more excitement in one day than she'd experienced in a long time.

Her eyes settled on her landline phone. Would Pete call? Would he stop by with the Tupperware containers? Did he have suspicions about her?

He'd never been in this house until today, but they *had* met before. She was sure he didn't remember. How old had he been the last time she'd spoken to him? Ten? They'd both changed so much since then.

When he'd caught sight of her lime Jell-O salad, however, the look on his face had nearly stopped her heart. She could see his mind working to solve an old, old puzzle.

She hoped he wouldn't. Not yet. Not until she knew he was going to be okay, even after what she'd done. He deserved to know what she knew, though, didn't he? She couldn't put it off forever.

But she could put it off a little longer.

nine

Thursday evening, Pete forced himself to drive to Wilma's house to return the empty Tupperware containers. It was easier this time, knowing Lily wouldn't be there. Windy Ray hadn't been subtle about wishing to accompany Pete on this mission, but Pete planned to talk to Wilma about Lily and didn't want any witnesses.

He parked and turned to Pearl. "This is all your fault, you know."

She made a squealing noise he could only interpret as a laugh and flicked her tail back and forth. He put a hand on each side of her face, leaned close, and whispered, "You're the worst."

He didn't actually blame her, of course. It was his own fault she'd snuck through the back door at Giorgi's. His own fault he'd been roped into taking Lily along for the trip back to Great Falls. And now that the ring had finally resurfaced, it was time to make plans.

The thought of sitting next to Lily for two hours made his hands clammy and his heart race.

Wilma opened the door with a smile. "What a surprise. Please come in."

He should've called. "I brought your containers."

She closed the door behind them. "You can set them on the counter. The food was just as good warmed up the next day, I hope."

He followed her to the kitchen. "It was great. Thanks. And I have something else for you." He didn't want to do it, but he'd promised he would. He pulled a smooth, round rock from his pocket and held it out. "This is from Windy Ray. Er, Raymond."

She put a hand to her chest. "For me? How thoughtful."

She took the rock, which was the size of her palm and the color of thunderclouds, and turned it over and over. "It's lovely."

"He has a thing for rocks."

"Please tell him thank you for me."

Pete nodded. "I also wanted to let you know I'll be heading to Great Falls Saturday morning."

Wilma's face brightened. She looked down at Pearl and spoke in that voice folks reserve for little kids and animals. "Somebody's tummy must be feeling better now, hmm?"

Pearl moved to lean against Wilma's legs in response, and Pete quickly intervened. "Oh no, you don't." She would knock poor Wilma over in no time. "Sorry about that."

"Why don't we sit down." Wilma gestured toward the table. "Then I don't have to worry about losing my balance."

Pete hesitated, but it wasn't like he had anyplace else to be. He took the seat across from hers, and Pearl pressed herself against his knees.

Wilma studied his face as if searching for something. "Can I make you some tea?"

He leaned his arms on the table. "No, thank you."

"Have you eaten?" She half rose from her chair. "I can fix you a sandwich."

He held up a hand. "No, thank you, I picked up a burger from Gunner's Griddle after work."

"Oh." She sat back down with a look of disappointment. "Do you do that often?"

He patted his stomach. "More often than I should."

He hadn't grown wider with age—his frame was still wiry as ever—but his body verified the years in other ways. His bald spot grew by the day, his hands were stiff and callused from years of manual labor, and his nose, which had been broken three times, had grown bulbous around the crooked cartilage so that it resembled a funnel cake from the county fair.

He was an ugly son of a gun.

"I make a pretty good burger myself, you know." Wilma spoke with enough insinuation, even he couldn't miss it.

He smiled. "I'm sure you do. I'm a big fan of your Christmas caramels."

"Oh." She waved a hand. "That's nothing. Just some cream, butter, and sugar. But I suppose"—she bent her head toward Pearl and lowered her voice—"I should rethink your gift card to The Hog House."

He laughed. "It does present something of a dilemma."

"There's a Chinese place in Shelby." Wilma nodded. "I'll do that next time."

"You don't have to—"

"Nonsense. You work hard out there every day. Where would Sleeping Grass be without you? Drowning under piles of garbage, that's where."

Pete shifted in his seat. She made it sound like he was doing something important, but he'd never done anything important in his life.

"Were you a garbageman before coming here?"

He looked at his hands. "No. I drove a cement truck for a while, though."

"You've done a lot of driving, then, hmm?"

That felt like an understatement. He'd crisscrossed half the country looking for a place to settle, a place to belong, with no success. "Yeah."

"And what about your family? Do you see them often?"

They were crossing into dangerous territory now. How could he explain to this woman that he had no family? His younger sister was the only person he had left, and he hadn't seen her since she told him to butt out of her life some thirteen years ago. His temper had cost him more than a job that day.

"Not much," he said. "What about your family?"

She sighed. "Herb's been gone almost five years now. My kids come when they can. Sleeping Grass isn't an easy place to get to, you know. It's not on the way to anywhere."

Pete knew. That was one reason he'd been willing to consider the job in Sleeping Grass when he started running out of options. A man could hide here.

"Anyway, about Saturday . . ."

"Right." She sat up straighter. "I should call Lily. Would you fetch me the phone, please?"

She held out her hand, and he tried not to frown. She wanted to call her right now? Pearl protested when he stood and she had to reposition.

He grabbed the phone and set it in Wilma's hand. He hadn't seen a landline in years. Wilma punched in Lily's number from memory, and Pete had no choice but to stand awkwardly by and wait.

"Hello, Lily, dear, it's Wilma." Wilma's voice rose as if she had to shout to be heard. "I've got great news. Pete—you remember Pete?—is driving to Great Falls Saturday morning, and he says he would be delighted to take you along."

Pete's face heated. He'd said no such thing. What would Lily think?

Wilma listened to Lily's response for a moment, then cupped a hand over the phone and whispered to him. "What time are you going?"

His face still burning, he cleared his throat. "Uh, ten. If that's—"

"He says ten." Wilma listened and nodded. "Mm-hmm. Yes. I see." Another pause. "Lovely, dear. Okay, see you then."

She hung up and handed her phone back to Pete. He dutifully returned the phone to its base and gave her a wary look.

"It's all settled." She grinned. "You can pick her up here at ten."

His brow furrowed. "Here?"

"Yes." Wilma's smile dimmed. "She said that would be best. I assume it has something to do with that boyfriend of hers." Her voice rang with disapproval.

He tried to sound unconcerned. "Have you met him?"

Wilma drummed her fingers on the table. "No. I don't get out much, and she's never brought him over. But I've gathered he's rather particular about things, if you know what I mean."

Pete nodded slowly as his thoughts bounded about like jackrabbits. He shouldn't get involved with a woman like Lily. She was younger than him. Better than him. In a relationship. Not that giving her a ride was the same as getting involved. He had a few things to pick up at Walmart, too. But the last thing he needed was to cross paths with Jerry.

He realized Wilma was staring at him with a funny look on her face. He turned. "I should get going."

She paused for a second, as if she wanted to say something but changed her mind. "Okay. I don't want to keep you." She rose from the table. "I'm sure you have more exciting things to do than entertain an old lady."

He didn't, but he was afraid to give Wilma the chance to ask any more questions, or Pearl the chance to start causing trouble. His house had been pig-proofed long ago, but

Wilma's had not. The knickknacks displayed around the living room wouldn't stand a chance against Pearl if she started thumping around.

At the door, Pearl waited patiently while he slipped on his boots.

"Good girl." He gave Pearl a scratch and Wilma a wave. "I guess we'll see you Saturday."

Her smile seemed thoughtful. "I'll be here."

Though the temperature had dropped back into single digits for the evening, she stood in the open doorway and watched until he pulled away from the curb. His heart felt a little tug. She was alone, like him. Maybe he could stop by again, and not just on Saturday morning to pick up Lily. He would be careful not to overstay his welcome in her life, though. He'd done that enough times when he was a kid to know it hurt less if you remove yourself from someone's life than if you wait for them to kick you out.

The wind howled as he and Pearl drove home, parked, and hurried into the house, but this time he didn't hear his mother. He heard other voices.

"We only have room for your sister, Pete. I'm sure they'll find another place for you."

"You're nothing but white trash, Pete."

The voices grew louder, screaming in his ears.

"You're lucky we kept you as long as we did, Pete."

"We just can't deal with these behaviors anymore, Pete."

Pete, Pete, PETE!

He slammed the front door on the wind, his heart pounding. Pearl nuzzled his hand, hoping for a snack, and he walked woodenly to the fridge for a banana.

"You'll never leave me, right, Pearl?"

She eagerly took the fruit from his hand and ate it loudly, drowning out everything else.

Pete nodded. "You and me need to stick together."

ten

Despite the cold, Pete's hands began to sweat as he neared Wilma's house Saturday morning. Lily would be there. She was going to ride in his truck. He should've vacuumed the interior. What if it smelled like garbage? What if she was allergic to pigs?

Windy Ray had offered to pig-sit, but Pete had been too afraid of being alone with Lily. He'd thought Pearl would provide a buffer. Now he wasn't so sure. How would he explain Pearl to Lily?

He'd be tempted to cancel the trip altogether if he wasn't so eager to get the diamond ring off his hands. It was worth more than his truck. He'd cleaned it a dozen times, and poor lovesick Philip was desperate to have it back. Pete hoped someday Philip and his future wife would be able to laugh about all of this.

He parked the Dodge in front of the yellow house with a resigned sense of doom and stuck a finger in Pearl's face. "You stay here and be good. I'll be right back." He opened the door and stepped out, then narrowed his eyes and reached back in. "I'll take these." He removed the keys from the ignition. No need to tempt fate.

Pearl turned up her snout.

Wilma opened the door when Pete knocked, and his stomach twisted like a cinnamon roll from Sunny's when he saw Lily standing behind the impeccably dressed older woman. She didn't smile or frown, just fixed her brown eyes on him. They reminded him of a doe standing on the side of the road, studying each car that passed as if trying to decide whether to leap in front of it.

"You made it," Wilma said. "Please come in."

Pete looked over his shoulder. "I shouldn't. Pearl's waiting in the truck."

"Of course. You'll want to get going, then." She stepped aside to let Lily pass. "I hope it's not too windy on 15."

Pete fumbled for something to say. "Uh, thanks."

Thanks? That was all he could think of? Thanks for what? For not hoping for *bad* weather? Windy Ray would rib him mercilessly for this if he were here. Thank goodness he wasn't.

Lily bent to pick up a camo-printed cooler just inside the door.

Pete jolted out of his daze and stepped into the house. "Here, let me." He lifted the empty cooler and glanced at Wilma. "This is a nice one."

She leaned against her cane and chuckled. "Herb fancied himself a mighty hunter. Nothing but the best gear for him when he was camping in the woods with his buddies." Wilma's face softened at the memory.

Lily stood in the doorway and waved back at Wilma. "See you later, Miss Wilma."

Wilma smiled. "Don't you forget those chicken-and-rice bowls, dear."

One side of Lily's mouth twitched. "I wouldn't dare."

She headed outside, and Pete was moving to follow when Wilma grabbed his arm and said, "Here." She shoved forty dollars into the pocket of his coat and whispered loudly, "Take Lily somewhere nice for lunch, hmm?"

He was too dumbfounded to speak. "I . . . uh . . ."

She gave Pete a meaningful look as she pushed him out the door. "You two have fun, now."

He stumbled toward the truck as she quickly shut the door behind him. It was abruptly very clear to Pete that he was in over his head.

Wilma's words rang in his ears as he carried the cooler down the short icy path to the Dodge. Fun? There were folks who found haunted houses fun. That must be the kind of fun Wilma was referring to because he felt like he was about to die. He kicked himself as Lily reached the truck ahead of him and opened the passenger door. He should've opened it for her. He should've asked her if she minded having Pearl along. He should've *warned* her at least.

Lily peered into the cab and smiled the first real smile Pete had seen.

"Hello, you must be Pearl." Lily tilted her head. "Can I sit by you?"

Wilma must have told her about the pig. Pearl squealed irritably.

Pete hefted the cooler into the back and called to the insufferable swine, "Come on, Pearl, move over." He rarely used a stern voice with her, but now seemed like the time. "There's plenty of room."

Pearl reluctantly shifted to the middle of the seat but turned her tail toward Lily with a snort. Pete hurried to the other side and climbed in behind the wheel. Pearl never acted like this with Windy Ray.

"She can't be left alone at home." Pete missed the ignition twice before getting the key inserted correctly, starting the engine, and pulling onto the road. "I'm sorry I—"

"I don't mind." Lily's voice was like the creek behind

Windy Ray's house in the summer. Unwavering and unhurried.

"Okay." He stared straight ahead, concentrating as if still learning to drive. He'd never been so aware of the duct tape he'd liberally applied to the rip in the seat. Why had he never replaced the fabric?

Pearl breathed noisily beside him, leaning closer than was necessary.

"Thanks for bringing me along," Lily said.

"You're welcome." Pete was grateful he had to watch the road so he wouldn't accidentally ogle her. He wasn't an ogler. He most certainly did not make a habit of ogling women. But he was so drawn to her face, so aware of her presence that he feared there were a lot of things he might do that he was not in the habit of doing. Like make a fool of himself . . . although that wasn't as rare an occurrence as he would like it to be.

Her hair was the same color as her eyes, like the bark of a snowberry bush. She folded her pale hands neatly in her lap, and he couldn't help but think of a verse from one of his favorite Edna St. Vincent Millay poems:

> By the dear ruffles round her feet,
> By her small hands that hung
> In their lace mitts, austere and sweet,
> Her gown's white folds among.

It was a poem about a ghost in a garden. Fitting for Lily.

The back of his neck began to prickle as several miles passed in silence. Should he say something? Everything in his truck suddenly seemed dingy compared to her. She was such a *woman*. This was nothing like sharing a cab with Windy Ray, who smelled like woodsmoke and sweat. Lily somehow smelled of sunshine, even in the dead of winter.

Finally, Pete couldn't stand it any longer. "How long have you known Wilma?" The words came out too forcefully, and she flinched. He frowned. "Sorry. I don't talk to many people other than Pearl and Windy Ray. I'm a little out of practice."

She looked at him. "Windy Ray?"

"He's my . . . uh, friend." He stopped himself from saying *only friend*. He didn't want her feeling sorry for him.

"You mean Raymond?"

"Wilma told you about him?"

"She showed me his rock." Her voice held a hint of amusement. "We both agreed it was a very sweet gesture."

Didn't that figure. Here Pete had thought it was the oddest thing he'd ever heard of, giving a woman a rock. He'd told his friend it was a terrible idea. He could never let Windy Ray know about this.

"Did Wilma also tell you about Pearl's—" he glanced at the pig—"adventure?"

Lily laughed, and he swore the whole truck momentarily lifted off the road.

"Yes." Lily patted Pearl's back. "That was a bold move, sweet girl."

In response, Pearl stood and emitted in Lily's direction a very rude noise from her hind end.

Pete went stiff with horror. "Pearl!"

An acrid smell filled the cab, and he began to panic as Lily's eyes widened. It was far too cold to roll down the windows. How could Pearl do this to him? Heat crept up his neck and enflamed his ears as his breathing became shallow. He'd been right. He'd entered the most haunted of haunted houses and he was about to die.

Wilma blinked at the man glaring down at her from the doorway as the wheels turned in her mind. This must be Jerry. What was he doing here?

"I said, where is she?" He narrowed his eyes. "You're Wilma, aren't you? Lily said you needed her help today."

Wilma refused to let him ruffle her. She thought fast. "Yes, of course. I don't know what I'd do without her."

"I need to talk to her."

"She's not here."

His scowl deepened.

Wilma drew herself up to her full height. "I sent her on an errand. It's really very kind of her to help me, don't you think?"

"When I texted her, she said she was here."

Wilma waved a hand. "She left only moments ago."

It had, in fact, been nearly four hours already. She hoped the Lord would forgive her for the lie.

"What was the errand?"

She put a hand to her chest. "I beg your pardon, but that is none of your business, young man. My personal needs are not your concern."

His nostrils flared. "Lily is my concern."

"I assure you I will send her home as soon as she has finished helping me. Now, if you'll excuse me, you're letting in the cold air, and my old bones would thank you if you'd please remove your foot."

He had wedged his boot in front of the door to keep her from closing it. He stared her down, and she stared right back, shivering like a freshly shorn sheep on the inside but determined not to let it show. This was *her* house. He had no right to show up here and intimidate her.

After what felt like far too long a time, his face relaxed into a smarmy smile. "No problem. Sorry to bother you, ma'am." He removed his foot from blocking the door.

She dipped her head. "Good day."

As the door clicked shut, she let out a long, shaky breath. Her legs wobbled as she made her way back to the kitchen.

How dare he speak to her like that. *Really*. Perhaps she should make herself some chamomile tea.

She ran water into the pot and set it on the front burner. Why hadn't Lily told him she was shopping for Wilma in Great Falls today? Something felt wrong about this whole thing, but far be it from her to second-guess the dear young lady. If she hadn't wanted to tell Jerry she was going to Great Falls with Pete, Wilma certainly wasn't going to tell him either.

The teapot began to whistle, and she turned the burner off, her mind still ruminating over the expression on Jerry's face. Why had he been angry with her? They'd never even met before.

The phone rang, and she absentmindedly answered it, her knees a little shaky. "Hello?"

"Hi. This is Sadie from Financial Assistance Services calling for Wilma Jacobsen."

"Oh. Yes. I believe you've called before, Sadie."

She hadn't yet called the number Sadie had left in her last message. It was easier to focus on other things, like Pete and Lily. But the bills kept coming, and Wilma knew something needed to be done, and soon.

"I sure have," Sadie said, her tone kind. "I wanted to tell you about a new law aimed at providing debt relief for people such as yourself. Do you have a minute to chat?"

Wilma hesitated. It would be better if her eldest son were here for this, or at least Lily. Numbers and budgets had never been her strong suit. She'd gotten herself into this situation, however, and she should be the one to get herself out of it.

"Yes." Wilma picked up a pen and notepad. "Go ahead, dear."

eleven

Pete was sorry to see the exit that would take his truck back to Sleeping Grass from I-15. Boy, was he sorry.

After the flatulence fiasco with Pearl, which he had *not* forgiven her for, the day had turned around. He'd somehow had the presence of mind to get Lily talking about flowers, and she hadn't stopped. She'd described all the different plants in her yard—when each one bloomed, which were her favorites—and he never once let on that he already knew about every inch of her garden.

On top of that, the sun had been shining, and the big blue Montana sky couldn't help but make anybody smile.

They'd delivered the ring to a very relieved Philip, who had given Pearl a wary look and asked if she'd had all her shots. Then there had been a slight hiccup when they arrived at Walmart and Pete realized he couldn't bring Pearl inside. He'd always had Windy Ray along in the past, who was more than happy to wait in the truck with the animals so long as Pete brought him back a box of Raisinets and a twelve-pack of Pepsi.

Lily had suggested Pete give Pearl his Carhartt vest and the grungy baseball cap in the back seat and put her in a cart.

Lily could've suggested they walk into the store in swimsuits, and he wouldn't have refused her. They'd gotten plenty of odd looks as they wandered the aisles, Lily pushing a cart for the food, and Pete pushing one filled with seventy-nine pounds of pork, but no one had said a word to them about it. Pete didn't figure there were many places left in the country where you could get away with a stunt like that, so God bless Great Falls, Montana.

"I can't believe that worked," Lily had said as they left the store. "I haven't had this much fun in years."

After transferring the frozen food to the cooler, Pete had taken Lily to lunch as Wilma suggested, but he had certainly not used Wilma's money. Driving home now, he brainstormed ways to give it back to her without making her mad.

Lily's voice cut through his thoughts. "How long have you had Pearl?"

"About three years now. She was a piglet when I found her."

"Found her?"

He hesitated. "At the dump. I got out of the truck to stretch my legs and heard a noise. I thought it was a sea gull at first, but it was Pearl."

Lily put both hands on her chest. "How awful. She's lucky you came along."

Pete shrugged, secretly pleased by her words.

"How did you choose her name?"

"It was Windy Ray's idea. I guess there's a story in the Bible about a man who finds a pearl of great price and sells everything to buy it. He said Pearl is kind of like that. Because when I found her, I knew she was worth something."

Lily gave Pearl a fond look and rested her hand on Pearl's back. "I like that."

Pearl stiffened and scooted closer to Pete. She hadn't warmed up to Lily as Pete had hoped, but Lily didn't seem to be bothered by the fact. Maybe Pete could forgive Pearl, after all, since they wouldn't even be on this trip if it wasn't for her.

Sleeping Grass came into view, and Pearl squealed.

"Are you happy to be home, Pearl?" Lily asked.

A series of grunts followed.

Pete slowed as the speed limit changed. "I think she mostly just misses the food when we're out. You wouldn't believe her appetite."

"She ate a diamond ring." Lily laughed. "I believe it."

Pete smiled. Everything about Lily fascinated him. The way she scrutinized everything with wide eyes as if it were brand-new. The waves in her hair that made it seem as though it was moving even though he'd never met anyone with such a sense of stillness. The tone of her voice, which could be a murmuring creek or a rushing flood but always reminded him of water.

There were hundreds of poems about beautiful women, but none could stand up to Lily.

He passed Sunny's Sweet Shop and glanced over at her. "Should I drop you off at your house?"

Something flickered across her face. "No, I need to give Miss Wilma her food and her cooler."

"Right." He was hoping she'd say that. He didn't want to risk seeing Jerry. Or Jerry seeing him. "That Wilma's really something, isn't she?"

Lily nodded. "After her fall the other day, I've been thinking. She should get a Life Alert button, or at least a cellphone. What if she'd fallen on a Tuesday? She might not've been found for days."

Pete frowned. "You're right. I hadn't thought of that."

"But I know what she'll say if I bring it up."

"What?"

Lily squinted her eyes like Wilma and wagged her finger

at Pete. "Nonsense, dear, everything is perfectly fine. Don't you worry about me."

Pete laughed at her perfect impersonation of Wilma. "That's what she'd say, all right."

Lily gave him an enigmatic look. "Maybe *you* should bring it up."

He gulped. "Me?"

She turned her face toward the window. "Well, I'm just the housekeeper."

Pete pulled up in front of Wilma's house and parked. "You're not just the housekeeper, Lily. You're her friend. She's lucky to have you."

Lily put her hand on the door handle but didn't open it. After a long moment, she said in a low voice, "I hope she doesn't come to regret it."

He wanted to ask what she meant by that. He wanted to ask why she lived with Jerry but hadn't spoken a word about him all day. He wanted to ask what her favorite color was and why she hadn't come to dinner the other night. But before he could muster any kind of response, she hurried out of his truck and shut the door.

Pete had never had much success as a deep thinker, but as he drove away from Wilma's house, he gave it a try anyway. Why had Wilma ordered Lily to walk home as soon as they'd brought the cooler into the house? Why had she agreed to take her money back only if he promised to come for dinner next Thursday? Why had Lily refused to look at him once they got out of the truck? He'd thought they'd had a nice day together.

He shouldn't be surprised he'd screwed it up somehow. That's what he always did. It would probably be another three years before he had the chance to speak to Lily again, and it was probably for the best. He was no good for her.

A dilapidated Mazda Hatchback was parked near his house. He'd never seen it before, but something about the car gave him a funny feeling. The back window on the driver's side had been replaced with cardboard and duct tape, and the front driver's-side tire was obviously a spare.

He pulled into his driveway and gave the Hatchback another furtive look. The sun was reflecting off the windshield, but it looked like there were two people inside, watching him. It had to be close to zero degrees with the windchill factored in. What were they doing?

He helped Pearl out of the Dodge, and her stumpy little legs made a break for the house. She was still wearing his vest, its zipper scraping along the ground. Pete hurried toward the front door to let her inside, then froze when he heard his name.

"Pete."

He turned around. A woman and a boy of maybe ten were standing by the Mazda. Her eyes were fixed on Pete, while the boy's eyes were on Pearl.

Pete blinked. "Danielle?"

Bear in a chair. It couldn't be.

The woman tugged on the boy's arm, and they walked closer. He could see her face clearly now.

"Dani, what are you doing here? Are you okay?"

She didn't answer. Pete shook his head. Neither she nor the boy were dressed for the chilly weather. They were going to freeze to death.

"Come on." He jerked his thumb toward the house. "Let's get you inside."

He let Pearl in first, then held the door open. Dani kept her hand on the boy's arm as they entered the house cautiously, like they might fall through the floor. They were both shivering.

Pearl approached the boy in her uninhibited, bull-in-a-china-shop way and snuffled at him. He stumbled back, his eyes wide. Pete was about to call her away, tell her to leave the poor kid alone, when the boy knelt and threw his arms around her neck.

Pete shook his head again. "I—"

"You keep a pig in your house?" Dani asked.

"Yes."

"And you have a baby?" She was staring at the baby walker in the corner, the one he'd rescued from the trash. Pete had cleaned it up and greased the wheels.

"No."

She continued to stare at it.

"How did you find me?" Pete inclined his head toward the boy. "And who is this?"

She moved to stand beside the kid and put her hand on his shoulder. "This is Braedon. Your nephew."

twelve

It was far too late at night for coffee, but Pete didn't say so. He watched Dani take sip after sip from a Coca-Cola Santa mug.

She had the same face as their mother. The same color hair. But her eyes were different.

"You don't have to look at me like that, you know." Dani peered at him over the mug.

He lowered his gaze. "You're the last person I expected to show up at my house."

Her last words to him still rang loud and clear in his memory. *"Just leave me alone, Pete. You're good at leaving, just like Mom."* He didn't like leaving all the time. He'd never wanted to leave his sister. They were supposed to stay together, but it wasn't long after their mother left before he'd learned an eleven-year-old boy had very little control over his life.

He thought of Braedon, sound asleep in the spare bedroom. He had just turned eleven, Dani had said. And see? He'd been dragged here to this nothing town in the middle of nowhere to his no-good uncle's house through no fault of his own.

"Is this your house?" Dani looked around. "You've never stayed anywhere long enough to buy a house."

The words were like sharp rocks under bare feet. "I'm renting."

"Will you get in trouble for having us here?"

"No."

If his landlord was okay with a pig, Pete didn't think she'd mind two humans staying with him temporarily.

A loud grating noise came from Pete's bedroom, and Dani raised one eyebrow. "I don't know how you can sleep in the same room as that creature."

He'd gotten used to Pearl's snoring long ago, although he'd never imagined anyone else having to put up with it. "I'm glad you're here, Dani."

The words just kind of came out. He'd thought about her so many times, worrying over whether she was okay. He hadn't even known about Braedon or he would've worried about him, too.

She stared at her mug.

"Have you been in Albuquerque this whole time?" he asked.

She nodded.

He pointed his chin toward where the Mazda was parked. "And you drove all the way here in *that* thing?"

Her laugh held no humor. "It wasn't pretty."

Silence fell, except for Pearl's snoring. Pete shifted in his chair. It had been hours since he'd arrived home, and yet he'd come no closer to figuring out what exactly was going on. Dani had made it clear she didn't want to talk about it in front of Braedon, but now that the boy—his *nephew*—was asleep, there were still no answers forthcoming.

Not that it mattered—why they were here, or how they got here, or what she wanted from him. It didn't. Because he'd failed to be there for her when their mom left and they'd been separated, when he'd run away from foster home after foster home to get to her but was never allowed to stay, and later when they were adults and he'd shown up in her life just long enough to cause problems before taking off again.

This time would be different.

"Do you want more coffee?" He decided to stick with easy questions for now. They had all the time in the world to talk about why she was here if he had anything to say about it.

She put down her mug with a thunk and stood from the table. "I already drank too much coffee. I'm going to bed."

"Okay." He'd offered her his room. She'd declined, opting for the floor in the spare bedroom. He would find her something more suitable first thing in the morning if he had to drive all the way back to Great Falls. He'd find warmer clothes for them, too.

She walked to the hall and stopped, her back to him, one hand on the wall. "Good night, Pete. See you when the morning wind blows."

His heart wrenched as a long-ago memory resurfaced. Suddenly he was eleven again, and everything was just as it should be.

Until it wasn't.

thirteen

Pete moved the joystick, and the Xpeditor's arm picked up a blue bin and dumped it. Lift, dump. Lift, dump. He felt the tedium. The passing of time on the road had slowed considerably since Monday when Braedon had begged Pete to leave Pearl at the house while he went to work. Pete had reluctantly agreed, thinking one day with Pearl would be enough to keep Braedon from ever asking again.

He had been wrong.

Now it was Thursday, and the time alone in the Xpeditor reminded him of the last hour of class on the last day of school. Never-ending.

As he finally drove back to the carport, he chastised himself. "It's only been a few days, and Braedon needs a friend more than you do. Quit your bellyaching."

He was going to have to ask Braedon to give Pearl up tomorrow, though. It wouldn't feel right to get ice cream at Sunny's without her.

He switched from the Xpeditor to the Dodge and headed home, thinking about his nephew. He'd proven to be a quiet kid. Timid. Never complained about his food, although thankfully Dani had taken over dinner duty. One look in Pete's fridge and she'd declared him unfit for the kitchen.

She still hadn't said anything about how she'd tracked him down or why, but he figured the explanations would come when she was ready. In the meantime, he was completely enthralled by his nephew. He looked nothing like Pete, but the lost and searching sheen of his eyes bore a strong family resemblance.

When Pete entered the house, Pearl trotted over to greet him. He bent down and rubbed her head and then her back. "What are you chewing on?"

Braedon appeared, plodding along the wall with prepubescent steps the way he'd done every day since his arrival. "I gave her an apple."

Pete straightened. "You recall what I said about how many apples she can have?"

Braedon nodded. "Yes, sir."

Pete didn't like the "sir" thing, but he wasn't sure what to do about it. His experience with kids was limited to the occasional child waving wildly at his garbage truck when he drove by. Maybe he could ask Dani about it later.

He looked Braedon in the eye. "Did you remember her vitamins at lunch?"

Braedon's face fell, and he hunched as if he'd been struck in the gut. "I'm sorry."

Before Pete could respond, Braedon disappeared down the hall. The spare bedroom door shut with a muted thud.

Pete stood in the middle of the living room, dumbfounded. What had he said?

Dani came out of the kitchen, wiping her fingers on a dish towel. "He'll be okay. He's . . . sensitive."

Pete threw up his hands. "I'm not mad. I was just asking."

"He doesn't know that. He's used to . . ."

Her voice dropped off, and Pete frowned. However she was

going to finish that sentence, he had a feeling he wouldn't like it.

"Can I go talk to him?"

Dani studied him for a moment before nodding. When Pete moved toward the hall, she held up a hand. "Wait."

He stopped. She studied him again, her hands twisting the towel and belying the stoic look on her face. "Never mind."

He huffed as he hurried from the living room. She'd been infuriating as a child as well, her four-year-old self annoying him constantly when he was eleven like Braedon. Their mom always told Pete to be patient with Dani. *"She follows you around because she loves you,"* she would say. *"You're the only brother she has in the whole wide world."*

Some brother he turned out to be.

He knocked on the spare bedroom door. "Can I come in?"

No reply.

He cracked it open. "Braedon? Can I talk to you?"

When he heard a sniff, he opened the door wide. His nephew was sitting on the bed with his arms wrapped around his knees. He stared at Pete with tears brimming in his eyes.

"Hey, buddy." Pete walked slowly to the bed and sat on the edge. "Did you think I was upset about the vitamins?"

"I'm really sorry I forgot." Braedon wiped his eyes with his sleeve. "I promise I won't do that ever again."

"It's okay." Pete scooted closer. He wanted to give his nephew a pat on the knee or something but didn't know if he should. "We can do it together before I leave for Wilma's house, no big deal."

"Really?" Another sniff.

"Sure. I forget Pearl's vitamins, too, once in a while."

Braedon straightened his legs. "You're not going to yell at me?"

"Of course not."

The anxious look on Braedon's face turned Pete's heart inside out. Why was this kid afraid of him?

"Look. Buddy. I promise I will *never* yell at you, okay?"

Braedon studied him in much the same way Dani had a few minutes ago. "Even if I mess up?"

One side of Pete's mouth lifted. "We all mess up sometimes. I guarantee I've messed up more than you ever will."

Braedon hung his head. "I don't know about that. My dad says I can't do anything right."

Pete felt his fists begin to clench and forced himself to take a deep breath. How dare *anyone* say such a thing about his nephew, especially his father.

Braedon's voice dropped to a whisper. "He says he doesn't know how he ended up with a loser like me."

Pete's jaw tightened. It had been a while since Pete's last fight, but if Braedon's dad were in the room right now, Pete would have a very big problem on his hands. Or rather, Braedon's dad would have Pete's hands around his neck. But getting angry wasn't going to help Braedon.

Pete cleared his throat around the unfamiliar feelings welling up from somewhere deep down. "Well, I think you're the coolest kid I've ever met. I wouldn't trust just anybody to watch Pearl while I'm at work, you know."

Braedon looked up at Pete. "You wouldn't?"

"Not a chance. I wouldn't even trust your mom with that job. Only you."

The smile that lit Braedon's face was gradual and beautiful, like the sun rising over the prairie. Then, just like that, his face fell again. "I wish you didn't have to go to that lady's house for dinner."

Pete hadn't expected he'd have company when he'd accepted Wilma's invitation on Saturday, but it would be rude to back out now. If he knew Wilma at all, she'd been working on dinner all day.

"I won't be gone long. If there's any dessert, I'll bring some home for you, okay?"

Braedon considered this. "Okay."

The boy's face remained glum, though. Pete racked his brain for something more to cheer up his nephew. He had so little to offer. With a flash of inspiration, he remembered the comic books he'd found in the box outside Sunny's a couple of weeks ago.

"Come on." He hopped off the bed and waved for Braedon to follow. "I've got something to show you."

Wilma surreptitiously watched Pete dig into the seconds she'd dished out. In some ways, he reminded her of Herb. Herb had never gained a pound no matter how much he ate. It seemed Pete was the same way. Absolutely infuriating. In other ways, the two men were night and day. Herb had been a jovial nonstop talker and prankster. The kind of guy who always had a story or joke up his sleeve. *"Have you heard this one, Willy Mae?"* he'd ask.

Pete was much more reticent.

"This is good, thank you." Pete took a drink of lemonade. "I haven't had homemade corn bread in years."

"You're more than welcome. I only wish Pearl was here so I could sneak her some, too."

He'd been vague earlier when she asked why the pig hadn't come along. She had thought they were inseparable, but he'd told her Pearl was spending time with someone else. Wilma didn't dare hope it could be Lily. The girl hadn't been herself on Monday, and Wilma had been too cowardly to ask what had happened with Jerry once Lily went home on Saturday. Wilma had prayed late into the evening that she hadn't gotten Lily into trouble.

"I've been enjoying those rice bowls you and Lily brought me," she said. "I can get two suppers out of one bowl."

Something she couldn't quite interpret flashed across Pete's face. Lovesickness at the mention of Lily's name, if she had to guess. He choked on a bite of meatloaf, and she nodded to herself. Definitely lovesickness.

When he gave no sign of responding, she continued, "If you happen to be going to Great Falls again soon, please let me know."

He looked at his plate. "I might be going sooner than I thought." His voice was pensive.

She leaned forward, her interest piqued. "Oh?"

He scraped the last crumbs of food from his plate. "I, uh, have a couple of unexpected guests living with me right now."

Her interest was downright captivated now. She almost fell off the edge of her seat.

He shifted in his chair. "My sister and nephew are here."

The words sank in, and Wilma stilled. "Dani's here?"

Pete gave her a surprised look. "How'd you know her name?"

Oh, what a foolish woman she was, letting her mouth get away from her like that. She scrambled to cover her tracks. "You mentioned her before, didn't you? When we were talking about our families?"

"Oh." Pete gave a little shrug. "I guess I don't remember. Anyway, I need a lot more food now, and Braedon, my nephew, needs winter boots, and who knows what else if they're going to stay for a while."

Wilma felt light-headed. Pete and Dani together again, just as they always should've been. It felt like a miracle. "*Are* they going to stay for a while?"

"I don't know."

Her thoughts swirled. That was all he had to say? She had

so many questions, her brain couldn't keep up. Why had Dani come? Where had she been? What did she remember of Sleeping Grass, and about what had happened?

Was Pete glad Dani was here? He appeared troubled by it.

Wilma settled on an easier question. "How old is Brandon?"

"It's Braedon." Pete set his fork on his plate and leaned back. "He's eleven."

Eleven. How much did Pete remember about being eleven? Too much, probably.

"Pearl is with them?"

"Yes."

"You should've brought them with you to supper." Even as she said it, she was glad he hadn't. She was too old for such a shock. But now that she had time to prepare . . . "Next time you should all come. I insist."

Though Pete seemed to wince slightly, she couldn't afford to consider too carefully what his feelings might be regarding a next time. He simply had to come again.

Wilma clapped her hands together before he could speak. "I'm so glad there will be plenty of leftovers to send home with you."

"That's very kind, but—"

"What about school, hmm?"

Pete rubbed his chin. "I hadn't thought about that."

"If they're going to stay, you'll have to enroll the boy in school." She wagged a finger at him. "Education is important, young man."

"Yes, you're right, but—"

"Do you need any linens? I've got stacks of towels and sheets I haven't used in years."

His expression turned sheepish. "Well . . ."

She pushed away from the table. "Of course you need linens. I'll get you some right now."

"Please." Pete stood as well. "Let me do it."

"Nonsense. I know where everything is."

She could hear him following close behind as she made her way to the linen closet. How many times had she wondered what it would've been like if she'd allowed him and Dani to be part of her life? She'd thought at the time that she was making the right decision for her family, but she'd struggled to convince herself ever since. It would've been tight here in the house, it would've been hard, but couldn't they have done it?

She opened the closet door and swallowed hard. Her voice quavered. "Hold out your arms."

Herb would tell her not to dwell on the past, but she couldn't help it if the past had come to her.

Pete did as she asked. As she passed neatly folded sheets and towels from the linen closet to his waiting arms, she fought back a vision of pulling a sheet up to Pete's chin to tuck him in at night. Drying his head with a towel when he came in from playing in the rain. She had those memories with her own kids.

She didn't deserve this second chance to be part of Pete's life, but she was going to make the most of it. She needed to tell him—

"I think that'll do, Wilma." Pete peeked at her over an armful of linens piled as high as his nose. "There's only three of us."

"All right." She shut the door reluctantly and leaned on her cane. "But I'm sending you home with a few things from my freezer along with the leftovers, and I don't want to hear a single argument out of you."

Wilma sat on the edge of the bed in her flannel nightgown and stared at the framed photo on the dresser. Two young women—their arms around each other's necks, their eyes shining with laughter—stared back at her.

Even with her best pair of wool socks on, Wilma's feet were cold. "I know I failed you, Rosie," she whispered. She reached over and touched her friend's face. "I'm sorry. But you failed me, too."

She slowly, wearily pulled her legs up under the covers and laid her head on the pillow. It had been almost twenty-five years since Rosie's last letter. She'd written from a town outside Chicago where she'd found herself once again in custody of the law. She only wrote when she was in jail.

Wilma had Rosie's five letters tucked away in the bottom dresser drawer. As usual, the final letter had been jumbled and difficult to read. Rosie had asked about Pete and Dani. How were they doing? Would Wilma send a picture to her? Could Wilma please tell them how much their mother loved them and missed them?

It wasn't fair. If she'd missed them so much, why had she stayed away?

If she'd known what Wilma had done, maybe she wouldn't have.

Sometimes when Wilma received a letter, she would be angry at how Rosie assumed she would take on her responsibilities, covering for her like she had always done before. Other times, Wilma would feel the crushing weight of guilt that she hadn't been able to do the one thing her best friend had counted on her to do. The one thing Pete and Dani needed most.

The other four times Rosie had written, Wilma had spent days agonizing over how to respond. How to tell Rosie her children weren't here. By the time she sent a letter back, she'd waited too long and the letters were returned, with Rosie's stint in jail for a drug-related misdemeanor already over and Rosie on her way to some new place with some new man who made all the same old promises.

The last time, though, Wilma sent her response right away.

The very next day. It explained everything, as much as something like this could ever be explained, and it begged Rosie to come back. Even though the kids were grown by then, Wilma thought maybe if Rosie came home, everything would be okay. They could all start over.

That letter was never returned, and Wilma never heard from Rosie again.

fourteen

Pete wasn't surprised by the first thing out of Windy Ray's mouth when he sat down at Sunny's on Friday.

"Did Wilma say anything about me last night?"

Pete shrugged off his coat and draped it over the chair. "No, but I saw your rock."

Windy Ray sat up taller. "Where did you see it?"

"In her kitchen. It was on the windowsill above the sink."

"Was there anything else on the windowsill?"

The corner of Pete's lips twitched. "I don't know, a couple knickknacks maybe, a plant? I didn't pay much attention."

Windy Ray fixed him with a solemn gaze. "I thought we were friends."

Pete laughed. "We must be or I wouldn't have brought you these." He pulled from his coat pocket the two doll slippers he'd converted into dog shoes and held them out. "For Apisi."

Windy Ray took them and turned them over, examining every inch. Pete had weatherproofed the fabric, but it was Dani who'd devised a plan to sew a snap into the overlapping flaps around the tops to help them stay on. She had seen him struggling with them and bossily demanded he hand them over to her.

Windy Ray picked up Apisi from the floor and slipped the faux red high heels on her front paws. "These will keep you warm and dry."

He never used a different voice when talking to Apisi, like most folks did when addressing their pets. Apisi sniffed the boots.

Windy Ray nodded at Pete. "Thank you for the gift. If I may ask, what about her other foot?"

Pete laughed again. "I'm working on that. I figured this was better than nothing."

"We are grateful."

"Here you go, boys." Sunny appeared with two cones and two bowls. "I went with Moose Tracks today."

"Ah, Moose Tracks." Windy Ray accepted his cone from her hand. "My favorite."

Pete took his cone, as well. "Thanks, Sunny."

"Is Pearl still doing okay?" she asked.

Windy Ray had wasted no time telling everyone he knew about the unfortunate incident with Pearl and the chocolate cake. Thankfully, he didn't know many people.

Pete watched Pearl slurp down her ice cream. "Seems to be."

"She wasn't in the truck when you picked up the dumpster the other day. I got worried."

"Oh. She's fine." Pete squirmed under Sunny's scrutiny. "She's been staying home with my nephew most days, that's all."

Sunny's eyes widened. "I didn't know you had a nephew."

"Neither did I."

Sunny was still the only person in Sleeping Grass who remembered Pete from childhood. He worked hard to avoid running into anyone who might bring up the past, but Sunny, who was two years ahead of him back in school, had studied his face when he'd come in with Windy Ray that first time and pulled his name from her bear trap of a memory. And for some reason, it didn't bother Pete that she remembered.

She put her hands on her ample hips. "He just showed up at your doorstep?"

"Pretty much."

He didn't want to get into it. He had no answers for the inevitable questions.

Sunny narrowed her eyes. "You'll have to bring him in sometime."

So I can meet him. She didn't say that, but Pete heard the words loud and clear all the same. He licked his cone and nodded vaguely, unwilling to make any promises. Unsure how far to let her in.

When Sunny had gone, Windy Ray tipped his head. There was a small dot of ice cream on his nose as he leaned closer to Pete. "Was the rock in the middle of the windowsill or off to the side?"

The house smelled like chili. Braedon came thumping into the living room when Pete shut the front door.

"Hey, buddy, how was your day?"

Braedon shrugged and poked his toe at the corner of the area rug. "Fine."

He had to be bored out of his mind stuck in the house all week. Pete felt guilty for taking Pearl with him today.

"Maybe tomorrow we can go sledding."

They'd had more snow than usual this winter. Still, it would be difficult to find a good sledding hill because the wind blew the snow into drifts, leaving large patches of bare dirt and dead grass. Not that there were many hills around here.

Braedon looked up. "Really?"

"Sure. If your mom will watch Pearl for us."

"Pearl can't come?"

Pete scratched his chin.

Have you ever seen a pig fly down a snow-covered hill
that sparkles in the sun?
Has anyone?

He chuckled to himself. "I'll have to think about it."

"Okay."

Pete left Pearl and Braedon together and made his way into the kitchen. Dani was standing at the stove.

He cleared his throat. "Hey."

She didn't take her eyes off the pot she was stirring. "Hey."

"I was wondering—"

"I got a job today."

He swallowed. *A job?* His heart swelled with something that felt an awful lot like hope. If she got a job, that meant she and Braedon planned to stick around, right?

His sense of hope morphed slightly into confusion. "How'd you do that?" She hadn't taken the Mazda. The dusting of snow that had fallen last night hadn't been brushed from the car's windshield.

"I walked."

"To where?"

"The gas station. They're desperate for help, I guess. I start tomorrow."

That answered the question about whether Dani would pig-sit. Pearl might get her chance to fly down a hill after all.

"You walked there in your tennis shoes?"

"Yep."

He frowned. It wasn't very far, but it must've been slippery and wet.

"I'll find you some boots."

"It's not a big deal."

"I'll give you a ride tomorrow."

She turned her back to him to slice a loaf of garlic bread. "No need. I'll be fine."

"It's no trouble."

She set the knife down and braced her hands against the counter. "I don't need your help."

He stared at her back. Clearly she did or she wouldn't be here. She must've thought the same thing because she turned and folded her arms across her chest.

"I don't need your help with *that*." Her voice held a hint of a pout, just like when she was four and didn't get her way.

He flinched at the memory, unwilling to think too much about when Dani was four. "What about the Mazda?"

She looked down. "It wouldn't start."

"I'll check the battery."

While she didn't look happy, she didn't protest. Even if he could get the battered Hatchback running, would he want her driving that hunk of junk around? If only Windy Ray had a car he could borrow.

"What time will you be done with your route on Monday?" Dani asked. She pulled three bowls from the cupboard. Pete had owned only one bowl a week ago, but he'd since gone to the thrift store and bought four more, along with several plates, cups, and forks.

"Around five. Why?"

"School gets out at three-thirty."

He blinked. School. More evidence his family—was he allowed to call them that?—wasn't going anywhere anytime soon. Despite having read pages and pages of poetry that eloquently described the human condition, he had no name for the feelings churning inside him.

Whatever story his face was telling as he sorted his thoughts, Dani misread it.

"I'm sorry." Her expression shifted as the words tumbled out. "I shouldn't have just showed up here. And I should've talked to you before making all these plans to see if it was okay—"

"No." He held up a hand. "It's fine. I'm glad you made plans. I'm glad you're here. I . . ."

She waited. He wavered. But he meant it, didn't he?

"I want you to stay as long as you want."

She stared at him in that unnerving way. "I got a divorce."

"Okay."

"It was a long time coming."

"You don't have to explain. It's none of my business."

"You're right." Her eyes sharpened. "It's not. My life stopped being your business a long time ago."

He looked away. She wasn't referring to when she was four. She must realize, looking back, as he did, that he'd done everything he could then. She was referring to the years that followed when he'd lost his right to be part of her life. Now she was here.

The sound of squealing and laughter came from the living room. Pete's mind raced in circles, looking for the right words to say.

Dani spoke before he could. "Braedon will have to walk home from school. How far is it?"

"Pretty far. About a mile and a half."

Sleeping Grass was small but sprawling. The old K–12 school, the one Pete had attended, had been located near the center of town, but a few years ago that building was condemned and a new school had been built on the outskirts. He wasn't comfortable with Braedon walking that far. It wouldn't be too bad when the weather was decent, but this time of year would be cold and windy nearly every day.

"I'll talk to my boss," he said. "Maybe I can take a quick detour from my route and pick him up. He can ride with me until I'm done. Work on homework or something."

She looked skeptical. "I don't know . . ."

"Yeah." Braedon bumbled into the kitchen, Pearl at his heels. "I could do that. Right, Mom?"

She looked back and forth between Braedon and Pete. "You want to ride in a garbage truck?"

Braedon glanced at Pete. "Yeah."

"It'll be a tight squeeze with Pearl," Pete said. "And it's loud and boring in there."

The boy was thin and gangly, hardly took up any room, but Pearl wasn't going to like sharing her seat with him. Braedon seemed eager to cram himself into a noisy, compact space, however.

He made pleading eyes at Dani. "Please, Mom?"

She pressed her lips together and gave Pete a look. "Only if your boss says it's okay."

Braedon pumped his fist. "Yesss."

Pete felt a bit triumphant himself. "Okay."

Dani turned to Braedon. "And only on days when I'm working."

He tried to look serious. "Okay."

Dani stared them both down for another minute before picking up a large spoon from the counter. "Fine. Now go wash your hands for dinner."

Braedon scurried down the hall to the single bathroom.

Pete watched him go before grabbing a carton of milk from the fridge. "I'm surprised he's so excited about a garbage truck."

"He doesn't care about the truck." Dani sighed the sigh

of an overburdened mother and shook her head. "He cares about *you*."

And that was how Pete wound up lying awake in bed until two in the morning, stewing over every stupid mistake he'd ever made while nearby Pearl snored away.

Pete got off early on Wednesdays because Wednesday was out-of-town day. The day he picked up the bins for the residents who lived outside of town but who were still within the purview of Sleeping Grass. The route consisted of a handful of lonely-looking homesteads spread far and wide, hence the knock-off time of one-thirty.

He helped Pearl out of the Xpeditor and into the Dodge, then headed toward Wilma's house. It was Windy Ray's fault. Over their Monday game of Chickenfoot, which Pete had lost, he'd made the mistake of telling Windy Ray that Lily had waved at him as he drove down her alley that morning. She'd been looking through her back window. He thought maybe she had smiled.

"She was watching for you," Windy Ray had said. Pete wasn't so sure. She probably just happened to be there and felt obligated to raise her hand when he looked over at her house like a creep while picking up her bin. Why would she watch for him? She had Jerry.

Windy Ray had sensed with uncanny ability Pete's inner torment over the issue of Lily. "Perhaps you should talk to

Wilma about it," Windy Ray had suggested. "And perhaps you should invite me and Apisi along."

Pete chastised himself as he pulled up to Wilma's house. There was no way he could ask Wilma about Lily without raising suspicion. And what if Wilma told Lily that he had asked? He was way out of his element here. But he couldn't stop thinking about her.

Tank in a bank.

He had dated three women in his life. When he was in his second group home, he'd had a brief relationship with a girl living in the girls' wing. The fight he'd started when another boy made her cry was the reason he'd had to leave that place.

Then in his twenties, he'd fallen for a girl with beautiful golden curls and an easy laugh. It had taken him far too long to realize she was purposely creating situations where he would get into fights over her. It made her feel good about herself or something. Dani had been the one to tell him how messed up that was.

And there was Sheila. The woman Pete thought he'd be with forever, until he found her with another man and ended up in jail for assaulting him. He'd only delivered a couple of blows and a shove, but the guy had pressed charges.

An alarming number of the fights he'd been in had to do with women.

For that reason, he'd steered clear of them since Sheila, admiring from a distance but not trusting himself to handle another romantic relationship. He was too screwed up. Had too much baggage.

And yet.

Lily was the last person on earth he should have on his mind, but the first person he thought of every morning.

He knocked on Wilma's door, and she opened it right away.

"I'm glad to see you, come in." She waved her free arm enthusiastically. "I've got a surprise for you."

The house smelled delicious, and Pearl raised her snout to sniff the air.

Wilma led them to the kitchen. "You're not allergic to pecans, I hope."

"No, ma'am."

She motioned for him to take a seat at the table, where she set a laden flowery tray down before him. "Lemon-pecan bars."

His doubts about coming here began to dissipate. He was glad he'd told Windy Ray not to come until a little later. "Those look amazing."

She put a small white plate and fancy silver fork in front of him. "Please, help yourself." She bent to look at Pearl. "And don't think I forgot about you."

A banana appeared, and Pearl squealed her delight. Wilma laughed. She'd asked Pete what she could give Pearl for a treat when he called her about coming over. There was already a plate on the floor by the vent—Wilma had planned everything out—and she set the banana there, then joined Pete at the table.

"I've been dying to hear more about this nephew of yours. I suppose you've enrolled him in school by now, hmm?"

"Dani did, yes." Pete cut a bite of his bar with the fork. He'd never eaten a bar with a fork before. "I have to pick him up at three-thirty."

"How is he liking it?"

It took a second for Pete to answer because the lemon-pecan bar tasted like a Wendell Berry poem about walking to the sun. "This is really good."

She smiled. "Wonderful."

"I think he likes it okay. He hasn't said much about it."

Pete had asked Braedon all kinds of questions when he

picked him up Monday, but the boy hadn't been interested in talking about school. He wanted to talk about the Xpeditor and the dump and the comic books Pete had given him.

"And how about Dani? What has she been up to?" Wilma leaned toward him intently. He was flattered by her motherly attention but also wary. In his experience, people's interest in him never lasted long.

"She got a job at the gas station."

Wilma nodded knowingly. "Sounds like they're settling right in."

Pete took another bite and thought that over. Yes, they'd settled in all right, but how long would Dani want to share a room with her son in her brother's rental? And how long would she want to work at a gas station when she had a bachelor's degree in communication?

"You've got smoke coming out your ears," Wilma said. "What's on your mind?"

Talking with Wilma about his personal life made him uneasy. Why was she so interested? Yet she seemed to genuinely care about him. Maybe she was just lonely.

"I worry about them," he finally said. "I wonder if they can be happy here."

"But you don't want them to leave."

"It's nice having family around," he admitted.

Dani had remained distant so far, while Braedon had already staked such a claim on Pete's heart that he couldn't imagine life without him. How could that happen in such a short time?

"Yes." Wilma gave him an odd look, and her voice grew heavier. "There's something special about having a family."

He hesitated for only the briefest of moments before helping himself to another bar. He didn't know what had caused the change in Wilma's demeanor, but he noticed the time and realized Windy Ray would be arriving soon.

Pete didn't want to miss his chance. "Does Lily have any family around?"

Wilma shook her head. "I don't think so. From what I can get out of her, they're all still in Omaha, where she grew up. Jerry brought her up here. I wonder sometimes if she shouldn't have stayed in Nebraska."

"Why's that?"

"It's probably nothing." Wilma worried the top of her cane with her thumb. "I just don't like the look in that man's eyes."

Pete narrowed his own eyes. "I thought you said you never met him."

Her shoulders drooped. "I hadn't. He just . . . well, he happened to stop by when you and Lily were in Great Falls."

Pete gripped the little silver fork. He happened to stop by? That didn't make any sense. "What did he want?"

Pete heard the gruffness in his voice, but Wilma didn't seem to notice. "Nothing. It was no big deal. He was looking for Lily, is all."

"With a look in his eye that you didn't like?"

"I shouldn't have said anything."

The lemon-pecan bar no longer tasted like hope and blessings. He set his fork down. He had to find a way to talk to Lily. To make sure she was okay. But what possible reason could he give for asking Wilma for her phone number? And even he wasn't dumb enough to show up at her house.

There had to be another way.

"I've been thinking about throwing a First Day of Spring party," Wilma said. "With tea and streamers and cupcakes with pink and yellow frosting. You'll help me, won't you?"

He stared at her. *Pink and yellow frosting*?

"I know we won't see any real signs of spring for weeks yet, but wouldn't it be fun? You could bring Dani and Brandon and Raymond. And Lily would come, too, of course."

He did the math in his head. It was just under two weeks until the first day of spring. Longer than he would like to wait to talk to Lily, but he had no better plan.

"Okay, sure. And it's Braedon."

"Yes, I apologize." Wilma tapped her head. "This old brain isn't what it used to be."

A loud knock echoed through the house. Pete stood. "I'll get it."

He opened the front door and nodded at Windy Ray. "Oki."

The grin on his friend's face dimmed. "It's only you."

"Don't worry." Pete stepped aside. "Wilma's in the kitchen."

Windy Ray carefully removed his shoes and Apisi's boots and set them neatly against the wall. Apisi bounded ahead when Windy Ray put her down, unaware she had only three legs. Windy Ray was close behind, followed by Pete.

"Good afternoon, wawetseka." Windy Ray bowed and held out his hand to Wilma. In his palm sat a piece of rose quartz the size of Pearl's ear. "Please accept this gift."

Pete rolled his eyes behind Windy Ray's back.

"My, how lovely." Wilma took the crystal and dutifully examined it. "It's beautiful."

"Its beauty can't compare to yours."

"Nonsense." Wilma gestured to the chair beside her. "Please have a seat. I made dessert."

"And I"—Windy Ray alighted on the chair like a robin on a post—"have died and gone to heaven."

When Wilma's phone rang at precisely eight o'clock that evening, she knew who it must be.

She shuffled over and picked up the receiver. "Hello, Michael."

"Hey, Mom. How are you?"

The truth was, she was tired. After spending the morning reading through all the paperwork Sadie from Financial Assistance Services—FAS, as Sadie called it—had sent her in the mail, she'd baked her famous lemon-pecan bars and then hosted her afternoon visitors. Once they had left, she'd started planning her First Day of Spring party.

She didn't want to tell Michael any of that, however. He would bring up her financial power of attorney if she mentioned FAS, have a conniption if she mentioned entertaining men in her home, and blow a gasket if she mentioned throwing a party he would adamantly insist she could not afford.

"I'm fine, dear, how are you? How are Paula and Yvette?"

"Good, as far as I know. Ever since Yvette started college, she's far too busy to call Paula or me. You know how it goes."

"Yes." Her kids had done the same. "Did you ever hear about that promotion at the office?"

"I didn't get it." His voice turned glum. "They gave it to some young upstart. But my boss said it was a tough call. It'll be my turn next time."

"That's too bad. You work so hard. What did Steven say?"

Her middle child had immersed himself in the business world on the East Coast and was always giving Michael advice about how to move up the corporate ladder.

"He can't even take five minutes to pick up the phone these days, Mom. You know that."

"He's very busy. His job is so demanding." She didn't want to admit he never called her either.

"It's all right. Look, Mom, I was wondering if you'd want to come down for a visit later this month. We haven't seen you in ages."

She winced. She couldn't possibly visit this month. Not

in this weather. Colorado was too far to drive in winter, and her party was coming up. It was her chance to check up on Dani. She'd lost track of the young lady over the years, after her aunt and uncle whisked her away from Pete, claiming one little girl was all they could manage.

It was also her intent to get Pete and Lily under the same roof again. She was convinced Lily would be better off with a man like Pete, and she was also convinced Pete's life would improve considerably with Lily in it. They needed a little help, however.

Her help.

"I don't know, Michael. You know I hate traveling in the winter."

"It's almost spring."

"Not here, dear. Sleeping Grass was still getting snow in the middle of May last year, remember?"

"I'll come up and get you myself, Mom. Drive through the night. You won't have to worry about a thing."

Ha. If only that were true. He had no idea how many things she had to worry about.

"Nonsense. With the price of gas, *really*."

He was silent for a moment. She could picture him pinching the bridge of his nose. It wasn't that she didn't want to see her family. She did. She loved them. But ever since Pete moved back to Sleeping Grass, she'd felt a sense of obligation. Like he needed her somehow. And since she'd failed so miserably when he needed her before, she had no desire to fail him again. No desire to add to her regrets. And now Dani was here, too.

"Does this have anything to do with that Lily person? I don't understand why—"

"Of course not." Wilma huffed. "Don't be ridiculous."

"I'd feel better about the whole arrangement if I could talk to her. How do you know she's trustworthy?"

Wilma raised one eyebrow. "She's as trustworthy as you or

I, dear. And you could always come up here to visit if you're so intent on meeting her."

He paused, and she knew what he was going to say.

"Now's not a good time for me to take off work, Mom. Not until I get that promotion."

She nodded, feeling victorious. "And now's not a good time for me to travel."

She could picture him rolling his eyes.

"Promise me you'll come in the summer, then."

She hesitated. According to Sadie at FAS, if Wilma decided to enroll in the debt-relief program by the March 31 deadline, she would see significant results in less than three months. By summer, therefore, Wilma should have returned to financial stability. She wouldn't need to be afraid of Michael looking too closely at her accounts anymore or asking too many questions.

"Okay. That would be lovely."

"Okay." He let out a long breath, as if whether his mother would visit was an enormous burden to bear. "Tom and Rachel will want to drive over and stay while you're here."

Wilma's heart twinged. She hadn't talked to her daughter, Rachel, in months. She'd tried to call a couple of times, but Rachel was always busy.

Or avoiding her mother.

"If Rachel can take the time off, of course."

"I'm sure she'll try, although she doesn't get paid time off for her new job."

New job? Wilma frowned. "I didn't know she changed jobs. She's not working at the hospital anymore?"

"She is. She had to get a second job. She didn't tell you?"

Wilma gripped her cane and jabbed it at the floor. No, she had not been told. One shouldn't keep such things from one's mother. "I thought she made good money at the hospital."

Rachel worked at the front desk in radiology. It was only thirty hours a week, but Wilma had thought that was plenty since Tom worked full-time repairing and installing windshields.

"When Tom went back to school in January, Rachel picked up a job at the fabric store. I thought you knew."

"Tom went back to school? What on earth for?"

Michael sounded resigned. "He realized windshields weren't his passion in life. He wants to become a missionary."

Wilma gasped. Michael might as well have said Tom wanted to take a vow of poverty. She had the utmost admiration for missionaries, of course—they were doing the Lord's work, after all—but it wasn't exactly a lucrative career. Thank goodness Tom and Rachel only had one child to put through college.

"Things will be a little tight for them while he's in school," Michael continued. "Hence the second job."

"She should've told me if they needed money. I could've—"

"No, Mom. You couldn't have." His voice was gentle but left no room for further discussion.

Her right arm began to tremble as it held the phone up to her ear. An achy feeling spread through her chest.

"Do you want me to tell Rachel to call you?" Michael asked.

"No, that's all right." The words sounded strained coming through the tightness in her throat. "I'm sure we'll catch up soon."

His voice dropped to a more pensive tone. "I don't understand what the deal is between you two."

"There is no *deal*, Michael."

She hoped she sounded convincing. Even if she didn't, she knew her eldest son would pretend to be convinced because he preferred not to talk about such personal matters.

"Okay, well, don't forget you promised to come down this summer." His voice was all business now. "I'm going to hold you to that."

"Yes, dear."

They spoke for another minute before saying goodbye. She let the phone drop to the table with a clatter. That achy feeling in her chest felt like disappointment and shame. What kind of mother didn't even know what her own daughter was going through?

Rachel had once accused Wilma of caring more about the women in "those rehab homes" than about her, but Rachel just didn't understand. And no wonder she had been so busy lately. Tom, a missionary?

She and Herb had raised their kids in the church and had been pleased when they married spouses who shared their beliefs, but Wilma never expected any of them to do something like this. It was one thing to go to church. Quite another to traverse into a snake-infested jungle or some such place with nothing but the Word of God for protection.

She clucked her tongue at herself. There she went again. Not trusting that God would take care of her family. Not willing to step out in faith when an opportunity to put her loved ones in God's hands presented itself.

It was hard now, looking back, to remember why she had thought adding two more kids to their family would be impossible. Why she had been so scared. Yes, it was hard to remember now. But it had been easy then.

All this time she felt she'd let Rosie, Pete, and Dani down, but now she had the distinct feeling she'd let her own kids down, as well. Her relationship with Rachel had been strained for years, and Wilma couldn't help but wonder how much her preoccupation with righting past wrongs was to blame. Now her daughter wouldn't even tell her she needed help.

Wilma pushed herself to her feet with a surge of determination. She couldn't rewrite history. There were problems she could solve in the present, however. She marched over to the kitchen counter and picked up the pile of FAS paperwork.

sixteen

Pete parked the Xpeditor a block away from the school. Braedon had never told Pete he was embarrassed to be picked up by a garbage truck, but Pete figured it was a safe assumption. The last thing he wanted was to be a source of embarrassment to his nephew.

Braedon appeared a minute later, backpack slung over his shoulder, and Pearl stomped her hooves in anticipation.

"I know he's way cooler than me," Pete said, "but you don't have to rub it in."

There were two steps to get into the Xpeditor, and Braedon stepped up on the first one to pull the door handle, then jumped back down to let the door swing open before climbing in. As soon as Braedon shut the door and buckled, which was not an easy feat considering Pearl took up so much space, Pete pulled back onto the road. His boss had reluctantly agreed to let Pete pick Braedon up from school when needed, but only on the condition that Pete waste as little time as possible doing so. And that Dani sign a waiver releasing the great city of Sleeping Grass from any liability whatsoever with regard to the young man.

"How was your day?" Pete asked.

"Fine."

"Do you have any homework?"

"Just vocab and a little math."

Pete didn't remember having homework in fifth grade, but Braedon had homework almost every day. Maybe Pete just didn't remember what school had been like. He'd had a lot of other things on his mind at that age, and many of his memories were blurry.

"How was the goulash?" There had been great deliberation this morning over whether Braedon wanted to try the cafeteria's offering for hot lunch or brown-bag it. Eventually he'd said, "You only live once," and decided to try the goulash.

"It was okay. Kind of mushy." He pushed at Pearl. "Scoot *over*."

Pearl didn't budge. Braedon was pitiful, wedged between a door and a pig.

Pete kept his amusement to himself. "It's probably hard for cafeteria food to compete with your mother's cooking."

"True." Braedon leaned back and rested his arm on Pearl, accepting his lot in life. "Those lunch ladies are nice, but they don't stand a chance against my mom."

Pete hadn't eaten so well as he had the last few weeks in his whole life. Dani had discovered the cookbooks in the cardboard box from the dumpster and had been making all kinds of things. Never anything fancy, but boy, was it good.

Pete stopped the truck beside a blue bin and activated the hydraulic mast. "Has she ever made goulash?"

"No." Braedon's voice changed. "My dad didn't like stuff like that."

"Oh." Pete felt as though he was always skirting around the issue of Braedon's dad. "What kind of stuff did he like?"

Braedon shrugged. "Nothing that was mixed together. No casseroles. Steak and potatoes. Hamburgers."

Pete drove on in silence, trying to picture this man who was blind to his own son's greatness and ate steak and hamburgers. Turned out silence was just what Braedon needed.

"He'd get mad if I couldn't finish my dinner. He'd say a real man knows how to clean his plate. I would take less food so I could eat it all, but then he'd call me a sissy and give me more."

Pete's grip on the steering wheel tightened as Braedon spoke, but he forced himself to keep his voice calm. "Did your dad ever get rough with you, Braedon?"

"Nah." Braedon looked out the window. "He never touched me. Not even for a hug. I guess I wasn't worth the effort."

Old, familiar voices slid unbidden and unwelcome into Pete's head.

"You're lucky we kept you as long as we did, Pete."

"We just can't deal with these behaviors anymore, Pete."

He shook his head.

"You're worth every effort, buddy." He stopped at the next trash bin, but instead of lowering the mast, he turned to his nephew. "You know what Windy Ray always says?"

Braedon had been captivated by the old man when he'd gone with Pete to Sunny's last Friday.

"What?"

"He says everything the Creator makes has value, but a man must choose whether he wants to see it."

"What do you mean?"

"Like with Pearl." Pete had told Braedon the story of how he and Pearl had come to be together. "One person thought she wasn't worth the effort, but I thought she was. And I don't just *think* you're worth the effort, Braedon. I know it."

While Braedon appeared to ponder this, Pete picked up the bin and moved to the next one.

"The Creator, like God?" Braedon asked.

Pete took a deep breath. "Yes. Windy Ray says there are many ways to describe God, but Creator is his favorite."

"My dad says there's no such thing as God. He says people who believe in God are stupid."

Pete had felt that way many times. If moms could disappear without a trace, if brothers and sisters could be ripped apart, how could there be a God? Other times, Pete felt differently. If places like the Hi-Line and the Rocky Mountains could exist, if words like Thoreau's could be formed and written down and shared, how could there *not* be a God?

"How many more days until Wilma's party?"

Pete smiled at the change of subject. "Five more days."

Braedon had been excited when Pete told him about it. Dani had not.

"Sweet." Braedon played with Pearl's ears, and she smiled. "We should get Pearl a party hat."

Pete pictured it and laughed. "Good idea. Maybe we can go to the dollar store this weekend and see what we can find."

"I want to help put up the streamers."

"I'm sure that can be arranged."

They came to the second-to-last trash bin of the alley and stopped. Several large, broken-down boxes were leaning against the bin.

Pete opened his door. "I'll be back in a few minutes."

He knew better than to say *I'll be right back* when he got out of the truck in this alley. Conrad Rountree lived on this block, and he never missed an opportunity to shoot the bull with anyone who came along.

Pete picked up the first box and paused. Huggies diapers, size one. He grabbed the second box. Graco Convertible Crib in Walnut Espresso.

"Well, I'll be." The nice young couple who lived here must've had a baby. Their first. Pete smiled. He'd fixed up the baby walker to be good as new. He'd drop it off for them next week.

Conrad appeared, just as Pete knew he would, his big belly leading the way, thumbs tucked behind his wide yellow suspenders designed to look like a tape measure. "Dang weatherman says gusts up ta sixty miles an arr tomorrow, d'ya hear?"

It had taken several visits with Con before Pete had grown adept at deciphering the gravelly words spoken around a large pinch of chew.

Pete tossed the cardboard into the hopper. "I heard it on the radio."

"I 'spect Windy Ray'll make the most of it."

Pete nodded.

Con jerked his thumb at the truck. "Who ya got in the cab there with Pearl?"

Pete found himself standing up taller. "That's my nephew."

"That right?" Conrad spit into the dirt, and some of the brown juice dribbled into his chest-length beard. "I got a nephew servin' time in Deer Lodge. My brother's boy. Right shame."

Pete had heard all about Con's brother's ne'er-do-well son before, but he didn't let on.

"It's hard on my poor ma," Con continued. "Bad for her nerves."

"How *is* your mother doing?" The last time they'd talked, Con told Pete he'd had to move his mom into the assisted-living place in Shelby.

Con leaned against the fence as if he weren't outside in the cold in nothing but a long-sleeve shirt rolled up to his elbows. "She's arright. Says she got nuthin' to do. The lady in charge of 'ranging events done up and quit on 'em. Right shame."

"That's too bad." Pete reached for the door handle. He knew from experience there was only one way out of this conversation. "I better get back to work. Good to see you, Con."

Con raised a grimy hand in response as Pete climbed into the truck. He quickly dumped the new parents' bin and moved to the last one in the alley, which was Con's. Like Wilma's, it rarely had much in it, especially in the winter. Folks sometimes assumed the amount of garbage collected increased in the winter compared to the summer because everyone was stuck inside, but Pete found the opposite to be true.

"Who was that?" Braedon asked.

"His name's Conrad Rountree."

"Cool suspenders. Do you have any suspenders?"

"Can't say that I do."

"Oh." Braedon sounded disappointed, and Pete hid a smile.

At ten o'clock, Pete was waiting in the dark outside the gas station even though Dani had told him not to come. He wasn't going to let his baby sister walk home at night by herself. Sleeping Grass was a pretty safe place, but he wasn't about to take any chances.

Dani pulled open the door and slid in. She laid her head back against the seat. "You didn't have to."

He wasn't sure what to say, so he said nothing.

"Is Braedon in bed?"

"Yes."

"Did he get his homework done?"

"Yes."

Her voice changed. "I hate not seeing him all day."

She'd been there this morning to take Braedon to school but had to leave for work before he got out. She'd dropped

Pete and Pearl off at the carport before Braedon was even awake so she could have the truck to drive Braedon to school. After she'd dropped Braedon off, she drove the truck back to the carport, left it there for Pete, and walked to the gas station.

Pete was keeping his eye out for a dependable used vehicle for her. He had a little money in savings.

"Didn't you say you'd be able to get better shifts once you've been there long enough?"

Dani sighed. "That's what my boss said, but better shifts won't make it any less boring."

"Business is slow, huh?"

"It's not that, it's just I don't really *do* anything. I stand there and press buttons. Not exactly rewarding work."

"You don't *have* to work, you know. I can support you."

"I appreciate that, Pete, but I want to be able to stand on my own two feet."

He parked in his driveway, and they walked into the house. Pete could hear Pearl snoring, but something was off.

He listened for a moment before scoffing. "The swiney little traitor."

The snores sounded different because they were coming from the spare bedroom. Pearl had defected.

Dani threw up her hands. "How am I supposed to get any sleep in there with that going on?"

"My offer still stands. You can have my room."

"I'll sleep on the couch." She plopped herself down on it as if to prove her point.

"Dani."

"I'll be fine. I'm tired enough to sleep anywhere."

She did look tired. Not just tired, but weary. Pete felt a surge of protectiveness. It was a feeling from deep in his soul that pushed other feelings and memories to the surface, where they glared at him with unblinking eyes.

He'd always been protective of Dani, even when she had annoyed him to no end. Maybe because they never had a dad around and Pete had been the man of the house. Maybe because, despite the love and affection their mother had showed them, Pete always somehow knew it was up to him to take care of Dani.

He'd tried. He'd done everything he could think of. When one social worker drove away with Dani while another held on to Pete's arms, he'd fought his way free and ran after the car, screaming her name. Screaming "Stop!" and "Come back!" until he couldn't breathe and blood roared in his ears and the car disappeared.

He'd been fighting ever since.

"Are you okay?" Dani asked. "You look like you're going to throw up."

He slowly lowered himself onto the other end of the couch. "Did you ever hear from Mom?"

Two deep creases appeared between Dani's eyebrows. Her lips turned down, and she stared at her hands in her lap for so long, Pete began to wonder if he'd spoken the words in his head and not aloud.

"No." When she finally answered, it was as if she were four again. "Did you?"

"No."

If he had gotten a phone call, a letter, anything from her saying she was okay or that she missed them or something . . .

"I don't remember her." Dani's voice was resigned. "All I remember is Aunt Ellie telling me she went away because she was sick and didn't want us to watch her die. She wanted to spare us. But I never believed that. I think she just left."

Pete's gut twisted. No wonder his aunt and uncle always warned him not to talk about his mom to Dani when he would visit. They'd thought they could make it easier for

Dani by feeding her a fantasy. Better for her to believe their mother had been too sick to care for them, right?

He wished that would've worked, for Dani's sake. Then they wouldn't *both* have to torture themselves over things they couldn't change.

"Maybe she did want to spare us."

"Oh, please." Dani rolled her eyes. "We both know she just decided there was a better life out there somewhere without us."

Pete winced, his sister's words sharper than a Dickinson poem. "You said you don't remember her. I do. She loved us."

Dani leaned forward and rested her elbows on her knees, her chin on her hands. She looked straight ahead, but Pete knew she wasn't seeing a dingy gray wall smudged with snout prints. He knew because he'd looked into the past like that himself, many times, wondering how things might've been different.

Dani shook her head and blinked, failing, as he always did, to envision that other life. The one where nothing had torn them apart.

"Then why didn't she ever come back?"

seventeen

Wilma patted her hair and smoothed the front of her floral silk blouse. Her guests would start arriving any minute now. Pete and Braedon first at five-thirty to hang up the streamers. Then Dani, Lily, and Raymond at six. She moved the platter of cupcakes a half an inch to the right.

There. Perfect.

Yesterday, Lily had come in the morning to clean as usual, and Wilma had reminded her about the party. Lily hadn't made any promises. Should Wilma have invited Jerry? She shuddered. No, one encounter with him had been enough.

"Lord." Wilma clasped her hands together under her chin. "Please let her come."

She heard a car door slam out front and hobbled to the door as quickly as she could, opening it before Pete could knock. "Happy spring!"

Her spirits were high. She'd mailed off her paperwork and first payment to FAS last week, and Sadie had called this morning to let her know it had been received and she would get started on it right away. Four payments of $199.99 were a small price to pay for the results Sadie had guaranteed.

"Happy spring." Pete smiled as he ushered Braedon and a festive-looking Pearl into the house like a hen shooing her chicks. "I guess Mother Nature didn't get the memo."

The sky was hazy with low, gray clouds. Wilma leaned on her cane. "It's forty-one degrees. That's about as springlike as we could hope for on March nineteenth. Now, you must be Braedon."

She spoke his name deliberately, having practiced it all day to be sure she'd get it right. She fixed her eyes on the boy, and he nodded shyly.

"Yes, ma'am."

"Oh, now, none of that. You can call me Miss Wilma."

"Okay." He was thinner than a lodgepole pine and seemed younger than eleven, but she supposed everyone grew up at their own pace. He had the skittish look of a stray cat afraid to approach the dish of food that had been set out for it. It wouldn't do to make him feel uncomfortable.

She shifted her attention to the pig, bending as far as she dared to address the creature. "What a wonderful party hat you have on, Pearl. Thank you for coming. It's an honor, as always."

Pearl bobbed her head and made a series of noises.

"That means *Thanks for inviting me*," Braedon said.

Pete put a hand on Braedon's shoulder. "No, I think it means *You'd better be honored*."

"Nonsense." Wilma straightened with great effort and leaned against her cane. "It means *The honor's all mine*."

A chuckle escaped Braedon before he stiffened and looked at the floor. Wilma took it as a victory. What a dear child.

She tapped her cane against the floor twice. "Shall we get to work, gentlemen?"

The half hour she'd allotted for decorating went by quickly. They had red, blue, yellow, and green streamers. Braedon made a grand show of fashioning a large bow from the yellow for the back of each chair, and he blushed when she applauded.

"Those are wonderful." She resisted the urge to pinch his cheeks. "Wherever did you learn to do that?"

He shrugged. "My mom's good at this kind of stuff."

"Well, she isn't the only one. Thank goodness you came along to help me."

He scrunched his nose in a pleased way, and Wilma's heart squeezed. Rosie used to do that. An image of her dear friend's face rushed toward her through the years. She'd soaked up praise like the prairie soaked up a late-August rain, and Wilma had never hesitated to give it to her. Though Wilma was several years older, they'd been more than best friends. They'd been like sisters.

It had never been enough.

A knock sounded, and Wilma cleared her throat. "Would you mind getting that, Pete?"

He answered the door while she adjusted her glasses and moved the tray of cupcakes half an inch to the left.

"Lily's here," Pete called.

Wilma smiled. She wasn't sure how she was going to tell Pete about her and his mother. She wasn't sure how she was going to get Lily out from under Jerry's thumb. As Pete and Lily came into the kitchen, trying not to touch each other, however, she was sure about one thing.

They were smitten.

Pete tried to look anywhere but at Lily as they finished eating dinner and Windy Ray fetched the cupcakes from the counter at Wilma's request. He couldn't believe she was here. He knew it had nothing to do with him, but his presence hadn't kept her away, at least.

Why did he have to think about her every day? Why did the way she laughed at Windy Ray's jokes make his stomach turn inside out?

He felt his sister's eyes on him and made the mistake of looking at her. She raised her eyebrows in Lily's direction and smirked. His ears burned.

Windy Ray stuck the tray in Pete's face. "Pink or yellow?"

"Yellow," he mumbled.

Windy Ray continued around the table, asking "Pink or yellow?" and presenting cupcakes to each person with the flourish of someone pulling out their wallet to show off pictures of their grandchildren. It was quite a feat considering the oxygen tank he had to lug around with him.

"Can I have one of each?" Braedon asked.

Windy Ray nodded gravely. "I believe that would be wise."

Dani looked like she wanted to protest but didn't have the heart.

When Windy Ray had finished his task and retaken his seat, Wilma held up her cupcake. "Thank you, Raymond. And here's to the first day of spring."

Everyone held up their cupcakes and pretended to clink them together like champagne glasses. Heat rushed to Pete's face as Lily held her cupcake out to him, and he tapped it with his. Had she done something different with her hair? Or was it her orange shirt that made her somehow appear even more beautiful than before?

He could never write a poem to do her justice.

"Don't you think so, Pete?" Wilma asked.

He jerked. Everyone was looking at him.

"Don't you think that's what Dani should've said to that horrible man who accosted her at the gas station?" Wilma elaborated, clearly trying to be helpful.

A horrible man accosted Dani at the gas station? Why

was this the first he was hearing about it? His muscles began to tense.

"Asking for my phone number hardly qualifies as accosting." Dani gave him a look he knew was meant to warn him—plead with him—not to get upset. He was familiar with the look. It was the same one she'd given him at her high school graduation when her boyfriend had been hanging all over her, right before Pete shoved the hormonal kid to the ground. The same one she'd given him when Uncle Ted asked him to leave Dani's twenty-fifth birthday party because he was drunk, right before he'd taken an inebriated swing at Uncle Ted's chin.

Yes, he knew that look well.

"Apisi and I were accosted at the gas station once," Windy Ray said. "A woman in a minivan didn't think I should park my bike in a parking space. Where else would I park it, I would like to know?"

Lily glanced at her phone with a frown and pushed away from the table. "Wilma, it was a lovely dinner, but I need to head home."

"So soon?" Wilma's face fell in disappointment, and Pete could understand the feeling.

Lily's smile seemed tentative. "Thank you for inviting me."

"Please, take a cupcake home with you." Wilma struggled to her feet. "I made so many."

"All right."

While Lily put on her coat, Wilma dug a white paper plate out of a drawer. She put two pink and two yellow cupcakes on the plate. "Here you go, Lily. And I'd feel so much better if you'd let Pete walk you home."

Pete stood abruptly, almost knocking over his chair. "Yes, good idea. It's dark."

"And it's so far," Wilma added.

Seven and a half blocks, Pete happened to know. Maybe not "so far," but far enough on a cold, dark night to need an escort, right?

Red spots appeared on Lily's cheeks. "I don't think—"

"I insist." Wilma tapped her cane against the floor. "All this talk about people being accosted leaves me feeling anxious for you, dear. You wouldn't deny an old woman a little peace of mind, would you?"

Lily glanced at Pete, then quickly looked away. "I suppose not. If Pete doesn't mind."

Pete opened his mouth to declare just how much he didn't mind, but Wilma beat him to it. "He doesn't mind one bit."

If Pete wasn't already fretting over what he and Lily might talk about and what she might be thinking, he might've had the good sense to be embarrassed. Instead, the only feeling his brain had room for was anxiety.

"Braedon, keep an eye on Pearl for me, would you?"

Braedon nodded solemnly.

As Wilma practically shoved him toward the door, Pete heard Windy Ray ask in an exaggerated whisper, "Does anyone know what Pete's favorite flowers are?"

Dani snickered. "Lilies."

Pete would deal with them later.

The street was dark. The clouds obscured any moonlight, and the streetlight on Wilma's block had burned out long ago. Pete had forgotten his jacket in his eagerness and, frankly, terror, but he hardly felt the cold as his blood charged through his veins like water over Niagara Falls.

"You didn't have to do this," Lily said softly, her voice floating easily through the night. She carried the plate of cupcakes with both hands.

He slowed down to keep pace with her, pleased she seemed to be in no hurry. "It's no trouble. I needed some fresh air anyway."

He was half-surprised his voice didn't squeak like a kid going through puberty. He felt as awkward as one.

"I like fresh air, too," Lily said. "Sometimes I crack open my bedroom window even when it's cold. Jerry hates it when I do that, but I love how the night sounds."

He would let her open every window in the house if he were Jerry. If that was what she wanted. How could he deny her anything?

He wasn't Jerry, though. He and Lily were barely more than acquaintances, no matter how much he wished otherwise, and to prove it he couldn't think of a single thing to say to her. He'd already asked all the obvious questions during their drive to Great Falls: *"How long have you lived here?" "Where did you grow up?" "Do you work at any other houses besides Wilma's?"* He'd even asked what her favorite place to eat in Sleeping Grass was, which had made her laugh.

It was Sunny's. Same as him.

"Sometimes I sit up and listen to the night and eat Skittles," Lily continued.

"Skittles?"

"I'm a sucker for Skittles. What's your favorite candy?"

"You know those gummy Coke bottles?"

"Gummy Coke bottles? Really?"

His ears burned. "You're a sucker for Skittles, I'm a sucker for all things Coca-Cola."

It was something his mom had collected. Coca-Cola hand towels, Coca-Cola magnets, and a Coca-Cola clock in the kitchen. She'd loved that thing. Whatever happened to it? The house eventually fell into foreclosure—just after Pete went into foster care—but he had no idea where all their belongings had ended up. He'd only taken a bag of clothes and a box of miscellaneous items from his room. He hadn't thought about that clock in years.

"Do you like those Coca Cola Santa mugs and everything?"

He grinned sheepishly. "I have a full vintage set of them."

She laughed.

"They're highly collectible." He tried to sound indignant but failed.

"I'm sure they are." She smiled. "Do you have the Christmas ornaments?"

"I used to, but I don't know where they are anymore. I haven't put up a Christmas tree in a long time."

"Oh." Her voice sounded sad. "Wilma had a beautiful tree at Christmas, covered in crystal snowflakes and red ribbons. I helped her take it down in January. It was the first thing she had me do when I started working for her, and I was so disappointed."

"I bet she would've left it up if you'd asked."

"I didn't want to be a bother."

"You could never be a bother." He dropped his gaze to the ground in front of him. She must think him ridiculous, talking like that.

"Did you ever talk to her about getting a cellphone or a Life Alert button?"

He cringed and hoped she couldn't see it in the dark. "I meant to, but . . ."

"You didn't want to risk upsetting her." Lily nudged his arm with her elbow, and there was a smile in her voice. "You big chicken."

He looked over at her. She was watching him. He chuckled. "I guess I am. What about her kids? Do you know them? Maybe they could talk to her about it."

"I don't have their contact info."

The seven and a half blocks were disappearing under their feet far too quickly. He slowed the pace even more. "I'll talk to her. I promise."

He shouldn't be making any promises, especially to a woman. Especially to *this* woman. He knew better.

Lily nodded. "Thank you."

A few steps passed in silence, and Pete began to panic. Soon they would reach her house and he would have to say good night and then it could be weeks—months—before he would see her again.

"I like your friend Windy Ray," Lily said. "How did you meet him?"

Pete laughed at the memory. "I was at the grocery store with Pearl just after I'd found her, and she got away from me. I started running up and down the aisles, looking for her. When I found her, she was sitting next to Apisi in a shopping cart, and Windy Ray was lecturing them about the difference between imported and locally grown beef. I said, 'That's my pig,' and Windy Ray pointed at Apisi and said, 'That's my dog.' We've been best friends ever since."

He'd never said that out loud, that Windy Ray was his best friend. He had the terrifying and exhilarating feeling he might say all kinds of things he'd never said out loud if he talked to Lily long enough. Something about her made the words fly straight out of his mouth instead of passing through his mind for inspection first.

She made a sound like the wind gliding over the surface of the Marias River. "You're lucky to have one of those."

Pete never realized how true that was until he heard the wistfulness in Lily's voice.

"We play Chickenfoot every Monday at his house. Apisi and Pearl are best friends, too."

"Chickenfoot?"

"It's a domino game."

"I've never heard of it. Sounds fun."

Lily's house came into view, and she stopped, though they were two houses away still.

He stopped as well and shoved his hands into his pockets. "Maybe I could teach you sometime, if you want."

She turned toward him. For a moment, there was a break in the clouds, and the moon shone on her face. Pete's heart thrashed in his chest like a bull trout stranded on the riverbank.

The moon reaches out
and paints the lily's face with silver,
touching its brush to the tip of her nose
and leaving a star in her eye.

He swallowed.

She glanced over at her house, and something changed in her face. "Maybe."

More than anything, he wanted to ask her to go with him to Windy Ray's house Monday night, yet that look on her face held him back. He thought of the time Jerry showed up at Wilma's house looking for Lily. What if Pete invited Lily, and Jerry didn't want her to go? Of course he wouldn't want her to go.

Pete wouldn't ask Lily to sneak around, but he desperately wanted to spend more time with her and how else could he do it?

Desire and duty yanked his heart in different directions, stretching it thin like pulled taffy until it sank in the middle. His shoulders sank, too. He couldn't ask. He shouldn't even be here.

"I guess I better get back to check on Pearl. Make sure she doesn't eat the rest of those cupcakes."

Lily nodded slowly, but the clouds had re-covered the

moon so Pete couldn't read her face. "Good night, Pete. Thanks for walking me home."

"Good night."

He waited until she entered the house and closed the door before turning away. She never looked back, never waved, and now he felt the cold.

eighteen

Pete sat on his couch Monday night and stared at the four-inch retro Coca-Cola truck in his hand. It had been sitting on top of the trash bin at Lily's house this morning, waiting for him. He'd hoped to see her through the window when he hopped out to get it, but there'd been no sign of her.

The toy truck was in good condition, though it had to be at least forty years old. Where had she found it? He spun its wheels with his finger.

"What's that?"

Pete practically jumped out of his skin. He must've really been lost in his thoughts if Braedon the elephant walker and Pearl the mouth breather could sneak up on him. "Just an old toy."

He held it out, and his nephew took it. "Cool. It's probably an antique or something."

"It's not *that* old."

Pearl climbed onto the couch and leaned heavily against him. "Easy, girl, you're squishing me."

Braedon set the truck on the coffee table. "Can we watch *Ninja Warrior*?"

Pete glanced at the time. Dani would be home from work soon. He'd left the Dodge at the gas station for her after he and Braedon had dinner with Windy Ray. "Your mom said she wants you ready for bed when she gets home, remember?"

"I already brushed my teeth. All I gotta do is put on my pajamas."

Pete waffled. "Did you finish all your homework?"

"Yeah."

Pete should have asked that question hours ago, but he'd been utterly consumed with the Coca-Cola truck. What did Lily's leaving it for him mean?

"Okay, but only until your mom gets home. As soon as she walks in that door—"

"I know, I know," Braedon grumbled. "You're going to turn it off."

Pete turned on the TV and found the show Braedon liked. He'd already gotten into trouble with Dani a couple of times for letting Braedon watch TV before he'd taken care of his responsibilities. He didn't want to endure that lecture again.

"Whoa, did you see that?" Braedon was on the edge of the couch, his body leaning and twisting in sync with the contestant on-screen. "I'm going to be that strong someday."

Pete covered up a smile. "I don't doubt it. Keep eating your vegetables."

Braedon made a face. "That's not how they got their muscles."

Pete didn't argue. Braedon's eyes were glued to the TV as he jerked from side to side and made sound effects. It was impressive what the competitors could do, but Pete couldn't imagine wanting to try it himself.

"You think that would be fun?" he asked.

"I think being strong would be fun."

"You're already strong."

Braedon sank back into the couch. "No, I'm not."

Pete grimaced. "Says who?"

Braedon mumbled something with a scowl on his face.

Pete picked up the remote and turned down the volume. "Who says, Braedon?"

He wrinkled his nose. "Everybody."

"At school?"

"I'm always the last one picked for teams."

"You're still new. You have to give it time. The other kids have been going to school together since kindergarten. I'm sure they'll want to be your friend once they get to know you."

"I don't need any friends."

Pete frowned. Where was this coming from? "I don't know about that. Aren't there any kids you'd like to hang out with?"

"No."

Pete's frown deepened at the hard edge in Braedon's voice This wasn't the Braedon he'd come to know the past few weeks. "Everybody needs friends."

"My dad says a real man doesn't need anyone."

A hole opened up in Pete's chest. He'd told himself the same thing when he was Braedon's age, every time he'd been passed around to a different place. And again every time he'd lost another job and been forced to move on. He'd wanted to believe it.

"Windy Ray says the Creator made us to need each other and to need Him."

Braedon stared at the TV, and Pearl breathed noisily in Pete's ear. He didn't know if everything Windy Ray said about the Creator was true, but his friend seemed to know what he was talking about most of the time. Except when it came to women.

Pete watched the glower shadowing his nephew's face,

trying to decide what he should say. He was unprepared and inadequate for this situation, but shouldn't he say something? Though he was the adult here, it felt as if he were still eleven years old. What right did he have to speak into Braedon's life?

A sound came from outside, and Pearl's ears perked up.

Pete was ashamed at his sense of relief. "Your mom's home. Better get in your pajamas."

Braedon grumbled but obeyed, trudging down the hall and slamming the bedroom door behind him. Pete clicked off the TV, feeling at a total loss. It was like Braedon had transformed before his eyes.

He leaned against Pearl. "What was that all about? What should I do?"

She didn't appear nearly as concerned as he was.

"You're no help at all."

Dani entered the house, hung the keys on a hook with a long sigh, and pulled off her coat. She noticed Pete and Pearl on the couch, watching her, and eyed them suspiciously. "What's going on?"

Pete shrugged. He wasn't about to throw Braedon under the bus. "Nothing."

"Is Braedon in bed?"

"No."

She stood there motionless a moment longer. "Is there anything I need to know?"

Pete tried to smile. "No. Everything's fine."

She looked skeptical. He fought the urge to glance down the hall toward the spare room. "How was work?"

Her shoulders drooped. "Ugh, mind-numbing."

"Has that phone-number guy come back to bother you again?"

She rolled her eyes. "I wouldn't tell you if he did."

He didn't understand—was it a crime if he wanted to keep an eye out for his baby sister?

"I can take care of myself," she added. "Just like I always have."

Something painful burned through him like a shot of whiskey. She didn't remember, but he certainly did. He remembered making her dinner. Washing her clothes. Walking her to preschool. Would she even believe him if he told her? Uncle Ted and Aunt Ellie had never wanted to talk about anything from before Dani went to live with them. They'd always been content to pretend all was fine with the world.

Braedon returned to the living room, skulking along the wall. "Mom, can I get a cellphone?"

Her head jerked back. "What? Why?"

He gave Pete a pleading look. "Other kids in my class have one."

Pete grew still, as if freezing in place would make him invisible. The last thing he wanted was to get caught in the middle of an argument between his sister and nephew.

"You're eleven." Dani rubbed her forehead. "We've talked about this."

Braedon threw his hands up dramatically. "But I need one."

"What for?"

"I just do."

Pete had never been a parent, but even he knew that wasn't an answer.

Dani was unmoved. "I told you before, we'll discuss it when you get to middle school."

Braedon wrinkled his nose. "But fifth grade *is* middle school here. Fifth through eighth grade."

Dani blinked, momentarily at a loss. Pearl heaved herself off the couch and hoofed over to Braedon, butting her head into his side.

"I think she's ready for bed," Pete said, then immediately

chastised himself for speaking when both Dani and Braedon turned to look at him. He gulped.

Dani shook her head as if clearing her thoughts. "Your uncle's right. It's late. Now's not the time to talk about this."

Braedon glared at Pete as if Pete had betrayed him. "Fine. I'm going to bed. Come on, Pearl."

The pig was more than happy to follow Braedon down the hall, never having been the type of swine to stay up late.

"Good night," Dani called, but there was no reply.

She sank onto the couch and closed her eyes with a groan. Pete shifted uncomfortably. He hadn't seen this side of Braedon before, but Dani likely had. He considered sneaking out of the room while she wasn't looking, but then she spoke.

"I thought switching schools would be good for him. Give him the chance to start over."

Pete ventured a guess. "He didn't have many friends at his old school?"

"Not exactly."

"They still sell flip phones, you know. I don't think he could get into too much trouble with one of those. . . ."

His voice tapered off as Dani sat up and gave him a look. "You're taking his side?"

"I-I, uh . . ."

"No offense, Pete, but you don't know anything about this or about Braedon." Her eyes flashed. "Eleven-year-olds aren't responsible enough to have their own phones. He's just a kid."

The words hit Pete hard. She was right, and boy, was Braedon lucky to have a mother who understood he was still a child—who understood she was the adult, not him.

Dani picked up the Coca-Cola truck from the coffee table and examined it. "His dad was always trying to get him to 'be a man.' Always trying to toughen him up, even when he was little. I saw the person he was trying to turn Braedon into, and that's why—"

"That's why you divorced him?"

"It wasn't the only reason, but it was a big part of it. He wasn't going to be happy until Braedon was just like him."

Pete kept his mouth shut. Like Dani had said, he didn't know anything about it. He hadn't been involved, which was his own fault. If he hadn't forced Dani to kick him out of her life, he might've been there for her and Braedon sooner.

Just add it to his long list of regrets.

"I'm really tired," Dani said.

That was Pete's cue. He stood. "One of these days I'm going to convince you to take my room and stop sleeping on the couch." He headed for the hall but stopped when he heard her voice.

"One of these days I'm going to convince you it's not your job to protect me anymore."

He didn't turn around. He didn't want her to see his face. It wasn't his job? She had no mother. No father. Uncle Ted and Aunt Ellie had both passed away years ago. Her ex was out of the picture. If Pete didn't protect her, who would?

nineteen

Pete stood in the candy aisle Wednesday afternoon and scratched his head. He'd never paid much attention to Skittles. Who knew there were so many different kinds? Did Lily prefer the original flavor? What about sour? There were even limited-edition St. Patrick's Day Skittles on clearance. Pearl grunted impatiently.

He picked up one of each kind and turned to leave. "Come on, Pearl."

He took three steps and stopped. Pearl bumped into the back of his legs with a snort. What was he thinking?

He backtracked and put all the candy back on the shelf. Lily would think he was a creep. But she had left *him* a gift, as if they were friends, maybe. A man could buy a bag of Skittles for a friend, couldn't he?

"Moose on the loose." He grabbed a bag of the original, muttering to himself.

"They're hard on my teeth, those Skittles."

Pete spun around, and Pearl squealed. Windy Ray leaned on a shopping cart behind them. Apisi stood on the child's seat and wagged her tail, wearing her red high heels despite the mild weather today.

"I'll stick with Raisinets," Windy Ray said.

"They're not for you." Pete snatched three bags of Raisinets from the shelf and tossed them into Windy Ray's cart. "Here."

Windy Ray looked at the candy in the cart. Looked at Pete. "I didn't know you liked Skittles."

There was a gleam in Windy Ray's eye as he said it, as if somehow he knew the truth. Pete considered telling his friend that he loved Skittles and dreamed about Skittles and couldn't get through the week without Skittles, but the old man would see right through him.

"I don't. They're for Lily."

"Ah. I see. But they're distressing you, these Skittles. Perhaps you should give her a rock instead."

Pete shook his head but couldn't hold back a smile. "You're crazy."

"Yes." Windy Ray nodded solemnly. "Crazy in love."

"You hardly know Wilma."

Windy Ray pondered that for a moment before responding, "That doesn't seem to matter much."

Pete couldn't argue with that. He nodded toward Apisi. "What are you guys up to today?"

"It's a good day to get out of the house, is it not?"

Pearl sniffed around the cart, causing it to roll forward. Pete moved it back. "We're headed to the school to pick up Braedon in a few minutes."

His stomach held a kernel of dread about that. All week it seemed like Pete never knew which Braedon was going to come home from school. The timid and respectful Braedon he'd first gotten to know or the hostile and sulky Braedon who recently had been making appearances. He had no idea whether this was normal behavior for a fifth grader.

"You are troubled," Windy Ray said. "Your forehead is as furrowed as a newly plowed cornfield."

"Ha, who's the poet now?"

"It's you."

Pete sighed. "Braedon's been acting weird the past few days. I think something's going on at school."

"This happened to my son once. Someone was stealing his lunch, as it turned out, and he didn't want to tell me. Of course, that was long ago, and I don't know if kids steal lunches anymore."

Pete gaped. Windy Ray had never mentioned a son. "I don't think that's it. And you have a son? Where does he live?"

Windy Ray glanced at the ceiling. "He's with the Creator now."

"Oh." Pete looked at the floor. "I'm sorry."

"He has his mother and the Creator to keep him company and fill his heart with joy. It is I who am alone."

Pete shifted on his feet and fumbled for words. "You've never talked about them."

"This is true."

"Was it . . . uh, how did . . . ?" Pete's hands raised slightly and then dropped. What could he say? Some friend he was.

"They were on a boat, and the wind took them away. It has been many years."

Pearl had found a giant plastic tub of licorice and was nuzzling it with her snout. Pete nudged her away from it with his foot and pondered his friend's words, suddenly understanding why his friend shouted into the wind as if demanding an answer.

He thought about his mother. Braedon was her grandchild. Her only one. Was she out there somewhere? Would she hear him if he howled into the wind and let it carry his voice across the prairie?

"How did you get your son to tell you about the lunches?"

The oxygen tube coming from his nose swayed back and

forth as Windy Ray bobbed his head, casting a line into the river of his memories for an answer. "I asked many questions until I found the right one."

The bag of Skittles crinkled in Pete's hand. He wouldn't even know where to begin. "That could take forever."

Windy Ray considered this for a long moment before nodding as if it had been decided. "Perhaps you should talk to the lunch lady."

Pete parked close to the school, not having to worry about embarrassing Braedon today since he was in the Dodge. He glanced over at Pearl. "You don't think I should talk to the lunch lady, do you?"

She was watching out the window for her buddy and gave no response. But it was a terrible idea. The lunch lady would think him an overreacting fool. Although in a school this small, she probably had a pretty good read on every kid. . . .

No. He couldn't do that. He would just have to try the other method and hope one of his questions would hit the mark.

Pearl's grunting alerted Pete to Braedon's approach. Braedon climbed into the truck with . . . was that a pleasant look on his face?

"How was school today?"

Braedon put his arm around Pearl's neck. "Good."

Good? Not fine? Pete put the truck into drive. Maybe he wouldn't need to worry about finding the right question or interrogating lunch ladies.

"How about PE?"

"It was good. This one kid picked me for his partner for tennis. We have to play tennis for two weeks."

Pete barely resisted the urge to pump his fist. He'd been

right. Braedon had just needed time to settle in and get to know some other kids.

"That's awesome, buddy. You'll have a bunch of friends in no time."

Braedon lifted one shoulder. "I hate tennis."

Pete chuckled. "Fair enough."

Maybe this parenting thing wasn't so hard after all.

Wilma puttered around her house in a mood no amount of tea could ever change, even if she did like tea. She'd straightened everything she could think to straighten, yet Lily had done far too good of a job cleaning on Monday, leaving Wilma with nothing to do.

She'd left three messages for her daughter, Rachel, since talking to Michael last week. Part of her was hurt that Rachel hadn't called back, while another part wondered what she would say if she did. She had no help to offer, and heaven knew her questioning Rachel about Tom's decision to become a missionary was destined to lead to disaster.

Her thoughts turned to Pete and Lily, then Dani and Braedon. If she couldn't do anything for Rachel, perhaps her assistance could be applied elsewhere. She'd been puzzling over Dani since last week's party. She was around Lily's age and was, for all practical purposes, new to town. Wouldn't it be wonderful if Dani and Lily could be friends? And if Lily started spending time with Dani, she might end up around Pete more often as well, and didn't that sound like an intriguing possibility?

Wilma hobbled to her landline and picked it up with a quick glance at the time. Still an hour or so before suppertime, so hopefully she could catch Lily before Jerry got home from work.

Lily answered after three rings. "Hi, Miss Wilma."

"Hello, dear. How are you?"

"I'm fine. How are you? Is everything okay?"

"Yes, of course. I was calling to ask if you had any plans Saturday morning?"

She remembered from when Dani was talking about the gas station that she usually worked the late shift, so if she was going to get the two young ladies together . . .

"No, I don't. Do you need me to go to the store for you?"

Wilma carefully pulled out a chair at the table and sat down. She should've taken a minute to think this through. She wanted to invite Lily over, but for what exactly?

"No, thank you, I just wondered if you, uh . . ." She looked around the kitchen for inspiration, and her eyebrows shot up. "I wondered if you'd join Dani and me for a ladies' tea party."

"A tea party?"

"Scones and everything. Doesn't that sound lovely? Can you come at, say, ten o'clock?"

Lily was quiet for a moment, and Wilma tapped her cane against the floor. Lily simply must agree to come. *Tap, tap, tap.*

"All right."

Wilma sat up straighter. "Yes?"

"Yes, I'll come. That sounds fun. What can I bring?"

"Not a thing, dear, not a thing."

"I could pick up some groceries for you."

"Nonsense. It's almost April. It's time for me to get the Corolla out of the garage."

"Are you sure?" Lily sounded skeptical.

"Don't you worry about a thing. Just be here Saturday at ten."

She hung up the phone with excitement and doubt battling for prominence in her mind. What if Dani couldn't come? What if Dani didn't *want* to come? Surely Pete would encourage her. He didn't want her moping around town without a single friend, did he? And who would turn down a tea party with scones?

Wilma laughed. All that tea was finally going to be good for something.

Next, she needed to call Pete and get Dani's number. She'd written down his cell number on a scrap of paper. Where had she put it? She pushed out of her chair and shuffled over to where the phone's base sat. She found a couple of pens, a Post-it notepad, and a stack of mail. That's right. She'd set the mail here when she was tidying up to keep it from cluttering the table.

There was no scrap of paper with a phone number, but what was this? She pulled a piece of mail from the middle of the pile. She'd quickly flipped through the stack earlier, assuming it was all junk mail and bills. She must've missed this one. The return address said it was from the Liberty County Treasurer's Office.

She studied it, her stomach suddenly queasy. It looked familiar, as if she'd received a letter like this before, but she couldn't remember. Grabbing her letter opener, she carried the piece of mail back to the table so she could sit down before slicing it open. Her hand shook as she pulled the contents from the envelope.

She frowned. "That's quite enough of that. Steady on, now." But her voice trembled as well.

She adjusted her glasses, then unfolded the sheet of paper. It appeared to be about property taxes. The words *delinquent* and *lien* shouted at her from the page, and her heart pinched painfully. She'd gotten a property tax bill in the mail . . . when was that? She struggled to remember. What had Herb once told her about property taxes? Why couldn't she *remember*?

A large number caught her eye. Impossible. She couldn't owe that much. And why were they sending this now? In the five years since Herb's passing, since she'd taken over the job of paying the bills, she'd never once sent a check to the treasurer's office. It had never been a problem before. Herb had never written a check for the property taxes because he'd said—

"Oh dear." The paper crumpled as her grip on it tightened. The mortgage. He'd said the property taxes were rolled into the mortgage payments every year. *"It's all taken care of, Willy Mae."*

Except the house had been paid off months ago, so there were no mortgage payments anymore.

twenty

Wilma watched out the window at a quarter to ten Saturday morning. She'd had the table set since seven. She'd hardly been able to sleep. At the last minute, she'd decided to invite her dear friends Edna and Gladys to the tea party as well, and everything was in order.

Once she'd finally found that pesky scrap of paper in the pocket of her housecoat, she'd convinced Pete to give her Dani's number. Dani had declined her invitation at first. She'd insisted she was too busy with work and didn't want to leave Braedon, which of course was a flimsy excuse since the boy was old enough to watch himself even if Pete wasn't available.

Wilma had found a way around Dani's refusal, however. When Wilma had needed Pete's help to get her Corolla started after its months-long stint in the garage, she'd impressed upon him how important it was for a woman to have at least one good friend, especially after a major life transition. She'd laid it on thick, and Pete had done the rest.

An ancient Chevy Bel Air pulled up in front of her house. It had been a while since she'd seen Edna and Gladys. How Edna could still be driving that old thing around was beyond her. Nevertheless, Wilma shuffled to the door and opened it with a smile.

"Good morning, ladies."

Edna bustled in first. "Just look at that blouse! Is it new?"

Wilma nodded. "A Christmas gift."

"Gorgeous."

Gladys practically flung herself out of her coat and handed it to Wilma. "I don't suppose there's going to be any coffee at this tea party."

Wilma hung the coat on a hook. "I made some just for you."

"You said Lily's going to be here? You know, I only recommended her because my cousin insisted. I hope it's working out."

"Like a dream." Wilma ushered the ladies toward the kitchen. "She's been a godsend."

"Maybe I should hire a cleaner," Edna said. "Dusting is such a chore."

Gladys sniffed. "If you want a job done right, you've got to do it yourself, I always say. But to each her own."

Edna ignored Gladys's comment, as one did after decades of friendship. "The table's beautiful, Wilma. Look at that fruit tray. You didn't miss a thing."

"Thank you. Please have a seat."

It was easier said than done. Gladys's large size and Edna's bad back worked against them, but Wilma didn't have time to fret over that. She thought she heard a car door slam shut.

"Make yourselves at home, ladies." She shuffled back toward the door. "I'll be right back."

She didn't see any vehicles out front except the Bel Air, but someone knocked on the door just as she reached it. She pulled it open.

"Dani, how lovely to see you. Did you walk all the way here?"

Dani looked over her shoulder. "Pete dropped me off."

"Ah, so you couldn't escape." Wilma clapped her hands together once and grinned. "How thoughtful of him."

Dani's eyes widened for a second, but then she laughed. "I'm sorry if I didn't seem eager to come. I've never been too keen on parties."

"We'll have to cure you of that ailment, then, won't we, dear?"

Wilma gestured for Dani to come in while peering around the young lady to see if there was any sign of Lily. This whole plan relied on Lily being here.

"Come and meet my friends." She led Dani to the kitchen. "This is Edna, and this is Gladys. Ladies, this is Dani."

Edna held out her hand. "How nice to meet you, Dani."

Dani shook it. "Nice to meet you."

"Isn't Danny a boy's name?" Gladys asked.

Wilma gave her a look. "It's short for Danielle, Gladys, *really*."

Gladys shifted in her seat and mumbled, "How was I supposed to know?"

Wilma encouraged Dani to take a seat and smiled smugly to herself when Dani chose to sit as far from Gladys as possible. The woman could be a handful sometimes, and Wilma would know. They'd been friends since grade school. Since long before Edna moved to town from Great Falls because her husband wanted to "get away from it all." Gladys had a big heart, however, even if she did have an equally big mouth.

There was a single knock on the door, followed by the sound of it opening. "Hello, Miss Wilma, I'm here."

"Lily." Wilma practically melted with relief. "Wonderful."

Now the party could begin in earnest.

Tea—and coffee—had been served, most of the scones eaten. Wilma had enjoyed the pleasantries exchanged by the women as they sipped from her Royal Albert china teacups, but she didn't want to waste any more time on small talk. She was eighty-two, for heaven's sake. Time was not exactly on her side, and she was on a mission.

"Dani, dear, what do you do for fun?"

Dani's fork froze halfway to her mouth with a strawberry stuck to its end. "Um, I'm pretty busy with work, so . . ."

"Yes, of course, but surely you must have hobbies. Interests. Reading, perhaps?"

Dani set her fork down. "I read sometimes."

"That's wonderful. Good for the mind. Lily, didn't you say you liked to read?"

Before Lily could answer, Gladys piped up. "I just finished this horrible book about a serial killer in Connecticut. I don't know how the librarian talked me into it. I've never been so thankful for all the cameras and alarms Ronald's got all over our house."

"Right." Wilma frowned. "He's very safety-conscious. Now, Lily, weren't you telling me—?"

"I prefer a good romance," Gladys continued. "But nothing too *detailed*, if you know what I mean."

"Do stop interrupting," Edna said, turning to Lily. "What kind of books do you enjoy?"

"Oh, anything really." Lily fidgeted with her napkin. "Romance, literary, Western. Mystery, fantasy . . ."

Gladys huffed. "There's enough to talk about in this world, I would think. I don't see the point in making up a whole new world just for a story."

When Wilma and Edna both gave her a look, she threw up her hands. "But to each her own." And then under her breath, "As long as I don't have to read it."

Wilma cleared her throat. "I bet you have a whole collection of interesting books, Lily."

Lily hesitated. "I have a few."

"Maybe Dani could stop by and borrow one from you sometime, hmm?" She gave Dani a hopeful look. "Wouldn't that be nice?"

Dani looked a little like she'd eaten some bad chicken, but Wilma forged ahead. "I'm sure Lily wouldn't mind, would you, Lily?"

Lily's expression was much more difficult to read as she glanced at Dani. "You might have better luck at the library. I would hate to disappoint you with my selection."

Gladys wagged her finger at Dani. "If you see a book about a serial killer in Connecticut, don't say I didn't warn you."

Dani laughed in a way that seemed to take her by surprise.

Gladys tilted her head. "You remind me of someone."

Wilma's heart stopped. Oh dear. She hadn't mentioned to Gladys that Dani was Rosie's daughter, but Gladys had always been sharp as a tack, and Dani did look strikingly similar to her mother. Gladys had never been as close to Rosie as Wilma, yet Wilma should've known her old friend would notice the resemblance.

Her chest constricted. This was not a conversation she could afford to have right now. Call her a coward, but she wasn't ready. Not to mention there was no telling what Gladys might say.

Gladys pointed a finger at Dani. "Wilma, doesn't she remind you of—?"

"Now, now," Wilma interrupted. "We don't want to bore anyone by talking about people they don't even know. We're talking about books."

Gladys was opening her mouth, no doubt to protest, when Wilma met her eyes with a silent plea. She couldn't be sure what Gladys saw on her face, but it was enough to cause her friend to close her mouth. When one had known another person one's whole life, sometimes no words were needed.

Wilma let out the breath she'd been holding.

Edna addressed Dani, "Have you been to the library? They remodeled it last year and added more windows."

"No." Dani clasped her hands together in her lap. "I don't have a library card."

Wilma jumped at the opportunity to take back control of the plan that had seemed to be deteriorating before her eyes. "It would be much more fun to borrow a book from a friend, don't you think? Who knows what else you young ladies might find you have in common."

Lily met Dani's eyes with a small smile. "I don't remember the last time I was called a young lady. I'm forty-one."

Dani smiled back. "I'm forty-two."

Gladys harrumphed. "My generation never felt the need to blab about our age."

Edna frowned. "Gladys."

"What?"

"Never mind." Wilma straightened her blouse and turned her full attention on Lily and Dani. "It's all settled, then, *young ladies*. Now you'll just have to—"

Her words were cut off by a pounding on the door. Her forehead wrinkled. Had Pete come to fetch Dani so soon? She would need to have a word with him about his manners. One must wait until one has been summoned, *really*. She'd started to push her chair back from the table when Lily hopped up and said, "I'll get it."

Wilma didn't object. After all, if it *was* Pete, perhaps he and Lily could have a nice little chat. Despite a few hiccups, everything was working out rather splendidly.

"More tea, anyone?" she asked.

The ladies all shook their heads, claiming to be stuffed to the gills.

An unpleasant voice shot down the hall. "I thought you said she wanted you to serve tea at her party."

Wilma flinched. That wasn't Pete. She glanced around the table. No one else seemed to be paying much attention, thankfully.

Lily's voice came next. "Yes, I—"

"There's only one car out front. Not much of a party. You lied to me."

It was Jerry. Wilma narrowed her eyes. Oh no, he didn't. She would not allow him to ruin this day. She hastened to her feet as Lily responded with muffled words she couldn't make out. She rounded the corner and shuffled down the hall as fast as her unsteady legs would carry her.

Jerry was standing very close to Lily, but when he saw Wilma coming, he took a step back.

"What is the meaning of this?" she demanded. "You're interrupting my tea party."

He glared past her, trying to see into the kitchen. Wilma knew that if he leaned far enough, he could see the chair at the end of the table where Gladys was sitting.

Jerry turned his attention back to her, apparently somewhat mollified. "I thought Lily might need a ride home, if you're done with her. The wind is picking up."

She forced charm into her voice. "That's very kind of you, but—"

Lily held up a hand. "The party was just wrapping up. I'm sure you can spare me now, can't you, Miss Wilma?"

Lily's eyes pleaded, and Wilma's heart sank. Something was wrong here. How did she always find herself involved with women in crisis? She wanted to say no, that she couldn't spare Lily. That she would need Lily to stay and help her indefinitely, as a matter of fact. But Lily's eyes continued to plead with her to let her go, and Wilma's resolve weakened. She couldn't exactly keep Lily here against her will. But what was the best way to keep Lily from getting into trouble with Jerry? What should she say?

Inspiration struck then, and she made her voice stern as if she *had* in fact hired Lily for this event as Jerry seemed to believe. "I can spare you for now, dear, as long as you come back on Monday to clean up the mess."

Her words had the desired effect. The suspicion faded from Jerry's face, and he wrapped his hand firmly around Lily's arm. "She'll keep coming back as long as you keep paying. She's good at cleaning up messes."

After they'd left, Wilma trudged slowly back to the kitchen, her knees trembling. What a wretched man. If he made her feel like this, how must he make Lily feel?

It was more imperative than ever that she find ways for Lily to spend time with Dani and Pete. There was no doubt Lily could use as many friends as she could get.

When she reached the table, Edna and Gladys were engaged in a discussion about JCPenney, of all things, but Dani studied Wilma with a knowing look. Edna and Gladys were too deaf to eavesdrop on a conversation at the other end of the hall, though Dani clearly was not. What exactly had she heard?

Wilma tried to smile, to ease the concern she saw in Dani's eyes. "Don't let me forget to give you Lily's phone number, dear. I'm sure she would be delighted to hear from you."

Dani didn't seem to share Wilma's certainty about that. "I think it would be best to let her call me."

"Yes." Wilma sank into her chair, not wanting it to be true but knowing it was. "You're probably right."

"I'll take a few of these scones home, Wilma," Gladys said. "They're already dry. No sense in saving them for tomorrow."

twenty-one

Pete drove the Xpeditor up to Lily's trash bin Monday morning with a squirming pile of worms in his stomach and a bag of Skittles in his hand.

He side-eyed Pearl. "This is a bad idea."

She stomped her hooves. The look on her face gave the impression she thought she had all the answers, while he was nothing but a poor, bumbling human who couldn't figure anything out on his own.

"Subtle," he said.

Pearl squealed.

He maneuvered the joystick to lower the mast and pick up Lily's bin. He could hear a stream of beer bottles clanking their way into the hopper. He glanced at Lily's back door but saw no activity inside the house. Despite it being the first of April, her yard showed no sign yet of spring. When would she start clearing out the flower beds? Mulching and fertilizing? He could picture her doing such things, a peaceful smile on her face.

The bright red bag of candy screamed at him.

He could always give it to Braedon. Or feed it to Pearl. Had the vet ever said *no Skittles*?

"This is ridiculous." He snatched up the bag and opened the door. He was fifty years old, for crying out loud. He'd survived two group homes. Had his nose broken three times. He'd lived out of his truck in several dangerous locations when he was in between jobs with nothing but his fists and a pocketknife for protection. He had no reason to be afraid of a bag of Skittles.

Before he could change his mind, he set the bag on top of the bin and slid back into the Xpeditor. He drove forward to the next house, keeping an eye on the conspicuous red bag from his side mirror. What if someone walking by stole it? What if it blew off in the wind? What if . . . ?

Ugh. What if Jerry found it first?

Pete's hands felt clammy as he worked the joystick and quickly moved to the next house, then the next. This April Fools' Day, he was the biggest fool of all. The last thing he wanted was to cause any problems for Lily. Dani had told him about Jerry showing up at Wilma's house Saturday morning. She'd said he seemed "put out," but what did that mean? Why didn't Lily know she deserved better than Jerry?

Not that *he* was any better. He with his dirty job, poor credit score, and tons of baggage. He would never hurt Lily, though.

Had Jerry?

Pete slammed on the brakes at the next stop with a growl deep in his throat. If he had and Pete ever found out about it . . .

He cranked up the radio, and Pearl gave him an annoyed look.

"Sorry, girl." He banged the steering wheel in time to the music. "I need a distraction."

The music didn't help. All he could see in his head was his fist in Jerry's face. What he never wanted to see, however, was the look on Lily's face if she ever saw him lose it like he'd done so many times before. He couldn't let that happen.

He pulled up to a house and blinked. The huge cottonwood tree in the backyard hadn't looked like that last week. The windstorm a couple of days ago must've snapped its branches. No surprise since the tree was overgrown and had probably never been trimmed. The woman who lived here was tiny, and her husband used a wheelchair to get around. An ATV accident, Sunny had said. How were they going to cut up the wood and get rid of it?

Pete rubbed his chin. He didn't own a chainsaw, but Conrad Rountree did. A twenty-inch Stihl Farm Boss MS 271 Con had proudly shown him more than once. And when Pete had passed Mr. O'Malley's house earlier, he'd noticed the old man's woodpile was getting awfully low. The solution was clear to Pete. He'd talk to Con about it when he passed through his alley on Thursday.

If only the problem with Lily could be solved so easily.

Pete opened the door of Windy Ray's house with Braedon close behind. "Oki."

Windy Ray smiled. "It's good to see you, Pete the Poet and Braedon the Brave."

Braedon stood up a little straighter. "Oki."

Pete had taught him the Siksika greeting. Pearl trotted over to Apisi, and they did a little playful chasing while Braedon took a seat next to Windy Ray at the small table. The boy's moods had remained unpredictable, despite Pete's hope the other day that things had turned around for him at school. It was probably normal to have some trouble adjusting to a new home, new town, new school. When Pete had been eleven and forced to adjust to a new home, it hadn't gone well at all. He'd raged, refused to eat, and run away multiple times. He could hardly fault Braedon for having a bit of an attitude occasionally.

Windy Ray mixed up the facedown dominoes in preparation for their game and looked at Pete. "Did you see Wilma today?"

"No."

"You drove right past her house."

"I can't stop and visit while I'm working."

Windy Ray began to draw his dominoes from the pile and set them up. "I haven't seen her in many days."

Braedon drew the double nine from his pile and plunked it down. He'd caught on to the game quickly. "Is Miss Wilma your girlfriend?"

Windy Ray made the next play. "That would be an honor I am not worthy of. However"—he winked—"it's an honor I would never turn down if given the chance."

Braedon scrunched his face, and Pete had a moment of thankfulness that his nephew was not yet interested in girls. The moment didn't last.

Braedon gave him a sly look. "Is Lily *your* girlfriend, Uncle Pete?"

He would never tire of the title *Uncle Pete*, but his mouth went dry as he set a domino down. "No."

"It is so in his heart, I believe," Windy Ray said.

"What? I don't . . ." Pete fumbled for a response. "It is not so. In my heart or anywhere else."

Braedon took his turn in the game. "I think she's nice." He glanced at Windy Ray. "Miss Wilma too."

Windy Ray nodded. "She likes my rocks. She puts them on her windowsill."

Pete stewed, thinking about the bag of Skittles. He couldn't believe he'd left it for Lily this morning. He shouldn't have.

At the same time, he wanted her to know someone was thinking of her. Someone cared.

Braedon laid his last tile down triumphantly. "I win."

Windy Ray leaned back from the table. "Perhaps I have met my match."

When Pete and Braedon got home, Dani was in the kitchen baking something that smelled like all of Pete's hopes and dreams.

Braedon shouted, "Banana bread?"

When Dani confirmed it, Braedon pumped his fist. "Yesss."

Pearl seemed just as excited. Anything involving bananas was automatically her favorite.

Pete couldn't remember whether his mother had ever baked such things as banana bread. He did remember that she'd had good days and bad days. What did she do on the good days when he was little? The years had made the memories hazy and uncertain.

Braedon took a granola bar from the cupboard, even though he'd eaten two servings of pulled pork at Windy Ray's.

Dani gave him an affectionate look. "Did you finish your homework?"

"In the truck."

She glanced at Pete for confirmation, and he nodded. "Pearl helped."

Dani smiled down at the swine. "I bet she did. Braedon, you should get ready for bed. It's a school night."

"Aw, man. It's not even nine o'clock."

"Growing boys need lots of sleep. And so do potbellied pigs."

"Fine," he grumbled. "Let's go, Pearl."

Pearl dutifully followed him down the hall. Pete leaned against the counter and watched Dani grease a glass loaf pan she must've picked up somewhere because he'd never owned one in his life.

She cast a worried glance in the direction Braedon had gone. "I got his third-quarter report card in the mail today."

Pete frowned at her tone. "And?"

"It wasn't great. He's a smart kid, but when he's struggling socially, his grades slip."

"I thought he made a friend."

She focused on the bowl of banana bread batter and muttered, "It's just like last time."

He didn't like the sound of that. "What happened last time?"

She wiped her hands on a dish towel he'd also never seen before. "Nothing. Never mind."

He crossed his arms over his chest. What happened to Braedon at his last school? Had he been bullied? Pete's blood began to boil. If someone was messing with his nephew . . .

No. Stop. This was why Dani didn't want to talk to him about it. She was afraid of how he'd react. He didn't want to confirm her suspicions that he was still a hotheaded jerk, so he decided to *never mind*, just as she'd said. For now.

"Everything go okay at the gas station today?"

She shrugged. "I guess."

"Nobody bothered you?"

She turned her eyes on him. "Pete."

"Sorry." He lifted his hands. "I just want to make sure you're okay. That everyone's okay."

Something he wouldn't even dare try to interpret passed over her face.

"Look, I'm sorry." He lowered his voice. "I know I caused you a lot of trouble back in the day. I was selfish and out of control. You were right to push me away. But I've changed."

She poured batter into the pan and took a deep breath. "I know. I can see it. I was afraid to come here at first, afraid of the example you might set for Braedon, but I'm not afraid of you anymore."

Her words struck him like a fist to the gut. She should've never had to fear him. He'd let his anger control him for so long, let his fear direct his fists, but the fight was going out of him now. It had never brought anything but pain to his life.

"You were so destructive for a while there," Dani continued. "You . . ."

"I know. I ruined everything. I'm sorry."

She slid the pan into the preheated oven. "Mom ruined everything, not you. I never should've said you were like her."

"Don't you ever wonder what happened to her? Where she ended up?"

Dani closed the oven door and winced. "No."

He wondered. Every day. What if she was still out there somewhere? She'd be in her late seventies now, and he didn't know if he'd even recognize her. What if she was all alone in some nursing home somewhere?

Why had she never come back?

"I don't want to talk about Mom." Dani set the oven timer. "I have something far more interesting to talk about."

He narrowed his eyes. "What?"

"I spoke to Lily today."

Just the mention of her name caused Pete's heart to leap, yet he tried to appear unconcerned. "She called you?"

Dani nodded. "From Wilma's phone. She's there every Monday to clean the place."

He knew that already, but Dani didn't need to know that he knew. "What did she say?"

"She invited me to stop by tomorrow morning to borrow a book."

It was all Pete could do to keep his eyes from bugging out.

Dani was going to Lily's house? He could find out so many things about her if Dani were to bring home a report. His spirits began to rise, but then an ominous thought sobered him right up. What if Jerry was there? He didn't want his sister anywhere near that guy.

"She said her boyfriend was going to be at work." Dani apparently had the same mind-reading ability as all the other women Pete knew. She gave him a meaningful look. "And she said to tell you thank you for the Skittles."

Well, that just floored him. Leveled him right down to trampled roadkill on the highway, which was probably what he looked like.

"You okay?" Dani asked.

He barely heard her because in his mind he was already picturing the candy aisle at the grocery store and trying to decide which kind of Skittles to get for next week. But when she asked again if he was okay, he looked up. "Oh. Yes. Just thinking."

"I know you have a crush on her."

"I—"

Dani held up a hand. "Don't try to deny it. I think she's cool. I only want you to be careful. This Jerry guy . . ."

He hung his head. "I know. Wilma said they've been together quite a while."

"I'll do a little digging when I'm over there tomorrow." Dani's eyes sparked with something akin to mischief, or maybe it was determination. "See what I can find out."

His lips turned down. He wanted to know everything about Lily, but he didn't need his sister's help embarrassing himself. He could do that all on his own. What did she plan to do?

"Don't worry." Dani grinned. "I won't even mention your name."

He raised his eyebrows.

"Trust me, I won't have to. I have no doubt she'll mention it for me."

twenty-two

Pete rubbed the baby oil with aloe vera and vitamin E into his hands and applied it to Pearl's back. He used to hate this task, but he'd come to appreciate the benefit to Pearl. She made happy pig noises as he finished the job and held her face between his hands.

"What would I do without you?"

She nudged his chin with her snout. He didn't deserve such a faithful friend, even if she did sleep in Braedon's room now. Every day she reminded him that not everything tossed aside by others was worthless garbage. Sometimes it was treasure.

He glanced at the time, though he'd checked it less than five minutes ago. Dani should be home from work any minute. He'd been distracted all day by the thought of hearing about her visit to Lily's house.

The front door opened, and he jumped up from the stool he was using in the kitchen. Braedon was in the shower—Pete had convinced him to hose himself off by telling him Pearl would be enduring a grooming regimen, as well—so Pete had a few minutes to talk to his sister alone.

He walked into the living room. "Hey."

Dani was taking off her coat. "Hey."

He wasn't sure how to bring Lily up without sounding desperate. "Did you . . . uh, how was your morning?"

Her lips twitched as she shrugged. "It was fine."

"Oh." He began to sweat. She was going to make him say it. "Did you go to Lily's house?"

"Yes."

He nodded. She set her giant mom purse on the coffee table and cupped a hand under Pearl's chin. "Hi, Pearl. You smell good." Then she walked past Pete and into the kitchen.

He clambered after her. "Well?"

She smirked. "Well what?"

He wanted to pull his hair out. "What did you do? What did she say? Did she give you a book?"

Dani's eyes danced with amusement, but she had the good manners not to laugh at him. "Go look in my purse."

He hurried back to the coffee table and paused. Normally he would never go near a woman's purse, but this was a critical situation. After a moment's hesitation, he opened the lumpy black bag like he would open a ticking backpack found under a bridge. He held his breath.

A book. *This House of Sky* by Ivan Doig. He pulled it out, and his heart swelled in his chest. It was one of his favorite books, a memoir written by a Montana man who'd grown up not far from here during a time when Montana was mostly wilderness. The prose was distinct and ruggedly beautiful. This was the book Lily had lent to Dani?

"She said it's one of her favorites."

Pete spun around to find Dani watching him from the hall. She appeared thoughtful. "Not the kind of thing I usually read, but she convinced me to try it. Now, keep looking."

Keep looking? He set the book down and peered back into the purse. He reached in with a sense of wonder and took out a vintage lapel pin shaped like a Coca-Cola crate filled with six Coca-Cola bottles. It was about the size of his thumbnail. He gaped.

"I told her you would like it," Dani said.

He didn't speak for a minute. Coca-Cola lapel pins weren't easy to find in such good condition. It was the nicest gift he'd ever been given. Why had she done this?

Dani read the look on his face far too easily. "She said you and Wilma are her only friends. And now me, I guess."

He stared at the little pin in the palm of his hand. He didn't have many friends either.

"I'm worried about her, Pete."

His sister's words snapped him out of his thoughts. "What do you mean?"

"I know the signs, okay?" Dani looked at the floor. "He checks her phone every day when he gets home. That's why she called from Wilma's landline. He gets mad if she goes anywhere unless it's to the store or to work. She lies to him about how much money Wilma pays her so she can tuck some of it away without him knowing. I think she might be planning an escape."

"She told you all that?"

Dani hesitated. "More or less."

Pete's mind raced. He'd suspected Jerry was far less than caring and considerate, but it rattled him to hear Dani's take on things. What could he do to help Lily?

"You said you know the signs." He took a step toward his sister. "Did your husband . . . ?"

She shook her head. "Jake was immature and selfish, but he wasn't like that. I dated a guy once, though. I dumped him when I realized he was trying to isolate me from everyone else and make me dependent on him. I knew where that was going, and I figured it out before it got too dangerous. I changed my phone number. But Lily . . ."

Every muscle in Pete's body was on edge. "What?"

"I don't think she figured it out until it was too late. Maybe not even until . . . well, until she met you."

Pete blinked in astonishment. "Me?"

"Sometimes it takes being around a decent guy to realize what a jerk your own boyfriend is." She gave him a half smile. "Don't let it go to your head or anything. The bar was set pretty low."

He squeezed his fist around the lapel pin until it bit into his skin. Tyke on a bike, what was he going to do? Part of him wanted to march over to Lily's house right this minute and give Jerry what he had coming to him, but that wouldn't reassure Lily he was the decent guy she supposedly thought he was. Plus he'd probably just end up in jail. Again.

"Has he hurt her?" He fixed his eyes on Dani. "Does he . . . ?" He couldn't bring himself to form the words, but Dani understood.

"I don't know for sure. She didn't say anything, and I didn't see any bruises."

"But you suspect he does."

Dani lifted one shoulder. "I've only just met her. I don't want to jump to conclusions. But there was a lot of alcohol in the house, and my guess is, when he gets drunk, it isn't pretty."

Pete heard Braedon come out of the bathroom. Pearl ran down the hall to greet him.

Dani leaned toward Pete and lowered her voice. "I only told you all this because you said you've changed. You're not the guy who goes around beating people up anymore. Promise me you won't do anything stupid."

It took every ounce of strength and will to loosen the hold he had on the lapel pin and take a deep breath. Dani was right. He'd given her a whole speech about how he wasn't that guy anymore. She'd trusted him with this information because she'd believed him, even after all the times he'd made her life miserable by starting a fight at the drop of a hat.

He couldn't use his fists to solve this problem. He would need to find another way. He would need help.

"I promise."

As soon as he got off work tomorrow, he would pay Wilma a visit.

Wilma gripped her cane in frustration and shivered. It was chilly this evening. Where had she put—?

The phone rang. It was eight o'clock. She shuffled over to the landline.

"Hello, Michael."

"Hi, Mom. How are you?"

"Freezing my tail off, if you must know. I'm trying to find my cashmere cardigan."

"The one I got you for your birthday?"

"Yes. I've looked everywhere."

Michael hesitated before responding. "Have you asked Lily if she's seen it?"

"She doesn't do my laundry, dear, *really*. Besides, the cardigan is dry-clean only."

"It's also worth over two hundred dollars."

Wilma sniffed, suddenly regretting ever bringing it up. "What exactly are you trying to say?"

"Nothing." He paused. "I just thought maybe she took it home. Uh, accidentally."

"She would never steal from me, if that's what you're implying."

Her tone was indignant, but deep down she wondered. She'd looked everywhere, even under the bed, though there was no reasonable explanation for it ending up there. Lily was the only person who'd been in the house since Saturday afternoon, when Wilma last wore the sweater to sit on the front porch for a few minutes of fresh air.

How well did she know Lily, really? She was mixed up with that Jerry fellow, after all, which didn't commend her judgment.

Wilma shook her head. Impossible. Lily would never do such a thing. "You should be ashamed of yourself, Michael."

"You're the one who brought up stealing, Mom, not me. And you're the one who insisted on hiring Lily because Gladys's sister or whoever insisted Lily needed the money. You said she was 'economically disadvantaged' and her clothes weren't much better than rags."

Wilma pursed her lips. "It was Gladys's cousin, and I know what I said, but Lily has become a dear friend, and I'd thank you to keep your unfounded opinions about her to yourself."

"I'm sorry. It's just, I worry about you. Did you get the email I sent about the financial assistance program for the elderly?"

She pressed her lips together. No, she had not. She hadn't turned on her computer—the computer Michael had set up for her after Herb passed away—in months. What would she do on there? She preferred keeping her records in paper form. In file folders. Besides, she'd already found help with her financial situation all on her own without Michael's interference. She'd sent her second payment to FAS yesterday.

"Not yet."

"Promise me you'll read it, okay? It sounds like a great program. I cross-checked it with the BBB."

"Okay." She could agree to that if it would keep him out of her hair. "How are Paula and Yvette?"

They talked about her daughter-in-law and granddaughter for a few minutes, then said goodbye. Wilma's phone-holding fingers were practically frozen stiff by the time she set the clunky receiver back on its base. One wouldn't know it was April by the temperature, that was for sure. The months of endless cold and wind seemed to last longer every year. She was getting too old to live on the Hi-Line.

She couldn't leave, though. Not yet. She still had unfinished business to attend to.

twenty-three

Wilma knocked on Gladys's door Saturday morning with an air of adventure. In the past few days, she'd become part of a plot. Pete's plot, to be precise. He'd stopped by unannounced—how exciting!—on Wednesday afternoon to enlist her help with regard to Lily, and together they'd come up with a plan.

The plan involved another trip to Great Falls, this time in Wilma's Corolla. It also involved Gladys because Wilma needed somewhere safe to be while Pete and Lily were gone in case Jerry were to stop by her house again. He needed to believe Wilma and Lily had gone to Great Falls in the Corolla when in fact Pete and Lily had dropped her off here before leaving town.

She could've gone with Pete and Lily, of course, but when Pete suggested it, she'd claimed it would aggravate her knee if she sat in the car for that long. In reality she wanted to give Pete and Lily the chance to spend time together without her peering over their shoulders. They had no need of a chaperone. Plus it was past time she filled Gladys in on who Pete and Dani were before her friend accidentally said something Wilma would regret.

Gladys answered the door in a gaudy long-sleeved blouse with a paisley print. "You made it. I was beginning to wonder."

Wilma glanced at her watch. She was only three minutes late. "Good morning."

"Come on in, the coffee's on."

Wilma followed her friend to the kitchen, half expecting to see Edna since the two ladies were practically inseparable, but no one else was around.

"I told Ronald to make himself scarce, so he took the car to Shelby for a tire rotation." Gladys waved her hand in a general westerly direction. "It's a guarantee he'll stop at the hardware store and the diner while he's at it to chew the fat with all the good old boys. He won't be back for hours."

Wilma took a seat at the table. "I don't want him put out on my account."

"Pfft." Gladys made a face. "He'll take any excuse to spend the day in Shelby."

Wilma poured herself coffee from the carafe already waiting on the table. Ronald had been a police officer in Sleeping Grass for thirty-five years. He and Herb had been friends in the way men were when their wives spent a lot of time together. Herb had admired Ronald's skill at hunting both animals and criminals. Wilma admired Ronald's ability to see past Gladys's often uncouth exterior.

"Time to spill the beans, Wilma." Gladys had taken a seat opposite hers and was giving her an exacting look. "Why are you really here, and what's it got to do with Rosie?"

Wilma's eyes widened briefly, but her friend had always been one to get straight to the point. "How did you know it had to do with Rosie?"

"Oh, please. That look on your face when I almost mentioned her name at the tea party? You've been hiding something from me. Honestly, I didn't think you had it in you."

Wilma stared into her mug. She'd never told anyone about how the state asked her and Herb to take Pete and Dani into their home. Never told anyone about Rosie's letters, or that Wilma had tortured herself by keeping tabs on Pete's disastrous journey through the foster-care system. She'd certainly never told anyone how the state had come to her and Herb again, when Pete was fourteen, to ask if they would reconsider. *"Our only other option at this point is a group home in Great Falls,"* the social worker had said. Pete had been running away and getting into fights and wreaking havoc in foster home after foster home.

The first time the social worker had asked, when Pete was eleven, Herb had been ready to say yes. They were about to move into a bigger house, the house where she lived now, and he thought Pete and Michael could learn to be friends. Herb had left the final decision up to her, however, since she would be the one caring for the kids. And she had said no.

The next time, Wilma had been desperate for a second chance with Pete, but Herb had put his foot down. *"It's too risky,"* he'd said. *"We're not equipped to deal with a kid that troubled."* No amount of pleading on her part could change his mind. To this day, she'd had to live with the knowledge there had been one brief open window and she'd slammed it shut.

"Well?" Gladys piped up. "Are you going to tell me or not?"

Wilma sighed. It had all happened so long ago, yet the memories were still fresh. "Do you remember the day we discovered Rosie had disappeared?"

Pete felt self-conscious driving Wilma's Toyota Corolla, which was an old-lady beige color. Between his Dodge and the Xpeditor, he was used to riding a lot higher on the road. Wilma's car smelled a lot better, though, which was one reason he'd left Pearl home with Braedon. Pearl didn't smell bad as far as animals went, but she was still an animal. Plus she'd made quite a stink last time he drove to Great Falls with Lily, and he wanted to avoid a repeat performance.

Lily gestured toward the top of his head. "The pin looks good."

He'd stuck it in his baseball cap, which he wore today to cover up his bald spot. "Thanks. It was really nice of you."

Her brown eyes studied him. "It was nothing."

It was everything, he wanted to say. He almost did.

She pointed out the window. "Look at the turbines."

The wind turbines in the field they were passing were spinning strong and steady. It was mesmerizing to watch their blades go round and round. At least a dozen of the turbines were spread out along a rolling hill as they neared Great Falls.

"Jerry had a friend once who worked as a turbine tech," Lily said. "Can you imagine climbing up there?"

"No." He shuddered, partly at the thought of climbing over five hundred feet to maintain a wind turbine with little more than a harness and helmet for protection, and partly at the mention of Jerry's name. She'd never brought him up before. But that's what this whole plan was about, wasn't it? Finding out more about Jerry and what kind of situation Lily was in.

Lily turned toward him. "If you could have any career in the world, what would it be?"

Any career? He'd never thought about it because what would be the point? A GED and a criminal record severely limited a man's options. He'd always been thankful for whatever job he could get.

"I don't know."

It was hard to think with her looking at him like that. Like she was interested in what he had to say. Like she could . . . see him.

"I would be a teacher." She smiled wistfully. "First graders maybe."

"I thought you might say horticulturist."

She laughed softly, water spilling over rocks. "Gardening is just a hobby. It makes me happy to watch things grow. Making it a job would ruin it."

"Did you go to college?"

"I got my AA degree at a community college in Nebraska, and then life sort of happened. You know how it is."

He did, but he heard the longing in her voice and wanted to give her . . . well, the sun, moon, stars, and universe. "It's not too late."

The words hung between them, suspended, as if unsure whether to rise or fall.

"It kind of feels like it is," she finally said.

He wasn't sure what to say. There were no colleges in Sleeping Grass. He didn't know if she could even get a teaching degree in Great Falls.

He turned off I-15. "What about online school?"

He would buy her a laptop. He would get a second job and pay the tuition. He would make sure she had the highest-speed internet Sleeping Grass could offer. At least he would do all those things if—

"I don't think Jerry would like it."

He frowned. "Why not?"

She shrugged. "It would take up a lot of my time."

Pete felt his blood begin to simmer. "It's your time, not his."

Her laugh held no hint of humor. "Everything is his."

His blood boiling now, Pete forced himself to focus on the road. They were almost to Walmart. "What do you mean?"

He needed to know. She looked down at her hands in her

lap. Slender and delicate hands a better man than he could write a hundred verses about.

"Nothing." She shook her head. "Forget I said anything. Please."

He might forget what his mother's voice had sounded like. He might forget the name of that place Windy Ray always talked about taking him to. But he would never forget what Lily said.

"All right." He parked the Corolla and killed the engine. He would go along with Lily's wishes for now. If he pushed too hard, he might never get the information he was looking for. But he wouldn't forget the quiver in her voice or the pulse in her neck, beating as fast as a scared baby bird's.

For once in her life, Gladys was speechless. Wilma wasn't sure what to make of it.

"I, you . . . huh." Gladys drummed her oversized fingers on the table. "And you have no idea where Rosie is now?"

Wilma sighed. "I'm inclined to believe she is no longer with us. The trajectory she was on wasn't one that typically leads to a long and fulfilling life."

"What's the point in telling Pete, then?" Gladys scrunched up her face. "Maybe you should let it be."

Wilma gripped her mug as a chill swept over her. She still hadn't found that cashmere cardigan. "I've considered that, but he deserves to have his mother's letters, and I can't very well give him the letters without explaining everything else."

Gladys harrumphed. "He might hate you if you tell him—did you ever think of that? Not worth the risk, if you ask me."

"Of course I've thought of that. It's all I've thought of since he plucked me off my kitchen floor that day in February. I don't want to lose him again."

The more time she and Pete spent together, the more she wondered how she ever could've turned him away. He'd been a child—a broken and abandoned child—and she'd been too afraid of how her life would change.

Gladys wagged a finger. "I doubt you'd ever get Dani to come back for another tea party."

"You don't know that."

"How else will Pete and Lily spend time together if they're not speaking to you? You said Lily had to pretend to be with you today."

Wilma frowned. "What does Lily have to do with anything?"

Gladys scoffed. "If she has feelings for Pete like you hope she does, then she might take his side against you."

Wilma drew in a sharp breath and gave her friend a look.

Gladys held up her hands. "What? You came to me for help."

"This is not helping."

"I just want to make sure you've thought everything through before you start meddling in other people's lives."

Wilma took an unsatisfying sip of lukewarm coffee. It was much too late for that. She was up to her ears in meddling. "I don't want him to stop visiting. I can't imagine my life without Pete and Pearl in it."

Gladys nodded. "Then you should let sleeping dogs lie."

"But I feel I owe him the truth. It's the least I can do."

"Then you should drop the bomb as soon as possible."

Wilma sniffed. "You're still not helping, Gladys, *really*."

Her friend leaned back in her chair, and her voice softened. "Have you prayed about it?"

Wilma jerked her head, startled. She and Gladys attended the same church but rarely spoke of spiritual things. "Yes. I've been praying about it for years. I prayed for a second chance with Pete and then out of the blue he moved back to Sleeping Grass."

"What have you heard God tell you in your heart about this?"

"To tell the truth."

"Then you must."

"But I'm scared." Wilma wanted to wring her own neck. "Even back then, I was such a coward. I didn't think I was strong enough to be their mother. I was afraid to upend my life."

Gladys reached across the table and covered Wilma's hand with hers. Her fingers were plump and warm, Wilma's cold and bony. "I used to think Rosie was the fearless one. You know how she was. Full of life and always ready to try anything. Go anywhere. I envied her some, I admit. But now . . ."

Her voice changed as it passed over the decades-long history between them. "I see things differently now. She wasn't fearless. She was just afraid of something far different from what we were. And you aren't a coward, Wilma. Anyone who wants to tell the truth must be brave."

Pete lay awake in bed that night, staring at the ceiling. It had been the kind of day that made a man feel upside down. As if things he thought were real weren't, and things he'd never believed suddenly seemed possible.

"*Thanks for being my friend,*" Lily had said before hurrying from Wilma's Corolla and heading home. It hadn't disappointed him like he might've expected, the idea that they were just friends. Instead, it had felt as if he'd been given not only a gift but also a grave responsibility.

They'd talked about animals and Butchart Gardens and the Montana prairie. Everything but what Pete wanted most to talk about, which was whether Lily was okay. Whether she was safe. Whenever he'd steered the conversation in that direction, she had deflected. When she told him she'd never read Kipling or Silverstein and he offered to lend her his copies, she had replied that it would be better if she checked them out from the library.

He hadn't gotten his questions answered, but he had learned what he'd already suspected. There was a line she wasn't able or maybe willing to cross. A line that separated the part of her life Jerry knew about and the part he didn't. Pete felt a deep sense of protectiveness.

He'd only spoken briefly to Wilma before heading home. She'd seemed quiet and distracted. He hoped it wasn't all too much for her. In fact, his protectiveness extended past Lily to the dear old woman. Aside from Dani, Braedon, and Windy Ray, he had no one else, and Wilma was beginning to feel like family.

He couldn't look out for his own mother, but he could look out for her. Maybe next Wednesday he would take her to the phone store in Shelby and help her pick out a cellphone. It was a dinky little place that didn't actually sell phones—you had to go to Great Falls for that—but on Wednesdays and Fridays, someone would be there whom they could talk to about phone plans and options. Not that there were many options on the Hi-Line.

He'd mentioned the possibility of a cellphone to Wilma the other day when he was jump-starting her Corolla, and she'd been resistant. He didn't know if it was the thought of learning how to use a cellphone or the thought of paying for one that held her back. Maybe a little of both.

He couldn't help but wonder what the deal was with her kids. Why hadn't they insisted on a cellphone already? Didn't they care? His forehead wrinkled. Did they even know about her fall? She wouldn't keep that from them, would she?

The digital numbers on the alarm clock by his bed read

1:12 a.m. Good thing he wasn't working tomorrow or he'd be in big trouble. As Lily's face floated through his mind, he was pretty sure he was in big trouble anyway.

The sound of Pearl's snoring rumbled through the house, and Pete thought of Braedon and how he let Pearl sleep right up on his pillow with him. Dani slept with a pillow *over* her head, trying to block out the loud, grating noise.

He turned onto his side. It was jarring to suddenly have so many people in his life he cared about. Kind of scary, too.

His eyes grew heavy, his body relaxed. His last thoughts before drifting off were of brown eyes and brown hair and a field full of lilies.

twenty-four

Wilma eyed Lily suspiciously Monday morning. "You seem tired today, dear. Are you all right?"

Lily covered up a yawn and laughed, but the laugh rang hollow as far as Wilma was concerned. "Didn't get much sleep last night. I made the mistake of drinking black tea a little too close to bedtime."

"Hmm." Wilma wasn't convinced. "I see. And what were you up to yesterday?"

She suspected there was a reason Lily was moving sluggishly that had nothing to do with tea and everything to do with Jerry being intolerable to live with.

Lily finished mopping the kitchen floor and wrang out the mop in the bucket. "Not much."

Really, that just wasn't going to cut it. *Not much*.

"You seem to spend a lot of time at home. Have you thought about getting a car?"

Lily's expression remained neutral. "I haven't driven in years. My license is expired."

"You could renew it."

"I'd have to go all the way to Great Falls to retake the test."

Wilma smiled. "I happen to know a young man who

wouldn't mind taking you there." She couldn't be sure, but she thought she detected a hint of color rising in Lily's cheeks.

"Everything in Sleeping Grass is within walking distance. I don't need a car."

"Don't you ever want to go anywhere besides Sleeping Grass? And I don't mean to Great Falls to run errands for an old lady. There's a whole big world out there, you know."

Lily's eyes grew wide for a moment, as if she could see the possibilities, and then she held up a rag and pointed down the hall. "I'll go take care of the bathroom now."

Wilma clucked her tongue to herself once Lily was out of earshot. Did the poor girl have any idea that both her trips to Great Falls with Pete had been something of a setup? Perhaps not, but Wilma doubted she would mind even if she knew. She seemed willing to accept Wilma's help deceiving Jerry but not willing to discuss the issue of Jerry any further than that.

She reminded Wilma of Rosie. She'd never wanted to talk about her problems or mistakes either. She always pretended everything was fine and she knew what she was doing. Even when the drinking and drugs began to prevent her from caring for her children. Even when Pete and Dani were home alone at suppertime. Even when she'd pushed Wilma out of her life for "too much meddling."

Wilma had tried to keep an eye on the kids from a distance. She'd seen them looking shabby and thin but had stayed away from their house for almost three years, telling herself Rosie would never let them go hungry. There was one time, however, after she'd served her own family their evening meal, when Wilma couldn't stand it any longer. She'd brought leftovers to Rosie's house, concerned the kids might not have anything suitable in their fridge.

Pete had stared at her, curious and confused, but had accepted the Saran-wrapped plates of baked drumsticks, rice, and lime Jell-O salad. The next day, Rosie had called to chastise Wilma. *"I can take care of my own children, Willy Mae."* Except she couldn't. And Wilma had stood back and prayed and hoped Rosie would figure it out, would shake whatever demons kept her from putting her kids before herself, until one day it was too late.

Lily reappeared in the kitchen with a teasing look on her face. "I swear you have the cleanest bathroom I've ever seen."

"Nonsense, it was perfectly filthy." Wilma hoped Lily would never discover she was not actually in need of a cleaning lady. "Perhaps you could wipe down the trim boards." She scoured her mind for any other chores the young lady could do. "And the guest bedroom hasn't been used in ages. It ought to be aired out and the bedding washed."

"Okay. I'd be happy to do that."

Lily turned to get straight to work, but Wilma wished she would slow down and chat a minute. "Lily."

She turned back around and waited expectantly.

"Those breakfast bars you got me from the Walmart. They were quite good."

Lily smiled. "I'm glad to hear that. You've got to make sure you're eating, Miss Wilma. You're nothing but skin and bones."

"I eat plenty."

Lily hesitated. "I worry sometimes—"

The landline rang, causing both women to startle.

"My." Wilma put a hand to her chest. "That's rather loud, isn't it?"

It rang a second time, and she considered letting it go to the machine but worried over who it could be. What if it was Sadie from FAS? What if she mentioned something about Wilma's debt in her message and Lily overheard? That wouldn't do at all.

"Would you hand me the phone, please, dear?"

Lily brought her the receiver, and Wilma answered the call. "Hello?"

"Hi, Mom, it's me."

Rachel. Wilma's shock must've shown on her face because Lily raised her eyebrows and whispered, "Is everything all right?"

Wilma covered the mouthpiece with her hand. "Yes, it's fine, dear."

"Is someone there?" Rachel asked.

"It's Lily."

"Oh." Rachel's voice held an edge. "I didn't mean to interrupt."

"You're not interrupting anything. She comes every Monday."

"So I've heard."

Wilma felt as though she'd said the wrong thing. She often felt that way when talking with her daughter. "How are you? I've called several times."

"I've been busy. I got a second job."

"Michael told me. At a quilt store?"

"A fabric store."

"I had no idea Tom wanted to be a missionary."

"Me neither."

"It's wonderful, of course. I'm sure you're very proud."

There was a pause. "Yes."

"You don't sound very sure."

"It's just going to be tough, Mom. We have to pay for school, and we're going to have to move to who-knows-where. And most sending agencies require you to raise your own support. I'm still getting used to the idea of going around to different churches asking for money."

"You'll send me a fundraising letter, I hope. I'd be glad to support you."

Her daughter's tone was difficult to decode. "I think you're writing enough checks every month as it is. That wasn't why I brought it up."

Wilma glanced around to find Lily had graciously made herself scarce. Such good manners. "I can't think of a better place to send a check than to Tom's ministry, dear."

"Really?"

The surprise in Rachel's voice caused Wilma to wince. She'd believed—hoped—that her children understood her desire to minister to women in crisis. To give whatever money she could. But perhaps it wasn't that simple. They never knew about Rosie's drug problem or the situation with Pete and Dani. Wilma had tried to shield them from all that. They had no idea of the guilt she carried.

Now here she was, wondering if she'd ever really helped anyone. Had all those checks made any difference or had they done nothing but deepen the hole she was in and widen the gap between her and her children? She wanted to give money to Tom and Rachel's mission work, but what about the letter she'd received from the county treasurer?

Her financial outlook would change soon, though. She would pay the back taxes she owed. Sadie from FAS was hard at work for her this very moment, making sure Wilma benefitted from every possible type of assistance available. Her kids would never have to know how bad her situation had become.

"Really," she said. "It will be my pleasure."

It never ceased to amaze Pete how much garbage twelve hundred people could produce in a week. He couldn't help but wonder sometimes if clearing it all away only exacerbated the problem. If no one came along to move the trash out of sight, out of mind, would folks be forced to face their own wasteful habits and find ways to reduce the amount of garbage they created?

He shook his head. Driving the Xpeditor for hours each day with only a pig for company gave him too much time to think. Thinking too much had never served him well. He'd done nothing but think about Lily all day.

"I'm pathetic, aren't I, Pearl?"

She appeared to nod in zealous agreement.

"I appreciate your honesty."

He checked the time. In ten minutes, he would need to head to the school to pick up Braedon. His nephew was never far from his thoughts either. Most of the time, Pete thought about what a wonder the kid was and how lucky Pete was to have him in his life. But he also thought about Braedon's dad, and Braedon's mood swings, and how much having the kid around took Pete back to his own childhood. Back to memories that wavered in the corners of his mind like shadows that couldn't be nailed down.

His cell rang. When he saw Dani's name on the screen, his heart dropped a beat. Pearl gave him a long-suffering look as he picked up the phone.

"Dani? Are you okay?"

He thought he heard an exasperated groan, but it was hard to be sure over the rumble of the Xpeditor.

"Everything's fine. I got off work early and was hoping you could pick me up and take me to the school to get Braedon."

Pete's face scrunched. That didn't make sense. "Your shift is over? It just started two hours ago."

"I'm aware of that. Can you come?"

Something fishy was going on. Pearl raised her snout as if she smelled it, too. He'd promised his boss he wouldn't take any more time than necessary to help out with his nephew, but how could he say no to Dani? His gut told him it was important.

"Okay, I'll be right there."

He had altered his Monday route to better accommodate picking Braedon up from school—which had caused consternation among several waste service customers that he'd had to smooth over—but the gas station was in the opposite direction of the school. The town office was going to get calls about this, and his boss was going to chew him out, but Pete wasn't too worried. There was no waiting list of folks gunning for Pete's job.

Dani was ready when he pulled up. She made a face as she climbed in. "There's no room in here."

"Pearl, scoot over."

"There's nowhere for her to scoot." Dani squirmed around trying to squeeze into the small amount of space Pearl didn't occupy. "How does Braedon ride around like this?"

"He's not going to fit today, that's for sure. Do you want me to take you to the carport to get the Dodge?"

"No, just drop me off at the school. Braedon and I will walk home."

"Are you sure?"

He'd already gone this far out of his way. He might as well drive all the way back to the carport.

"I'm sure. Braedon and I have a lot to talk about."

Her voice was grim. Uh-oh. Pete remembered his previous suspicions about Braedon being bullied and frowned. "Is everything okay?"

"It's fine, Pete." She glanced at the time. "Let's go."

Minutes later, Pete parked a block away from the school.

Dani hopped out of the garbage truck. "Thanks for the ride. See you at home." She slammed the door and began to walk briskly toward the building.

Pete exchanged a look with Pearl. "What was that all about?"

The pig had no idea. Pete pulled away from the curb. With any luck, he could finish his route without any complications, get to Windy Ray's by five, and be home by seven. Then, even if Dani wouldn't talk to him about what was going on, maybe Braedon would.

Pete's wish for no complications didn't come true. Somehow the blue bin at the house on the corner of Fifth and Clark had lost its lid. The lady who lived there, the one who always wore a pink robe and pink slippers, had refused to accept that Pete didn't carry around replacement lids in his truck.

Then another bin was missing entirely. The tall, gaunt man at 112 Birch had peered down his long nose at Pete and insisted he'd pulled the bin out that morning and now it was nowhere to be found. *"How a garbage bin of that size could disappear into thin air is beyond me,"* the man had said in a nasally voice.

Pete suspected foul play.

At Windy Ray's house, he'd lost the Chickenfoot game in record time. "You're not focused," Windy Ray had said. "Your mind has pulled up a chair at another man's table."

"My mind's far too restless to sit in a chair" had been his response.

It was cold when he climbed out of the Dodge at his house, but there was still light in the sky, sure evidence summer was coming despite all other signs to the contrary. Though it was nearly mid-April, Sleeping Grass showed no signs of new life.

Pete expected to find Braedon sitting on the couch doing

his homework when he opened the door, but Braedon was nowhere to be seen and a feeling of dissonance filled the house. He'd read a Japanese poet once whose poems all ended abruptly with no resolution and left Pete feeling unsettled. That was how he felt now in his living room.

Pearl stomped her hooves and paced a couple of times as if she noticed, too.

Dani appeared in the living room entryway with a dish towel in her hand. "He's in his room."

"Oh."

"Did you eat?"

"Yes."

She nodded and went back to the kitchen. Pete looked at Pearl, looked at the hallway, and whispered, "Something's going on."

Pete's fears about what might be happening to Braedon at school resurfaced with a vengeance as Pearl trotted down the hall to Braedon's room. One part of Pete's heart wanted him to march directly to his nephew's room with Pearl and find out if he was okay. Another part felt compelled to talk to Dani first. She had been a parent for eleven years. Pete had been an uncle for only a month and a half.

She was sitting at the kitchen table, facing the hall as if expecting him. "How was Windy Ray today?"

"Fine."

"You should invite him here one of these Mondays." She wrinkled her nose. "It isn't fair *he* always has to cook for *you*."

Pete's lips twitched. "I think he finds it more than fair. He's tried my cooking."

"He hasn't tried mine."

Pete lowered his head in acquiescence. "True enough."

He joined his sister at the table. Pearl came snuffling into the kitchen, hanging her snout.

"What's the matter?" Pete scratched her ears. "Braedon wouldn't let you in?"

Dani sighed. "He's not really taking visitors at the moment."

Pete could feel the muscles in his neck and shoulders begin to tense. "Are you going to tell me what happened? I know they're short-staffed at the gas station. There's no way they sent you home early."

Dani rubbed her eyes. "I asked to leave because the principal called me. There was . . . an incident." She covered her face with her hands and groaned. "Blood was shed."

Pete scowled. He *knew* it. "Who was it? How bad is he hurt?"

Dani dropped her hands and stared at him. Something he couldn't read was in her eyes. Was it fear? Was she still afraid he would lose his temper like all those other times?

"Look, Pete, I should've told you before." She hung her head. "We had the same problem at his old school. It was another reason I wanted to get out of Albuquerque. Braedon's dad didn't think it was a big deal, so he always—"

"What?" Pete pushed back from the table and stood as anger coursed through him. "He didn't care that someone was bullying his son?"

Dani's eyes widened. "No, Pete, you don't understand."

He began to pace, and Pearl watched him uneasily. "You're right, I don't understand. I don't understand why Braedon's dad didn't want to protect his own son. I can't believe he thought someone hurting Braedon was no big deal. And now it's happening again?"

"Pete. Stop." Dani's shoulders sank, and she gave him such a pained look that he stopped pacing and braced himself. Maybe Braedon had been hurt worse than he thought.

"Nobody hurt Braedon, in Albuquerque or here." Dani's voice was frighteningly quiet. "It's the other way around."

twenty-five

Pete was quiet as he drove Wilma back from Shelby Wednesday afternoon. Their brief stint at the phone store, if you could call it a store, had been less than successful. Whatever type of phone or plan the guy had looked up on his computer to show Wilma, she'd found something unsatisfactory about it. Pete didn't know why she'd even agreed to the trip.

It was Pete's turmoil over his nephew that weighed him down the most, however. Never in a million years would he have thought Braedon to be the bully. It left a sick feeling in his stomach to imagine Braedon striking another child. Drawing blood.

Something Pete had done more times than he could count.

"A penny for your thoughts, dear," Wilma said. "I know you can't be this upset over my giving that slick salesman a run for his money."

Pete hesitated. How could he possibly tell this genteel woman his nephew had terrorized a fellow student? Then again, she'd raised three children and was a grandmother. Maybe she would understand. Or maybe she would be horrified.

She looked over at him intently when he didn't answer. "If a penny is insufficient, how about a dollar?"

Mole in a hole. He'd vastly overestimated his ability to master the parenting thing—not that he was technically a parent—and he wanted to talk to someone about it. Why not this lady who had never been anything but kind and generous to him?

"It's Braedon. On Monday, he . . ." The words were hard to say. "He hit another student. Several times."

Wilma gasped. "Oh my."

"He's currently suspended."

"He's awfully young to be harboring that much anger." Wilma's voice was pensive. "Was he defending himself?"

Pete shook his head. "From what I can get out of my sister, it was basically an unprovoked attack. I guess he'd been picking on this kid for a while—making his life miserable—then the other day, *boom*. Fists started flying."

"That doesn't sound like the young man I met at my First Day of Spring party."

They entered the Sleeping Grass city limits, and Pete slowed the car. "I know. There's got to be more to the story. But Dani said the same thing happened at his old school. Next time, he'll be expelled."

"Have you talked to him about it?"

"Not yet. Dani grounded him and told me to give him a couple days to think about his choices. He spends all his time in his room and won't even look at me."

"He's ashamed of himself, I expect."

Pete pressed his lips into a line. He knew that feeling. "I'm worried about him."

"Of course you are. But he's young—he'll learn from this."

Pete gripped the wheel. It had taken him over thirty years to learn that fighting others never got you any further in the fight against yourself. He didn't want it to take Braedon that long.

"I don't want him to end up like me."

"Nonsense. He would be fortunate to end up like you. A fine, upstanding citizen. You shouldn't be worried about that."

Pete winced. If Wilma knew the truth about him, the things he'd done, no way would she say such things. "I've been in a few fights myself."

This news didn't seem to surprise her. "None of us is perfect, Pete. God is the only One who never makes mistakes."

From where Pete was sitting, it seemed as though God had made plenty of mistakes. But Pete wasn't just talking about "mistakes." He'd injured other human beings. On purpose. He'd served time for it. He'd made his own sister's life miserable, the only person he had in the whole world after his mom left. He'd tried all manner of drugs and alcohol to quiet the voices, and nothing had ever helped. What could Wilma know about regrets like that?

"He loves you, you know," she continued. "The Lord. Because you're you, and because you are His creation."

It sounded like something Windy Ray would say.

Wilma must have sensed his doubt. "It's true." Her voice was so calm, so full of assurance. "You are a treasure."

He continued to drive in silence. She made him feel as if it *could* be true. There was no reason for her to say these things if she didn't mean it, was there? But then why had no one ever wanted him? Not even his own mother?

"Braedon is lucky to have you in his life," she added.

They arrived at Wilma's house, and he steered the Corolla carefully into the garage, shaking his head. He'd been glad when Wilma suggested they take her car today, because he couldn't quite imagine her climbing into his Dodge.

Wilma picked up her purse and raised her eyebrows at him. "Won't you come in for some tea?"

He hesitated. He didn't like tea, plus he should really get home. He had a lot to think about, and Braedon had been home alone all day. Well, alone except for Pearl.

Wilma somehow raised her eyebrows higher. "Or perhaps a glass of cranberry juice? We hardly got to visit."

"All right." He chuckled to himself. He didn't like cranberry juice either, but he could hardly deny her. "Just for a few minutes."

She bustled out of the car and into the house. He hurried after her. She still had a lot of get-up-and-go for an eighty-two-year-old woman. He found her struggling to pull off her heavy coat.

"Let me help you with that."

"Thank you, dear." She gestured for him to hang it on the back of a chair. "I'd prefer to wear my lighter jacket and my nice cashmere cardigan, but I can't find the cardigan. I'm stuck wearing this ugly old thing." She waved a hand at the coat. "At least until the weather changes."

He was grateful for a change of subject. "It's supposed to be in the fifties all next week."

She pulled two glasses from the cupboard. "Won't that be nice. Please, have a seat. It's such a treat for me to have a visitor."

He obeyed and didn't protest when she set a glass of cranberry juice in front of him. He could tolerate the stuff for Wilma's sake.

"Now." She settled herself next to him. "Dani's still working at the gas station, hmm?"

"Yes."

"I suppose there aren't many other job opportunities around here. What about at the school?"

"I don't know."

"She's a smart young lady. I'm sure she'd prefer something more intellectually stimulating, don't you think? Something more meaningful?"

"Well, yes, but—"

"Perhaps she should expand her job hunt to include Shelby." Wilma tapped her cane thoughtfully. "It's only a thirty-minute drive."

Pete didn't think his sister was job hunting at all, in Shelby or otherwise, but he wasn't sure what to say. He knew Dani could do better than the gas station. Better than Sleeping Grass, for that matter. He would probably spend the rest of his life here, cleaning up other people's messes and being slowly eroded by the wind, but what about Dani and Braedon? They deserved more.

"We'll have to keep our eyes and ears open for opportunities, now, won't we?" Wilma continued. "A suitable job is bound to come along eventually."

Eventually. The word sank into Pete's soul and embedded there like a pebble stuck in the heel of his shoe, clicking against the pavement with every step. Did Dani plan to stick around long enough for *eventually*? He wanted the world for his sister and nephew.

But.

He didn't want them to leave.

He took a sip of juice, giving himself time to think of a way to change the subject once again. His eyes scanned the kitchen, taking in Windy Ray's rocks on the windowsill and stacks of papers on the table. The house was in such neat order that the papers stood out.

He set his glass down. "Have you been working on your taxes?"

She stilled and folded her hands on the table. "Whatever do you mean?"

He pointed his chin at the stack of papers. "It's almost

Tax Day. I thought maybe you'd been working on your taxes."

His eye caught on one of the envelopes. *Liberty County Treasurer's Office*, it read. What could that be about? The only thing he could think of was property taxes. He didn't have to worry about those himself, being a renter, but he knew property taxes in Liberty County had risen the past few years despite a lack of growth in the local economy.

"I filed my taxes early." Wilma's voice sounded strained. What had he said? She straightened the papers and slid them away. "They make it so confusing, you know, but Lily helped me. Such a dear."

The mention of Lily's name hit Pete hard. He hadn't had the nerve the other day to ask her what kind of Skittles she liked best. It was like if he brought it up, he'd have to face how it might look, his leaving gifts for her on a garbage bin. He'd have to risk hearing something in her voice or seeing something on her face that told him it was a foolish and futile thing to do.

So he hadn't brought it up. But he'd left her a bag of Wild Berry Skittles on Monday.

Wilma slid her glass of juice to the left, then back. Her hand appeared to tremble. "Pete, I was hoping I could talk to you about something."

His eyes returned to the envelope from the Treasurer's Office, and a knot formed in his gut. That envelope gave him a bad feeling. "Is it about your property taxes? Is the county giving you trouble? I'd be happy to look at that letter if it would help."

Her face paled. "No. I mean, yes, but—"

"Have you talked to your kids about it? If you were my mother, I'd want to know if you were having trouble."

She stiffened. "It's nothing they need to worry themselves over. I've got it under control."

He held out his hand. "Can I see it?"

He could see she was torn, but after a moment she gingerly picked up the envelope and handed it to him. “It’s not a big deal. I have a plan.”

He pulled out a sheet of paper and skimmed it quickly, then swung his eyes back to the top and read it again. This didn’t look like “not a big deal.”

“You owe over three thousand dollars?”

“The money’s in savings.” She clasped her hands together. “All I have to do is transfer it and send a check. I just haven’t gotten around to it yet.”

Pete drummed his fingers. Something didn’t feel right about this, but what did he know? “You’re sure?”

“Of course I’m sure. It’s all going to be taken care of.” She smiled but it didn’t seem to reach her eyes. “Not to worry. Now, I was hoping we could—”

His cell rang, and he flinched. He pulled it out of his pocket. “Sorry, I just want to make sure it isn’t important.”

It was Mrs. Nelson, his neighbor. Uh-oh. “Hello?”

The voice was high and tight. “Uncle Pete?”

Pete’s heart clenched. He’d told his nephew to go next door and use Mrs. Nelson’s phone if there was an emergency. “What’s the matter, Braedon?”

“I’m sorry. Pearl accidentally ate my Snickers, and now she’s throwing up. I’m really, really sorry.”

“It’s okay, buddy. I’ll be right there.”

He ended the call and scrambled to his feet. This had happened before. Keeping Pearl away from candy was like keeping raccoons away from trash bins.

“Is everything all right?” Wilma asked, one hand on her chest.

“I don’t mean to run off, but Braedon and Pearl are having a bit of a situation.”

She waved a hand. “Of course, go, go. We can talk another time.”

He hesitated, hating to leave like this. "Thanks for the juice."

She pointed at the door. "Go. Your nephew needs you."

Wilma sat at the table for several long minutes after Pete left, her thumb scouring back and forth across the top of her cane, her heart quavering inside her. She'd almost told Pete about Rosie. She'd come within inches. Was she relieved her efforts had been interrupted . . . or disappointed?

Mostly relieved if she was being honest with herself. *"If you were my mother . . ."* he had said. What would Pete think if he knew she almost was?

It was so nice having him check in on her once in a while. So nice that he was concerned about her having a cellphone to call for help if needed. His concern over the property taxes had alarmed her, however. She shouldn't put off payment any longer. She had been waiting for the debt-reduction program Sadie had enrolled her in to be complete so she would know exactly what her financial standing was before withdrawing any money from her savings account. Should she keep waiting or make the payment?

Sadie might be able to help her with this decision. Wilma nodded to herself. Yes, Sadie would probably know better than anyone.

She rose with a groan and shuffled to the phone. She dialed the number for FAS and entered the extension code Sadie had given her.

A bright and professional voice came on the line. "Financial Assistance Services. This is Sadie, how may I help you?"

"Sadie, it's Wilma Jacobsen."

"Mrs. Jacobsen, I'm glad you called. I was just checking the status of your case file. What can I do for you?"

"I'm in a bit of a pickle with my property taxes, and I was wondering if you might be able to help me."

"I would be happy to. What's the problem?"

Wilma explained about the notice from the county and the money she owed. She explained how she forgot the property taxes had previously been rolled into the mortgage payment. When she had finished, she took a deep breath.

"That's my pickle, you see."

"This is good news," Sadie said.

Wilma wrinkled her nose. "It is?"

"Yes. I'm glad you told me. I can update your file to include the taxes as debt you owe and possibly get them reduced, as well."

"Oh, that *is* good news. Does that mean I should wait to send the payment?"

"Yes. I expect your paperwork to go through in the next four to six weeks. Once it does, then you can pay the tax if there's any left."

Wilma leaned against her cane. Hadn't Sadie said "four to six weeks" last time they'd talked? Well, these kinds of things moved slowly, of course. Bureaucracy was never in a rush.

"Is there anything else I can help you with, Mrs. Jacobsen?" Sadie asked.

"No, dear, thank you. That was all."

"All right. I'll be in touch as soon as I hear anything, okay?"

After she'd returned the phone to its place and sat down in her favorite chair, Wilma nodded to herself. How fortunate she was that the government had passed this new law to help people like her. What a thrill it was going to be when she could tell Rachel she was going to give all the money she'd been using for credit card payments to Tom's ministry instead. All she had to do was wait four to six more weeks.

twenty-six

When Pete walked through the door, the smell hit him like a fifty-pound bag of garbage.

"Ugh." He braced himself. "Braedon?"

His nephew appeared from the kitchen and took a couple of steps along the wall, his head hanging low. "I'm sorry. It was an accident. Don't be mad. I'm really sorry."

"You can stop apologizing, buddy. Pearl's always been a sneak. It could've happened to anyone."

Pete decided not to mention that Dani had been clear Braedon was not to eat any candy while grounded.

Braedon jerked a thumb over his shoulder. "She's in there."

Pete took long strides across the floor and entered the kitchen. Pearl was lying on the floor, looking spent. Near her, a towel lay across what Pete could only assume was a nice, sloppy pile of puke.

He knelt beside her. "One of these days, you're going to learn your lesson."

She groaned.

Pete turned to Braedon. "Can you get the mop and bucket from the closet, please?"

As Braedon hurried to the closet, Pete rubbed a hand down

Pearl's back. His instinct was to make her drink water, but he'd learned from the vet that he was supposed to let her stomach rest for a few hours before giving her anything to eat or drink.

He gently rested a hand on her cheek. "You're a real pain in the butt, you know that?"

Braedon returned, his face scrunched up and red. "Is she going to die?"

"No way, she's going to be fine." Pete stood and put a hand on Braedon's shoulder. "Don't worry."

Braedon flinched at Pete's touch. "I'm sorry."

Pete sighed. "I'm not mad. I promise. Now, let's get this cleaned up, okay?"

The two of them worked together mopping up the mess. The smell was awful, though the look on Braedon's face was worse. Pete didn't know how else to reassure his nephew that he wasn't in trouble. That Pearl would be good as new by bedtime. That if anyone was to blame, it was Pete for leaving his pig in the care of an eleven-year-old.

By the time they finished cleaning, Pearl had trudged over to the beat-up dog bed in the living room for a nap. Pete checked the time. Dani wouldn't be home for a while yet.

Technically it had been a "couple of days," right? Braedon had been given plenty of time to consider his life choices, and if he disappeared into his room now, who knew how long it might be before Pete had a chance like this again.

Pete gestured toward the table. "Why don't we sit and talk for a minute."

Braedon didn't look happy about it, but he sat. Pete felt for the kid, knowing his heart must be a jumbled-up mess. Even after all this time, Pete could remember enough about his younger years to know there was a lot that didn't make sense at Braedon's age.

Not that everything made sense now that he was fifty.

Braedon scowled at the tabletop and slouched. "Are you going to tell my mom about the Snickers?"

"No, but I think you should."

Braedon's eyes flicked up for a second, but he said nothing.

Pete was out of his element here. "Just think about it, okay?"

Braedon mumbled, "Okay," and began hitting his left heel against the leg of the chair.

Pete noticed the knuckles on his nephew's right hand were swollen and bruised. "Did you ice your hand when you got home from school the other day?"

"No."

Pete wished Windy Ray were here. He would know what to say. "I hit someone once."

Braedon's heel stopped banging.

Pete cleared his throat. "Actually, I've hit a lot of people."

Braedon ventured a glance at him from the corner of his eye. "Why?"

"Because I didn't know what else to do with my anger, I guess. But I regret every single swing."

No response. Braedon turned his face away and sniffed.

"How about you?" Pete asked as gently as he could. "Why did you do it? I've seen how you care about Pearl and how you try to look out for your mom. You don't seem like the kind of kid who likes to hurt people."

Another sniff. A stifled sob. Pete waited.

"Tyson said if I was really his friend, I would hate the same kids he hates. I told him I did, but he wanted me to prove it."

Tyson? That must be the kid who'd picked Braedon for a partner in PE. Braedon's only so-called friend. "Who's the kid you punched?"

"Cole."

"Tyson hates Cole?"

Braedon nodded.

"Do you know why?"

Braedon hesitated. "Not really. Tyson said Cole is a loser, and anyone who's friends with him is a loser, too."

Pete was beginning to get the picture. "You're not a loser, Braedon."

His nephew stiffened, his shoulders hunched forward in a posture all too familiar to Pete. Braedon was fighting the voices, like Pete. Only Pete's voices had been many, and Braedon was probably only hearing one. His father's.

"Do you remember when I told you about finding Pearl at the dump?"

Braedon didn't answer, but Pete could tell he was listening.

"What if I had left her there?"

Braedon frowned.

Pete scooted a little closer. "Would that have meant she really was trash?"

Braedon's eyes flashed. "No."

"But if whoever threw her out thought she was nothing, and I thought she was nothing, wouldn't that make her nothing?"

"No." Braedon's voice sounded heated now. "It doesn't matter what anyone thinks. Pearl isn't garbage."

"That's right. And it doesn't matter what anyone thinks about you. You are not a loser. Remember what Windy Ray says about the Creator?"

Braedon's fist loosened slightly. "Everything God makes has value, whether we choose to see it or not."

Pete nodded. "If Tyson chooses not to see Cole's value, that's on him. You can still choose to see it. And if anyone chooses not to see your value, that's their loss. Big-time. But I see it. Your mother sees it."

He wished he could add *Your father sees it*, but instead he let silence reign—except for the sound of Pearl snoring in the other room. Pete shifted in his chair. He had no idea what he was doing. No idea if anything he said was getting through. All he knew was that he wouldn't allow the voice in Braedon's head to go uncontested.

"I love you, buddy." How many times had he longed to hear someone say those words to him after his mom left? How many times had he struck out in anger trying to silence the voices that told him he wasn't wanted? Wasn't worthy? He thought of all the words that had been said to him—the words he'd tried to fight his way through—and spoke the opposite to his nephew. "You mean the world to me. I love having you around. I don't ever want you to leave."

Words he'd never heard.

Braedon's body began to shake. He wiped his arm under his nose. "I shouldn't have done it. I shouldn't have hurt Cole."

"You're right. You shouldn't have." Pete thought of all the people he'd hurt and cringed. "You need to apologize."

A sob shuddered through the boy. "Then Tyson won't be my friend anymore."

Pete's heart sank. Braedon's only friend. A crummy friend by all accounts, but still. "I'm real sorry about that, buddy. Real sorry. But you'll still have Pearl and me. And Windy Ray."

Braedon made a face.

"What?" Pete threw up his hands in mock indignation. "Don't we count? Aren't we cool enough?"

Braedon's nose was running, his eyes red, but Pete thought he saw the faint hint of a smile pass over his nephew's face. "Windy Ray's pretty cool, I guess."

Oh, brother. His friend would have a field day with that if he were here. "You've got to be kidding me. Windy Ray? That old fogey?"

Braedon's laugh was halfhearted, yet it was music to Pete's

ears. Then the boy's face fell, and he said, "I don't want to go back to school tomorrow."

Pete nodded. "It's not going to be easy."

"Do you think Mom would let me stay home?"

"I doubt it."

"Would you ask her?"

"No way, buddy." Pete reached over and tousled Braedon's hair. "You're on your own with that one."

Braedon huffed. "Ah, *man*."

"How about we surprise your mom and make dinner?"

Braedon's lip curled. "That would surprise her, all right. She said you're not allowed to cook anymore."

"I think it'll be okay—if you help me. What do you say?"

Braedon didn't seem too enthusiastic, but he agreed to give it a try. As they pulled out everything they'd need for boxed mac and cheese with hot dogs—the meal Pete was willing to attempt—Pete thought about his dad.

He tried to imagine standing in the kitchen of their old house with his dad, making dinner, but he couldn't. He couldn't even picture the man's face. All he could see were other, unhappy faces. Faces that wanted him to know everything he'd done wrong. Faces that saw the trouble he caused but never saw the hurt and anger underneath.

His heart wrenched. Maybe they had. Maybe some had tried, like Arnie at the group home, who gave him his copy of Thoreau. Pete had been so intent on sabotaging every relationship he had that it was possible he hadn't seen how hard some of his foster parents had tried. How much they had cared.

Boy, he hadn't made it easy. He'd pushed them away. He'd fought them. But no matter how hard Braedon pushed and fought, Pete was determined about one thing. He wasn't going anywhere.

twenty-seven

Sometimes the relentless rumble of the Xpeditor was mind-numbing, hour after hour, alley after alley, turning Pete's brain to mud. Stop-lift-dump, stop-lift-dump . . . until *stop-lift-dump* became the cadence of his life. Today was one of those days.

He looked over at Pearl and shook his head to clear the sludge. "How do you think Braedon did at school?"

Just as Pete suspected, Dani had refused to let Braedon stay home this morning.

"Do you think he apologized to Cole?"

Pearl didn't have an opinion on the matter. She'd bounced back from yesterday's stomachache and had been her usual self all day.

Pete checked the time. His route was nearly complete. He wondered what kind of Braedon Dani had found when she picked him up from school and wished he could've been there. Of all the days for Dani to work the morning shift, it had to be today.

He finished at one house and drove forward to the next. As he approached the blue bin, he saw a white envelope taped to its side. He shifted the truck into park and jumped out.

Inside the envelope was a thank-you card for the baby walker. *He's too small to use it now*, it read, *but we know he's going to love it when he's bigger. Thank you for thinking of us*. Pete smiled. They'd had a boy. He wondered what they'd named him.

"S'posed to snow down south this weekend, d'ya hear?" Conrad Rountree appeared and leaned against the fence, his long beard blowing sideways in the steady breeze. "Down 'round Bozeman. Nuthin' here, though."

Pete tucked the card into his back pocket. "That right?"

"Ma says she wishes it'd snow here, too, and cover up all the dirt."

Pete nodded. The Hi-Line was a dull and dirty stretch of desolation in April. "Is your mother still bored at her new place?"

"Outta her mind." Con spit and tucked his thumbs behind the yellow straps of his suspenders. "She calls me ten times a day. 'Con, what're you doin'? Con, where'd I leave my knitting needles? Con, bring me some licorice.' They don't let 'em have no sweets there 'cept on special 'casions."

Pete thought of Pearl puking Snickers all over the kitchen and nodded. Moderation had its benefits. "I'm sorry to hear that."

"You saw the woodpile at Old Man O'Malley's, I 'spect?"

Pete smiled. "Thank you for taking care of those branches. Did you have any trouble?"

"Naw. That lady that lives there—Celia, I think—'bout cried all over me. Gave me a plate of cookies."

"And Mr. O'Malley?"

"Oh, you know how he is. Crabby old mule. Said I ain't packed the wood tight enough. Made me restack it."

"He didn't."

Con cackled and slapped his leg. "Shore did, the son of a gun. I always wunnered what crawled up his—"

"Well, I sure appreciate your helping out, Con. I don't know when I would've had time to get to it." Pete liked helping people when he had the chance, but his life had been pretty full lately. He couldn't remember the last time he had so much going on and so many people to think about.

Con shrugged. "It weren't nuthin'. I got that Farm Boss, you know. Cut them branches up like they's nuthin' but whittle sticks."

Pete glanced at the truck, thinking he better get back to work, when a thought struck him. "How long have you owned your place, Con?"

Con tugged at his beard. "It's my ma's place still, but I take care of it'n pay the taxes'n everthing."

Pete's ears perked up. "The property taxes? You happen to know anything about what happens if you don't pay?"

"Yer not behind on yer taxes, are you?" Con shook his head. "That's a bad deal."

"No, not me. But I have a friend who's behind. She got a notice about owing money. It said something about a lien."

It was something he'd considered asking Windy Ray about, but he feared what his friend might do if he thought Wilma was in dire straits of any kind. He wouldn't put it past Windy Ray to sell one of his kidneys on the black market if he thought it would help Wilma.

"Buddy a mine once, he couldn't pay." Con pushed off the fence and kicked at the dirt. "Right shame. Car accident. Couldn't work. He got one of them notices but didn't do nuthin' 'bout it. After 'while, disability finally kicks in and things're gettin' better so's he contacts the county and asks, 'How much do I owe?' And they says, 'Someun's paid the taxes and holds the lien on yer property now. If'n you don't pay them back after so many months, they'll own yer house.'"

Pete's eyes grew wide, and Con nodded solemnly. "Like I said, it's a bad deal."

"Did he lose his house?" Pete asked.

"Purt near, 'cept his uncle died'n left him some money and he paid it off just in time. Only thing 'at saved him."

Pete gave a low whistle. It was worse than he thought. "I had no idea."

"If'n yer friend's an old gal, she could prolly get her taxes reduced. Elderly assistance program. That's how my ma done it. But tell her she better not put it off 'less she wants someun else gettin' their hands on her property."

"I'll tell her." Pete held his hand out, and Con shook it. "Thanks a lot, Con."

"Yer welcome."

Pete pondered Con's cautionary tale as he drove away, which had dropped a stone into the pit of his stomach. He didn't want Wilma to lose her home. She'd told him she'd lived there for almost forty years. If only there was a way to talk to Lily about this so they could come up with a plan.

"I don't like it, Pearl." He finished his last alley of the day and headed back toward the carport. "I don't like it one bit."

Dinner had been a quiet affair. Braedon had sulked and picked at his food, Dani never had much to say anyway, and Pete couldn't stop thinking about Wilma. And whenever he thought about Wilma, he thought about Lily.

Dani watched him clear the table as she wiped down the counter. "What kind of bee got in your bonnet tonight?"

He set a stack of dishes in the sink. "Huh?"

She set the dishrag down. "Something's bothering you."

He wasn't sure he wanted to involve his sister. She had enough problems of her own. "Just thinking about Braedon. Did he say anything about his day when you picked him up?"

She leaned her hip against the counter. "He said no one

would talk to him and that it was the worst day of his life. But he's said that before."

Pete plugged the sink drain and started the hot water. "I told him he should apologize to the kid."

"I told him he had to."

"Did he do it?"

"Not yet. He'll get there. But I don't think that's the only thing on your mind, Pete. Is it Lily? Have you talked to her lately?"

He could feel his cheeks warm up. He kept his back to his sister as he started scrubbing the dirty plates. Having two more people around resulted in a lot more dishes.

"No, not for a while. Have you?"

"No. But I finished that Ivan Doig book and need to return it."

Her voice was full of implication, but he didn't know what she was getting at. "I'm sure you could leave it at Wilma's for her."

"I thought you might want to return it yourself."

"You want me to bring it to Wilma's?" He rinsed the plates and set them in the drying rack. "I could leave it on her bin, as long as it's not supposed to rain."

A bag of Skittles was waterproof. A book was not.

Dani laughed. "There must be some way to return the book that would involve you actually talking to Lily."

His brow furrowed. "She didn't loan the book to *me*."

"I'm trying to help you out here, big brother. Don't you want to see her?"

He saw no point in denying it, but he couldn't bring himself to say yes, afraid of what Dani might hear in his voice.

"Of course you do," Dani continued. "The book would give you an excuse."

"To do what? Show up at her house? You know that's not a good idea." He rinsed the last of the dishes and unplugged the drain. If Dani and Braedon were going to stick around, he might have to talk to his landlord about installing a dishwasher.

"Jerry always goes out drinking Friday nights. At Arrow's. She said he never gets home before midnight."

Pete cringed. He'd seen Jerry at Arrow's. Pete had only the occasional beer these days, having long ago lost his appetite for drunkenness, but when he'd first moved back to Sleeping Grass, he'd gone to Arrow's a few times to size up the town. You could learn a lot by sitting on a barstool and listening. Jerry had been there one Friday night, just like Dani said. The man was loud and obnoxious while playing a game of pool, patting the waitress's behind when she walked by. The waitress had shrugged the incident off as if it happened all the time, but Pete had made a note of it. He hadn't been back to Arrow's since.

Dani walked closer, so Pete was forced to give her his attention. "Look, it's none of my business, but don't you like her?"

He hesitated.

"I know you do. So why don't you stop by tomorrow night and return her book?"

It *would* give him the chance to talk to Lily about Wilma. "I thought you said it was none of your business."

"And I thought you said she deserves better than Jerry."

His blood pressure spiked just hearing the man's name. "I never said that."

"You don't think she does?"

"I do."

"Then go see her."

"I can't show up uninvited."

"Sure you can. If she's not up for company, she'll just take the book, say thanks, and close the door. No harm done."

"You make it sound simple."

"Maybe it is."

He knew it wasn't. He knew his feelings for Lily, the situation she was in, his track record with women . . . none of it was simple. But Dani kept giving him a look far too intent for someone supposedly minding her own business.

"You've got nothing to lose, Pete."

His heart pounded. That's where she was wrong. For the first time since his mother walked away and never looked back, he had everything to lose.

twenty-eight

They say ice cream tastes better when shared with a friend, and Pete had to admit it was true. It also tasted better when it wasn't twenty below zero.

Sunny stood beside the table with her hands on her hips. "Well? What do you think?"

She'd brought him and Windy Ray a new flavor today. One the company she ordered from had recently started carrying called Blueberry Bliss.

He took another bite. Though his stomach was in knots, it tasted good. "I like it."

Windy Ray had a purple spot of ice cream on his nose. "It's my new favorite."

Sunny smiled. The ice cream tasted like blueberry pie and had chunks of dough in it like piecrust.

She put her hands down and moved a little closer to the table. "How's your family doing, Pete?"

He swallowed. Her question made him think of Dani, which made him think of Lily, which made him think of the promise his sister had managed to extract from him about stopping by Lily's house tonight. He was all kinds of terrified. But he said, "Fine."

"How come your nephew didn't come with you today?"

Pete focused on his cone. Braedon was still grounded until further notice. "Uh . . ."

"I believe the young man is on house arrest, Sunshine in the Sky." Windy Ray nodded gravely. "It's very serious."

Pete groaned inwardly. He wasn't sure if Sunny could be trusted with that information.

"Boys can be a handful sometimes." Sunny shook her head. "You remember my brother, Skip? He got grounded every other week when we were kids."

Pete leaned toward Sunny. "And he turned out all right?"

Sunny laughed. "He lost one and a half fingers to an auger, and his brain cells have been reduced to minimum capacity from all his concussions, but otherwise he's all right."

Windy Ray looked up from his cone. "These fingers he lost, which ones were they?"

Sunny held up her left hand and pointed to the ring and pinky fingers. Windy Ray bobbed his head as if this was very important information. "I see."

Sunny turned back to Pete. "Tell Braedon if he shapes up, I'll give him a double cone next time he comes in."

Pete nodded. "Thanks, Sunny. I will."

Windy Ray munched on the last bite of his cone as he watched her walk away. "She prefers to talk to you, I think. She's a very kind woman."

Pete shifted in his chair, not liking the way his friend was looking at him. "Yeah, she's nice."

Windy Ray tilted his head. "Hmm."

No. Pete turned his attention to his ice cream. There was no room in his life for *hmm*. He and Sunny were just friends. She wouldn't be interested in a guy like him anyway.

He racked his brain for a different topic. "How is Apisi's constipation?"

Windy Ray picked up Apisi from the floor and held her

close to his face. "She's doing much better. Aren't you, Apisi? Pooping every day."

Pete chuckled. "Glad to hear it. And hey, before I forget, Dani wanted me to invite you over for dinner."

This made Windy Ray sit up with a jolt. "Will Wilma be there?"

"What, you're only going to come if Wilma's there?"

"Of course not. I would never refuse an invitation to eat your sister's cooking. Braedon told me about the banana bread."

Pete shook his head in amusement. "It was pretty good. You want me to put in a request?"

Windy Ray considered this for far longer than he would have if he had realized Pete was joking. Finally, he folded his hands on the table in front of him and blinked. "No."

The knots in Pete's stomach loosened a bit as he fought back laughter. What would he do without Windy Ray? "Okay, how about next week?"

"I believe I'm available."

"Sounds good." Pete finished his cone and wiped his fingers on a napkin. Blueberry Bliss was sure tasty. He leaned over to check on Pearl, then sat back up to find Windy Ray staring at him. "What?"

"Will Wilma be there?"

Pete threw up his hands in exasperation but couldn't keep a grin from spreading across his face. "I'll see what I can do."

The street was dark and empty. Jerry's truck was nowhere to be seen. Pete looked down at the book in his hands, and it felt like so much more than it was. A book, yes, but also a connection to Lily. Something she had touched, spent time with, loved.

He walked closer to the house. He'd parked two blocks away, and he'd told himself it wasn't because he was afraid of Jerry—he'd fought bigger men—but he was. Not for his own sake, but for the misery the man could cause Lily. Funny how a man could charge into a fight without a second thought when only his own safety was at risk but cower in the shadows when someone else's well-being was involved.

Standing at her door, he raised a fist to knock, then held back. Maybe he should leave the book on the front step and walk away. He had no reason to believe Lily wanted to see him. But what if Jerry found the book and started asking questions?

Pete's hands were sweaty. He knocked.

His senses, on high alert, took in a rustle of movement in the house, the flutter of a curtain, a dead bolt being turned. Lily opened the door and stared at him. "Hi."

"Hi."

She wore sweatpants and an oversized sweatshirt, her hair pulled back in a ponytail. She seemed so young.

He realized he was staring and held up the Ivan Doig memoir. "Dani asked me to drop off your book."

Lily's expression was enigmatic as she reached to take it. "How did she like it?"

Idiot. Why hadn't he asked her? "I'm not sure." He thought he saw a flash of disappointment on Lily's face and hurried to add, "But it's one of my favorites. I've read it three times."

At that, she clutched the book to her chest. "Isn't it beautiful?"

"Yes. Like poetry."

"Doesn't it make you feel as though you're standing on the plains surrounded by wildflowers and sheep, listening to the wind?"

Pete shoved his hands in the pockets of his jacket. That was precisely how it made him feel. "Yes."

"Have you read any of his other books?"

"Yes."

She watched him for a moment, and he realized with a sinking feeling that she was waiting to hear which of Ivan Doig's other books he had read. But before he could extricate any other titles from his befuddled brain, she looked at the sky and said, "I was thinking of going for a walk."

The stars were starting to come out. The air was cold, but the wind remarkably calm.

Pete took a step back. "Oh. Okay. I won't keep you."

One side of her mouth lifted. "Do you want to come?"

"Me?"

She made a show of peering around his left shoulder, then his right. "I don't see anyone else."

Her voice held a hint of teasing, and his eyes widened. "Oh. Yes. I want to go with you."

He couldn't think of anything he wanted more, in fact.

She held up a finger. "I'll be right back."

She closed the door and left him standing in the dark. Of all the possible scenarios he had tortured himself with the past few hours, this one hadn't crossed his mind. A truck came rumbling slowly up the road as he stood there, and Pete held his breath until he saw the truck was gray. Jerry's truck was black. A dumb little Chevy S-10 Jerry had put oversized tires on.

The man in the gray truck was wearing a cowboy hat and seemed to glare at him as he drove past. Pete forced himself to take a deep breath. He didn't know that guy. His nerves were playing tricks on him, was all. He wasn't doing anything wrong. Just returning a book to a friend.

The door opened again, and Lily stepped out of the house. "Ready?"

He made an embarrassing yelping noise that was meant to be a yes, though the truth was that he wasn't at all ready.

She didn't seem to notice. He followed her down the walk to the street and hung back to let her choose which way to go. She turned right.

"Remember when Ivan was living in Ringling with his grandma? In that dumpy old house?"

Pete startled, Lily's words sounding loud and sharp in the hushed evening air. "Yes. And he would visit the Brekkes to read their magazines."

"I wonder sometimes what it would've been like to live back then." Her voice seemed wistful. "Everything was so simple."

"And hard."

She laughed softly. "True. Montana has never made it easy on anyone."

Her words were like a pebble dropped in a pond, the ripples stretching out and out, the tiny waves reaching the shore long after all signs of the pebble had disappeared. Montana certainly hadn't been easy on him. He guessed it hadn't been easy on her either.

"Before you moved to Sleeping Grass, had you ever been to Montana before?"

She shook her head. "I'd never been anywhere. How about you?"

Pete watched the ground pass underfoot. There were so many things he could say, so many places he'd been, but the roads he'd taken weren't ones he was proud of. "I've traveled a bit."

"Have you been to the coast?"

"Which one?"

"Either one. It's a dream of mine to see the ocean."

"I spent some time in Oregon, so yes."

The ocean was only about seven hundred miles away. A person could drive there in one day. Why hadn't Jerry ever taken her?

An unfamiliar feeling wobbled in his chest. Maybe she'd never told Jerry about her dream. He wanted to ask what other dreams she had, what else she wanted to see, but something held him back.

"Do you ever wonder what your life would be like if you'd made a different choice once upon a time?"

He looked over at her, and her face was tilted toward the sky. The stars were out in force now, and Pete didn't think anyplace he'd ever been could compete with the Hi Line for stargazing. He looked away before she could catch him staring. There were so many choices he'd made that could've altered his life if he'd chosen differently. He'd never wondered about just one. What choice was Lily thinking about?

"I guess I mostly wonder why I was such a fool for so long. I'm not a very fast learner."

"Your days of being a fool are behind you?"

He laughed. "I wouldn't say that."

She laughed, too, and he thought of his mother. She'd seemed happy most of the time. Laughing and singing. Squeezing his hands and trying to get him to dance. Kissing his forehead at night and whispering, "*See you when the morning wind blows.*" Even after all this time, he couldn't figure out why that had been a life she needed to run away from.

Lily slowed to a stop and sighed. "We should probably head back."

Pete looked around in bewilderment. How had they gone so far? "All right."

They turned around, and his fingers itched to pull out his phone and check the time to make sure they were still safe from the possibility of Jerry's return, but he was afraid she would interpret the check as something else. He replayed the evening in his mind instead, reassuring himself midnight was still far away. Was this what Lily's life was like? Examining every move she made through the lens of where Jerry was and what he was doing so she could avoid trouble?

She read his mind—it no longer shocked him when women did that—and pulled out her own phone. "It's a little after nine."

Her phone beeped. She frowned and quickly responded to a text, then tucked the phone away. Silence fell between them, but it wasn't heavy or awkward. The steam of their breath hung in the air.

Pete walked close to her but not close enough their arms would touch. He let her set the pace as he worked up the courage to say what he felt needed to be said. He chewed on the words, trying not to bite his tongue, and thought about what Dani had told him. *"I think she might be planning an escape."* Finally, hoping the darkness would keep his face from giving too much away, he spoke.

"If you ever need anything, *anything*, I hope you'll let me know. Doesn't matter the time, I will be there, and you'll be safe with me."

The tips of his ears burned. He kept his eyes on his feet.

She nudged him with her elbow. "I don't have your number."

His eyes widened, and he patted his pockets. "I could write it down."

"I'll find my notebook when we get to the house."

He understood why she didn't want his number saved in her phone, and he knew better than to ask for her number in return. They continued walking at a slow pace, talking about Pearl and Sunny's Sweet Shop before circling back to Ivan Doig. As Lily's house came into view, Pete remembered Wilma and barely stopped himself from smacking his forehead. He'd almost forgotten.

"Has Wilma mentioned anything to you about her property taxes?"

Lily scrunched her lips to the side. "No, but she told me on Monday that you talked to her about a cellphone. Thank you."

"She owes a bunch of money." He blurted it out in a guilty way, not sure if it was right to share the information but not knowing what else to do.

Lily frowned. "I've wondered about her finances, but she always pays me every week. I'd hoped I was imagining it."

"Why did you wonder?"

"Well . . ." She gave him a sheepish look. "It's not like I mean to check out her mail or anything, but when I carry it in for her, I can't help but notice there seems to be a lot of mail from credit card companies. Bills, from what it looks like."

Pete made a face. Did Wilma owe more money than the three thousand to the county? "She's never said anything?"

"She's much too polite to talk about money. She's very old school, you know."

He remembered how uneasy Wilma had been when she brought it up the other day. He narrowed his eyes. Wait a minute. She hadn't brought it up at all. He had. What had she been planning to say?

"A friend of mine was telling me how you can lose your house if you don't pay the property taxes."

Lily grimaced. "Jerry takes care of all our finances. I don't really know anything about that. But I know Wilma wouldn't like us bugging her about it."

"I know." Pete kicked at a rock. "It's none of our business, but . . ."

They reached Lily's house and made their way up the walk to the front door. Lily put one hand on the doorknob and looked at him. "It's nice that you care so much about her."

I care about you, too, he wanted to say.

"Let me grab my notebook and another book for Dani."

She shut the door before he could respond, and he found

himself waiting in the dark once again. It didn't bother him that she didn't invite him in—he didn't want to see the home she shared with Jerry anyway—but the door closing in his face felt uncomfortably symbolic.

She reappeared after a minute, and he tried to look like it was the most natural thing in the world for him to be standing on her front step. When she handed him a notebook and pen, he wrote down his number, almost adding his name underneath before thinking better of it.

He handed it back to her and kept his voice low. "I mean it. Anytime. For anything."

She acted like she hadn't heard and held out a book. "Here. Let's see what Dani thinks of this one."

Peace Like a River by Leif Enger. Pete blinked. He'd had a lot of time to read since his wilder days had ended. Especially since moving back to Sleeping Grass, which offered many long, dark nights with nothing else to do. Poetry was his favorite, but some stories, like the Ivan Doig book and the one he now held in his hands, gave him the same kind of feeling.

"I love this book."

Lily's smile almost seemed sad as she looked over his head at the sky. "Me too."

twenty-nine

As Pete neared Lily's house Monday morning, he eyed the bag of Tropical Skittles sitting on the control box between him and Pearl. They made him think of Lily on an island vacation in the ocean, standing under a palm tree. Wouldn't she love that?

"I've never been to an island."

Pearl looked over at him with a suspicious glint in her eye.

"Don't worry." Pete held up a hand. "I would take you with me."

An empty promise, to be sure, since pigs were not allowed on airplanes. But Pearl didn't need to know that.

He'd spent the weekend stewing over his walk with Lily. Would she call him if she needed help? He'd given Dani a summarized version of their conversation after much prodding, and she'd been surprised Lily let him write his number in her notebook. "*She must hide it somewhere,*" she'd said.

Pete didn't like the idea of Lily having to hide anything, but it gave him a small sense of satisfaction to know she could get ahold of him if she needed to.

He pulled up to her house, Skittles on his mind. He'd never been a fan of the candy, but maybe he should give them another try. He dumped the blue bin, then shifted the Xpeditor into park so he could hop out and leave his gift. Maybe someday he'd get something for Lily that cost more than $1.29.

He reached for the handle, but the truck door flew open before he could grab it, and suddenly a man was there.

"What are you doing hanging around my house?"

Jerry.

Pearl squealed, and Jerry narrowed his eyes at her before returning his attention to Pete.

Every muscle in Pete's body grew taut. "I'm picking up your trash. It's my job."

"What about Friday night? My buddy said he saw you at my house. *Loitering*, he said."

Pete's insides turned to ice. The man with the cowboy hat in the gray truck. He should've known word would get around somehow. It was a small town. He should've never let Dani talk him into going to Lily's.

Jerry scowled at him, inches from his face, and Pete wanted to shove him out of the truck and onto the ground, but he thought of Lily and held back.

"You got a thing for my girl or something?" Jerry's voice was hard and tight like a fist. He grabbed the front of Pete's shirt. "You peepin' on her? Maybe I should tell your boss about that."

Pete's heart pounded as Pearl squealed again and stomped her hooves. Was Lily watching from the house? He took hold of Jerry's wrists and jerked on them so Jerry had to let go. "Don't touch me."

Jerry had a couple of inches and forty pounds on Pete, but Pete had the better position. He leaned toward Jerry, forcing him back. "Get out of my truck."

Jerry's foot missed the top step, and he flailed backward. He landed on his feet on the ground, cold fury darkening his eyes.

After a tense moment, he took a step back. The element of surprise was gone. Pete had the upper hand now, and Jerry knew it.

"You stay away from her or you'll be sorry. I'll be watching you."

There were so many words Pete wanted to say, but instead he slammed the door shut and put the truck into drive, breathing deeply to keep his anger in check. He couldn't endanger Lily. He couldn't lose his job. He needed to remain calm. Younger Pete would be scrabbling in the gravel with Jerry right now, unconcerned about the consequences. Older, wiser Pete had a job to do and a family to think of.

His family.

Looking straight ahead, he forced himself to drive to the next bin. He would not allow Jerry to rattle him. Pearl snorted and stomped in distress.

"It's okay, girl." Pete reached over the control box to give her a reassuring pat on the head as his eyes fell on the bag of Skittles that had fallen to the floor. "Everything's going to be okay."

Wilma contemplated Lily as the young woman let herself into the house and entered the kitchen.

"You're late."

She didn't mind—heaven knew she had no other plans to work around—but she was surprised. Lily had never been late before.

"Sorry." Lily's face was pinched. "It won't happen again. You can take it out of my pay."

"Nonsense, it's no trouble. I was beginning to worry, that's all. Is everything all right?"

Lily clasped her hands behind her back and nodded, but when she tried to speak, nothing came out.

Wilma's forehead wrinkled as her motherly intuition kicked in. Everything was most certainly *not* all right. She tapped the chair beside her with her cane. "Come sit at the table with me, dear."

Lily hesitated, but Wilma pulled the chair out and pointed. "Please."

Once Lily was beside her, Wilma could see her eyes were red and puffy. "You've been crying."

"It's spring allergies."

"Don't be ridiculous. There's not a single thing blooming in the whole county. Why don't you tell me what's bothering you?"

"I'm just tired. I didn't get much sleep this weekend."

Wilma sat quietly, waiting. She would *not* press. Usually when a young lady had something on her mind, all she needed was a little open space to fill with words.

"Jerry gets mad at me sometimes." Lily picked at a fingernail. "I know better than to make him angry, but . . ."

Wilma did not like the sound of that one bit. "Did he hurt you?"

"Not really. He just yells a lot and throws things."

"At you?"

Lily lowered her voice. "Near me."

Wilma's face scrunched. "How near?"

Lily didn't answer, didn't move.

"How near, Lily?"

The young woman slowly reached up and pulled back the collar of her shirt, revealing a bright red gash on her collarbone. Wilma gasped.

Lily quickly pulled her shirt back over the wound. "He didn't know the glass would shatter like that."

Wilma's hands began to shake as she leaned closer to Lily.

"That's hogwash. You know as well as I do, he knew exactly what would happen."

Lily hung her head and mumbled, "I should've sent Pete away the second I saw him at my door. Then none of this would've happened."

Wilma didn't know what Lily was talking about, but she knew one thing. "It's not your fault." She put her hand over Lily's. "It's Jerry's. You should call the police."

Lily's head jerked up. "No. He never laid a hand on me, I swear."

"He still hurt you. I can't send you back to that house—"

"Miss Wilma, you don't understand. I have nowhere else to go. He's made sure of that."

"You could stay here."

"He would come."

"Let him." Wilma waved a hand. "I've turned him away before."

"I can't let you get hurt. I can't let you support me. I need to figure this out on my own."

"But you're not on your own, dear. You have friends who care about you. Who want to help. There must be something—"

"I have a plan." Lily lifted her head and met Wilma's eyes. "You've already helped more than you know by hiring me for this job. I just need a little more time to put away enough money."

The mention of money made Wilma stiffen. If only she could write a check and solve Lily's problems. But how much would it take? She already owed so much. She thought of Rachel and the resignation in her voice. *"I think you're writing enough checks every month as it is."*

"I've sold a few things secretly that Jerry doesn't know about," Lily continued. "Items I've picked up here and there. I'm getting close."

Wilma stilled as her son's question about her cashmere cardigan returned unbidden to her mind. *"Have you asked Lily if she's seen it?"* No. Lily would never steal from her. The young lady was in a desperate situation, however. People often did unseemly things in desperate situations.

"What kinds of items? Clothing perhaps?"

Lily's forehead wrinkled. "Sometimes. Mostly things I find at the thrift store that people don't realize are valuable."

"I see." Wilma considered asking more questions but shook her head. She should only think the best about her friend. "What if you had more cleaning jobs?"

Lily stared at her hands. "I don't know . . ."

"My friend Gladys, remember her? She could hire you. And Edna too."

Lily's tone was skeptical. "Are they looking for a cleaner?"

Wilma huffed. "They will be soon."

"I don't want charity, Miss Wilma."

"Nonsense. They would be lucky to have you. They'll never know how they got by without you. Let me talk to them."

Lily looked unsure, yet there was a spark of hope in her eyes.

"Leave it to me, dear." Wilma nodded, already planning what she would say to her friends. None of them were wealthy—no one in Sleeping Grass was—but perhaps together they could make a difference. "Now, what's all this about Pete at your house, hmm?"

The young lady blushed, and Wilma's heart warmed. Even Herb wouldn't have objected to her so-called meddling in this case, she was sure. The thought of her husband made her smile inside, though another thought worried her. If it happened that Lily left Jerry—and Wilma certainly hoped it would—how far away would Lily have to go?

thirty

When Pete arrived home Thursday after work, he let Pearl out of the Dodge and leaned over the side of the truck bed to peer at his latest find. The bike would need a lot of work. Both tires were blown out and there was no seat, not to mention the sparkly pink swirls that would need to be painted over. But when Pete had seen it leaning against the trash bin at 713 East Fourth Street, he'd known immediately it was for Braedon.

It hadn't been an option to load the bike into the Xpeditor and drive it around all day—Pearl would've staged a mutiny if he even tried—so he had tucked it away behind a bush in the alley and returned for it after he finished his route. Now if he could just keep it hidden from Braedon until it was ready.

By the time he stowed the bike under a tarp in the shed, Windy Ray was pulling up to the house on his big red tricycle. He parked next to Pete's truck and carefully dismounted, picking up the oxygen tank with his left arm and Apisi with his right.

"I'm hungry."

Pete jerked his chin at the house. "I don't know what all

Dani's been cooking up in there, but I'm sure there will be plenty."

"Is Wilma here yet?"

"Not yet."

Pearl was waiting at the door, impatient to get inside. Pete let everyone in and smiled at the smells coming from the kitchen. He was still getting used to having such a wonderful thing as dinner waiting for him when he came home from work. It only happened when Dani wasn't working the evening shift, but still, he didn't take it for granted.

Pearl headed straight for Braedon, who was waiting in the living room. Braedon knelt so he could hug her around the neck.

Windy Ray watched the reunion with a thoughtful expression. "You're no longer her favorite, I see."

Pete hung up his coat and grumbled, "I'm still the one who pays for her food."

Windy Ray set Apisi on the floor. She ran over to her porcine friend and sniffed around all the most embarrassing places, then yipped at the laces on Braedon's shoes.

Braedon stood. "Windy Ray, I've got something to show you." He started toward the hall and waved an arm. "Come on."

Windy Ray ambled after him, followed by Pearl and Apisi, and Pete chuckled to himself. The other day, Pete had taken Braedon to the creek to throw rocks, and Braedon had found one with unique markings that he'd been dying to show Windy Ray. Pete wondered if he should be offended that his pig and his nephew were both more interested in hanging out with someone other than him, but he didn't feel offended. He felt . . . well, like a blessed man, truth be told.

He was about to head to the kitchen to see if Dani needed any help when there was a dainty knock at the door. He hurried to open it.

"Hi, Wilma. Thanks for coming."

She beamed as she shuffled into the house. "I wouldn't miss it, dear. Not for anything. This is quite the treat for an old woman like me. Something smells delicious."

"I can't take any credit." He helped her with her coat, and she glanced around the house with a sharp eye.

"It's tight quarters around here for the three of you, hmm?"

"Four, if you count Pearl. But we manage."

"I see." She leaned closer to him and lowered her voice. "Now, I've got some news about Lily."

Pete stiffened. Dani had wanted to invite Lily tonight, too, but after Pete told her about his encounter with Jerry on Monday, they decided it wouldn't be a good idea. He wished she were here, though.

"Is she okay?"

Wilma eased herself down onto the couch. "She will be soon, I think. Gladys and Edna have agreed to hire her on—isn't that wonderful? She'll be able to earn more money."

Pete remembered what Dani had said about Lily's money. She gave most of it to Jerry and had to lie about the amount so she could hide some away for herself. Would Jerry agree to Lily taking on more jobs?

"Don't look so worried." Wilma patted his hand. "Everything's going to work out."

He wasn't so sure. Jerry's scowling face flashed in his mind, but he didn't want to get into all that with Wilma. "What about you? Have you worked out the problem with your property taxes?"

She clucked her tongue. "It barely even qualifies as a problem. Don't give it another thought."

"But I heard you can lose your house if you don't pay. Someone else can pay the taxes and take the house if you don't pay them back."

Wilma looked a bit surprised. Pete hated to add to her worries, but Con's story about his friend compelled him to continue. "A friend of mine said there are programs available for older folks who need help. Financial-assistance programs that can get your taxes reduced. I could help you get signed up."

"That's very kind of you, dear, but I'm already enrolled in a financial-assistance program. They're helping me sort everything out."

Relief washed over him. "That's great."

"Yes, so you can put it out of your mind."

A happy squeal caught their attention, and they both turned toward the hall to see a boisterous procession headed their way. Pearl was in the lead, followed by Apisi, Braedon, then Windy Ray.

Wilma smiled. "Hello, everyone. How lovely to see you all."

Windy Ray's face lit up, and he walked faster. When he reached the couch, he stuck his hand into his pocket, and Pete rolled his eyes. Not again.

Windy Ray pulled out a reddish-colored rock. It had a stripe of white around the middle and was shaped roughly like a heart. He held it out to Wilma.

She lifted it gently from his palm as if it were made of fine china instead of sediment and iron. "Why, thank you, Raymond."

He bowed. "My heart is in your hands."

Oh boy. Pete exchanged a look with Braedon, who was making a funny face but managed to keep from laughing out loud. Thankfully, before Windy Ray could embarrass himself any further, Dani poked her head out of the kitchen.

"Dinner's ready."

Braedon pumped a fist. "Yesss. Finally."

As they all made their way into the kitchen and crowded around the tiny table on mismatched chairs he'd rescued from the dump, Pete smiled to himself. How many times had he sat at this table alone, eating soup from a can or a frozen dinner? Talking to a pig and turning up the volume on the TV to drown out the loneliness? And now?

Walt Whitman's words sprang to his mind: *"Happiness . . . not in another place but this place, not for another hour but this hour."* Pete had read Whitman's *Leaves of Grass* several times, but now the words meant something to him they'd never meant before. If only Lily were here, "this hour" would be one of the happiest of his life.

Wilma pulled her heavy coat on slowly, not wanting the evening to end. What a blessing it was to spend time with friends. What a gift the Lord had given her by bringing Pete back to Sleeping Grass and showing her what a fine man he had become. And to think she'd never even dreamed of getting to see Dani again, and Rosie's grandson, too. To think Rosie would never meet Braedon.

Wilma knew she didn't deserve all of this, but she was thankful anyway. "My goodness, it was the best meal I've had in a long time." She grasped Dani's hands. "Thank you so much."

"It was my pleasure. I hope you'll come again."

"Oh!" Wilma hugged her. "What a dear."

She said goodbye to Braedon and Raymond, and Raymond caught her eye and held it. His smile was different from Herb's—it had a seriousness behind it she wondered about—yet she found it very pleasant. She'd never expected to enjoy his company so much.

He bowed. "I'll count the days until I see you again."

"My." She put a hand to her cheek. "I hope it won't be too many, then."

His dark eyes widened and danced. "I hope that, as well."

She remembered his rock and stuck a hand into her pocket to make sure it was there before turning to Pete. "Would you mind walking an old lady to her car?"

He opened the door and offered his elbow. "Of course not."

Outside, the sun was about to set. She thought of all the evenings she and Herb had watched the sun go down together and took a deep breath. She missed him.

"I don't suppose you'd be able to take me back to that phone place in Shelby next Wednesday, would you?"

Pete helped her navigate the walk like a true gentleman. "Sure. Have you made up your mind?"

She had, but not about a phone. She'd decided to ask Lily to help her at the phone place, as well. She would tell Lily she needed her to choose for her. She would insist on it. Then she would make an excuse to stay home and let Pete drive Lily to Shelby without her tagging along.

"Yes. I've made up my mind."

"All right, I'll come by around three if that works."

"That works perfectly."

They reached the Corolla, and Pete cleared his throat. "Do you want me to drive you home? It's no trouble."

"Nonsense. I can drive a few short blocks."

He seemed unconvinced, but he nodded. "Okay."

He opened the car door for her, and she slid her cane in first before lowering herself onto the driver's seat. Despite her words of confidence, she was glad she was going to get home before dark. In years gone by, she would drive home from Great Falls at night, snow pelting the windshield, without blinking an eye. Now, even getting around Sleeping Grass was a chore. How much longer before Michael put his foot down and took her car away?

Pete stepped away from the Corolla and waved. "See you next week."

She waved back. "Bye now."

The street was still and empty except for a little black truck with big wheels parked under a cottonwood tree that shrouded the truck in shadow. She drove slowly and made wide turns until she had the Corolla back in her garage. Once inside the house, she let out a long breath. The house always seemed quieter after she'd been somewhere. After she'd been reminded of what it was like to be surrounded by voices and laughter.

It would be nice to go down and stay with Michael for a couple of weeks this summer. She'd almost forgotten the joy of family time, but tonight's supper at Pete's had made her long for her kids. Why hadn't she made more of an effort to visit them?

It was partly because traveling *anywhere* from Sleeping Grass was difficult. Eternally long stretches of lonely road if one should drive. Expensive flights with long layovers if one should fly out of Great Falls. But it was also because every time she was with her family, she was reminded of Pete and Dani, separated and without a mother. Of Pete being passed around, unwanted. Of calling the social worker and saying, *"No, I'm sorry, it's just not going to work for us to take them,"* and then going about her life as if they hadn't been counting on her.

Guilt had been a persistent and disagreeable companion. Things seemed to be turning around for Pete now, however, and since he and Dani had been reunited, Wilma could be reunited with her children, right? It had been far too long since she'd seen them.

Money also had been an issue the past few years, of

course, but she hoped she would hear from Sadie at FAS soon so she could make her travel plans.

The kitchen table was bare because she had moved all her papers and bills to her bedroom after Pete had seen her property-tax letter. As she sat down in her favorite chair, the papers were merely out of sight, not out of mind. It had been sweet of him to be concerned about her, but she should be the one concerned about him. She had a duty to ensure he was well situated and happy. She owed it to him.

She tapped her cane against the floor. Owing others was something she was all too familiar with. She had mailed her final FAS payment this morning and had only to be patient a few more weeks.

The phone rang, startling a high-pitched yelp out of her. She put a hand to her chest. *Goodness*. It wasn't eight o'clock, so it wouldn't be Michael on the phone. Who could it be?

She shuffled to the dresser and pressed the talk button on the receiver. "Hello?"

"Hey, Mom, it's me."

Her heart swelled. "Rachel. How wonderful to hear from you. How are you? How's your new job? How's school going for Tom?"

Rachel laughed. "One thing at a time, Mom. Everything's fine."

"You must be so busy."

"Yes. And now all of Callie's graduation stuff is ramping up. I can't believe my baby's going to be moving out and going to college. It doesn't seem possible."

Wilma knew that feeling all too well. "It's amazing how quickly life changes. Is she excited about graduating?"

"I can hardly get her to slow down long enough to talk to me, but yes, I think so. That's what I wanted to talk to you about."

"Oh?"

"I know you told Michael you would come visit this summer, but we were thinking if you came down at the end of May, you'd be here for Callie's graduation and her party and everything."

Wilma gripped the receiver. May was rapidly approaching, but surely she would have everything squared away with her finances by then, right?

"When is the graduation?"

She hadn't yet received an invitation. While Michael and her business-minded son, Steven, always organized their lives down to the smallest of details, Rachel had never been one to plan ahead.

"The last day of May, but I think we're going to have the party the Sunday before. Or maybe the Sunday after."

"I see." Wilma told herself not to be frustrated at Rachel's indecision. It didn't matter which Sunday the party was scheduled for, she would be as available one week as the next. "Well, I think that could work, dear. I'll need to talk to Michael."

"Great." Rachel sounded pleased. "Callie will be happy. Hey, did you ever find that sweater?"

Wilma winced. Michael must have mentioned the sweater to Rachel. She tried to keep her voice light. "Oh, it's around here somewhere, not to worry."

"Lily comes every week, right? Maybe she could help you look for it."

Wilma didn't like her daughter's tone. Michael must be souring Rachel toward Lily. How could her children think so poorly of her judgment that they would assume she didn't know whom she could trust? Then again, she'd kept many things from them, and she'd wondered about Lily herself. Would she steal from her? Wilma would've happily given the cardigan to her if she would've asked.

"Yes, Rachel, I'm sure she'll help me look. It'll turn up."

There was a long pause before Rachel finally said, "Okay."

After they'd said their goodbyes, Wilma brushed her teeth and changed into her nightgown. She looked at the picture by her bed with a sigh.

"It's hard getting old, Rosie."

She thought of her kids and Rosie's kids, all grown up now. She thought of all Rosie had missed. Life was such a strange and wonderful thing.

It was time to tell Pete about his mother. She knew that. It had been in the back of her mind the whole evening as she watched him talk and joke with his friend and nephew and make his sister blush with his praise of her cooking. After he returned from Shelby with Lily on Wednesday, after Lily had gone home, she would tell him.

"'Rosemary, Rosemary, cheeks like a cherry. Eyes like the moon, what a treasure you are.'"

She sang the song under her breath as she turned off the light and climbed into bed, but her heart wasn't in it. The real treasure had been right there under Rosie's nose the whole time, and she'd missed it. Thrown it away. Even Wilma hadn't seen it for what it was at the time. She'd mistaken the treasure for a burden.

She could see it now. Oh, how much easier it was to look back using the lens of time and see the coarse grains of sand would someday be pearls.

thirty-one

Pete and Braedon were on their own for dinner Sunday night because Dani had to work an extra shift to cover for a sick employee. After much deliberation, they had decided to open a bag of Doritos and nuke frozen mini-pizzas in the microwave. Real gourmet stuff. They also sliced an apple in case Dani asked if they'd eaten anything besides junk food.

Pearl had somehow managed to eat most of the apple herself.

Braedon's face was covered in orange powder from the chips as he helped Pete clear the table. "Why's it called Sleeping Grass?"

Pete picked up the dishrag. "Windy Ray says it's because the wind is always bending the prairie grass so it looks like it's lying down. Like the prairie is sleeping."

"Oh. I don't want to go to school tomorrow."

Pete held back a sigh. This had been an ongoing issue since the fight and suspension. "I know, buddy, but you have to."

"Why?"

"You've missed enough school already, that's why. You know, avoiding your problems won't make them go away."

"My mom's doing it, so why can't I?"

Pete folded the top of the chip bag and clipped it with a clothespin. He thought preschoolers were the ones who asked *why* about everything, not eleven-year-olds. "Your mother's not avoiding anything."

"She's avoiding my dad."

"What makes you say that?"

"Why else would we come all the way up here? We're almost in Canada."

Pete knew it was because they had nowhere else to go. He knew Dani and Braedon had needed somewhere to stay for a while to figure out what they were going to do. But if Braedon didn't know any of that, Pete sure wasn't going to be the one to tell him.

"To see me and Pearl, that's why." He winked.

Braedon didn't seem to buy it, but he kept his thoughts to himself and started sweeping the floor. Dani had stipulated from the beginning that Braedon would help with chores around the house, but at first the boy had seemed terrified to do so. Once he'd realized he wasn't going to get yelled at for tying the garbage bag wrong or missing a crumb on the counter, however, he and Pete had become a good team. Dani did the food planning and buying and making, while Pete and Braedon were the cleanup crew.

Pete had no complaints about the arrangement. "Soon as you're done with that, I've got something to show you outside."

"Okay."

Pete sidestepped Pearl, who liked to make cleaning up as difficult as possible, and headed for the front door. The other day, when he'd checked the forecast for the upcoming week—sunny and upper fifties through Friday—he'd decided to get Braedon's bike ready over the weekend so Braedon could ride it to school.

Pete already had a bike seat in the shed he'd saved from the trash months ago. When he'd driven to Shelby for bike tires, he'd come up empty. Thankfully, Norman's Outdoor Sports in Cut Bank had come to the rescue. It was an hour's drive from Sleeping Grass, but it beat a trip to Great Falls. And Tim, expert waste-management specialist for the town of Cut Bank, had happened to be at Norman's buying a softball glove for his daughter. They'd spent forty-five minutes talking trash.

As for painting the bike, Windy Ray had told him to ask Sunny. Pete had been skeptical that she could help, but it turned out her cousin had an auto-body shop that handled custom paint jobs. He was happy to take Braedon's bike from sparkly pink to midnight blue with silver thunderbolts in exchange for a dozen apple-streusel bars from Sunny's. Pete couldn't wait for Braedon to see it.

He wheeled the restored bike out of the shed but kept it covered under a tarp. It was a nice night, cold but clear. While the Hi-Line was still largely barren and lifeless, the first hints of spring could be found, if a person knew where to look. Like a daffodil poking up through the ice.

The front door squeaked open, and Braedon and Pearl came tumbling out of the house. Braedon was laughing. "What's under the tarp?"

Pearl trotted over and sniffed at it.

Pete waved an arm. "Why don't you pull it off and see?"

Braedon's face was eager as he tore off the tarp. His eyes grew big. "Is this for me?"

Pete nodded. Braedon's jaw dropped as he stared at the bike. He ran over and threw his arms around Pete's waist. "Thanks, Uncle Pete."

Pete stiffened at first, his arms out to the sides. In the two months his sister and nephew had been here, he'd never hugged Braedon. He couldn't remember the last time he'd hugged anyone. But after a second, he let his arms encircle his nephew and squeeze.

"You're welcome, buddy. I thought now that it's getting nicer, you could ride it to school."

Braedon pulled away and grabbed the handlebars. "I really like it, but I still don't want to go to school."

"I know. Have you apologized to Cole yet?"

"Yeah. Sort of."

"Sort of? What did you say?"

"I said, 'Sorry I hit you' and walked away."

It was more than Pete had said to those he'd hit, even when Dani had begged him to apologize to her creeper high school boyfriend. "I'm proud of you."

"Tyson won't talk to me."

"That's his loss."

Braedon straddled the bike and ran his hand over the painted thunderbolts. "Did you say sorry to the people you hurt?"

"No, but I should have."

"Why didn't you?"

"Well . . ." Pete paused, wanting his answer to be a good one. "Partly because I didn't have anyone in my life at the time telling me I should. And partly because I wasn't sorry—I thought it was their fault for making me mad. I didn't want to take responsibility for my actions."

Braedon looked up from the bike, his expression inscrutable.

"But those days are over," Pete continued. "I'm not a fighter anymore because now I know it's not worth it. It never gets you anywhere. And I want you to promise me you're not going to be a fighter anymore either."

"My dad says sometimes you have to put a man in his place."

The words made Pete squirm. What kind of behavior had Braedon's dad justified using those words? Like Pete was one to criticize. After everything he'd done, he wasn't any better of a role model. He could only hope to be one in the future, to keep trying every day he was fortunate enough to have Braedon in his life.

He spit in his hand. "Let's shake on it."

Braedon eyed Pete's hand warily before climbing off the bike. He stood in front of Pete.

Pete reached out. "I solemnly swear, no more fighting."

A timid smile slowly spread across Braedon's face. He brought his hand to his mouth and looked at Pete, eyebrows raised. When Pete gave him an encouraging nod, Braedon spit.

"I solemnly swear, no more fighting."

They shook hands, and their saliva sealed the deal. Braedon giggled and said, "Ew." Pearl wedged herself between them and squealed.

Pete wiped his hand on his jeans. "Do you know what time it is now?"

Braedon shook his head.

"Time for you to take your bike for a test ride."

His nephew whooped and was disappearing down the street before Pete could shout at him to be careful. He crossed his arms over his chest with a shake of his head. Dani was going to lecture him about not giving Braedon a helmet, but for now he'd let the boy enjoy his moment.

After a few minutes, Braedon came riding back and passed the driveway waving and pedaling furiously. Pete's heart swelled.

Take a boy and a dark blue bike
Throw them together and you might
Make him laugh
Make him smile
Make him forget
For a while
That not everything's as easy as
Spinning wheels at night.

thirty-two

Wilma tried to read the clock through blurred vision. It must be almost three. Pete would be here any minute.

"Ohhh." She rubbed her temples. "Fiddlesticks."

As it turned out, she would not need a fabricated excuse to get out of accompanying Pete and Lily to Shelby this afternoon. The stabbing pain in her head was all too real.

"I know what you would say, Herb, but that stuff tastes awful."

Her husband had sworn by ginger tea for headaches.

There was a knock at the door, and she gave a feeble "Come in" from the couch, hoping whoever it was would hear, but the door didn't budge. After a moment, there was another knock, and she groaned. She didn't want to stand up.

"Hello?" The door cracked open, and Pete's misshapen nose poked into the house. "Wilma?"

"Yes, I'm here." She waved a hand. "Come in."

He stepped inside and frowned. "Are you okay?"

"I'm afraid I've come down with a bad headache. I think you and Lily are going to have to go to Shelby without me."

"What are you talking about?" Lily appeared in the doorway, startling Pete. "Are you okay, Miss Wilma?"

"Yes, yes. Goodness' sake, everyone needs to stop asking me that. I've just got a headache and will be staying home today."

Pete looked at Lily, then turned to Wilma with a question on his face.

"I asked Lily to come along." Wilma's voice was strained from the pain. "I want her to choose for me."

Lily bustled over to Wilma's side and took her hand. "We can reschedule. You need to rest."

"Of course I need to rest. That's why I'm staying here and you're going with Pete."

"But—"

"No buts. I need a cellphone for my safety. Tell her, Pete."

Pete's cheeks reddened. "Actually, it was Lily's idea to begin with."

Wilma chuckled despite her discomfort. "Oh, you two. I should've known."

"I don't want to leave you here like this." Lily's eyes were filled with concern, but truth be told, Wilma didn't think Lily looked much better off than she did. Her face was pale and drawn.

"Nonsense. I'll be fine, and I will look forward to hearing all about the phone you pick out. Maybe next week we can go to Great Falls and pick it up."

Lily looked over at Pete, who responded with a slight shrug. They clearly didn't know what to do, so she decided to take the commanding approach.

"Close those curtains on your way out, please. And lock the door. I'll see you in a couple hours."

She felt a bit like Gladys, bossing people around like that, but it worked. Lily closed the curtains, and Pete turned the lock on the doorknob.

He looked at Lily. "Is it all right if we take my truck, then?"

Her voice was quiet. "It's fine with me."

They both glanced back at Wilma one last time and hesitated, but she flicked her wrist and mustered as big a smile as she could. "Bye now."

When they were gone, she sank back into the couch with a groan. Of all the rotten luck. She couldn't even enjoy the success of her scheme due to the pounding in her head. She needed to rest so she'd be ready to talk to Pete later. She couldn't put it off any longer.

She remembered Gladys's words. *"Anyone who wants to tell the truth must be brave."* She didn't feel brave, yet she'd prayed fervently for courage. For wisdom. For the right words to say. She'd even dared to pray that God would soften Pete's heart toward her and help him understand that she'd never meant to hurt him. Never meant for him to suffer.

She certainly hadn't prayed for a headache, but if this was a test of her commitment, she was determined to pass it. Right now, however, she would close her eyes for a few minutes and be feeling better in no time. Everything was going according to plan.

Pete hadn't expected to see Lily today. He was completely unprepared. He hadn't brought a hat to cover up his bald spot. He hadn't cleaned his truck. Maybe they should've taken the Corolla, after all. But he couldn't leave his truck at Wilma's house. Jerry would know Lily had gone there, and if he or one of his buddies saw Pete's truck . . . It was too risky.

"Where's Pearl?"

Pete looked over at Lily and tried to act normal, though his blood was pumping unusually fast. "I left her at home."

"I thought she couldn't be left alone."

He nodded. "It's just for half an hour. Braedon will be home from school at three-thirty. I'm hoping for the best."

Yes, he was hoping against all hope that Pearl wouldn't make him regret his decision.

Lily shook her head. "Oh, Pearl."

"I gave her a stern talking to about being on her best behavior."

One side of Lily's mouth lifted. "Then I'm sure you have nothing to worry about."

Pete laughed. It did worry him. Immensely. He'd never left Pearl alone for more than a few minutes, but Braedon had begged to play with Pearl after school, assuring Pete that he'd ride his bike home as fast as he could. "Not *too* fast," Pete had warned and handed him a helmet.

They drove in silence for several miles. Pete wanted to explain to Lily why he hadn't left any Skittles the past two Mondays, but he didn't know how to do that without bringing up Jerry, which was the last thing he wanted to do.

"Do you think Miss Wilma's all right?" Lily asked.

"I don't know. She acts tough."

"I'll need to hurry home when we get back, but you'll stay with her and make sure everything's okay, won't you?"

"Yes. I promise."

"You didn't know I was coming today, did you? I didn't know you were coming either."

Pete's eyebrows shot up. "She didn't tell you I was going to drive?"

Lily chuckled. "I assumed *she* was going to drive, but I guess she never actually said that. I should've known, I'm sorry."

"Don't be sorry. I'm glad you came."

It was true. He'd been dying to talk to Lily ever since his confrontation with Jerry, but he'd had no way to do it. He'd hoped Dani could talk to her, at least once she finished reading *Peace Like a River*, but she was only halfway through the book. It had been all he could do to keep from hounding her to read faster. He could only imagine how badly she'd tease him if he did.

Lily didn't respond to his statement. Instead, she started asking questions about Braedon and Windy Ray and Pete's job. He let her control the conversation, content to just be in her presence, though part of him wondered if her questions were covering up what she really wanted to say.

Their time at the faux phone store had gone by quickly. Pete had watched with admiration as Lily interrogated the salesclerk until she was confident about which phone and plan would be the most cost-effective for Wilma but still meet her needs. The clerk placed the order and told them they could pick it up in Great Falls the day after tomorrow.

Pete had offered to buy Lily a cupcake from D' Cake Lady before they headed back to Sleeping Grass, hoping to extend his time with her, but she'd politely declined, saying she needed to get back home.

It bothered him when she called Jerry's house *home*.

Shelby was fading from sight in the rearview when Lily started fidgeting. Pete kicked himself over driving the Dodge. He could've parked it somewhere else and taken the Corolla. The Corolla was far more comfortable.

"Sorry about the seats in here." He kept his eyes on the road. "I'm used to riding with Pearl, and she never complains."

Lily stuck her hands under her legs and looked out the window.

"Not that you were complaining." He blurted out the words and felt his ears turning red. "And not that I'm comparing you to a pig. I just meant . . . oh, fig on a twig, I'll stop talking now."

He shouldn't have opened his mouth. He glanced at her from the corner of his eye and saw her face pinch like she'd just received bad news.

"I'm sorry." Why did he keep talking? What was wrong with him? "I didn't mean—"

"I have to tell you something, Pete." She looked over at him, then down at her lap. "And it's something that's hard for me to say."

Oh no. His chest constricted. His mind flew through a dozen possibilities, each one worse than the last. "Okay."

That was all he could say? *Okay?* He barely restrained himself from smacking the steering wheel in frustration.

She took a deep breath and hung her head. "I'm pregnant."

The road, stretching out like a gray ribbon through the plains, continued to disappear under the wheels of the Dodge, but Pete's world came to a standstill. *Pregnant?* How could—? What was—? Why did she—?

"Jerry doesn't know, and I can't let him find out." Her voice held an edge that Pete hadn't heard before. "I need your help."

He swallowed hard. He'd known she and Jerry lived together, but somehow he'd managed to keep himself from imagining Jerry touching her like . . . *that*. How could he possibly help her?

"Okay." *Okay* again, ugh. He sat up straighter and steeled himself. He had to do better than that. Lily needed him. "Yes. Anything. What do you need? What can I do?"

She didn't answer for a minute. Two minutes. His hands grew sweaty. Finally, she spoke, and it sounded like the kind of rain that falls on a dismal, gray day in February.

"I need you to drive me to the clinic in Great Falls."

Yes, that made sense. She couldn't go to the doctor in Sleeping Grass or Jerry would find out. Even Shelby was too close, but what about Cut Bank? It would be closer than Great Falls, at least.

"Isn't there a—" oh boy, what was the word for it?—"a baby doctor in Cut Bank?"

She turned toward her window. "I don't need that kind of doctor. I need the other kind."

Other kind? Pete's brow furrowed. What other kind?

Oh.

His heart twisted. *"I can't let him find out,"* she'd said. There was only one way to make sure Jerry never found out. Pete's stomach twisted. She must be so afraid.

"Please, Pete." Her voice was nothing but a vapor now. A mist. "There's no other way."

Pete used to wonder why he loved poetry so much. What it was about it that drew him in. Over the years, he'd realized it was because it took things that were untouchable, intangible, and formed them into something he could hold in his hands. Something he could make sense out of or go back to again and again until it did. But there were some things too vast and immeasurable to be confined to language. Even the most intricate of words and the most competent of poets had limits.

He slowly reached over and rested his hand beside Lily, palm up, heart exposed. "I want to help you."

She hesitated only a moment before placing her hand in his, and it was like grasping a moonbeam. He held on tight, his spirit crying out inside him with utterances far beyond human words, and he knew.

There was no poem for this.

thirty-three

A noise startled Wilma awake with a snort. Goodness, she was worse than Pearl. How embarrassing. What time was it?

The noise came again, and she realized someone was knocking at the door. She squinted at the clock. Was she expecting company?

"Wilma, it's Pete. Is everything okay?"

Oh, Pete and Lily must be back. Confound it all, she shouldn't have told him to lock the door earlier. With a grumble, she pushed herself to her feet and leaned heavily on her cane. Her head swam, and her throat hurt.

"I'm coming." The words came out as little more than a croak. She cleared her throat as she reached the door and unlocked it. Her nap hadn't helped at all. She must've caught a bug somewhere.

Pete opened the door cautiously. "Wilma?"

"Yes, dear, I'm here. I was just resting on the couch."

His eyes widened in alarm. "You sound terrible."

"Why, thank you." She meant it wryly, but the words fell flat as Pete put his hand under her elbow.

"Let's get you off your feet." He helped her back to the couch and frowned when a moan of misery escaped her lips. "Can I get you anything? I can make you some tea."

She couldn't even laugh. "No tea. A glass of water would be lovely."

He hurried to the kitchen and returned with the water. "Do you have a fever? Maybe I should take you to the doctor."

"I'll be fine. Just a spring cold, I suspect." She tried to give him a reassuring smile, even though at her age catching a cold wasn't the harmless annoyance it used to be.

Pete appeared suspicious. "How about some chicken-noodle soup?"

"I'm fine, really. Where's Lily?"

Something changed in his face, but she was too tired and unsteady to figure out what it was.

"She had to get home. I dropped her off."

"Did she choose a phone for me?"

"Yes. We'll go get it when you're feeling better."

"That's very kind of you." She wanted to go on to say that Lily should ride down to Great Falls with them and did Wilma really need to tag along for that, but her throat protested. She took a drink of water, and her hand trembled.

Pete sat down beside her. "I think we should go to the doctor."

"I just need a couple Tylenol and a good night's sleep. I'll be right as rain in the morning."

"Where's the Tylenol? I'll get it for you."

She opened her mouth to say *nonsense* but closed it again. She was in no shape to go traipsing around the house if she didn't need to. "In the vanity in the bathroom."

He jumped up to retrieve it, and she held her wrist to the back of her neck. Yes, it seemed she might have a fever, but she was sure it was nothing serious. Pete returned and held out the Tylenol bottle.

"Thank you, dear."

She shook two pills into her hand and drank them down. The pressure in her throat was building with each swallow. It wasn't even suppertime yet and she wanted to go to bed. She thought of her light-headedness and the number of steps from the couch to her room and sighed.

"Would you help an old lady to bed, Pete?"

"I'd rather help you to the doctor."

She waved a hand weakly. "I'll be fine."

He hesitated, clearly unconvinced, but eventually put a hand behind her back and another on her elbow and helped her stand. "I'm going to come back in a few hours and check on you."

That won't be necessary, she wanted to say, but her throat wouldn't let her.

Together they shuffled down the hall. Despite her discomfort, Wilma had to chuckle to herself. How frustrating to make it through the whole winter without so much as a sniffle and then come down with a cold just as the weather was finally starting to turn around.

Once they'd entered the bedroom, a look of panic crossed Pete's face as they reached the side of the bed.

"Don't worry," she said. "I can do it myself."

She sat first, then pulled up her feet. Oh, the bliss of laying one's weary head on a familiar pillow. She reached a hand toward the foot of the bed. "If you could hand me that blanket."

He moved the golden chenille throw so she could reach it, then stepped back.

"Thank you, dear." She felt a little better already. "Now, I'm sure you have better things to do than . . ."

Her raspy voice fell away as she caught a glimpse of Pete's stricken expression. She might've taken it as concern for her well-being, except he wasn't looking at her. He was staring at the clock on her wall.

Oh dear. Rosie's Coca-Cola clock. The one thing Wilma had taken from Pete's old house when it was foreclosed on.

Her chest tightened. She was supposed to tell Pete about his mother today. All the thoughts and plans and practiced speeches she'd prepared came rushing back to her mind. She'd woken up disoriented and had forgotten all about it. Her head was a fuzzy muddle.

"Pete, I . . ."

His eyes moved from the clock to the picture on the dresser, and her breath caught. Though the clock continued to tick, time stood still. Or perhaps it rewound.

"That's my mom." There was no question in his voice, only shock. He looked at her, then back at the picture. "Is that you?"

She could only nod. The backs of her eyes began to hurt as tears formed. Why hadn't she told him the truth? Why had she thought she had any right to be part of his life now after refusing to be before? This was not the way she wanted him to find out.

He picked up the picture frame and stared at the photo. "You knew my mom? Why didn't you say anything? Do you know what happened to her?" He stiffened and looked at her with wide eyes. "Do you know where she is?"

That last part was spoken in a whisper that nearly tore Wilma's heart in two. "Pete, I'm so sorry."

There were many more things that needed to be said, but her voice cracked, her throat throbbed, and the room spun. Pete set the picture frame down carefully, reverently, and swiped a hand over his face. "You need to rest, Wilma," he said, confusion and pain and disappointment on his face. "We'll talk about this another time."

He looked at her as if she'd betrayed him in the worst way.

She supposed she had. *I never meant to hurt you*, she wanted to say. But emotion constricted her throat even more than it already was so that the words wouldn't come.

When she didn't answer, he turned his back to her and took three steps toward the door, his shoulders sagging. Then he stopped. "Dani will check on you tonight."

Tears fell sideways and onto her pillow as she lay motionless. She heard Pete's footsteps move through the house and then draw near again. She held her breath.

He entered the room. In his hand he held the landline phone, which he put on the dresser, where she could reach it. He looked one more time at the picture, then left the room and was gone.

Pete didn't see the houses he passed or hear the songs on the radio as he drove home. He saw only his mother's face, young and happy and beautiful. He heard only his mother's voice. Had she gotten that line about the wind from Thoreau? "*The morning wind forever blows, the poem of creation is uninterrupted; but few are the ears that hear it.*" Maybe she had loved poetry, too.

How could Wilma never have mentioned that they'd been friends? How could she never have shown him the photo and said, "Look, this is from the time your mom and I spent the day at the river." Or "This photo was taken the day your mom and I went shopping for your baby clothes." Or at the very least "Here, you should have this picture."

He didn't know what to think. His head had already been a jumbled mess when he entered Wilma's house because of Lily and what she'd revealed to him. Now the thought of Lily becoming a mother and the thought of his mother's picture on Wilma's dresser combined to form a lump in his throat he couldn't swallow.

How long had they been friends? How had Wilma ended up with that clock?

Anger began to fester deep in his soul. It lurched around indiscriminately, lashing out at him and at Jerry, then at Wilma, his mother, his social worker, his life. He pulled into his driveway in a cold and heavy fog of unanswered questions and opened his door.

"Uncle Pete." Braedon came running up, his face red. "It's all my fault. I'm sorry, I'm sorry, I'm sorry."

What now? Pete shook his head to clear it and looked closer at his nephew. His eyes were also red, his nose running. Alarm kicked in, and he hopped out of the truck. "What happened?"

"I looked everywhere. I even set out bananas and Snickers, but she never came back."

No. Not Pearl. *No, no, no, no.* "How did she get out of the house?"

Braedon sniffed and wiped his sleeve across his nose. "I wanted to show her my bike. I went for a ride, just a little one, that way"—he pointed to his left—"and when I came back, she was smiling and I waved. So then I went that way"—he pointed right—"and when I came back, she was gone."

Pete's jaw tensed. His voice rose sharply. "You were supposed to watch her. Why didn't you call me?"

"I thought I would find her. I thought she'd come back." His voice broke, and his body heaved. "I'm s-s-sorry."

"Darn it, Braedon." Something snapped in Pete's head, and he rammed his fingers into his hair and roared, "What were you thinking?"

Tears welled up in his nephew's eyes, and his chin quivered. Pete lowered his hands. Shoot. "Braedon, I . . ."

The boy spun around and fled, his sobs trailing behind him. Pete growled in frustration. How could this be happening? He should talk to Braedon, apologize for yelling at him, but Pearl could be anywhere and it would be dark soon. Where could she have gone? How far would she go? She'd never been on her own before.

He climbed back into the truck and slammed the door, determined to find Pearl.

The keys were still in the ignition. As he jerked the Dodge into drive and backed up, a seventy-nine-pound weight pressing down on his chest, he could only hope and pray that this day wouldn't get any worse.

thirty-four

By the time Pete returned to the house, it was late. He'd driven up and down every road and every alley, calling for Pearl. He'd enlisted Windy Ray's help, and his friend had ridden his tricycle all over town until it was too dark to see anything. There'd been no sign of her.

"She's a smart pig," Windy Ray had said. *"She'll be okay. Thank the Creator this didn't happen in February."*

Maybe Pete should be grateful it wasn't freezing cold outside tonight, but he couldn't muster up any thankfulness toward anyone, especially the Creator. The Creator who allowed Lily to get pregnant with Jerry's child. Who never brought his mother back to him. Who couldn't even keep one single potbellied pig safe. If everything the Creator made had value as Windy Ray claimed, why didn't He take better care of it?

He tossed his keys onto the coffee table with a loud clunk, and Dani gave him a wary look from the couch.

"Any luck?"

"No. How was Wilma?"

He'd asked Dani to check on Wilma when she got off work. Stopping at Wilma's added several extra blocks to Dani's walk home, but she hadn't hesitated to agree. Pete kicked himself for not buying a car for her by now. Just add it to the list of things he was failing at.

"She was asleep. She was breathing fine and seemed comfortable. I refilled the glass of water by her bed, felt her forehead, and locked the door behind me."

"Thanks." He hadn't told Dani about the picture. He knew she'd never recognize their mother in the photo. She'd told him she didn't remember her. He needed to talk to Wilma again before he mentioned anything to his sister. "Is Braedon in bed?"

Dani nodded. "He's really upset. He blames himself, but he's just a kid, you know."

Pete hung his head. "I know. I shouldn't have yelled at him."

"What are you going to do?"

He let out a long breath. "I don't know. I guess keep my eye out while I'm driving my route tomorrow. Windy Ray said he'd ride around town again."

She didn't answer for a moment, and he felt a pit open up in his stomach as he imagined Pearl alone and hungry somewhere. Wondering where he was. Wondering why he didn't come.

When Dani finally spoke, her voice had changed. "Do you think it's strange that she would run away like that?"

He narrowed his eyes at his sister's tone. "What do you mean?"

She picked at a nail. "I mean, has she ever done this before?"

"No."

"Why would she take off right before dinner? She's not the kind of pig who misses a meal. It doesn't make sense."

He was on the edge of the couch now, every muscle taut. "It's been a long day, Dani. Just tell me what you're trying to say."

"Jerry said he was going to be watching, right? He threatened you. Maybe . . ."

Pete's body went cold, then hot. He jumped to his feet and grabbed his keys. "I'll kill him. I'll kill him with my bare hands. I'll—"

Dani grabbed his arm. "Stop. We don't know anything for sure. And what about Lily? What will happen to her if you show up at her house throwing accusations around?"

Pete's heart continued to pound, but he set the keys down. "We could call the police. Ask them to search Jerry's house."

Dani tapped her chin, probably thinking through options Pete's brain would've taken hours to get around to. "If Pearl is at Jerry's house—and that's still a big *if* at this point—then she's safe. Lily would take care of her. And if Pearl's not there, sending the cops could be bad news for Pearl *and* Lily. I don't think we want to make Jerry mad or tip him off until we know more."

Pete threw up his hands and thought of the menacing way Jerry had looked at Pearl the day he cornered Pete in the Xpeditor. "How are we going to know more? It's not like I can call Lily and ask her."

"We'll have Wilma call her. Get Lily over to Wilma's house somehow."

"She's sick. I'm not sure we should involve her in this." He didn't know when he'd be ready to face Wilma again. There had to be another way.

Dani frowned. "I know, but maybe she'll be better tomorrow."

"Maybe she'll be worse."

"Pete." Dani shot him a look of exasperation mixed with pity. "We're getting nowhere. I think we should try to get some sleep and see what tomorrow brings. You never know, Pearl could be waiting at the front door when we wake up in the morning."

They both knew the chances of that happening were slim to none, yet Pete appreciated the thought. "Okay. You're right. I just . . ."

"I know." She put a hand on his shoulder. "I'm worried about her, too."

He got ready for bed, his stomach in knots. He'd missed dinner, but he couldn't eat knowing Pearl was out there somewhere, hungry. Maybe even with Jerry. The thought made sparks of red pop in his brain like fireworks.

As he lay in bed, loud and insistent voices shouted at him.

"We just can't deal with these behaviors anymore, Pete."

"I need you to drive me to the clinic in Great Falls."

"You stay away from her or you'll be sorry."

"I promise I will never yell at you, okay?"

The voices were jagged and sharp and rattled around in his mind like crushed stone, and the worst part was that there wasn't the faintest hint of a swiney snore to drown them out.

thirty-five

The hours passed with agonizing slowness as Pete drove his route, his thoughts jumping from Pearl to Lily to Wilma and back like pinballs. He had no bright ideas about what to do regarding any of those situations, but as he'd driven down alley after alley with Pearl's empty seat tormenting him, one thing *had* become clear.

He couldn't take Lily to the clinic in Great Falls.

He didn't want her to carry Jerry's child. Didn't want her tied to a man like that for the rest of her life. He especially didn't want to tell her no or let her down or lose her from his life. But Windy Ray had said everything the Creator makes has value, and a man must choose whether to see it.

Everything. Even if God wasn't going to look out for His creation, Pete still would.

He thought of Pearl in a pile of garbage, her bones nearly crushed by the compactor, her breath nearly snuffed out, and he gritted his teeth. He just couldn't do it.

Finally, *finally*, he drove the Xpeditor into the carport. He'd kept a sharp lookout all day. He'd gotten out of the truck both times he dumped a load at the landfill to walk around and call Pearl's name but hadn't seen hide nor wiry hair of her. He'd even lingered at Conrad Rountree's house so the crusty fellow would make an appearance and Pete could let him know Pearl was missing. *"Right shame,"* Con had said and promised to keep an eye out.

Pete hurried from the Xpeditor to the Dodge. Boy, he wished he didn't, but he needed Wilma's help. He stopped by Windy Ray's to see if he'd turned anything up during the day. He hadn't. Next, he pulled up in front of Wilma's yellow house. He didn't want to go inside, but every hour that passed without finding Pearl only brought her increased danger. Time was not on their side.

He knocked and opened the door. "Wilma?"

A frail voice responded, "In the kitchen."

It was an awkward reunion as he entered the kitchen and saw her sitting at the table. Yesterday's events stood between them, and he shifted on his feet. "Uh . . ."

"I'm feeling much better today." She sounded hoarse, but her color had improved. "Please, won't you sit down? We need to talk."

He didn't want to sit down. He didn't have time to unravel whatever mysteries were tucked away in Wilma's past. Pigs could start to become dehydrated after only two hours without water, and it had already been twenty-four hours since Pearl's disappearance. "I can't talk now."

"But I—"

"I need you to call Lily. Pearl is missing."

Wilma put a hand on her chest. "Oh my. What terrible news. You want Lily to help you look, hmm?"

He scratched the back of his head, unsure how much to tell her. "Something like that. Would you call her?"

"Of course." She nodded toward the phone, and he retrieved it for her.

As she dialed, he paced the floor, imagining horrible scenarios and then kicking himself for thinking the worst, and then bracing himself for it all the same.

"Hello, dear, it's Wilma."

He strained to hear the other side of the conversation, but he couldn't make out Lily's voice.

"Yes, much better, thank you, but we need your help. Can you come over?" A pause. "Pete." Another pause. "Mm-hmm. Wonderful, thank you." She hung up the phone and turned to him. "She's on her way."

He let out a breath, then stiffened. His truck. If Lily was coming here, he needed to hide it. "I've got to move the Dodge. I'll be right back."

He was out the door before Wilma could respond. He drove two blocks west, then turned down an alley to park. He walked the alley back to the yellow house and slipped through the gate into Wilma's backyard, feeling as if every pair of eyes in town was watching him.

Wilma didn't seem surprised when he came through the back door. "You must be worried sick."

He fidgeted, his nerves frayed. "Yes." And not just about Pearl. He was worried about Lily, too, more than he wanted to admit. What was she going to do?

"Pete, I know you must have questions for me."

He did. So many. But he'd already waited nearly forty years for answers. He could wait a little longer. "Right now, I just want to find Pearl and help Lily, okay?"

The wrinkles on her forehead deepened. "What's wrong with Lily?"

He looked at the floor. That was not his story to tell.

She folded her hands in her lap. "I apologize. Sometimes I'm too nosy for my own good."

The front door squeaked open. "Hello?"

Wilma's voice barely carried. "In the kitchen, dear."

When Lily appeared, Pete's throat went dry. She was so thin, but somehow there was a child growing inside her. It seemed impossible. He fought to keep himself from staring at her belly.

"I came as fast as I could." She looked at him. "Wilma said you needed my help."

"It's Pearl. She went missing yesterday and . . ." He glanced at Wilma and hesitated for a moment, but knowing he was running out of time, he finished the sentence. "And I was wondering if you knew anything about it."

Her face scrunched in confusion. "How would I know about Pearl missing?" Seconds later, realization dawned and she slumped into a chair. "You think Jerry had something to do with it." Lily's voice was flat and resigned.

Wilma gasped. Pete longed to say no, to reassure Lily, but the truth was there at the table with them. All three of them knew Jerry was capable of pignapping, and much worse.

Lily caught his eye. "When did it happen?"

"Yesterday. While we were gone. Braedon said she was in the yard when he rode his bike down the street, but when he came back, she was gone. It was almost dinnertime. It's unlikely she would've taken off on her own."

"I'm sorry, Pete," Lily said. "Jerry didn't say anything to me. I-I don't know where Pearl is." She looked as though she might burst into tears.

He wanted to snatch her up and hold her close and keep her from crying, but instead he folded his arms across his chest.

"He *was* really irritable last night," she managed to add. "Even more than usual. I thought it was because he ran out of his favorite beer and had to go to the gas station." She squared her shoulders and locked eyes with him. "What can I do to help?"

He waffled. What *could* she do? She certainly couldn't ask Jerry about it. In fact, it would be better for her to pretend she knew nothing of the situation. She was already in a precarious situation of her own.

"Perhaps the best thing for you to do is keep your wits about you," Wilma said. She sounded tired, but she nodded crisply. "Be on the alert for any clues."

"All right, I will." Lily nodded, then turned back to Pete. "Look, I don't know if Jerry did this or not, but there was this stray cat I talked him into taking in once. She was a tiny little thing and never caused any trouble, but every time he saw her, he would lunge at her and yell so she would be afraid of him. He thought it was funny. Then one day she was gone. He said the cat ran away, but there were scratches on his hands."

Pete's heart sank. What defense did Pearl have against Jerry? The poor pig didn't even have claws. Still, could Jerry have scooped her up and carried her off in the blink of an eye? Pearl was a heavy and cumbersome creature. What if she *did* just wander off on her own?

"We'll find her." Lily stood and grabbed a notepad and pen from beside the phone. "I'm writing down my phone number, but please"—she glanced at Wilma—"call me from here if you can, and only if . . ."

"I understand." He knew the risk she was taking and would never endanger her if he could help it. He'd have Dani call if he used his cell just in case. He wouldn't put it past Jerry to answer Lily's phone if he saw a number pop up he didn't recognize.

As Lily handed him the paper, their eyes met again. Unspoken words passed between them. There was so much he wanted to say, but not with Wilma listening.

Lily looked away. "I'd better get back now."

Wilma wanted to plead with Pete to stay a little longer, but she didn't. It would be useless. His thoughts were clearly consumed by questions of Pearl's whereabouts, plus Wilma hadn't missed the look that had passed between Pete and Lily. She might be ill, but she wasn't blind. Something had changed between them. Something had happened.

"What are you going to do?" she asked.

Pete paced the floor. "Whatever it takes."

"Desperate times call for desperate prayers. I will ask the Lord for Pearl's safe return." Though the words were sincere, they sounded trite to her. Pete probably had no use for her prayers. Had he spent years praying for Rosie's safe return, as she had? "I really am sorry."

She left it up to him to decide whether she was referring to Pearl or to her long-standing and willful withholding of information. Truth be told, she was deeply sorry about both things.

Pete nodded and slipped out the back door without so much as a backward glance. Perhaps Gladys had been right when she'd told Wilma to "let it be." There was no going back now, however. If only Herb were here.

Wilma's head still pained her, though not as badly as yesterday. Regardless, she braced her hands on the table and rose to her feet. She would not sit idly by while Pearl was missing, possibly even stolen. Thoughts of Gladys had given her an idea. If anyone could organize a search party for Pearl's rescue, it was her bold and intrepid friend. It was just the kind of thing Gladys would jump into with both size-eleven feet.

Wilma shuffled to the hall for her light jacket. It was sixty-one degrees outside, a heat wave by Hi-Line standards, and she felt she could finally wear the coat without a warm sweater underneath. She pulled the jacket off the hook and tried to slip it on.

What was this?

Her arm struggled to go through the sleeve, and she tugged on it in frustration. She didn't have time for this. She tried the other sleeve with no luck, then held the coat out in front of her and examined it.

A chuckle that irritated her raw and swollen throat bubbled up. It was her cashmere cardigan, stuck inside the jacket. It must have come off with the coat the last time she wore it and she hadn't even realized. She never should've suspected Lily. The sweater had been hanging in the hall this whole time.

"Hold on, Pearl." She separated the sweater from the jacket, pulled on the sweater, and picked up her car keys. "We're coming for you."

thirty-six

It felt wrong to be at Windy Ray's house without Pearl. For three years, she'd been Pete's constant companion. When he'd played his first game of Chickenfoot with Windy Ray, she was there. Every time he'd bought Raisinets for his friend, she was there. As he had waterproofed Apisi's booties one, two, three times, she had snuffled around his feet and rammed her head into his knees.

He'd let Dani know he wouldn't be home for dinner. Windy Ray and Apisi came out of the house and joined him in the truck. Without Pearl, it felt like there was unlimited space for three bodies. Apisi sniffed the seat and gave him a questioning look.

"I don't know where she is." He petted the top of Apisi's head. "Will you help us find her?" The dog gave a mournful and drawn-out coyote cry, and Pete thought that if he could make a sound that would convey what he felt in his heart, that would be it.

Windy Ray's face gave nothing away, but his voice was deep and thoughtful. "I don't know what I would do without Apisi. I have asked the Creator to open our eyes and show us what we do not yet see."

Pete didn't want to waste any time discussing what God's role might or might not be in all this, so he simply nodded and pulled onto the road.

The plan was to spend the evening hours canvassing Sleeping Grass yet again, stopping anyone they came across to ask if they'd seen anything. If Pearl had wandered off, she wouldn't be far from a source of food and water, and someone might've seen her. Maybe camped out behind the bar and grill or by the grocery store's dumpster. If Jerry had taken Pearl, however, she could be anywhere. Where would he take her if not his house? Where to hide a seventy-nine-pound pig?

The unthinkable prodded at Pete's mind with the bony finger of doom, but he refused to acknowledge its presence. Jerry couldn't have harmed her. She couldn't be . . . gone. He had to have stashed her somewhere to make Pete mad, maybe even draw Pete out.

Pete smacked the steering wheel with the palm of his hand. "If we don't uncover any clues in two hours, I'm going to track him down."

Windy Ray didn't have to ask whom Pete was referring to. He picked Apisi up with both hands and held her in front of his face and nodded. "We'll find her."

Pete wondered what it would be like to have faith like that. To look at this huge mess of a world and still believe in something bigger. Something that made every little thing somehow more than it was, even someone like him. He allowed himself, for a moment, to believe. They would find her.

Having his friend beside him gave him strength and caused a spark of hope to ignite in his spirit. Windy Ray spoke to God, after all. Emily Dickinson once wrote that "hope is the thing with feathers," but today hope had long raven hair and a three-legged dog.

Time was a funny thing. Two hours could start off slow like a freight train leaving the station, then pick up speed until it was hurtling faster and faster down the tracks. It could meander like a lazy river, steadily progressing but taking its time bending this way and that. Or it could just disappear like a pile of dry grass set on fire, leaving nothing behind but the smell of smoke.

"It's almost dark," Windy Ray said.

Pete checked the time. Clenched and unclenched his fists. Inwardly scolded his stomach for grumbling about food at a time like this. "Let's start looking for his truck."

Jerry didn't limit his time at Arrow's to Friday nights. He'd been known to spend time there any day of the week. That would be the place to start.

Pete and Windy Ray had talked to many people, none of whom had anything helpful to tell them. Their most painful encounter had been with Sunny. Her blue eyes had misted over, and she'd offered him a huckleberry cream-cheese turnover. On the house. *"I'm so sorry, Pete,"* she'd said, her hand touching his arm. *"Let me know if there's anything I can do."*

He drove by Arrow's slowly, scanning the parking lot. Business didn't appear to be booming on this Thursday night in April, and the little truck with the big tires was nowhere in sight.

"I wonder if he frequents The Snorting Horse," Windy Ray said.

They drove by The Snorting Horse, Gunner's Griddle, and the gas station. They drove by Jerry's house and the HVAC office where he worked. No sign of the truck.

Windy Ray rested his hands on his knees and looked off into the distance. "Do you suppose he could be in Shelby?"

Pete stared at him. Of course. He should've thought of that sooner. Not only might Jerry be in Shelby, but Pearl might be there, as well. She couldn't have gotten to Shelby on her own, but she might've unwittingly hitched a ride there in a black Chevy S-10.

"You're a genius."

Windy Ray lifted one side of his mouth. "It has been said."

Pete compressed the thirty-minute drive to Shelby into twenty. As they entered the city limits, he briefly considered driving around to look for signs a pig had recently passed through but decided against it. Dusk was fading swiftly into twilight, and Pete was tired of searching. He didn't want to search anymore. He wanted answers.

There were several bars in Shelby. At the fourth one, they spotted the S-10.

"There it is." Pete jerked his chin toward the pickup.

Windy Ray's tone was matter-of-fact. "Yes."

"I'm going in there. You wait here."

He hopped out of the Dodge and marched toward the front of a squat brick building with the neon words *Waterin' Hole* glowing in the window. Both E's had burned out.

He put a hand on the door. In the twenty minutes it had taken him to drive here, he'd tried unsuccessfully to come up with a plan. Now that he'd arrived, he thought maybe plans were overrated. He didn't need a plan; he just needed to look Jerry in the face and ask him a question.

The inside of the Waterin' Hole was dim and smelled like a man who'd spilled beer on his shirt, then fallen asleep sprawled in a recliner in front of the TV. About a dozen folks milled around, some murmuring quietly into near-empty mugs, others laughing raucously as if there were voices they needed desperately to drown out. Pete knew from experience that would never work.

Pete scanned the room: a rickety-looking pool table in the corner, three TVs showing men's basketball, rodeo, and ax-throwing. Jerry had to be here somewhere.

He heard him before he saw him. "Hole-eee cow! Look

what the cat drug in. Strayin' kinda far from your garbage pile, don't you think?" Jerry's voice had the effect of fingernails on a chalkboard.

Pete shuddered and searched the murky depths of the bar. There. Jerry was coming out of the bathroom. As Pete drew a deep breath, he reminded himself he was here for information only.

He approached the scowling man. "What have you done with my pig?"

Jerry slapped the back of the man next to him and laughed. "Did you hear that? *My pig.*"

"I know you took her."

Jerry held his arms out wide. "Now, why the heck would I do that? Unless, of course, I was hungry." He made a broad gesture and shouted, "Anyone up for some tenderloin?"

Anger flared in Pete, but he tamped it down. Pearl was counting on him. "Just tell me where to find her, and I'll pretend this never happened."

Jerry's smile faded. He stepped closer to Pete and jabbed a finger into his chest. "If I took her, and I'm sayin' *if*, you ain't never gonna find her."

Pete swatted his finger away, his adrenaline spiking. "I swear—"

"If there's a problem, boys," the bartender called, "you can take it outside. I don't want any trouble in here."

Jerry raised both hands in a mocking way. "Don't shoot, Bert. I was just leavin'." He sniffed a couple of times and lowered his voice. "You smell like you been rolling around in the trash." He bumped Pete with his shoulder as he walked by and headed for the door.

Pete's blood was a river of lava in his veins, yet he forced images of Lily and Pearl into his mind to calm himself. They were both in danger. He couldn't do anything to jeopardize their safety.

He followed Jerry outside. Night had fallen, and clouds covered the moon. "Get away from that truck, Jerry. You're not going anywhere until you answer my question."

Jerry turned with a vicious glare. "Oh yeah? I got a question. You've been spending too much time breathing garbage fumes. I think it's starting to mess with your brain."

Pete moved closer, his eyes flicking over the bed of Jerry's truck for any sign of Pearl, his body trembling with barely contained rage. "That's not a question."

"Fine, here's one. That's your sister working at the gas station, right? How long's it been since she been with a real man? 'Cause I think I'd like to—"

His words were cut off by a hard shove. Pete looked at his hands. He hadn't meant to do that, but it had felt good.

Jerry lunged at him. "You're gonna regret that."

Their bodies made a muffled sound as they collided. Jerry had the advantage in size, but Pete had more experience. They wrestled on the ground for a minute before Pete landed a hard knee to Jerry's stomach and scrambled to his feet.

"Just tell me where she is."

Jerry jumped up, panting. "I don't know where your dumb pig is, but I hope she ends up on the butcher block where she belongs."

Pete's fist struck Jerry's face like lightning, and Jerry staggered back. Pete knew he shouldn't do it, but anger and adrenaline took over. *Bam*. Another punch to Jerry's face. *Thud*. A blow to his side. An old familiar battle cry burst from his mouth as he charged forward, lowering his shoulder and wrapping his arms around Jerry's waist. He slammed Jerry into the side of the S-10, then stepped back to let him fall.

Blood oozed from Jerry's nose, and his eyes darted wildly as he tried to draw in air after having it forcibly expelled from his lungs. Pete heard a growl that sounded like a small dog and stilled.

Apisi. Windy Ray. He stared at his hands again. *Oh no, what have I done?*

He'd made promises. He'd told Braedon he wasn't a fighter anymore. Promised Dani he wouldn't do anything stupid. Assured Lily she would be safe with him. Now she would see Jerry's face and know what Pete was capable of.

He took a step back. It had felt good to take Jerry down, righteous and just, but now regret overwhelmed him. He'd let everyone down, and fighting Jerry was like trying to fight his past. Futile and hopeless. He turned away, then back. Should he leave Jerry there? Should he call for an ambulance? How could he have done such a thing?

He turned away again and paced, breathing hard. How would he ever face his nephew after this? Or Dani or Lily? A scraping sound caught his ear, and he spun to look at Jerry. The man's right hand was pulled back, and it whipped forward, releasing something that sailed toward Pete.

Time was a funny thing. Two seconds could vanish in the blink of an eye or stretch like a rubber band, growing tighter and tighter until it snapped back to bite you. Pete jerked his body to the side and watched as a jagged rock the size of a child's shoe grazed his ear and flew by as if in slow motion. It rotated once, twice, then connected with a tall, lean figure with long raven hair.

Windy Ray crumpled to the ground silently, like a sheet falling from the clothesline to the grass, and Apisi began to bark.

thirty-seven

Pete had taken only one day off since moving back to Sleeping Grass. It had been his first summer, and he'd eaten dinner at Gunner's Griddle and spent the rest of the night puking his guts out from some bad chicken. Nate Harding, another town employee, had filled in for him and intimated afterward that he would rather not do that again.

Pete had done his best to oblige. He preferred sitting in the Xpeditor over sitting around his house anyway. But Friday morning at five, while it was still dark and the temperature was twenty-nine degrees, he called his boss from the Shelby hospital.

"Sorry to wake you, Clint, but I can't make it in today. Nate's going to have to cover my route."

Clint coughed, trying to clear the sleep from his throat. "What are you talking about? You sick?"

"No."

Clint waited.

Pete pressed his fingers between his eyes. "Call it an emergency or personal day or vacation, I don't care. I'm not going to be there."

After a moment of silence, Clint sighed. "Will you be back Monday?"

Pete wasn't sure, but he said, "Yes."

"All right."

Pete hung up the phone and went back into Windy Ray's room. It was dark, and a small lump at the foot of the bed stirred.

"Come on, Apisi." Pete scooped her up. "Let's go pee."

Quietly, he made his way outside. Windy Ray hadn't woken up since the rock struck him in the head. A couple of times he had started to thrash around and moan, causing the doctor to administer more sedatives. Windy Ray soon fell back into a deep sleep. It wasn't technically a coma, the doctor had explained. "*We want to bring down the swelling,*" he'd said, "*and give his brain a chance to heal.*"

The words had been spoken with confidence and optimism, but Pete had seen the concern etched into the lines of the doctor's face. He'd seen the nurse frown when she made her rounds to check vital signs.

This was all Pete's fault. Windy Ray was the best kind of friend to ever walk the earth, and Pete was the worst. He should've known better than to get close to anyone. He should've moved on from here before something like this could happen. Before he could screw it up and prove everybody in his past right about him.

He set Apisi down in the frosty grass to do her business. While she wasn't enthusiastic about getting her paws cold and wet, she quickly found a nearby bush and relieved herself. Back in the hospital room, Apisi circled twice next to Windy Ray's feet, then curled up into a ball. The hospital staff hadn't been happy about Pete or Apisi spending the night in the room. Only family was allowed, they'd told him. "*We are his family,*" Pete had responded. "*Go ahead and call security if you have to.*"

They hadn't.

Pete didn't know what had happened to Jerry. At some point, while Pete was kneeling beside Windy Ray's motionless body and calling 911, Jerry had climbed into his Chevy and driven off.

"Why'd you get out of the truck?" Pete whispered. "I told you to wait."

Oxygen pumped through the tube into Windy Ray's nose as monitors beeped and flashed. Pete had dozed off in the visitor's chair a couple of times during the night but otherwise hadn't slept. He'd never felt so alone, and he had no one to blame but himself.

Pearl had been missing for thirty-seven hours.

His phone buzzed, and he blinked at it bleary-eyed for a second before realizing it was a text from Dani. What was she doing up at this hour?

Are you awake?

His fingers were sluggish, but he managed to reply.

Yes. Why are you up so early?

Couldn't sleep. Too quiet around here. I've got your phone charger, some snacks, and a change of clothes. What else do you need?

Need? He rubbed his eyes, his brain processing slowly as a result of both exhaustion and regret. He wasn't the one in need. Wait, she was coming to Shelby?

How are you going to get here?

Borrowed car from friend at work.

He didn't know she had any friends at work. His eyes fell on Apisi.

Apisi's food from Windy Ray's house. It's in the cupboard next to the fridge.

Will his house be locked?

No.

Okay, anything else?

Pete yawned and caught a whiff of his breath.

Toothbrush please.

Okay. Be there after I drop Braedon off.

He returned his phone to his pocket and shook his head. Maybe he wasn't as alone as he'd thought, though he didn't deserve help. Didn't deserve a second chance at having family in his life. He peered through the darkness at Windy Ray. Look what happened to people who spent time with him. And what was Braedon going to think? After Pete had made Braedon solemnly swear to never fight again, he'd savagely beaten another man. He'd pummeled him like some hotheaded twenty-year-old.

He'd told Dani he was different now, that he'd grown up, but apparently after half a century he was still trying to become a man. Inside, he was still an eleven-year-old kid fighting against the social worker to break free and run after his little sister. Fighting against circumstances he never asked for. Fighting to be good enough that his mother would want him again.

One thing was different now, though. Now he could see that Dani had been better off without him all those years ago.

Wilma was still in bed at eight o'clock in the morning, much to her chagrin. Goodness, that bug she'd picked up must have really taken it out of her. She was feeling much better except for a pervasive weariness. Bouncing back from an illness was never easy at her age, she supposed.

She thought she'd heard a knock at the door, but she wasn't expecting anyone. Who would stop by unannounced at this hour? The front door creaked open, and her eyes widened. Had she not locked the door last night? And here she was in her pajamas, *really*.

"Miss Wilma?"

Oh, thank heavens. It was only Lily. "Be right out, dear."

Her voice was stronger today, her throat only a little sore. She carefully slid out of bed and decided against taking the time to get dressed. Her housecoat would do. What on earth was Lily doing here?

She found Lily in the kitchen, looking rather pale. "Good morning."

"Good morning, Miss Wilma. I'm sorry to drop in like this."

"Nonsense. Have you had breakfast?"

Lily hesitated. "I'm not hungry."

Wilma put her hands on her hips. "Breakfast is the most important meal of the day, dear. Why don't you start the coffee while I make some scrambled eggs and toast."

She set to work, her body moving slowly, and thought about her son Michael. A few weeks after Herb had died, Michael had mentioned to Wilma that he and Paula would like her to consider selling the house and moving in with them. *"There's no reason to stay up there in the middle of nowhere all by yourself,"* he'd said.

She'd had plenty of reasons. How could she leave the house she and Herb had shared for over thirty years? How could she impose on her family like that? She was capable of taking care of herself. And then Pete had reappeared in Sleeping Grass and given her yet another reason to stay.

She'd raised such a fuss about it at the time that Michael never brought it up again. Now, however, as she struggled to whisk the eggs with one hand while leaning on her cane with the other, she wondered. How long could she keep this up?

"I owe you an apology, Lily." She turned the heat off on the stovetop and scraped the eggs onto a plate as Lily took the sugar bowl from the cupboard.

Lily set the bowl on the table. "What for?"

Wilma indicated the cashmere cardigan hanging on the back of her favorite chair. "I lost my cardigan for a time, and I entertained the idea that you might've taken it. To sell. That was wrong of me."

Lily eyed the sweater. "That's why you asked if I was selling clothes."

"Yes. I'm sorry."

"I was desperate enough to have done it. I was starting to think I'd never be able to get away. But it doesn't matter now."

"What do you mean it doesn't matter?" Wilma set a plate of food on the table and motioned for Lily to sit.

The young woman obliged. "Nothing. Never mind."

Wilma sat down with her own plate of food and buttered her toast.

"All right." She didn't like the look on Lily's face, but she wouldn't press. "Now, what brings you here this morning?"

Lily hadn't touched her food. "Have you heard any more about Pearl? Have they found her?"

"That's a good question. I haven't heard anything. Gladys is having flyers printed today, and we're going to hang them up all over town." Wilma peered at Lily over her glasses. "You can help us if you'd like."

"You haven't talked to Pete?"

"Not since you were here yesterday."

Lily stared at her hands. "I'll never forgive myself if something bad happens to Pearl."

"My goodness." Wilma set her fork down with a clank. "It's not your fault, you hear me? Don't you dare blame yourself."

Lily hopped out of her chair. "Coffee's ready."

Wilma watched Lily pour a cup of coffee and set it near Wilma's plate with trembling hands. The poor girl was clearly distressed.

Wilma stirred two spoons of sugar into her mug. "Perhaps after breakfast, we can call Pete and get an update, hmm?"

Lily looked downright miserable as she nodded. "Okay."

"Are you not feeling well? You haven't eaten a thing."

"I'm fine."

Wilma had had enough of this. She set down the crust of her toast, took a sip of coffee, and for once she pressed. "Anyone can see plain as day that you are not fine. Now, you're going to tell me what's going on or I'm going to invite Gladys over here to drag it out of you."

Lily looked up, too startled to speak for a moment. "I, uh, I'm worried about Pearl."

"You mean to tell me all this moping and not eating is because of Pearl?"

"It's my fault."

"It most certainly is not." Wilma pursed her lips together. Aging had caused her eyesight to weaken, her hearing to deteriorate, but her intuition regarding young women in crisis hadn't yet faded away. She softened her voice. "I don't think that's the only thing bothering you."

There was a sharp intake of breath, then a choking sound as Lily's shoulders began to shake. "I don't know what I'm going to do."

A sob burst from the poor girl's mouth, and everything became clear. Wilma had been a young woman once, too, after all.

She took a deep breath. "You're having a baby."

Lily's sobbing escalated, which was all the confirmation Wilma needed. She placed a gentle hand on Lily's arm. "How many weeks?"

"S-s-seven. I didn't think . . . I mean, at my age . . ."

"Your age? Nonsense. I was a little up in years when I had my babies, too, but I promise, you are still young and full of life."

"I'm forty-one. I can't . . ."

Wilma waited. Lily studied her hands and sniffled. After a minute, Wilma clucked her tongue. "You're sure? You've been to the doctor?"

"I can't go to the clinic here. But I've had three positive tests."

"And morning sickness, clearly."

Lily nodded.

"You've been unusually tired, I suppose."

Lily nodded again.

"I still think you should go to the—"

"What am I going to do?" Lily pressed her palms into her eyes. "How could this happen?"

"A baby is a blessing, dear."

Lily shook her head. "This one isn't."

Wilma chided herself. She shouldn't have said that about a blessing. Even if she believed it, it had been a thoughtless comment. "I'm sorry. How can I help? Does Jerry know?"

"No."

So many questions swirled in Wilma's head. How was Jerry going to react? Would the baby be in danger? Was Lily still planning her escape? Everything would be harder now. More complicated.

Wilma straightened abruptly. What if Lily felt she had no choice but to . . . "My offer still stands, dear. You and the baby can come live with me."

Lily was silent.

"There's nothing I would love more," Wilma added. "I don't need all this space for myself, and I've always loved babies."

Lily didn't move. It was as if she'd sent her spirit elsewhere while her body sat at the table. Wilma couldn't guess what was going through her mind. She only knew she didn't want Lily to feel she had no other choice than to make an irreversible decision.

Finally, Lily spoke. "I wouldn't be safe here. You wouldn't be safe. And I couldn't afford to pay rent."

"That doesn't concern me."

"I know about the trouble with your taxes." Lily looked up now, a guilty expression on her face. "Pete told me."

"Oh, that." Wilma waved a hand. "That's nothing to worry about. I've signed up for assistance. I thought it might've come through by now, but it's only a matter of time. I expect to hear from them any day now."

"When was the last time you talked to them?" Lily asked.

Her tone suggested suspicion, and Wilma sat up straighter. "They have lots of other people to help besides me, you know. I called not long ago. Sadie assured me help was on the way."

"Maybe you should call them again."

Wilma bristled. She had enough people concerned about her finances already. She didn't need any more. Yet Lily was in a sensitive situation. It wouldn't do to upset her. "Perhaps I will. Then would you consider moving in with me?"

Lily's face had that look she used as a cover-up, the one that gave nothing away. But her knuckles were white. "Okay. Call this Sadie person right now, and I'll consider it."

For goodness' sake, all this to-do over nothing. Wilma barely held back an unladylike huff, then inwardly chided herself. Lily was feeling overwhelmed and frightened. The least Wilma could do was reassure her.

"All right." At Wilma's request, Lily fetched the phone and the paper on which Wilma had written the number for FAS. Wilma dialed the number carefully and waited.

Four rings. Five. Six. She glanced at Lily, who was watching intently.

Seven rings. Eight. Her heart squeezed, but Wilma told herself there was no cause for alarm. As she'd told Lily, FAS was surely helping plenty of other people, many of whom were likely in a much worse position than she was. Even so, why didn't Sadie have an answering machine? Perhaps she was talking to someone on the other line. Yes, that must be it.

After ten rings, Wilma hung up. "I guess they're busy today. I'll try again later."

Lily's red-rimmed eyes searched Wilma's face. "Promise?"

A small seed of unease planted itself in Wilma's chest, but she nodded. "Yes, dear, I promise. *Really.*"

"Can we call Pete now?"

Wilma had nearly forgotten about Pete and Pearl. She would need to get dressed and do something about her hair before Gladys showed up for their flyer-posting excursion.

"Of course. Let's call him right now."

thirty-eight

Pete was getting restless. The hospital room was slowly shrinking, Windy Ray hadn't woken up, and his fear for Pearl grew with every passing hour. Speaking of hours, it had now been forty-seven since Pearl was last seen alive and well. The thought of her alone and hungry somewhere, waiting for him to come, made him feel sick.

He shook out his aching right hand. The knuckles were swollen, and the pain was welcome. Coleridge's words from *The Rime of the Ancient Mariner* echoed in his head:

> The other was a softer voice,
> As soft as honey-dew:
> Quoth he, "The man hath penance done,
> And penance more will do."

Yes, he would. Whatever penance it took to atone for the harm Pete had caused Windy Ray. Even Pearl's predicament was his fault. He should've known better than to spend time with Lily. He knew it wasn't a good idea, and Jerry had warned him, but he'd been selfish. He wanted to be near her, to be within hearing distance of her voice, and look what had happened.

It had been easy to blame God for not taking care of His creation, but was it God's fault Pete insisted on making bad choices?

It was a small consolation that Jerry would probably not file charges against him for assault. Pete wouldn't mind going to jail, however, if it meant the police could help Lily get away from Jerry. But he knew that wasn't how it would work out. Guys like Jerry were good at covering their tracks and manipulating others to get what they wanted.

Pete's thoughts returned to Wilma's phone call earlier. *"Lily and I are eager for an update,"* she'd said. *"Any news about Pearl?"* It had killed him to admit he not only hadn't found Pearl but had landed Windy Ray in the hospital. Out of shame, he almost hadn't told her how Windy Ray had been injured, yet he didn't deserve to escape condemnation so he'd relayed every sordid detail.

Wilma had absorbed the news with a great deal of "oh mys" and "oh dears" and promised to pray. He was willing to accept that, for Windy Ray's sake. But not for his own.

Once Wilma had recovered from Pete's update, she'd told him of her and Gladys's plan to hang posters all over Sleeping Grass. He thanked her, but he couldn't help but wonder. Was she only doing it because she felt guilty about deceiving him? Now that he knew something of what she'd kept from him, all the kindness she'd shown—the meals, the invitations, the opportunities to spend time with Lily—felt tainted. She'd told him "You are a treasure," and he'd almost believed it.

Not anymore.

His stomach rumbled. He'd refused the breakfast and lunch the nurse had kindly offered because it didn't seem fair to enjoy a meal while neither Windy Ray nor Pearl could do the same. He'd skipped dinner last night, as well. But now, as he began to feel weak and light-headed whenever he stood up, he reconsidered. It wouldn't do Windy Ray or Pearl any good if he ended up in a hospital bed, too.

He examined Windy Ray's face for any sign of stirring, but his friend was resting peacefully. While the doctor had been weaning him off the sedatives throughout the day, Windy Ray still didn't seem inclined to wake up. Pete hated to leave him alone to hunt down a meal, however. Windy Ray loved Apisi, yet Pete didn't want him to open his eyes and find no one there but a dog.

As Pete deliberated on how to proceed, the door opened. He sat there stunned as Dani, Braedon, and Wilma entered the room. It took him a few seconds to find his voice. "What are you all doing here?"

Their faces looked grim, and he glanced at Windy Ray, feeling like his mistakes were on full display. Why had they come without telling him? Why did they seem so serious?

He looked at Dani, panic starting to grow as he imagined the worst. "I thought you'd still be at work."

"I left early because . . . well, I'll explain everything in the car. Come on, we've got to go."

He stood but didn't take a step. "I can't leave. I've got to—"

"Your sister knew you wouldn't want to leave Raymond alone." Wilma walked over to the bed and set her purse down. "That's why I'm here."

The lack of sleep and food worked against him to make his thoughts sluggish. What was going on? But when Wilma pointed at the door, and Braedon said, "Hurry up, Uncle Pete," he finally got his body to move.

"Is this about Pearl? Did you find something?"

"Maybe." Dani held open the door. "Let's go."

With adrenaline pumping through his veins, Pete looked

back once, still anxious about leaving his friend. But when he saw Wilma pulling rocks from her purse and setting them on the bedside table, he managed a small smile. Windy Ray was in good hands.

Outside, the sun was blinding, and Pete staggered like a drunkard. He followed Dani and Braedon to Wilma's car, which they had parked next to his Dodge.

Dani grabbed a paper bag and a bottle of water from the passenger seat of the Corolla, then shut the door and turned to him. "Give me your keys. We're taking the truck."

"I'll drive."

She handed him the bag and water. "No, you're going to eat while *I* drive."

His stomach began clamoring for attention at the mention of eating. Okay, fine. He pulled the keys from his pocket and gave them to Dani. They piled into the truck with Braedon in the middle, and Pete opened the bag. It contained a turkey sandwich, an apple, and two chocolate-chip muffins. He thought he'd never seen more beautiful food in his life.

He quickly unwrapped the sandwich. "Thank you."

"Sunny dropped off the muffins. She's worried about you."

Braedon watched wide-eyed as Pete took a huge bite. "Mom said you probably didn't eat all day."

Pete spoke with his mouth full as Dani pulled out of the parking lot. "She was right."

After he'd eaten enough to take the edge off his hunger, he dared to ask, "Where are we going?"

Dani kept her eyes on the road. "I don't want you to get your hopes up. We don't know anything for sure."

She was speeding, but Pete didn't care. "Just tell me."

"I was at the gas station, right? Working there, you see all kinds of people coming and going, and sometimes they talk to each other like you're not even there."

Pete chewed and nodded.

"So this one guy came in—I'd seen him before—and he's talking to this other guy about a pig."

Pete swallowed, and his body froze. "A pig?"

Dani nodded. "He said something about a cabin down by Tiber Lake and a pig, and I just, I don't know, had a feeling. So I clocked out and went to Wilma's to call Lily. To see if she knew of anyone who had a cabin by the lake."

Pete crammed half a muffin into his mouth. "Did she?"

"Stop talking with your mouth full. Yes. She said Jerry goes to the lake with a buddy sometimes. She gave me his name and told me he worked at Andy's Auto doing oil changes."

"And?" He took a swig of water.

"She felt bad she never thought of the cabin when we were all looking for Pearl. She seemed really . . . I don't know, sad or something."

It caused a physical ache in his chest to think of Lily, and he stared out the window as they passed Sleeping Grass. "Did you find the friend?"

"Yes. It was the guy from the gas station. And I got the approximate location of the cabin."

He gaped. "How?"

Dani didn't answer.

"How'd you get him to tell you?"

Her face flushed. "It wasn't hard, okay? I just flirted with him a little and told him I was looking forward to going to the lake this summer. He blabbed all about his cabin by Bear Rock."

"I can't believe you did that."

"You owe me fifty bucks for the oil change."

Pete laughed, then caught Braedon's eye and sobered. He had no right to be laughing after everything he'd done. "Hey, thanks for being here, buddy. I'm sorry I yelled at you."

Braedon mumbled, "It's okay."

"No, it's not. I promised you I wouldn't do that. I shouldn't have lost my temper."

Braedon looked down at his lap. "What happened to Windy Ray?"

The air in Pete's lungs suddenly felt scarce. He exchanged a look with Dani over Braedon's head. She must not have told him the whole story. Pete knew he'd need to come clean with Braedon about what happened, but he couldn't bear to do it now. "He got hit in the head, but he's going to be fine."

He hoped it was true. He hoped Pearl was at the cabin. He hoped Lily was going to be okay. He hoped, he hoped, he hoped, and somewhere deep down in his soul, he prayed.

Dani raised her eyebrows but said nothing as the truck took a right-hand turn south toward Tiber Lake.

Wilma sat in the ghastly burgundy chair beside Raymond's bed. She felt almost back to normal after her illness, aside from a lingering soreness in her throat and a slight fuzziness in her head. Under her breath she sang an old song:

"'Rosemary, Rosemary, cheeks like a cherry. Eyes like the moon, what a treasure you are.'"

Rosie's letters were in her purse. She wasn't entirely sure what had compelled her to take them from the drawer and bring them along when Dani had asked her to come to Shelby. Perhaps she hoped she might have the chance to talk with Pete and wanted to be prepared. Perhaps it was because the hospital in Shelby reminded her of Rosie. She'd been here for both of Rosie's births, and Rosie had been here for each of hers, keeping vigil, holding her hand, making her laugh through the pain.

There was so much pain involved in being a mother.

She pulled out the first letter Rosie had ever sent. It was

short but full of unspoken words Rosie had no doubt believed Wilma would understand. The return address was for Spokane County Detention Services, a mere seven-hour drive from Sleeping Grass, and yet a world, a life, an inexplicable choice away.

Dear Willy Mae,

Thank you for everything. I'm sorry. Tell the kids I love them and can't wait to see them. Tell them to be good.

Love, Rosie

Wilma remembered reading the letter a hundred times, searching for clues, searching for answers. She remembered writing draft after draft of a letter in response, each one inevitably ending up crumpled in the wastebasket. Herb had urged her to tell the truth, and she'd wanted to, she just hadn't known the right way to do it. Hadn't known the right way to say, "Your children aren't here. They've been split up, and Pete is in foster care. Please come back."

Perhaps it wasn't so hard after all.

Raymond stirred, and Wilma tucked the letter away. She rose and leaned against the side of the bed, her hands nearly touching Raymond's arm. He made a low guttural sound, and she frowned. What if he was in pain? What if he didn't remember who he was or how he got here?

Apisi hopped up on her three little feet and made her way to the head of the bed. She licked Raymond's neck and whimpered. It sounded a lot like *Wake up, wake up*.

Hesitantly, Wilma put her hand over his and squeezed gently. It was hard seeing him this way. All she'd ever known of him had been smiles and exuberance, but now his face was drawn and still. What a handsome face it was.

Her eyes drifted to their hands touching, and her cheeks warmed. How forward of her. How foolish. She tried to remove her hand, only to find Raymond was holding it. She gasped and looked up at his face.

His eyes twinkled. "I have died, and you are my—" he struggled to find the word—"my angel."

She pulled her hand away and swatted his arm lightly. "Nonsense. You're in the hospital, not heaven. We're both still very much of this earth, thank you."

He grinned. "If I couldn't be with the Creator when I woke up"—his eyes closed for a long moment before snapping back open—"then being with you is the next big thing." He shook his head. "Next *best* thing."

"You must have hit your head harder than we thought. You're half delirious."

"It's true I hit my head. It's more true that my head hit a rock."

She sighed. She'd been shocked by Pete's recounting of the incident in the bar parking lot. "Pete told me what happened. I'm very sorry."

"I'm not sorry." He looked earnestly in her face. "You're here."

She couldn't help but smile, and she didn't protest when he once again took hold of her hand. Only to humor him, of course. The poor man was in the hospital, after all.

He winced as he turned his head toward Apisi. "My faithful friend. How are you?"

"She's been worried sick."

He nodded solemnly at the dog, though it surely must have pained him. "I owe you many treats."

Apisi licked his nose, then lay down on his shoulder. Raymond caught sight of the rocks Wilma had brought, and his eyes widened in wonder. "My rocks."

"Dani and I chose a few from your house. We thought

it might make you feel better to be surrounded by familiar things."

His face became more serious than she'd ever seen it. "They are very special stones. Thank you."

She'd been bewildered by all the piles in his house. They'd seemed like nothing more than a childish collection at first, but as she walked around choosing which to bring, she'd become certain they were more than that. "What do they mean?"

He reached over with great difficulty and picked up one of the rocks. "In the Scriptures, in the book of Joshua, the Creator commands the men of Israel to gather twelve stones from the Jordan River to commemorate their crossing. You have heard of this?"

When she nodded, he continued, "The stones were meant to serve as a sign of what the Creator had done. So that when their children saw the stones and asked, 'What do these stones mean?' the men could tell them of the Creator's mighty deeds."

Raymond grew quiet for a moment, studying the rock in his hand. It was flat and green. "After my wife and son were taken by the wind, I didn't want to remember anything. I wanted only to forget. Then one day I went to the Marias River. I went to the place where the massacre occurred. You know of this also?"

Wilma's heart crumpled, and she nodded again. The US Army had slaughtered nearly two hundred Blackfeet women and children on the bank of the river in 1870.

Raymond's eyes burned with intensity. "I stood by the river and knew the things that had happened there should never be forgotten. I heard the cries of each *aakíí* and *oko's* carried on the wind, and I found a hundred and seventy-three stones and stacked them up, one by one. And I've been stacking stones ever since."

Wilma pondered this. "All the rocks in your house are for remembering?"

"Yes. Some to remember hard things, some to remember good things. And now I've become quite fond of rocks. They are pieces of the earth, which the Creator holds in His hands, and they are also memories."

She pictured the rocks Raymond had given her. "Whenever I see your rocks on my windowsill, I think of you."

"Yes." He bobbed his head. "I don't want you to forget about me."

She thought of Herb. She never wanted to forget him. As if sensing her thoughts, Raymond squeezed her hand. "There's room on the earth for many rocks."

At that moment, a nurse in faded blue scrubs opened the door and scurried inside. She stopped short when she saw Raymond.

"Oh! You're awake. How do you feel?"

Raymond pursed his lips to the side as if he really had to think about it. Finally, he said, "I'm a little hungry."

The nurse laughed. "Okay, then. I'll let the doctor know you're up. He'll need to examine you before I can give you anything."

"All right. I'll wait here."

She hurried off, shaking her head, and Raymond turned his attention back to Wilma. A gleam of humor had returned to his dark eyes. "Please tell me, Wilma. Where's my friend, Pete the Poet?"

thirty-nine

Tiber Lake wasn't technically a lake. It was a reservoir formed by the Marias River and the Tiber Dam. Tiber Lake wasn't technically its name either. Its official designation was Lake Elwell. Pete remembered his mother taking him and Dani there every summer. He hadn't seen it since he was ten.

As the expanse of water came into view, the hollow pit of hunger that had previously been in Pete's stomach was replaced by a different kind of pit. One that wasn't hollow at all but filled with a slinking, swarming, and vile creature waiting to tear him to pieces.

Fear.

"What if she isn't here?" he asked.

Dani didn't answer, but a different question echoed around the cab. What if she was? What if they found her and she was . . . ?

His throat went dry, and he swallowed hard. He couldn't think like that. "You know how to get to Bear Rock?"

Dani nodded. "I googled it."

"I want you and Braedon to stay in the truck when we get there."

The only thing worse than Pete finding Pearl's lifeless body would be Braedon finding it.

"Okay, but—"

"I want to go with you," Braedon interrupted.

"I don't think that's a good idea, buddy. Someone might be there."

"I want to go. It's my fault she's gone."

Pete shook his head. "No, it's not. Whoever took her, that's whose fault it is. And mine. I shouldn't have given you that kind of responsibility." Another choice he couldn't blame God for, if he was being honest. The next time he got the urge to punch someone, he should just punch himself.

Braedon slumped and sulked but didn't argue further.

Dani turned down a rugged dirt road and pointed. "There's the rock."

It had the look of a lumbering black bear. Dani pulled off onto a turnout, muddy from last night's unexpected rain, and parked the truck. They hadn't seen anyone on their way here. It was too cold for swimming, and ice-fishing season was over. In a couple of months, there would be campers and hikers and boaters, but today the lake was a desolate place.

He gave Dani a questioning look.

She shrugged. "He said he jumps off the rock in the summer and that his cabin is shaded. That's all I know. Are you sure you don't want us to come with you?"

He was very sure. What if Jerry was in the cabin? A jolt of alarm zapped Pete's body like a Taser as he remembered what Jerry had said about his sister. "I can't leave you in the truck alone. It's not safe. I should've dropped you off in Sleeping Grass on the way here."

"There's nobody around. We'll be fine."

Pete wrestled with himself. He didn't want to be responsible for anyone else getting hurt.

"We'll keep the doors locked the whole time," Dani reassured him. "And if we see anyone, I'll lay on the horn."

That could work. The sound would carry for miles.

"You know what Jerry's truck looks like?"

Dani nodded.

"Who's Jerry?" Braedon asked.

"No one."

Braedon scowled.

Dani elbowed him. "Watch your attitude, mister."

Pete wadded up the paper sack Dani had given him and stuffed it into the garbage bag hanging from the console. "Thanks for the food. Braedon, I need you to keep an eye out for anything suspicious."

"Like what?"

"I don't know. Just help your mom keep watch, okay?"

"Okay," he grumbled.

Pete understood Braedon's displeasure at being left behind. He would feel the same way. He opened the door and slid out. "You got your phone?"

Dani held it up. "Only one bar out here."

Pete's jaw clenched. Maybe he should drive them back home and return by himself.

"Just go." Dani waved him off. "We'll be all right."

Pete took a deep breath. If Pearl was here, he didn't want to leave without her. "I'll hurry."

He shut the door behind him and waited until Dani and Braedon pushed down the locks before heading toward Bear Rock. There were a couple of wind-damaged trees and a lot of scraggly bushes. If there was a cabin around here, it shouldn't be hard to find. He trekked toward the rock and thought of Lily. Was she safe?

He reached the rock and skirted around it, looking back to see if the Dodge was still visible. It wasn't. He checked his phone. No service. He scanned the area looking for signs of life. Where could a cabin be so it would have shade? Not near the water. He turned and peered up the hill. There. A small stand of trees with some kind of building half hidden behind it. That had to be it.

He was no athlete, but he climbed the steep, rocky hill like it was nothing, all the fear and worry and guilt from the past couple of days hastening his steps. Lengthening his stride. As he approached the building, it became clear it was more of a shack than a cabin, and a dilapidated one at that.

A tarp covered the front window of the shack. Pete stood facing the closed door, listening carefully but hearing nothing. No voices. No chairs scraping or floorboards creaking. No one was here.

The door was locked. It was a flimsy building, however, and Pete kicked the door in on the first try, fueled by anger and desperation. Inside, it was dark and smelled like rotting garbage. As his eyes adjusted, he saw a small table with two chairs, a ten-gallon water jug on the counter, and a chewed-up couch that looked like it had been home to a family of mice. There was another door leading to what must be a bedroom.

"Hello?"

His voice sounded loud and out of place. Nothing stirred. The floor complained as he approached a large cupboard and pulled it open. His eyes narrowed. The shiny stack of modern electronics inside the cupboard stood in sharp contrast to the dinginess that marked the rest of the shack. What was this stuff doing here? Where had it come from?

Jerry's job at the HVAC company gave him access to other people's homes, didn't it? Pete shook his head. He couldn't worry about that now. He was on a mission. He closed the cupboard.

Next, he hurried to the bedroom door and opened it. This room had a window facing the back, which let in a little light.

There was a fire-blackened pot tipped over on the floor, a cot frame with no mattress in the corner, and a heap of something that smelled like manure along the wall.

Flies buzzed, and he blinked. No, it wasn't a heap of something. His breath caught. It was . . .

"Pearl."

She didn't move. Fear gripped his heart and squeezed mercilessly.

"Pearl, it's me."

There was no response. He moved toward her, his arm outstretched, and almost tripped over a rope tied to the cot. The other end was tied to Pearl's back left leg, where it had rubbed her hide raw. Something between a moan and a keen came out of his mouth.

He was too late.

"My pearl of great price." He pressed a fist to his mouth. "I'm so sorry."

He knelt beside her and put a hand on her side, his eyes stinging. She was . . . warm? He gasped and leaned closer. She was still breathing. It was shallow and wheezy, but she was alive.

"Pearl, can you hear me?"

Her eyes opened and rolled about wildly. When they caught sight of him, they pleaded. His heart was in his throat.

"I'm going to get you out of here."

He remembered the pot and carried it quickly into the other room. The ten-gallon jug was almost empty, but he filled the pot halfway and hurried back to Pearl. She struggled to lift her head, so he tilted the pot carefully and dribbled water into her mouth. Due to numerous lectures from the vet, Pete knew dehydration was one of the biggest health threats to a pig like Pearl. He also knew better than to give her too much water at once.

He dribbled water into her mouth three more times, then

set the pot down. He needed to get her to the vet immediately. He cut the rope around her leg with the Leatherman strapped to his belt, his heart pumping fast.

"Can you get up, girl? Can you walk?"

She gave him a pathetic look and grunted weakly. He was going to have to carry her. He wished now for Dani and Braedon's help, but he wouldn't waste time running back to the truck. He worked his arms around Pearl's middle and heaved with no luck. He repositioned, braced himself, and tried again. His back protested, but she made no complaint as he lifted her off the floor.

He'd left both doors open, and he staggered through them with his precious cargo, out into the open air. Sweat was already dripping from his forehead. This was an impossible task. Her weight was unforgiving. How would he get her back to the Dodge?

"I'm sorry, girl. I've got to move you onto my shoulder."

He laid her in the dirt as gently as possible and adjusted himself so he could drape her front legs over his shoulder. With a loud growl and all his strength, he lifted her again so that she hung on his shoulder like a large sack of potatoes. He started toward the Dodge, watching the ground carefully, knowing he couldn't afford to stumble.

When he reached Bear Rock, he stopped, his lungs sucking in rapid gulps of air. His shoulder ached. It was going to take forever to reach the truck.

The coarse hairs on Pearl's back rubbed against his ear, and the sound of her wheezing made his heart sink. Then another loud and insistent sound pierced the stillness around him. He stiffened.

A horn.

Beep, beep, beep-beep-beeeep . . .

Pete steeled himself and took off at a run.

forty

By the time Pete reached the Dodge, sweat poured from his face, and his lungs burned as if he'd run five miles instead of five hundred yards. He could see a black dot in the distance, followed by a trail of dust. Someone was coming.

Dani had continued to honk the horn until she spotted him getting close, and then she leaped out of the truck and opened the passenger door. Her face was grim. "Is she . . . ?"

"She's alive. Barely." He motioned for Braedon to scoot over and laid Pearl on the seat while Dani rushed back around to the driver's side.

His nephew's eyes were wide. "What happened to her? Is she going to be okay?"

It was the voice of a scared little boy hiding in the closet. Pete wanted to reassure him, but what could he say? What promises could he make? All they could do was get her to the vet as fast as possible.

"I hope so, buddy."

"I'm going to pray for her. And Windy Ray, too."

"That's a good idea."

"My dad was wrong about a lot of other stuff. Maybe he's wrong about God."

Pete nodded. "Maybe so. Now buckle up."

Dani shoved the truck into drive and stepped on the gas. The wheels spun out in the mud at first, then gained traction. Pete braced himself against Pearl to keep her from rolling off the seat as the truck bumped over rocks and potholes. To the northeast, the black dot grew bigger.

Dani leaned toward the steering wheel. "Hold on."

The Dodge gained speed until the black dot in the distance took on the shape of a small truck with big wheels.

Jerry. Pete strained against his seat belt. He knew Jerry would recognize his Dodge, but there was no other way back to Shelby except around the lake.

The S-10 swerved and came to a stop, blocking the dirt road ahead of them. Jerry climbed out and leaned against the Chevy, arms crossed over his chest.

"Stop," Pete said.

Dani hesitated. "I can try to get around him."

"No. There's too much mud, and we can't risk getting stuck. Just let me out."

She hit the brakes. "What are you going to do?"

"I don't know."

"Who's that?" Braedon asked. "What's he doing?"

"That's Jerry." Pete slid out of the Dodge. "Whatever you do, don't get out of the truck."

Dani shook her head. "Pete, I don't—"

He slammed the door on her words, his blood roaring in his ears. He'd had enough of this guy. Dani had stopped about fifty yards from the S-10, and as Pete strode forward, he could see the black eye and split lip on Jerry's face.

"Cuts both ways, Pete!" Jerry shouted. "You wanted a fight, and now you've got one."

Pete came to a halt a few paces away, his nostrils flaring. "Move your truck."

"It'll move when I want it to move."

Pete didn't have time for this. He took a step forward.

Jerry lunged, fury burning in his eyes.

Pete grew still.

He knew how to put Jerry down. He could use Jerry's momentum against him and get him on the ground, his head smashed against the uneven road littered with rocks. His body vulnerable to the steel-toed tip of Pete's boot. It would be easy. It would feel like justice.

He thought of Pearl tied to a cot. Lily, afraid to leave the house or make a phone call. Windy Ray, lying in a hospital bed.

He braced himself. And flung his body out of the way.

As Jerry stumbled past in a stream of curses, Pete raced toward the S-10. He could no longer be a scared little boy who knew no other way to face the world than with his fists. There was too much at stake. Maybe that's what Jerry was, on the inside. But not Pete. Not anymore.

Pete threw himself into Jerry's truck, which was still running. Jerry chased after him as Pete drove the truck into the ditch.

Jerry pounded on the passenger window. "You idiot!"

Pete killed the engine and climbed out. Jerry came around the S-10 with a sneer, and Pete held the keys out to the side. "Stop."

Jerry looked at the keys and stopped, unsure what Pete was planning. "I'm gonna kill you."

"If you ever come near me or my family or lay a hand on Lily again, my friend is going to press charges. Assault with a deadly weapon. And I will press charges for theft, animal abuse, and whatever connection you have to that stockpile of electronics I saw in that cabin."

Jerry's eyes shifted. "You can't prove anything."

Pete shook the set of keys. "I bet one of these fits the lock at the cabin."

Jerry blanched, and Pete raised his arm. He threw the keys as far as he could. As Jerry watched them sail into the mud on the other side of the road, Pete caught a glimpse of the Dodge pulling up out of the corner of his eye. For once, he was glad Dani had read his mind.

The passenger door flew open. "Get in," Dani called.

He dove in, and she took off before he'd even closed the door.

"Will he follow us?" she asked.

"No. He's going to be busy for a while."

Once Jerry retrieved his keys, Pete had no doubt he would head straight to the cabin to remove all evidence of his recent activity.

"He looked mad," Braedon said.

"Don't worry. He's not going to bother us anymore."

Pete hoped it was true. The water bottle Dani had brought was rolling around by his feet, and he picked it up. Only a couple of sips left. Why hadn't he thought to save the water? He put one hand gently on Pearl's cheek and used the other to pour the rest of the water into her mouth.

"Hang on, Pearl." The vet's office was forty-five minutes away. Pete strained against the passing miles as if he could get them there faster. "Just a little longer."

After eating a little supper, Windy Ray had dozed back off, and the nurse had encouraged Wilma to let him rest as much as possible. Apisi had moved to her lap, and she stroked the dog's back as darkness fell outside. What had happened with Pete? Had he found Pearl? When would someone come for her?

Pete was right. She needed a cellphone. When this was all over, she would ask him to take her to Great Falls to pick up the phone Lily had ordered.

Wilma's heart sank. If Pete was still speaking to her by then, that is. Her heart sank even further. And what about the cost? She'd called the FAS number again just as she'd promised Lily she would—twice, in fact—and had been dismayed to hear a recorded voice say, in far too upbeat of a tone, that "The number you have called is no longer in service. Please hang up and try again."

At first, she thought she had misdialed, but she hadn't. Had FAS gotten a new number? Would Sadie contact her when her paperwork went through? A bad feeling gnawed at Wilma, but she couldn't spare many thoughts for her financial troubles right now. She was too concerned about other things, such as Pearl's whereabouts and Lily's future.

Wilma didn't know everything about Lily's situation, but she knew enough to suspect Lily might need more help than Wilma could offer. She thought of the dozen or so women's ministries she supported. Many of them were exclusively for women with addictions, but not all. Perhaps one of them would be a good place for Lily and her baby. But that would mean . . .

Oh dear. Those places were all so far away. Lily would have to—

"There's a joke about a horse."

Wilma gasped, her hand flying to her chest as she looked up. "My goodness, Raymond, you scared the stuffing out of me."

"A man asks the horse, 'Why the long face?'"

Apisi whined to return to her owner. Wilma stood and leaned against the bed, setting the dog down by Raymond's shoulder. "Was my face that long?"

"Yes. And I don't believe it is my health you're worried about."

"Of course I'm concerned about your health, but you're right. There are also other things."

He caught hold of her hand. "I would be honored to help carry your burdens, Wilma. I care for you very much."

She raised her eyebrows. "My, we are rather forward this evening. I think we need to ask the doctor to tone down the medication, hmm?"

His eyes never left her face. "My brush with death has removed my restraint, but it has not revealed anything I didn't already know."

"Brush with death?" The corners of her lips twitched. "That sounds a little dramatic, don't you think?"

"Love is dramatic."

She harrumphed. He had a point. How dull and predictable life would be without love. Yet she felt too old for drama.

She thought of Herb and all their years together. Wonderful years, for the most part. He always made her laugh, and once she'd accepted that he would always leave his cereal bowl on the counter and the cupboards in the garage open, she had found little to complain about. He'd been a good man.

She missed having someone to share life with. Without someone else to talk to, someone else to respond to the ordinary events of one's day, one sometimes began to feel as if one were invisible. As if she simply didn't exist.

"I'm very flattered, Raymond." She gave him a small smile. "And I consider you a friend, but . . ."

Instead of the disappointment she'd expected, resolve sharpened his expression. "A dear friend?"

She considered this. "I suppose so."

He nodded gravely. They looked at each other, and she wondered if he, too, was pondering the many years they'd already left behind and the very few that still lay ahead. Then the door flew open.

Braedon came barreling into the room first. "Guess what?"

Pete was next. "Shhh, keep it down. Folks are resting."

They looked at Raymond, who was grinning. "Wilma and I are dear friends."

Wilma blushed, suddenly very aware of her hand still in Raymond's grasp. Braedon smiled.

"You're awake." Pete moved closer to the bed and frowned at Raymond. "I'm really sorry I got you into this mess."

Raymond glanced down at Wilma's hand in his. "It's the best thing that's happened to me in a long time."

Pete looked tired, but he chuckled. "I can see that."

Wilma pulled her hand away, embarrassed. "Did you find Pearl?"

"Yes. She was in bad shape, but she's doing better already. We've been at the vet the past couple of hours. He said we could take Pearl home if we keep a close eye on her."

"That's wonderful news."

He nodded. "Dani stayed with Pearl in the truck, but Braedon wanted to come in and see Windy Ray real quick."

Raymond tipped his head at Braedon. "I am honored."

Braedon held his hand out so Apisi could sniff it but kept his eyes on Raymond. "You look like a mummy."

Wilma stifled a smile. The white bandage wrapped around Raymond's head did indeed give him a mummified look.

Braedon leaned closer. "I prayed for you."

Raymond grew solemn and still. "Another honor. You bless me, Braedon the Brave."

"Do you think the Creator helped us find Pearl?"

"I do."

"Then why didn't He help me get back before she was taken?"

Pete put an arm around his nephew's shoulders. "Let's not wear him out, okay? It's been a long day."

"Wait." Raymond held up a hand. "Maybe it was to keep you from getting hurt. Maybe it was to reveal something important to one of us. We may never know the reason."

Braedon's face scrunched in thought, but before he could respond, Pete tilted his head toward the door. "You really should go, buddy. Your mother asked you to come right back, and Pearl needs to get home."

Braedon sighed. "Okay. Bye, Miss Wilma. Bye, Windy Ray."

Wilma waved. "Goodbye, dear."

Raymond nodded at Braedon. "We'll talk more another time. And I will think of you when I'm counting bison tonight."

Braedon grinned and slipped out the door.

Pete turned to Wilma. "I'm sorry it got so late."

"It's quite all right. I was happy to help." Without intending to, she looked out the window at the night. Sleeping Grass seemed awfully far away.

"She can't drive home alone in the dark." Raymond's voice was firm. He jerked his chin at Pete. "And I don't need you moping around the room all night while I sleep. You will drive Wilma back."

Pete shifted. "But—"

"Apisi and I will be fine without you."

Pete glanced at Wilma, and Wilma's stomach did a little flip-flop as she thought about the letters in her purse. "I can stay."

"No." Raymond shook his head. "You must go home and get some rest, wawetseka. You've been ill."

"He's right." Pete plucked Wilma's jacket from the chair. "We can come back tomorrow."

She let him help her into the coat, her pulse quickening.

For years, she'd prayed for a second chance with Pete. She'd asked for courage. She'd allowed the weight of what she'd done to anchor her to the Hi-Line even after her family had all left. And now it was finally time.

"Ready?" Pete asked.

She took a deep breath and nodded.

forty-one

Wilma buckled herself into the Corolla. "Thank you for driving me home."

Pete started the car. "I don't know what I was thinking before. Haven't had much sleep the past few days."

"I understand."

"Thanks for staying with him for so long."

"It was no trouble. I'm just glad Pearl is okay."

"Yes."

"Do you know what wawetseka means?"

The corner of Pete's mouth lifted. "Pretty lady."

"Oh."

Silence fell. She wished she knew what he was thinking.

As the lights of Shelby faded behind them, Highway 2 stretched out ahead, dark and empty. Wilma gazed at the stars, which seemed close enough to touch, and at the prairie that unfolded around them like a golden quilt. She drew a deep breath and released it. "I owe you an apology."

Pete sighed. "It's been a long day."

"Please, I need to tell you—your mother and I grew up together. We were very close, but when I got married, things started to change between us. I can't explain it exactly; we just ended up on different paths. She never wanted to settle down."

"I thought it was my dad's fault they were never married."

"No, it was her decision. Then after Dani was born, he took off and she used his abandonment as evidence she'd made the right choice. Oh, Rosie." Wilma shook her head, memories jumping out at her like deer on the highway. "She loved you two. She really did. But she was always looking for trouble, and you know trouble isn't hard to find."

"No." Pete's tone was hard to interpret. "It's not."

"I knew things were starting to get bad when she stopped inviting me to your house. You were seven or eight, I think. I should've done something then, Pete. I should've intervened somehow. I suspected she was using drugs, but I had no way to prove it. I'm ashamed to say I stopped calling her. Stopped checking in. If I did run into her, I would tell her I was worried and she would say, 'Everything's right as rain, Willy Mae.'"

Pete's brow furrowed. "Willy Mae?"

"My middle name is Mae. She and my Herb were the only ones who still called me that after high school."

His voice lowered. "I remember that name. Willy Mae. She talked about you." He drew a sharp breath. "You brought us dinner once. I can't believe I didn't recognize you."

Wilma took a deep breath. "I had long hair back then. And no glasses. But I was there when you were born, Pete. I held you. I bought you birthday presents."

"What did you buy?" He sounded like a man searching for solid ground. She wasn't sure what good it would do him to know, but she scoured her memory.

"It was so long ago. The only thing I remember is a red wagon, and I only remember because the first thing you did was fill it with rocks until it was too heavy to pull, and Rosie and I laughed and laughed."

"I remember the wagon. I have a picture of me sitting in it."

"You were such a dear child. Dani too. I'm so sorry."

"Wilma, did you know she had disappeared once before?"

She shook her head. "No." It felt as though she were falling.

"She went out after dinner one Friday and told me to put Dani to bed. I fell asleep on the couch waiting for her. She didn't come back until Sunday night."

"You must have been terrified."

"You had no idea she was thinking of leaving us?"

"Perhaps I should have. But I had three kids of my own by then, and we had just closed on a new house. We were in the middle of moving. I hadn't talked to her in months." Wilma looked out the window, sorrow and regret thickening her voice. "I should've done more."

He didn't speak, and the silence prodded her. "There's something else you need to know."

A cat appeared in the road, eyes shining, and Pete slowed down. After a moment, it ran away.

"She wrote to me after she left. Five times."

"What?" Disbelief colored his voice.

Wilma held open her purse. "I have the letters right here."

His words came fast. "You knew where she went? Why didn't you tell the social worker? Why would she write to you but not to me?"

He was angry and confused, and she didn't blame him. "As for your first question, no, I didn't know where she went. It was months before I heard from her. She wrote me from a jail in Spokane, but she was only there briefly. I did tell the social worker, but there wasn't much she could do. Rosie just kept disappearing."

"But she would write to *you*."

This was the part Wilma had dreaded the most. The facet of the truth that was smooth as a mirror and reflected her failures.

"She was really writing to you, Pete. She thought you were with me."

"With you? Why?"

She clasped her hands in her lap. "Did the social worker ever ask you if you knew of any friends you could stay with? Anyone who might take you in?"

"I don't remember. They asked a lot of questions, and I was in shock, I guess." Pete's voice broke as the realization washed over him. "They asked you, didn't they? They asked you about us, and you said no."

Wilma's throat constricted. She swallowed, but it didn't help. "I'm so sorry. It's the biggest regret of my life that I didn't say yes to you and Dani. That you had to be split up. I thought we didn't have enough room. I thought five children would be too hard. I was afraid."

"We were afraid, too. Dani and me."

"I know." She sniffed, her head bobbing up and down. "I-I know. I'm sorry. Can you ever forgive me?"

He didn't answer. He turned north off Highway 2 at the Conoco sign and entered Sleeping Grass. They would reach her house in less than three minutes. She wanted to say more, but she couldn't. She wished he would answer, but he didn't.

Pete pulled into her driveway and shifted the car into park.

"Go ahead and drive it home for the night," she said. "You can bring it back tomorrow."

He nodded wearily. She pulled the letters from her purse and set them on the seat, patting them as if they were a little boy's head. By the time she carefully opened the passenger door and secured her cane, Pete had come around to help. He offered his arm, and as he walked her to the house, she thought of Rosie. It should be Rosie taking his arm, handing him her key, letting him unlock the door. How could a mother abandon her own children?

Wilma stiffened. In the long list of *shoulds*, there was

another. It should be her kids she counted on. Michael or Steven who gave her his arm. Why had she allowed the distance between her and her children for so long? She had pushed them away. Kept them at arm's length. Was she any better than Rosie?

No more.

She flicked the light on in the entryway and turned to thank Pete, but he was already climbing back into the car.

"Good night." Her voice was soft and quiet and disappeared into the night. "I'm sorry."

forty-two

Pete sat in the kitchen Sunday night, head in his hands. Pearl's snoring reverberated through the house like a freight train passing, and he'd never heard a more wonderful sound. He longed to tell Lily about Pearl's safe return.

Five letters lay on the table. He hadn't read them yet, though he hadn't been able to stop thinking about them. He had replayed in his mind a hundred times all the things Wilma had said. All the ways everything he thought he knew had changed.

He'd been angry at first. He'd pictured himself fighting against the social worker and running down the road after Dani and wondered what it would've been like if they had moved in with Wilma's family instead. What would that life have been like? Who might he have become?

It was tempting to dwell on the wondering. Tempting to believe that if only Wilma had said yes, everything would have been better. No group homes. No fights. A high school diploma. A family. But he would never know, would he? And if things had been different, he might not have these moments now with his sister and nephew.

His anger was beginning to subside. Wilma had been

younger than he was now when she'd been faced with that difficult decision. Would he have said yes if he'd been in her shoes? It hadn't been fair for his mother to put Wilma in that position to begin with. From this distance, he could understand that. What he didn't understand was where he stood with Wilma now. Had he been nothing but a charity case to her these past few months? A way for her to assuage her own feelings of guilt? If she hadn't cared enough to step in before, why did she care now?

"What's that?"

He raised his head. Dani was leaning against the wall, her eyes on the five envelopes. He'd thought she was asleep.

"Oh. Uh . . ."

He hadn't yet told Dani about Wilma and their mother. He'd thought it was because he wanted to figure it all out first before he tried, but maybe it was because he was afraid to bring it up and make it real.

"How long have you been sitting there?" Dani asked.

He glanced at the clock. "Too long. Sorry if I've been keeping you up."

"It's fine. It takes me a while to wind down after work."

"I thought they were going to start giving you better shifts."

She crossed the room and joined him at the table. "About that . . ."

He frowned. "What?"

"I put in my two weeks' notice."

His eyebrows rose. He'd known she wasn't happy working there, but he hadn't expected this.

"I should've talked to you first," she continued. "But I was getting a lecture from my boss about leaving work early again, and he was going off about not giving me better shifts if he can't count on me. Anyway, I snapped—I gave him my notice right then."

"When did this happen?"

"Yesterday."

Pete groaned. "You got in trouble for leaving work to help me. I'm sorry, Dani."

"Don't be. We found Pearl, and I hated that job anyway. And don't worry, I don't expect you to pay—"

"I can support you. I've told you that." It wouldn't be a grand life—things would be tight—but he could do it. All he'd ever wanted to do was take care of his sister.

"That's not what I want, Pete. I'm going to find another job." She looked away and shifted in her chair. "But I might need to expand my search a little."

Due to the late hour and all the other things on his mind, it took a minute for Dani's words to sink in. When they did, they just kept right on sinking, along with his heart. "You're going to leave?"

She made a face. "I didn't say that. I don't know what's going to happen. I just know there aren't many options for me around here. I was thinking maybe in Great Falls or . . ."

He thought of his house being empty again. He thought of his nephew and tried not to panic. He didn't want to lose him. What about Shelby? Shelby wasn't that far away.

He sat up straight. "I have an idea. Do you know Conrad Rountree?"

"I don't think so."

"His mom lives in the assisted-living place in Shelby, and he said they're looking for a new activities director. Someone to arrange events and schedules or something."

Dani leaned forward. "Is it full time?"

"I don't know."

"Does it come with benefits?"

"I don't know." He chuckled. "You'll have to call, I guess. I just know Con said his mother's been bored 'outta her mind' since the last director left."

"I could actually make a difference in people's lives." Dani was animated now. "I could make those people happy."

"I'm sure you make people happy when you sell them beer and cigarettes at the gas station." He raised one eyebrow. "I can't believe that's not fulfilling enough for you."

She swatted his arm. "I'll call them in the morning."

"Who?"

"The assisted-living place, of course." She gave him a look. "Any idea what the name of it is?"

"No. Sorry."

"I'll figure it out. Thanks for the tip. Now, about those envelopes . . ."

His stomach twisted. He picked them up and took a deep breath. "Wilma gave them to me. They're letters from Mom."

Dani's eyes widened. "You're kidding."

He shook his head. "Wilma knew her, Dani. All this time she knew about our mom and what happened to us and never said a word."

"Wow." His sister drummed her fingers on the table. "It's not the kind of thing that comes up over tea, I guess."

"I don't know why she would keep it from me. From us."

"She didn't. She told you."

"Yes, but why didn't she tell me sooner? Why did she pretend she cared?"

"Pete." Dani gave him a look. "She wasn't pretending."

He frowned at the letters. "How do you know?"

Dani tapped them with her finger. "If she didn't care, she never would've given them to you."

"But—"

"Have you read them yet?"

"No."

A long minute of silence passed as they both stared at the letters. Finally, Dani stood.

Pete looked up. "Don't you want to know what they say?"

She lifted one shoulder. "I told you, I don't even remember her. I think those letters were meant for you."

She slipped out of the kitchen, leaving him alone with his thoughts. There were many. About Braedon and the promises Pete had broken. About Lily and her baby. About his mother. She had run away, searching for something. Had she ever found it? Windy Ray told Pete once that the only thing a person can find that will make them stop searching is peace with the Creator. "*When you have that,*" his friend had said, "*it's enough. But without it, nothing is ever enough.*"

Pete rubbed a hand over his face. What had he spent his life searching for? Whatever it was, something told him he wouldn't find it in his mother's letters. But maybe he would find some closure.

It was almost midnight now, and five o'clock would come quickly. Without hesitation he picked up the first envelope and opened it.

forty-three

Pete parked a block away from the school at three-thirty Monday afternoon. Braedon was already waiting. Pearl squealed in delight as he climbed into the Xpeditor. Aside from her bandaged leg and refusal to leave Pete's side—even when he showered—she was back to her old self.

"Hey, buddy."

"Hey." Braedon put his arm around Pearl's neck. "Did you miss me?"

Pete understood his nephew was talking to the pig. He pulled back onto the road. "How was your day? Any progress with Tyson or Cole?"

"They both talked to me today."

"That's great."

Braedon shrugged. "There are only seventeen kids in the whole fifth grade. You can't avoid anyone for long."

"True." Pete smiled to himself. "But still, that's good news."

He yawned as he turned down an alley and stopped for the first blue bin. It had been a while since he'd had a good night's rest. Windy Ray was home now, though, and Pearl was doing well, so maybe tonight he would sleep.

His thoughts turned to the letters. Wilma and Dani had been right. With each one, he'd felt more and more that his mother was really addressing him. She'd been so sure he was safe and sound with Wilma, and that had made it easier for her to stay away. If only she'd known the truth.

Would it have made a difference? She'd made her choice, and he'd made choices of his own. Many that still haunted him.

He stopped for another bin. "I need to tell you something."

Braedon looked over Pearl's head at him. "Okay."

"It's about Windy Ray. You know how I told you he got hit in the head?"

"Yeah."

"Well, that was true, but it wasn't the whole story. I lost my temper and got in a fight."

Braedon's eyes widened. "With Windy Ray?"

"No, with Jerry. But when Jerry threw a rock at me, I ducked out of the way, and it hit Windy Ray instead. It was my fault he got hurt."

"Did you win?"

Pete gripped the wheel. "That's not the point. What I did was wrong. I said no more fighting—we even spit-shook on it—but I did it anyway. That makes me a loser whether I won the fight or not."

Braedon leaned on Pearl's back in silence for a minute before responding. "You're not a loser. You're the coolest guy I know. You don't become worthless just because you mess up."

Pete looked over at his nephew in surprise. "You sound like Windy Ray."

"No, I got that from you. I'm not garbage, and neither are you. And neither is Pearl."

Pete drove on—stop-lift-dump, stop-lift-dump—a warm

feeling in his chest. For the first time, he thought maybe he understood what Windy Ray meant when he talked about grace. Pete had done nothing to deserve a nephew like Braedon, and yet . . .

"You've got to take it easy on Windy Ray today, okay?" Pete smiled. "Let him win Chickenfoot for once. He's hurt."

At eight o'clock, Wilma's phone rang, as she'd hoped it would. She could've called her son over the weekend, but she had wanted to wait until Monday night to talk to him so she could try the FAS office again. She'd called Sadie's number five times today and had gotten the same "Please hang up and try again" message every time.

She could no longer pretend everything was all right.

"Hello, Michael."

"Hey, Mom. How are you?"

"I was sick last week. Had a nasty cold."

"Are you okay? Did you go to the doctor?"

"I'm fine. It was nothing. But there's something else."

She could hear him frowning through the phone. "What's wrong?"

If she told him, there would be no turning back. He would get power of attorney and take control of her finances. Scold her and baby her. Nag her about selling the house and moving to Colorado to live with him and Paula. She would lose her independence.

Would that be so bad?

"I think I've been tricked, Michael."

"I knew it. I *knew* hiring a housekeeper was a bad idea."

"Don't be silly. I found my cardigan. It was hanging in the entryway the whole time. That's not what I'm talking about."

"Oh. Then what?"

She hesitated. She still didn't have any real evidence. She could still get a phone call from Sadie, who had such a nice voice, and she might say something like *Sorry for all the fuss, we just moved to a new office. Your paperwork has been approved.*

"Mom?"

Wilma sighed. "I don't suppose you've heard of a new law that helps people reduce their debt?"

He groaned. "Oh no, Mom, you didn't."

"I don't know anything for sure."

"Someone called you?"

"Yes."

"How much did you send them?"

"Four payments of $199.99 each."

He was quiet for a moment, and she could picture him scowling and pinching the bridge of his nose.

"Okay. We can work with that. Did you give them access to your accounts?"

She thought back to all the paperwork she'd filled out and tried to remember. "I don't think so."

"Good."

"I gave them a list of all my credit cards."

"Have they made charges on them? Have you checked the balances?"

"I . . . uh, well, no." Her voice wobbled as tears began to form. "It's hard to keep track. I'm sorry, Michael."

"It's okay, Mom. We'll figure it out. It's not your fault, it's mine. I should've insisted . . ."

Wilma sniffed and tucked a tissue up under her glasses to wipe her eyes. "She seemed so nice and helpful. Really."

"I know. It's okay." He sounded resigned now. "What else did you tell her?"

Wilma tried to think back. What had she told Sadie? It

all seemed blurry and made her feel flustered. She'd never felt so old. "I told her I was behind on my property taxes."

Michael groaned again. "You're behind on your property taxes? Why didn't you tell me?"

"I didn't know until recently."

"How could you not—? Never mind. How far behind?"

"I'm not sure." She was not a woman given to demonstrations of emotion, but her voice became choked. "They sent me a notice."

"Don't cry, it's okay. I'm going to fix this. Steven will help. I'm going to need all the information you have on these people. Did they give you a phone number? Address?"

"The phone number is no longer in service. The address was on the paperwork they sent, but I mailed it back."

"Mom, listen to me. I'll arrange for a financial power of attorney tomorrow as soon as my lawyer's office opens, but it's going to take some time. You're going to need to call the bank and all your cards and let them know you've been scammed so they can freeze your accounts. Can you do that?"

She clutched the top of her cane and bolstered herself. Tears wouldn't get her anywhere. "Of course I can do that."

"Okay, I'll call you again tomorrow. And Mom?"

She braced herself. "Yes, dear?"

"You did the right thing telling me. I'm sorry if I ever made you feel like you couldn't. Paula says I'm becoming abrasive in my old age, but I'm working on it."

"You're a good son, and you're *not* old."

"You're a good mom."

She let out a long breath. "I haven't visited in ages. I haven't been . . ."

"Well." There was a hint of a smile in his voice now. "Good thing you're coming down for Callie's graduation, then, right?"

After they hung up, she wiped her eyes again and tapped her cane against the floor. She and Herb had never told their children about Rosie abandoning her kids or the state asking them to take them in. It had seemed like a burden their children weren't equipped to carry. She hadn't even known how to handle it herself. She knew one thing, though. When she went down to Colorado at the end of May, she would tell her children everything.

forty-four

Pete sat in his truck outside Wilma's house Wednesday afternoon. He hadn't talked to her since Friday night and maybe he wasn't ready, but he thought of the Henry van Dyke poem about time.

> Time is
> Too slow for those who Wait,
> Too swift for those who Fear . . .

He was half a century old. His mother had been gone for thirty-nine years. Time continued to pass.

The letters, which he'd read several times now, had evoked many feelings, but in the end they had mostly just made him sad. With each one the penmanship, the spelling, the tone deteriorated until the final letter was barely legible and the meaning difficult to decipher. It was clear she hadn't been well. He hoped she hadn't been alone.

Dani had refused to believe what Aunt Ellie used to tell her about their mother leaving to spare them from having to watch her die. She thought their mom simply decided there was a better life out there without them. But even if that were true, Pete knew she never found it. And maybe she never thought there was a better life. Maybe she just thought they would be better off.

He wished he could tell her she'd been wrong.

Pearl began to get antsy on the passenger side, and Pete wiped a hand over his face. "All right, hold your horses."

He slid out of the Dodge and opened the door for Pearl. He had to help her down so she wouldn't put too much pressure on her injured leg.

Wilma opened the door as they strolled up the walk. "Hello. What a lovely surprise."

She held the door open wide, and Pete and Pearl crowded in.

Pete nodded once. "Hello."

She looked down at Pearl. "You gave us quite a scare, young lady. I'm pleased to see you out and about, none the worse for wear, I hope?"

Pete rubbed Pearl's ear. "She's okay. Scared of the dark now, though."

"I shouldn't wonder." Wilma motioned for them to follow her to the kitchen. "After an ordeal like that."

Pete's head reared back when he saw boxes and folders covering Wilma's table. "What's all this?"

"Oh, that." She flicked her wrist. "Just looking for something."

"Do you need any help?"

"Don't be silly. I have a system, really."

He sat down in one of two chairs that wasn't occupied by paperwork and nodded when Wilma surreptitiously held up a banana with a questioning look in Pearl's direction. Pearl squealed with joy when Wilma peeled the banana and set it on a plate on the floor.

"Her appetite hasn't been affected, I see."

"No."

"How's Raymond faring?"

"Good. Out howling in the wind like his old self."

"Wonderful. And Dani and Braedon? How are they?"

Pete slumped a little. "Dani had an interview this morning for a job in Shelby. Activities director at the assisted-living place."

Wilma clapped her hands together once. "What great news. But you don't look very happy."

He shrugged. "I don't like the idea of her driving back and forth every day in the winter. I'll need to find her a decent used car that's not going to leave her stranded on Highway 2."

"Hmm."

"Look. Wilma." He took a deep breath and let it out. "I read the letters. Thank you for giving them to me."

"Of course."

"Why didn't you tell me before? Why did you wait so long when you knew I had so many questions?"

Her face was drawn and showed her age. She met his gaze. "I was afraid if I told you what I'd done, you wouldn't speak to me anymore, and then it would be like losing you all over again. It wasn't fair of me, Pete. I was a selfish coward."

He sat back. "My mom never should've expected that of you. You did what you thought was best. So did she, I guess, in a way."

"Sometimes we don't know what's best for ourselves."

"Windy Ray says that's why we should always ask the Creator to show us."

"Ah. Very wise." Wilma chuckled. "I did ask God what I should do about you, and do you know what He did?"

"What?"

"He brought you back to Sleeping Grass and set you right outside my house every Monday morning."

Pete chuckled. "I'm glad He did."

"Me too."

"I forgive you."

She blinked, and her mouth puckered.

He cleared his throat. "I never answered you before, when you asked, but I forgive you. And I understand."

She looked up at him with wide eyes. "Thank you, dear," she said quietly.

They sat in silence for a moment while Pearl snuffled around the kitchen searching for any crumbs that Wilma might have dropped, as if Wilma were the type to drop crumbs. Pete glanced around at the old-school filing system that had taken over the kitchen.

"Did you ever get your property taxes straightened out?"

She tapped her cane against the floor. "It's a little more complicated than I realized. My son Michael is helping me."

"That's great. Where does he live, again?"

"Southern Colorado."

A knock sounded at the door, and Pete looked over his shoulder. "You want me to get that?"

Before Wilma could answer, the door squeaked and Lily's voice rang out, "It's just me."

Pete's cheeks warmed, and he felt his ears turning red. He hadn't seen Lily since his fight with Jerry. How could he face her? What if she was afraid of him?

Wilma gave him a knowing look and whispered, "I called her while you were sitting in your truck trying to make up your mind. Told her to stop by. She's been wanting to talk to you."

Lily entered the kitchen with a shy smile. "Hi."

Pete swallowed. "Hi."

"I've been dying for a slice of cinnamon-raisin toast," Wilma said. "Would you both be dears and run to the store for me?"

Pete gaped at her.

She smiled. "Oranges too. I'd love some oranges."

"We'd be happy to, Miss Wilma." Lily raised one eyebrow at him. "Right, Pete?"

He fumbled to his feet. "Sure. I mean, yes. Uh, no problem." He picked up his keys from the table and turned to Wilma. "Anything else we can do for you?"

She shook her head and waved them away. Pete called for Pearl and wiped his sweaty palms on his jeans.

He was woefully unprepared for Lily.

The grocery store wasn't far away. Lily spent the short two-minute drive doting on Pearl, and to Pete's surprise, Pearl didn't seem to mind.

"I'm glad she's back." Lily leaned her face close to Pearl's. "You were such a brave girl, yes you were."

Pearl stomped her hooves.

Pete huffed. "Don't let it go to your head."

He chose a parking spot behind the store, aware of what could happen if the wrong person saw Lily climbing out of his truck. Lilac bushes with buds just beginning to form hid them from view of the main road. He turned off the Dodge, but Lily made no move to get out.

"I'm sorry for what Jerry did."

He flinched. "You have nothing to be sorry about. I'm the one who's sorry. I shouldn't have gone after him like that."

"He said it was an accident at work, but I knew it wasn't."

Pete pressed his lips together. "It was rash what I did, and wrong. I don't want you to think . . ."

"All I think about is being scared. All the time. I'm always wondering what he's going to do. What he's going to think."

She hung her head. "I can't live like this anymore. I made an appointment in Great Falls. For Saturday."

Pete focused on the steering wheel. When a man has spent years—decades—living by himself and moving from place to place without attachments, he gets used to feeling as if he has some control over his life, some control over his heart, even if it's all an illusion. What he wouldn't give for that feeling now.

"Lily, I won't be able to take you."

She looked down at her lap. "Do you have plans for this Saturday? I can reschedule."

"No, I-I don't have any plans."

Her hands shook. "Don't do this, Pete. Please. I need you."

It was a special kind of pain. What man doesn't long to hear a beautiful woman say those words to him? What kind of a man was he to refuse her? He heaved a heavy sigh. "There has to be another way."

"You don't understand." Her eyes flashed, and her voice hardened. "Jerry doesn't want a baby."

"Do you?"

She wouldn't meet his eyes. "I never thought . . . I-I don't know. Not if it means being stuck with Jerry for the rest of my life."

"You can leave him."

Her face contorted. "I've tried."

"I'll help you."

"Are you going to help me raise it, too?" Her tone was harsh now. Desperate. "Are you going to find me a place to live and buy baby clothes and take me to all my doctor appointments?"

He imagined such things. Turned them over in his mind and studied them. "I'll do whatever it takes."

Her shoulders drooped, and she leaned her head against the window. "You're still not getting it, Pete. If I leave him,

I'll have to leave Sleeping Grass and move somewhere far away." She lifted her head and looked over at him. Her eyes shone with unshed tears. "And I can't ask you to do that."

Pete thought of how it had felt when they held hands. Thought of the smell of her hair and how her voice was like water. Imagined her watching the sky through the window at night, eating Skittles.

Then he thought of his sister, a single mom. And Windy Ray and his Raisinets. He thought of Braedon and how he wanted to be the one to teach his nephew how to fish and how to work hard and how to find better ways to cope with life than fighting. They had so much to teach each other. And he thought of the noisy, smelly old Xpeditor, which had given him the kind of stable life a man with his history would struggle to find anywhere else.

"Let's go." Lily opened the door with a resigned voice and a sad smile. "Miss Wilma needs her toast and oranges."

forty-five

Wilma had never tolerated a messy house. Tidiness was not, as some people believed, overrated. Nevertheless, her kitchen looked like the office of one of those scatterbrained private detectives in the old movies. It had been no small feat to lug the boxes of folders and piles of envelopes from what had been Herb's office to the kitchen table.

Some of these bill stubs and bank statements dated back to before Herb died. Wilma was always afraid of throwing away something important, and now she was glad for that. Everything she'd needed had been right here, filed by month and year. She'd never made so many phone calls in her life.

She'd started yesterday with her bank and all the credit card companies. Some of the people she spoke with had been kind and sympathetic, others brash and condescending. This morning had been spent searching for and setting aside anything related to her property taxes for Michael, then pulling out every letter she'd received in the past three years from any ministry related to helping vulnerable women.

If she could type faster and see better, she could've found all the information she was looking for on the googlenet.

Instead, she had made more phone calls. *"What services do you provide?"* she'd asked. *"How much does it cost?" "Do you have any openings?" "Do you accept pregnant women?"*

It had been a laborious process, but she had narrowed the options down to two women's homes. The only two that had immediate openings and seemed to be what Lily needed. One was in Washington and boasted extensive music therapy, the other in Colorado, just an hour's drive north of Michael's house. Both specialized in helping victims of domestic violence start a new life. Both were nonprofits funded by donations such as the ones Wilma had been making for years.

There was a knock on the door. She waited a moment, expecting Lily to enter as she always did, but nothing happened. She shuffled to the entryway and pulled open the door. The air outside felt fresh and pleasant.

"Oh. Hello." She peered past Pete's shoulder. "Where's Lily?"

He looked somewhat like a little boy who'd lost his baseball. "She . . . had to go home."

Wilma squinted. "Is something wrong?"

He held up a bag of groceries, and she waved him into the house. Pearl followed closely on his heels.

"I was hoping to talk to her about something. Is she coming back?"

Pete lifted one shoulder. "I don't think so."

He sounded dejected.

She put her hands on her hips. "What did you do?"

"It's what I wouldn't do," he mumbled as he set the bag on the counter.

Wilma didn't know what to make of that. The obvious follow-up question stuck in her throat because she, of course, didn't want to press.

Pete threw up his hands. "I'm not sure I can talk about it. You'll have to ask her."

"Does it have anything to do with the baby?"

His eyes widened. "You know about that?"

"Of course I know about that. Here, I want to show you something." She gestured toward the table, where she'd left the letters for the women's homes in Colorado and Washington. When he bent to look at them, she jabbed the paper with her finger. "Haven of Hope and"—she jabbed the other one—"Redemption House."

"Churches?"

"No. Places for women who are fleeing domestic violence. Transition homes."

He snatched up the letters and pulled out his phone. In no time he had pulled up a website and turned the screen toward Wilma. "They don't have many pictures."

"For safety reasons, dear. The woman on the phone explained they must be careful to keep the location of the homes confidential. No identifying information or pictures on the computer or the brochures."

Pete nodded. "Makes sense."

The woman had also given her the number for a domestic-violence helpline. Apparently, there were programs that specialized in helping women relocate safely, and Wilma could only thank God she'd never had occasion to know such a thing existed. Quite a charmed life she'd had. Such an abundance of grace. The more she got to know Lily, the more she realized it.

"Can you call her to come over tomorrow?" Pete asked. "So you can show her all this?"

"She's working for a friend of mine tomorrow. You know Gladys Dunwell? Perhaps I'll stop by there."

Pete clutched the letters in his hand. "Both these places are so far away."

"Everything is far away from Sleeping Grass."

"I know, but I don't . . ." He slowly lowered his chin.

"I don't want to see her go either." She patted his elbow. "But what we want is not the important thing here, now, is it?"

On Monday when Lily was cleaning, Wilma had seen bruises that looked an awful lot like fingerprints around her wrist. They needed to get her out of that house. They needed to get her somewhere she'd be safe.

An idea began to form in her mind, and she couldn't believe she hadn't thought of it sooner. "Would you hand me the phone, please?"

She'd made what felt like a hundred phone calls the past couple of days. What was one more? Pete brought her the phone, and she dialed a familiar number.

"Gladys? Yes, it's Wilma. We need your help."

Pete jiggled his knee at nine-thirty that night, about to burst from the waiting. He could've sent Dani a message earlier to ask how her interview went, but he didn't want to bother her at work. And texting was a chore. Smartphones weren't made for the cracked and callused fingers of the working man, which moved sluggishly across the screen and hit two or three letters at once. The phone autocorrected, doing what it could to fit the man into its sleek high-tech world, but those *fingers*.

He'd already had three, but he shoved another peanut butter cookie into his mouth as he stared at the door, willing it to open. When he'd stopped by Sunny's the other day to let her know Pearl had been found, she'd hugged him and boxed up a whole smorgasbord of goodies for him to take home. A guy could get used to that kind of treatment.

Dani opened the door with a clunk, and he sprang up from the couch. "You're home."

She narrowed her eyes. "Did you do something bad?"

"No."

"Then what are you so hyped up about?"

"How'd the interview go?"

He followed her as she dropped her purse on the coffee table and crossed the room toward the hall.

She stopped abruptly. "Is Braedon asleep?"

"No. He said he was going to listen to music until you got home."

"Okay. I'll go say good night."

She disappeared into Braedon's bedroom, and Pete began to pace. Why was it so hard for women to answer direct questions? He heard voices murmuring behind the door and realized Dani didn't need to find him waiting in the hallway when she came out. He moved himself to the kitchen. He began to pace again, then thought better of it and sat down.

He was drumming his fingers on the table when she appeared, and he shot to his feet again. "Well?"

She seemed somewhat amused at his expense, but other than that he couldn't read her face. How long did you have to live with someone before you had a reasonable idea of what they were thinking?

"I'm hungry."

"But how did—?"

"Sit." She pointed at the chair he'd just vacated. "Give me a second, for crying out loud. You're acting like an annoying big brother."

He plopped himself down. "Because that's what I am."

She ignored him as she took a bowl from the cupboard and filled it with cereal. She shared his childish affinity for Froot Loops. He waited impatiently as she poured milk and rummaged through the silverware drawer—which had grown fuller and more diversified over the past few weeks—before joining him at the table. With a smirk, she started scrolling on her phone as she took a big bite of food and chewed slowly.

He couldn't stand it any longer. "Aren't you going to tell me? What did they say? What was it like?"

She rolled her eyes and set her spoon down in an exaggerated way that he was pretty sure was all for show. "If you must know, it went pretty well."

He waited, eyebrows raised.

"They asked a lot of questions and gave me a tour. I met some of the residents. And they offered me the job."

He braced his palms on the table. "They did? How could—? Are you—?"

She smiled and let him squirm a minute before continuing. "They'd already checked my references, since I emailed my résumé over on Monday. The pay isn't great, but the benefits are good, and the hours are all daytime. No more night shifts."

"You already said yes?"

"I said I'd get back to them, but it seems like a good opportunity for me. I really liked it there."

"Wow. That's . . . that's great."

She scrunched up her nose. "You don't look like it's great."

"No, it is, I just . . ."

"How about 'Wow, Dani, congratulations, I'm so happy for you'?"

He moved his hands under the table and squeezed his knees. "I'm happy for you. I knew they would love you. But what about a car? I've been calling around, but it looks like we're going to have to go to Great Falls or maybe even Helena to find one. We need to make sure it's reliable."

"We?"

He leaned back in his chair. "I want to help."

She studied him the same way she had when she first moved in. Like she was trying to determine what kind of man he was. "I appreciate everything you've done for me and Braedon. I don't know what we would've done if you hadn't taken us in. But I don't want to keep relying on you for everything."

And why not, he couldn't help but wonder. Would that be so bad? But he held his tongue.

"I looked at a couple of apartments while I was in Shelby," she continued. "They were small but livable. And the school there is bigger. I'm hoping it will be easier for Braedon to make friends."

Pete opened his mouth, then closed it. A dozen different things to say crossed his mind, yet none of them seemed right. She'd made up her mind. Though he didn't like it, he wanted what was best for her, didn't he? Just like he wanted what was best for Lily.

Finally, he let out a long breath and raised one side of his mouth. "Pearl is going to miss you."

"She's sleeping with you again." Dani fidgeted with her spoon. "She'll be fine."

Ever since she'd been pignapped, Pearl had switched back to sleeping on Pete's bed, and she twitched and wheezed her way through nightmares almost every night. It pained him to witness it. It pained him to think about what one man could do to another. What he himself had done.

He'd wondered why God didn't take better care of His creation, but he was beginning to wonder if the creation was more to blame for its own suffering than God.

He awkwardly patted his sister's shoulder. "When do you start?"

"The thirteenth."

He bobbed his head. "All right."

And it was.

forty-six

Wilma wished she could've been there to see it happen, though she was sure she would've been frightened out of her wits. Yesterday, while Lily was supposed to be cleaning Gladys's house, she was really loading all her belongings into Ronald's truck with Gladys's help and moving into the Dunwells' guest room. Not long afterward, according to Gladys, Jerry had shown up at the house looking for Lily, and Gladys had given him an unrestrained piece of her mind while Ronald called the police.

Today, Gladys had taken Lily to file for a restraining order. Lily still planned to move away—she didn't want to live in constant fear of running into Jerry, of course—but now that she lived with Gladys, she could leave town whenever she was ready without Jerry knowing. She could be gone for weeks before he realized. Gladys had even come up with ideas to make it appear as if Lily still lived there, like leaving a pair of her shoes outside the front door and putting the guest bedroom lights on a timer.

"*I dared him to try and come near her,*" Gladys had said, and Wilma could just picture Jerry cowering in her friend's overpowering presence.

What Lily was going to do about her baby, though, Wilma couldn't picture. She'd given Lily the information about the women's homes, and Lily had immediately been drawn to the one near Michael's house because of its gardens. She hadn't said a word about her child's future, however. While Wilma had a lot of opinions on the matter, she kept them to herself and prayed every night that Lily would have hope.

Luckily, the Lord didn't mind if she pressed.

The phone rang, and Wilma knew it was her son despite it being only half past seven. "Hello, Michael. You must be eager to talk to me."

"Have you received the power of attorney papers in the mail yet?"

"You know how long it takes the mail to get here, dear. It's like they still deliver it with a horse and buggy."

"I know. Just sign them as soon as they arrive, okay?"

"Of course. And how are you? You seem stressed."

He laughed. She couldn't remember the last time she'd made him laugh, and she tapped her cane against the floor in triumph.

"I'm okay," he said. "It's you I'm worried about."

"I'm perfectly fine."

"Listen, I've got good news and bad news."

She didn't like the sound of that. She wasn't in the mood for more bad news. "Good first, please."

"Okay. The good news is, your stubborn refusal to sign up for autopay or any kind of online account means those fake FAS people weren't able to get anything out of you except the checks you sent. And my lawyer assures me they tried."

"Well, good. They should be ashamed of themselves, preying on poor old ladies."

"I agree. Now the bad news . . ."

She cringed. "Oh, fine, go ahead."

"Because you were behind on the taxes, a lien was placed on the property and—"

"Yes, yes, I know about that."

"Listen, Mom. The lien on your house was sold to a third party. Sunrise Investments. My lawyer says there's no way to prove it, but he's sure Sunrise Investments is connected to the fake FAS. Once they found out you were delinquent, all they had to do was swoop in and pay the back taxes. Now they have a claim to your house."

She pressed a hand to her chest. "My goodness, that does sound bad."

"It's not as bad as it could be. The investors can't take ownership of your property until three years have passed, according to Montana law. We'll need to pay them whatever they paid for the lien plus whatever fees or interest they've applied to it. Then the lien can be removed."

"I see."

He hesitated. "Look, I've seen your savings account and credit card bills. You should've told me—"

"Michael, I—"

"I know, I know, there's no sense in arguing about it now. The important thing is getting this lien removed. Paula and I would like to make the payment."

She made a sound embarrassingly similar to a surprised chicken. "Certainly not."

"We're in a position to do it. We can't let you use money on this that needs to go to the credit card companies."

"*Let* me." She tightened her grip on the phone. "I don't need your permission."

He sighed. "Once you sign the power of attorney, you will, actually. I'm not trying to be cruel here, Mom. I'm trying to keep you from becoming homeless."

Homeless? She blinked and looked around the house. Her

memory wasn't what it used to be, but she remembered the day they moved in here. Michael had been ten, Steven eight. Rachel had been only five, and she'd stood at the front window and covered it in smudges while everyone else unloaded boxes. They had been happy here.

And yet.

Who was going to roll her garbage bin back in now that Lily was leaving? How many more subzero winters did she want to shiver through? Would she ever grow accustomed to the empty rooms and empty halls? How much was happening in her children's lives and *their* children's lives that she was missing?

"I'm sorry it has to be like this." Michael's voice was weary. "The only other option is to—"

"Sell the house."

He sighed. "Yes."

"No, I mean I want you to sell the house. I've been holding on to it long enough, don't you think?"

It all seemed clear now. She had stayed all this time for a reason, but things had changed. She would miss Pete and Pearl, Dani and Braedon, but her second-to-youngest grandchild was about to graduate from high school, for heaven's sake. What else might she miss if she stayed up here on the Hi-Line? One could see miles and miles of prairie from Sleeping Grass, but one could certainly not see Colorado.

"I don't want you to rush into anything, Mom."

"Nonsense. You don't have the luxury of taking your time when you get to be my age, you know. You were right to bring it up to me before. I just wasn't ready."

"And now you are? Just like that?"

"Yes."

"You're ready to give up your home."

"Yes. And my car, too. There's this lovely young lady named

Dani, and she hasn't had her own car since she moved here in February. I want to give her the Corolla. I hardly use it."

"You're going to give your car away to someone you just met in February?"

"Just met? Oh, my dear boy." Wilma smiled to herself and thought of Rosie. "I have so much to tell you."

forty-seven

The past week had flown by like a flock of geese headed south for the winter, except every day showed more and more evidence that spring had finally arrived. Pete noted the green grass starting to poke up in front yards as he drove through town. Pearl had been spending extra hours outside, and since a potbellied pig and a well-kept lawn didn't mix, she had to settle for the backyard when she wanted to play.

Pete parked in the Dunwells' driveway, feeling like a gawky teenager at his crush's house. Wilma had spoken to Lily several times since she'd moved in with Gladys a week ago, but Pete had not. He'd hoped maybe she would call now that she had no one looking over her shoulder and checking her phone, but maybe it was better that she hadn't. He hoped she could understand the decision he'd made.

A large woman he assumed must be Gladys answered the door with a rolling pin in her hand and a look on her face that could freeze the feathers off a Canada goose. "Who are you? What do you want?"

"I-I'm Pete," he stammered. "I just, uh . . ."

"Oh. Pete. Wilma told me about you." She noticed Pearl, and her expression brightened. "You can come in."

After letting him and Pearl into the house, she stood in the doorway a moment longer and glared up and down the road, gripping the rolling pin in one hand and slapping it into the other.

"You didn't see a little black truck, did you?"

"No, ma'am."

"Good." She slammed the door, reset the security system, and raised her voice. "Lily, you have a visitor."

She caught him staring at the rolling pin and smiled grimly as she leaned it against the wall by the door. "I prefer it to the cast-iron skillet because you can jab someone in the eye with the handle and it's easier to swing."

He swallowed.

She narrowed her eyes. "It took you long enough to come by."

"Uh, well, I just . . ."

"It's a good thing your job doesn't require any communication skills."

"Hi, Pete." Lily appeared, the scent of sunshine reaching him just after the sound of her voice. She knelt down. "Hi, Pearl."

Pearl rammed Lily's shoulder, almost knocking her over.

Gladys frowned. "My house has not been pig-proofed. How about I take Pearl to the backyard while you two talk?" She didn't wait for an answer, instead marching toward the back of the house. "Come on, Pearl. Let's go."

She was a woman accustomed to being obeyed, and miraculously, Pearl obeyed. Pete waited until he heard a door open and close before turning to Lily.

"Hey."

"I was wondering if you'd come."

"Wilma says you're leaving soon."

She nodded. "This week has been a whirlwind. Gladys knows how to make things happen."

It had been a whirlwind for him, too. Wilma had conscripted his help to get her house listed for sale, and Dani had started packing up her and Braedon's few belongings for their move to Shelby, which was scheduled for tomorrow afternoon. Somehow, all the people who had so suddenly and completely appeared in his life would soon be gone.

"About the other day. I wanted to say I'm sorry."

She tilted her head. "For what?"

He shifted on his feet. "For saying I would help you, and then . . ."

"It's okay, Pete. I understand." She gestured toward a chair in the living room, and he sat. She sat on the couch across from him. "I canceled the appointment."

Relief raced through his veins, but he tried not to show it too much. "You're not going to go through with it?"

"I don't know yet." She looked down. "I'm scared. This isn't what I wanted."

He rubbed the back of his neck. Windy Ray or Wilma would probably have some wise response, but he didn't.

"Will you hate me if I decide I'm not strong enough to be a mom?"

His head jerked back. "I could never hate you. But you're much stronger than you think."

She fidgeted. "Redemption House is close to where Wilma's son lives—did you know that? She says she's going to visit me."

"I'm glad."

"If you ever came down"—she blushed—"to see Wilma, I mean, you could maybe come to the house, too. If you want."

"Yes."

It was one of the easiest answers he'd ever had to give, but Lily seemed surprised. As if he hadn't thought of her every day for the past three years.

"I appreciate everything you've done for me."

It was his turn to be surprised. "I didn't do anything."

"You were my friend. No questions asked, no strings attached." She smiled. "Not to mention all those Skittles."

He could feel his ears turning red. The Skittles had been paltry gifts, offered sincerely but in complete ignorance of what she really needed. His friendship, however . . . though imperfect, maybe that had been a worthwhile gift. He was just a high school dropout who picked up other people's trash for a living, but he had been there. He had cared.

He forced out the words he'd come here to say, the words he'd practiced all week. "I'm going to miss you."

She laughed, the waves of Tiber Lake breaking gently on the shore. "I'll miss you, too."

There wasn't much else to say. For all that had happened since February, they hardly knew each other. He had memorized the movement of her hair and hands, the sound of her voice, the color of her eyes, but who was she really? Maybe she didn't even know herself after so many years of being erased by Jerry. If you think you're nothing for long enough, you start to disappear. He would know. Maybe he wasn't who he thought he was either.

After a few more minutes of small talk, Pete pushed himself out of the chair. "I promised Wilma I'd help her with some boxes today."

Lily stood. "I threw away my phone. I'm going to get a new number, but I still have yours."

He gave a small smile. He would be content with that.

She watched from the front steps as Pete helped Pearl into the Dodge. He shut the passenger door and walked around the front of the truck, raising an arm in farewell. She raised one in return, then lowered it slowly and placed her hand on her stomach.

The open box tipped off the end table and hit the floor with a crash. Wilma's hand flew to her mouth. "Oh dear."

Pete hurried around the corner to see what the hullabaloo was about and groaned. "Pearl."

"It's not her fault." Wilma leaned over the wreckage. "I never should've left it there. She didn't know not to bump it."

Pete came up beside her and looked down. His face blanched. "I'll replace them."

"Nonsense. Michael will say Pearl did him a big favor. There's not enough room at his house for me to bring all these silly old knickknacks. All they do is collect dust."

"Still, they're probably antiques."

"Ha." She pushed her glasses up on her nose. "Only the same ones every other old lady in America has in her living room."

Raymond marched into the room from the garage, where he'd been boxing up tools. He carried his oxygen tank on his back in a small pack. "What did I miss?"

Pete snorted. "Pearl broke some of Wilma's figurines."

Wilma waved a hand in the air. "She made my job easier, that's all."

"I'll glue them back together for you, Wilma. Every piece."

"That won't be necessary, Raymond. Thank you."

She hadn't been expecting Raymond to be here today. Pete had brought him along, and she was grateful for the extra help, though somewhat discomfited by his presence. He had already given her a black-and-white-speckled rock that shimmered in the light. *"Diorite,"* he'd called it. He seemed back to his old self after his "brush with death," though a mark remained on the side of his forehead where he'd been struck.

"What's it like in Granger, Colorado?" he asked.

Pearl chased Apisi behind the couch, and Pete cringed. "Watch it, Pearl."

"I haven't been down there in a long time, but it's a very nice city." She leaned on her cane, and Apisi zipped around it like a barrel horse. "Everything you need is close-by. No two-hour drives to stock up on supplies, and as far as I know it has never once been twenty below zero there."

"In a city like that, a man on a tricycle could get around to many places."

Pete huffed. "You wouldn't know what to do without the wind."

"Perhaps I don't need it like I used to."

"Then *perhaps* I will take you with me when I go down to visit." Pete glanced over at Wilma. "If Wilma says it's okay."

All eyes turned to her. *Really*. She studied Raymond and thought about how he'd held her hand in the hospital. It was a solid, strong hand. He was different from her Herb in almost every way, yet somehow he still reminded her of him.

"I suppose that would be all right."

Raymond beamed, and Pete rolled his eyes. She had half a mind to smack them both, but she had more urgent concerns. "Raymond, back to the garage, if you will. Pete, I need your help with something."

Raymond dutifully ambled toward the garage as Pete followed her in the opposite direction down the hall. She shuffled into her bedroom and pointed at the wall.

"Could you take that down for me, please?"

When he hesitated, she nudged him. "Go on. It's for you."

He approached the wall as if it might topple over on him. She waited patiently. She had no right to rush him when she'd taken this long herself.

He reached up and took the clock down with both hands, though it was scarcely bigger than a five-by-seven photo frame. He stared at it for a minute. “She kept it above the kitchen sink. She used to say it was because that’s where she spent the most time.”

“That’s where I found it. Herb got it down for me since I couldn’t reach.”

“How did you get in there?”

Wilma wasn’t proud of that exactly. “Well, we broke in.”

His eyebrows shot up. “You did what?”

“It wasn’t as sinister as it sounds. The house had been abandoned, as you well know. It had gone into foreclosure. I told Herb I couldn’t stand the thought of Rosie’s things being hauled away. Or worse, taken over by the new owners as if they’d never been hers. I mean, what if she came back?”

It seemed kind of silly now, but at the time, Wilma had still believed Rosie would return someday. She didn’t want her friend to find all her special things had disappeared.

“It was Herb’s idea. It was the one and only time that man ever broke a law in his life. But he was adamant I only choose one thing. One thing I knew she would miss the most.”

Pete looked down at the clock, and Wilma thought back to that day. There had been plenty of other Coca-Cola memorabilia in the house, of course. Some big, some small. It had been an easy choice, however. Just as it was to give it to Pete now.

“I was with her when she found that.” Wilma chuckled. “At a garage sale in Shelby, if you can believe it. Her face just lit up. The man said he didn’t know if it even worked, but she didn’t care.”

“But it did.”

Wilma nodded.

“And it’s been in your bedroom all this time?”

She raised one shoulder somewhat sheepishly. "I couldn't let anybody *see* it. I didn't want to go to *jail*."

Pete laughed, his amusement building until his shoulders shook and a grin split his face. "No, you're right, we wouldn't want that."

It did her heart good to see him happy. She tapped her cane against the floor and smiled, then winced as a loud crash came from the direction of the kitchen, followed by a squeal.

Pete's shoulders slumped, and he shouted, "Per-earl!"

forty-eight

Pete stood in the front yard, his thumbs hooked in the belt loops of his jeans. It was sixty-four degrees on this twelfth of May, and the wind, for once, had no teeth. All along the street, new leaves opened tentative faces toward the sun.

Braedon came up beside him. "You'll be there on Wednesday, right?"

Pete tousled his hair. "I wouldn't miss it."

Dani had insisted they didn't need his help moving into their new apartment today, but she *had* invited him for dinner this Wednesday night—and every Wednesday thereafter. He'd wheedled his way into picking Braedon up from school on Wednesdays, as well. This week they'd be going to Norman's in Cut Bank to buy Braedon his own fishing pole.

Dani slammed the trunk of the Corolla. "Braedon, go check your room one last time."

He made a face. "I did."

She gave him a look.

"You'd better listen," Pete said.

Braedon trudged off, grumbling to himself. Dani walked over to Pete and looked back at the car. She and Braedon had accumulated a surprising amount of stuff in three months, and the vehicle was packed to the top.

Pete crossed his arms over his chest. "I still don't understand why you couldn't wait three weeks until the end of school."

"I told you. Braedon wants to meet the kids from Shelby before school lets out, so he'll have someone to play with over the summer." She put on a brave face and held up crossed fingers. "Hopefully. Plus I'm ready to sleep in my own bed, in my own room."

In addition to the Corolla, Wilma had offered Dani the beds from the spare rooms in her house and her kitchen table. It had taken some convincing to get Dani to accept the gifts, but Wilma had eventually gotten her way. As usual. Pete had already dropped the furniture off at the apartment yesterday with his truck.

"Are you sure you don't—?"

"We'll be fine." She elbowed his arm. "I promise. And so will you. I saw the way Sunny was looking at you this morning."

He squirmed. They'd started going to Sunny's every Sunday for sausage casserole and cinnamon rolls. More often than not, Windy Ray happened to show up at the same time.

"I don't know what you're talking about." He appreciated Sunny, but Lily was always in the back of his mind. "We're just friends."

"You can never have too many of those, that's all I'm saying."

He narrowed his eyes. "Really? That's all you're saying?"

She laughed. "You can take it however you want, but it wouldn't kill you to branch out a little."

"I'm not a tree."

"You're not an old man either. You don't have to act like one. Live a little."

"You always were the bossy one. Even Mom used to say so."

"Did you ever read those letters?"

"I did, yes."

"And?"

"And we should talk about it sometime. When you're ready."

They fell silent for a minute, listening to the wind blow around them. He didn't know if it was because of the temperature or the sun shining or that things had changed, but there were no condemning voices on the wind this time, voices telling him he was worthless. Reminding him of his mistakes.

Dani pulled the car keys from her pocket. "Thanks, Pete. For everything."

He was the one who was thankful, but he didn't respond. He couldn't. Something seemed to be wrong with his throat.

Braedon came out of the house, followed by Pearl. She'd avoided the front yard ever since her harrowing ordeal, but she was a smart pig and had the swine-sense to understand this was an important moment.

"I didn't find anything," Braedon said.

"Okay." Dani checked the time on her phone. "We better get going. Say goodbye."

He shoved his hands into his pockets and kicked at a rock. "Bye, Uncle Pete. Bye, Pearl."

Pete's arms reached out to fold his nephew into a hug, but Braedon turned and slouched toward the car. A desperate feeling began to well up in Pete's chest. He didn't want to let them go. Then, with a wipe of his eyes, Braedon turned around and ran back. He knelt beside Pearl and held her tight, whispering something into her neck that Pete couldn't hear and didn't need to. When Braedon finally stood, he threw his arms around Pete.

"I love you, Uncle Pete."

Pete's throat still wasn't working correctly. He swallowed hard and squeezed Braedon back. "I love you, too, buddy."

Dani and Braedon got into the Corolla and waved as they backed onto the street. As Dani turned the wheel and shifted into drive, Pearl squealed, and for a brief moment panic shot through Pete's body. His mind flashed to another time when a car took his sister away and he had screamed and fought and chased after her with all the strength in his eleven-year-old body, believing his only hope was in holding on.

And he had. He'd held on to his anger, his loss, his shame. His failure. Not realizing true hope, the kind Windy Ray talked about, could only be found in letting go.

This time he stood at the end of the driveway and watched until the car was out of sight, Pearl at his side, snuffling through the grass. A gust of wind blew past his face, and he didn't run.

Acknowledgments

I'm beyond thankful for the whole team at Bethany House, every person who played a part in getting this book out into the world. You are so appreciated. Special thanks to Rochelle for your vision and encouragement, and to Luke and Hannah for your attention to detail.

A big thank you to my brother, Tim, for answering a million questions about trash and trucks without getting annoyed. Not enough people know what a great guy you are. The whole Struiksma clan is lucky to have you.

Thank you to all the waste management specialists out there doing an often-thankless job. I appreciate you, and I know you probably noticed the liberties I took with the logistics of your profession. I hope you understand.

Thank you to my early readers, Sarah Carson, Emily Conrad, and Kerry Johnson. Special thanks to Emily for brainstorming that problematic middle section with me. Thanks also to my agent, Keely Boeving, whose insight, encouragement, and faithfulness mean so much to me. You ladies are a bright spot in my life.

Thank you to Jenn Wright for being responsible for my

favorite scene in the whole book. Pearl would not have been the same without you!

More thanks than can be expressed go to my husband and kids, who have sacrificed for this dream, loved me unconditionally, and made me a better person. You guys are the best.

And thank you to the Creator of all things, who offers hope and peace to all no matter how hard the wind blows.

For more from Katie Powner, look for

Where the Blue Sky Begins,

available wherever books are sold.

Sometimes the hardest road of all is the road home. When Eric Larson is sent to a rural Montana town to work in the local branch of his uncle's company, he's determined to exceed everyone's expectations, earn a promotion, and be back in Seattle by the end of summer. Yet nothing could prepare him for the lessons this small town has in store.

At forty-six years old, Eunice Parker has come to accept her terminal illness and has given herself one final goal: seek forgiveness from everyone on her bucket list before her time runs out. But it will take more courage than she can muster on her own.

After an accident pushes Eric and Eunice together, the unlikely pair is forced to spend more time with each other than either would like, which challenges their deepest prejudices and beliefs. As summer draws to a close, neither Eric nor Eunice is where they thought they would be, but they both wrestle with the same important question: *What matters most when the end is near?*

"Katie Powner's engaging story will pull you in and leave you in wonder at that deep, blue sky."

—CHRIS FABRY, author and radio host

"Wholesome, charming, poignant—*Where the Blue Sky Begins* is a story of a man full of ambition who has something to prove, a woman full of regret who has amends to make, and a town full of delightful characters who have lessons to teach them both."

—ERIN BARTELS, award-winning author of *We Hope for Better Things*

About the Author

Katie Powner, author of *Where the Blue Sky Begins* and *A Flicker of Light*, grew up on a dairy farm in the Pacific Northwest but has called Montana home for over twenty years. She is a biological, adoptive, and foster mom who loves Jesus, red shoes, and candy. In addition to writing contemporary fiction, Katie blogs about family in all its many forms and advocates for more families to open their homes to children in need. To learn more, visit her website at www.katiepowner.com.

Sign Up for Katie's Newsletter

Keep up to date with Katie's latest news on book releases and events by signing up for her email list at the link below.

FOLLOW KATIE ON SOCIAL MEDIA

Author Katie Powner

@authorkatiepowner

@katie_powner

KatiePowner.com

More from Katie Powner

After an accident brings businessman Eric Larson and eccentric Eunice Parker together, the unlikely pair spend more time with each other than they would like while facing challenges beyond what they imagined. As Eunice comes to accept her terminal illness, they both wrestle with an important question: *What matters most when the end is near?*

Where the Blue Sky Begins

Widower Mitch Jensen is at a loss for how to handle his mother's odd, forgetful behaviors, as well as his daughter's sudden return home and unexpected life choices. Little does he know Grandma June has long been keeping a secret about her past—but if she doesn't tell the truth about it, someone she loves will suffer, and the lives of three generations will never be the same.

A Flicker of Light

Forced to sell his family farm after sacrificing everything, 63-year-old Gerrit Laninga no longer knows what to do with himself. Fifteen-year-old Rae Walters has growing doubts about The Plan her parents set to help her follow in her father's footsteps. When their paths cross just as they need a friend the most, Gerrit's and Rae's lives change in unexpected ways.

The Sowing Season